THE
LEVIATHAN
EFFECT

Also by James Lilliefors

Viral

THE
LEVIATHAN
EFFECT

JAMES LILLIEFORS

Published by
Soho Press, Inc.
853 Broadway
New York, NY 10003

Library of Congress Cataloging-in-Publication Data

Lilliefors, James
The Leviathan Effect / By James Lilliefors.
p cm
ISBN 978-1-61695-249-5
eISBN 978-1-61695-250-1
1. Natural disasters—United States—Fiction. 2. Extortion—United
States—Fiction. 3. Human-machine systems—Fiction. 4. United States.
Office of Homeland Security—Fiction. 5. Psychological fiction. I. Title.
PS3562.I4573L48 2013
813'.54—dc23
2012041037

Printed in the United States of America

10 9 8 7 6 5 4 3 2 1

Dedicated to the victims of natural disasters

"Intervention in atmospheric and climatic matters will . . . unfold on a scale difficult to imagine at present. Such actions would be more directly and truly worldwide than recent, or presumably future, wars, or the economy at any time. All this will merge each nation's affairs with those of every other, more thoroughly than the threat of a nuclear or any other war would have done."
    —Mathematician John von Neumann, *Can We Survive Technology?*, 1955

"Current technologies that will mature over the next thirty years will offer anyone who has the necessary resources the ability to modify weather patterns and their corresponding effects. . . . The technology is there, waiting for us to pull it all together."
    —*Owning the Weather in 2025*, a report produced for
    the US Air Force Chief of Staff in 1995

"May those who curse days curse that day, those who are ready to rouse Leviathan."
    —Job 3:8

THE
LEVIATHAN
EFFECT

PROLOGUE

Chittagong District, Bangladesh, September 25, 8:17 A.M.

DR. ATUL PRADHAN HAD just poured himself a cup of black tea when he heard what he thought was distant thunder. He glanced up curiously, saw the bright, cloudless blue sky through the second-story windows, observed the motionless leaves of the betel palms, and decided that he had been mistaken.

But as he went to lift his tea cup, he heard the sound again. And then he began to feel it; shaking the floor boards beneath his feet, rattling the bone china cup against the saucer.

Dr. Pradhan set his cup on the credenza and stepped out onto the teak-wood deck. He leaned on the rail of the colonial-style apartment house and saw the commotion below: people running chaotically, shouting. He looked where they were pointing—toward the blaze of sunlight to the southeast, and the palm-lined road that stretched to the long tourist beaches at Cox's Bazaar—and he saw the crest of the first wave.

Moments later, dark torrents of seawater pounded through the streets, smashing shop windows, sweeping away food carts and merchant stands.

Dr. Pradhan stumbled back inside and closed the door. He stared at the tidy stack of textbooks on the Chinese oak table; his notebook opened beneath a reading lamp to a chart of twentieth-century weather patterns in the Bay of Bengal; the framed photograph of his wife and two grown daughters, taken on a mountainside in Southern India three years earlier. Beethoven's Sixth Symphony still played on the stereo.

At 8:22, Dr. Pradhan felt the floor boards shaking again, violently this time, and he staggered to the window of his rented room. The sky suddenly darkened, and then he saw the second wave—this one much larger, at least fifty or sixty feet tall, he guessed, taking down trees and utility poles and beach shacks as it raced toward his building.

On the streets below, people stood waist deep in seawater now, many of them screaming. He heard a man shout, "God help us!" three times. Already, bodies floated on the receding waters.

Several blocks to the east, a four-story apartment collapsed against the rushing water. *It will take down this building, too*, Dr. Pradhan thought. *It will take down all of these buildings. Everything along this shoreline will be swept away.*

Still, when it happened, at 8:29, the suddenness was stunning—the wood and plaster crumbling beneath him, the furious rush of cold and greasy water flushing him with it. That was when Dr. Pradhan thought about who had sent him here—the man he was scheduled to meet that afternoon. The American.

And then, for several seconds, it seemed that he might be safe. Dr. Pradhan opened his eyes, gasping for air. He felt his face bobbing like a buoy above the current. Tasted the cold, salty water and the warm air as he kicked his legs.

He looked up for a moment, just before the next wave took him under, and saw a white sea bird flapping frantically into the cloudless blue sky.

It was the last thing that Dr. Atul Pradhan would ever see.

ONE

WHEN YOU AGREE TO serve at the pleasure of the most powerful man in the United States, you enter into a contract of unspecified duration and largely unstated terms. You join an elite team with only fifteen members, chosen for your experience and expertise, although everything you do during your tenure will be seen as a reflection of the man you serve. Many strong-willed and highly talented leaders have become disillusioned by the degree of scrutiny, public criticism, and compromise that go with the job.

The trade-off is that, for a short bridge of time, you have the opportunity to help shape your country's history. What you make of this opportunity depends on myriad factors, some of which you control, many of which control you.

Catherine Blaine understood all of this when she agreed to accept a Cabinet post in the administration of President Aaron Lincoln Hall. It was, to people who knew her, a surprising decision—even more surprising than President Hall offering her the job. Blaine was independent-minded and had been, at times, famously outspoken. Although she'd served nearly five years in Congress, she had a low tolerance for Washington's political machinery—its blind partisanship and storied inefficiency, in particular. On the other hand, she was a three-star general's daughter who believed in the principles of service and loyalty. She began the job with the measured enthusiasm that most Cabinet members carried to Washington—a belief that she could bring something new to the post, that she would seize her opportunity and make a difference.

The first seven months of Catherine Blaine's term as secretary of Homeland Security had been unexceptional, marked by modest achievements and often weighted down by minor disappointments and frustrations.

But on the afternoon of Sunday, October 2, all of that began to change.

Logan County, West Virginia, 2:23 P.M.

As the rotor blades of the UH-60 Black Hawk stopped spinning, Catherine Blaine hopped down from the right side of the helicopter cabin and loped across the asphalt parking lot of the mountain heliport, two paces behind her press secretary, Lila Hernandez, to a waiting Town Car limousine. The rains had finally stopped and the flood waters were receding, but the steel-gray skies were still thick with moisture, the trees all dripping rain.

Blaine and Hernandez had just taken an aerial tour of a flood-engorged valley with the governor and several state emergency management officials, after a brief press conference at the capitol. They were now being whisked back to the airport, where Blaine would make a quick statement for the cameras and then board a plane to Washington.

Jamie Griffith, Blaine's chief of staff, was waiting in the limousine, typing on his laptop. Hernandez slid in first, followed by Blaine. Hernandez immediately pulled out her mobile to check messages.

"How was it?" Jamie asked, without looking up.

"Familiar," Blaine said. The car began to move. "Dozens of homes lost. A couple hundred people will be sleeping on cots in the high school gymnasium tonight."

"At least we have some positive news."

"Yes." At *least*. Blaine watched the waterlogged landscape while the Town Car climbed the rough, mountain road: Wood-frame houses set back in the sparse, shedding woods. Cars on cinderblocks. Old appliances in a clearing. A depressed area before, made much worse by the flooding.

There was a primal beauty to this hill country, though, that Blaine understood. Even after spending years in the belly of Washington politics, after teaching political science and foreign policy at Princeton and Georgetown, she was still a mountain girl at heart, raised in the foothills of western North Carolina. These long, misty mountain vistas awakened an irresistible emotion in her.

She was here today as the face of the federal government, and as a bearer of good news—the promise that tens of millions of dollars in Federal Emergency Management Administration aid would be distributed to homeowners and renters devastated by the floods.

Homeland Security, which oversaw FEMA, was, by definition, charged with the overall safety of US citizens and soil. It was a broad definition, encompassing everything from airport security to border patrols to natural disasters. DHS was a branch of government that hadn't existed before March 1, 2003, its creation part of the reaction to the 9/11 attacks. With two hundred thousand employees, Homeland Security was now the third largest Cabinet department, after Defense and Veterans Affairs. Often its duties overlapped those of other Cabinet agencies.

Blaine's interests ran more to foreign affairs than natural disasters, but she understood that visiting flood sites went with the territory. A week earlier, she had taken a similar tour of flooded regions in rural Kentucky. In between, there had been a border inspection in Arizona, a speech to the International Association of Fire Chiefs in Seattle, and a meeting with the US Customs and Border Protection Commissioner in Wyoming—which, during an interview with a local reporter, Blaine had mistakenly called Montana.

She gazed up now and saw the name of the town they were entering whoosh by: BENDERVILLE.

Ahead, the patchy, potholed road flattened out among the wet trees. Travel fatigue was setting in again, and Blaine was anxious to return to Washington.

"We *are* in Montana, right?" Jamie Griffith deadpanned, still looking at his laptop screen.

Blaine smiled. She had made it clear that humor was welcome in her administration, even when it was at her expense. She was in good company, anyway: in 1982, President Reagan had famously raised his glass at a banquet in Brazil and toasted "the people of Bolivia."

"Did I tell you Kevin and I are finally getting away this weekend?" she said.

"Mmmm. Not the details," Jamie said.

Blaine listened to her staffers' fingers typing on their keypads, the windshield wipers slow-thumping back and forth.

"Just a mother-son bonding thing. Planning to spend a couple days on the Shore. Biking, kayaking. Crab cakes."

Jamie made a grunting sound but didn't look up. Blaine decided to just enjoy the scenery for a few minutes, reminding herself that her chief of staff had served her well over these past seven months. In fact, Jamie Griffith and Catherine Blaine had become a surprisingly effective team, even if they struck people as the odd couple: Blaine, tall and fit with dark blonde hair, green eyes, and strong classical features; Jamie, a couple of inches shorter, pasty skinned, paunchy, and perpetually disheveled. But, in fact, they weren't what they seemed—Blaine, who gave off an air of order and efficiency, could be scattered and impulsive, while Jamie was methodical and meticulous. Griffith was a family man with two young children; Blaine, the mother of a nineteen-year-old, had occasionally struggled with the responsibilities of parenthood.

As the limousine rolled through the gates of the tiny airport, Jamie closed his laptop and surveyed the small crowd in the parking lot—about as many media people and town officials as onlookers.

A beat-up, lopsided lectern had been set up on an edge of the airfield. A half dozen public works crew members were lined up to the left side of the lectern, all wearing their orange municipal rain slickers. Behind the lectern was a C-20F Gulfstream twelve-seat executive transport plane, waiting to ferry them back to Reagan National.

Jamie stepped out first and walked interference, holding out his arms to keep back a female reporter who rushed over shouting "Secretary Blaine! Secretary Blaine!"

Blaine stopped at the lectern, leaning down to speak into the microphone, which seemed to have been set for someone four feet tall. "I'd like to commend all of the local agencies for the first-rate job you've done in dealing with this disaster. We've had a productive tour of the flooded areas, and I have assured the governor that we are fully committed to providing the necessary federal aid, including individual assistance and housing assistance."

She then delivered a brief message from the President and took three questions from the local media. Washington had become more diligent about its response to natural disasters ever since the chorus of criticism following Katrina in 2005; Catherine Blaine had been asked by the President to stress the government's "commitment" to these West Virginia flood victims and she wanted to leave them with a sense of assurance that Washington would be there for them. But Blaine was thinking already about her next day's appointments. They traveled to Ohio in the morning for a meeting on levee recertification. Then back to D.C. for a luncheon at the State Department and an afternoon briefing with the President.

As she walked out to the plane, Catherine Blaine heard a frantic clacking of heels on the wet pavement behind her.

"Secretary Blaine? Secretary Blaine! Could I get a quick comment from you before you go?"

Her chief of staff quickly stepped between them, but Blaine stopped him. "It's all right, Jamie," she said, summoning a smile for the reporter.

It wasn't one of the locals, though. It was a reporter she recognized—a Washington correspondent named Melanie Cross, who wrote for the *Wall Street Review*.

The reporter took a moment to catch her breath.

"Do you have any comment, Secretary Blaine, on the reports coming out of Washington this afternoon about the security breaches?"

"The—?" Blaine studied the reporter's face as she repeated her question, pen poised above her notepad. An intense woman with thick dark hair, smooth, lightly freckled skin, big doe eyes. "Which reports are these now?"

"The AP is quoting intelligence sources. Saying there have been unprecedented security breaches at CIA, Department of Defense, State Department and the White House." She paused again to catch her breath, watching Blaine. "Do you have any comment?"

Blaine frowned, and glanced at Jamie, who was standing at the base of the steps to the Gulfstream. She *had* been briefed on several cyber security breaches in recent days, but they hadn't been "unprecedented"—and it wasn't something that should be known by the media.

"Is that the word they're using—'unprecedented?'"

"Yes. That's—" She looked again at her notepad and what seemed to be a crumpled printout of a news story. "—and I quote, um, 'one security source characterized them as potentially the most serious cyber threats the government has ever faced.'"

Blaine shook her head. "No," she said. "I couldn't comment on that." She gazed at the printout in the reporter's hand, which fluttered in the wet breeze. "Is that the story? Could I have a look?"

Instead of showing it to her, though, Melanie Cross continued to read, her damp hair falling over her face. "'Unprecedented cyber breaches at Department of Defense and the State Department.' Um, let's see, 'renewing fears that the country may be vulnerable to an attack that could paralyze power grids across America.'"

Blaine shook her head. In fact, every day foreign intelligence services tried to hack into US government websites and computer networks.

"I don't think our power grids are all that vulnerable," she said. "I think that's been overplayed. But, again, I'm not able to comment on your specific question."

Jamie cleared his throat loudly and Catherine Blaine turned toward the plane, as if noticing it for the first time. It was beginning to drizzle again, chilling the air.

"So are you saying then that you have *no knowledge* of these breaches?"

Blaine smiled, feeling a momentary exasperation at this leading question. A brief biography flashed up—Melanie Cross: business and tech reporter, who had helped break a story about illegal pharmaceutical networks in Africa; her boyfriend was, or had been, Jon Mallory, investigative reporter for the *Weekly American* magazine.

"My immediate concern today," she said, "is the flooding here and these good people of West Virginia who are suffering."

"Mmm hmm." Melanie Cross pretended to scribble something in her notepad. Jamie widened his eyes.

"Walk with me to the plane, if you'd like," Blaine said.

"Okay."

They moved toward the Gulfstream, the reporter walking sideways, half a step ahead.

"Off the record? I am aware that there have been some breaches in the past couple of weeks," she said. "But if there is a comment, it would need to come out of the White House. As you know, our cyber command operation is based at Fort Meade and we now have a cyber security coordinator at the White House. A so-called cyber czar."

"Yes. And how do you feel about *that?*"

"About what?"

"Cyber command. Appointing a cyber czar."

"Oh." *Clever reporter.* "Well, that's another story, isn't it?"

Melanie Cross stopped walking and tilted her head, pen poised again. For years, there had been a philosophical tug of war between Homeland Security and the military over which should take the lead on cyber security issues. During her tenure in Congress, Blaine had spoken out against what she considered wasteful duplications of efforts.

When she said nothing else, Melanie Cross prompted, "Off the record?"

"Off the record, I think cyber security is still a poorly defined frontier, spread out across all of our intelligence branches. I think we're doing better than we were but we're still more vulnerable than we should be. Okay?"

The reporter was writing furiously.

"You said off the record."

"It is."

"Then why are you writing it down?"

She lifted her pen. The marks on the page seemed gibberish to Catherine Blaine. Some kind of shorthand.

"I know you pushed for more centralized efforts when you were in Congress," she said, raising her chin. "And that you've talked about so-called unanticipated threats."

Blaine smiled, surprised that the reporter knew this. She had written an article for *Foreign Affairs* magazine three years earlier—a free-wheeling, somewhat controversial essay about the need to anticipate "unexpected threats." She had been a government foreign policy professor then, never imagining she'd be out on the front lines again like this. "Well, yes. I think it's important to look for things that we haven't imagined before," she said. "There are many potential threats that we haven't adequately considered simply because nothing like them has ever occurred before. That's what happened on 9/11. We hadn't seriously imagined that possibility. We didn't think about putting sky marshals on airplanes."

The drizzle was suddenly becoming rain, misting the trees. Jamie Griffith stood in the doorway of the plane now, waiting. "Look," Blaine said. "Why don't we sit down sometime in Washington and talk about it under more proper conditions? When we have a little more time."

"I'd like to."

"Call Jamie and he'll set up something."

"Thank you. I will." The reporter stood there, scribbling, as Catherine Blaine began to climb the steps. Blaine couldn't imagine what she was writing.

She took her seat across the aisle from Jamie, who was immersed in his laptop.

"Would you find out what the hell she's talking about with those breaches?"

"Already have." He handed her his computer. "AP and Drudge have it."

Blaine squinted at the screen. The Drudge Report headlined it CYBER 'GROUND ZERO' IN D.C.?

She clicked the link and got the AP story. Scrolled through it quickly. It was cool in the plane and her suit felt damp and clammy.

Unconfirmed reports say the breaches may have originated in Beijing.

"'Unnamed sources.' 'Unconfirmed reports.' 'Reportedly.' That's not news," Blaine said, handing it back. "I mean, there are breaches every single day. Can you put in a call to Director DeVries? I'd like to know why I haven't been briefed on this."

"Of course."

"Where's my BlackBerry?"

"I'm not sure. Did you—?"

"Never mind. I'm sitting on it."

Blaine clicked on her government-issue mobile, typed in her code, and checked the message screen. Although she called it her Black-Berry, it was actually an SME-PED, or Secure Mobile Environment Portable Electronic Device, a custom unit developed by the National Security Agency for communications at the top secret level—verbal and secure encrypted email. Similar devices had been developed for high-level officials at the State Department, Defense, and CIA.

Blaine carried a second encrypted mobile device as a backup, along with her own standard-issue cell phone, which she considered her lifeline to the real world.

There were three messages for her on the SME-PED. One was from the assistant to the undersecretary of state, responding to her inquiry about border crossing statistics for Arizona. Another was from White House Chief of Staff Gabriel Herring: the President reminding her about her briefing the next afternoon.

The third was a message from her son, Kevin.

Hi Mom—jst ud on ES sat

That was odd.

Catherine Blaine stared at the two and a half inch screen in her left hand, trying to make sense of what she was seeing. Her son Kevin had never sent a message to her on the government mobile device before. In fact, he *couldn't* have sent her one. SME-PED was part of a secure, top-secret-clearance network. Only nineteen people had access.

But there it was—her son's quirky abbreviations: *ud* meaning "update." *ES* for "Eastern Shore."

Jamie's voice tugged her away: "Cate, here's the DNI's office. I'll transfer."

She pressed the phone feature on her SME-PED and took the call as the plane moved toward the slick, open runway. "Catherine Blaine."

"Secretary Blaine? It's Susan Romero. The director is just coming out of a meeting and would very much like to speak with you. He said he will call you in three minutes. And he asked me to extend his apologies. There's a lot going on at the moment."

"I'm sure." She sighed. "It's a little disconcerting to have to learn about a national security breach from the media."

"He's very sorry. Three minutes."

"All right, thank you."

Blaine clicked off, and glanced at her watch.

The call from Harold DeVries, the director of national intelligence, came sixteen minutes later, as the plane was climbing through gray stratus clouds above the West Virginia mountains.

"I'm sorry, Cate," he said. "I understand you had to hear about this thing from the press?"

"I'll survive. What's going on?"

"It isn't much. We're more concerned about the way it got out than the breach itself."

"That's what I thought." She waited. DeVries had been a mentor to Blaine when she was first elected to Congress, a shrewd man with a broad knowledge of international politics and an ability to quickly grasp complicated issues. She'd found him her best ally on the Cabinet, even if he was occasionally unreliable. "It must be a high-level source if the media's taking it this seriously," she added.

"Yes, unfortunately. We'd like you to attend a briefing in the morning before you issue any statement. What's been leaked to the media is inaccurate, Cate. I can't go into details right now, but it's something very specific. And it has nothing to do with the power grid. Gabe Herring will give you details on the briefing."

"Okay." Blaine nodded to herself. It meant that they would have to postpone the meeting in Ohio. She'd have to stay in Washington. "Thank you, Harold. We're on our way back now."

"Good. We'll see you in the A.M., then."

Jamie came up the aisle with two coffees and bags of peanuts.

"Thanks," Blaine said, taking one of the coffees. Looking up at her chief of staff, whose tie, per custom, had been loosened three inches, the knot shoved to one side, she said, "Think I could I have a vodka tonic instead?"

"Sorry. Dry flight."

"Shucks." Blaine sipped. "Oh," she said, feigning distress. "We're going to have to scrap Ohio tomorrow. I'm going to be in on a briefing instead."

"Rats."

They shared complicit smiles. Then Blaine closed her eyes. She thought about her brief exchange with the reporter, Melanie Cross. She had enjoyed talking off script, even just for a couple of minutes. Talking about real issues, the kinds of things that had first lured her into politics.

Six minutes later, Catherine Blaine opened her eyes. She saw the wisps of sunlight through the gray rainclouds below the plane's left wing, the drops sliding across the window. She felt the drone of the plane's engines. Heard the sounds of keyboards clicking.

And remembered the third email message she'd received on her SME-PED.

TWO

HAD KEVIN SOMEHOW OBTAINED her secure email address? The thought stirred unpleasant memories: Blaine flashed to those months when Kevin had seemed to be slipping away from her, struggling to assert himself, talking to her defiantly, in other people's voices, it seemed. Blaine had come to a humbling realization during that time—that her work as a politician meant nothing if she couldn't fix the problems at home with her only child. That had suddenly become priority number one, the most important work in her life.

She had chosen not to run for re-election to Congress four years ago, and soon afterward accepted a long-standing offer to return to academia, as a part-time visiting political science instructor at George-town. Parenting had been a challenge for Blaine at times, and it was one she had mostly undertaken alone. She hadn't always been the best parent, she knew, tending to underestimate what was required. But it was something she'd been determined to learn, and she—and Kevin—had come a long ways since her step back from politics. He was in school now and working three nights a week in a Georgetown restaurant. But she was also aware how easily it could all slip away.

Blaine pulled out her SME-PED mobile device.

She clicked open the email screen.

Saw the subject line: the abbreviations that no one but Kevin would have used. Then she clicked on the message, and stared at the words on her screen.

It took her a moment to fully comprehend what she was seeing. Then she felt her skin prickle.

No, it wasn't Kevin at all.

It was some kind of prank.

But a serious prank.

Blaine listened to the tapping sounds of Lila Hernandez's finger-nails beating on her laptop keys one row in front.

Someone had hacked into her secure SME-PED and left a message.

Was this part of the "unprecedented" series of breaches the reporter had questioned her about?

She focused on the two-and-a-half-inch screen, studying the words more carefully. A message clearly intended for Catherine Blaine:

Madam Secretary. On 9/25, 9/28, & 9/30, three "natural disasters" occurred in three very different regions of the world. I assume that you heard about them. None of them, in fact, were natural.

The pattern will continue Monday with an event in Western Europe.

You have the ability to stop this pattern. Details will follow—but only if this communication is kept within the circle of you and the recipients of my previous messages.

If you choose not to stop this pattern, the events that occur after Monday will devastate your country.

—Janus 158Y49P83T9

CATHERINE BLAINE LISTENED to the engine hum in the cabin as the plane climbed to its cruising altitude of twenty-one thousand feet. A prank, obviously. But how had someone managed to hack into her secure mobile device?

During her time in Congress, Blaine had pushed for more effective cyber security safeguards, both in the federal government and in the private sector. Technological capabilities were constantly evolving and America's intelligence and military branches had not prioritized cyber security as they had other matters, including the conflicts in Iraq and Afghanistan. There had been numerous high-level breaches of government computer systems and military networks in recent years, most of which the public never heard about. But, as far as she knew, there had never before been an infiltration of a private secure internal network.

The fact that someone had composed the subject line using Kevin's quirky abbreviations was deeply troubling to her. Somehow, someone had infiltrated her private life. Her *son's* private life.

She studied the name and numbers at the end of the message.
Janus.

Roman god of beginnings and endings. Doorways and gateways. Often depicted as a two-headed figure—gazing forward and backward.

Past and future.

But Janus was something else, too.

It was a name she recalled from her time on the House Permanent Select Committee on Intelligence, and which had resurfaced more recently in an inquiry from a colleague. A nickname that had been given to one of the most notorious computer hackers in the world. A renegade product of the Chinese military, groomed to infiltrate the networks of foreign intelligence services.

She looked down at the blue screen glowing in her hand and read the message again, memorizing it. "The events that occur after Monday will devastate your country."

Monday is tomorrow.

"What is it?" Jamie asked. He was staring at her, two frown lines creasing his forehead. A row in front of them, Lila Hernandez stopped typing.

"I think someone's hacked into my BlackBerry," Blaine said.

There was a protocol to follow in the event of a network infiltration. First, she contacted the cyber security coordinator at the Department of Homeland Security on her other encrypted mobile. In a drone-like voice, he instructed her to disable the SME-PED and to use her other mobile device only if necessary.

Six minutes after Blaine reported the breach, a call came in on her secure phone. It was the head of the Cyber Crime Command. Not at DHS—this time, it was the cyber security coordinator at the White House. The man the media called the US cyber czar, Dean Stiles, a gruff, blunt former military intelligence officer.

"Your device has been fatally compromised," he informed her. "We have remotely accessed and deactivated it. Proceed with caution in any further communications. You will be met at the airport with further instructions."

"What's going on?"

"You'll be briefed and questioned upon your return."

Catherine Blaine clicked off and stared out at the dark gray clouds.
Questioned?

"We have Internet access here, right?" she said to Jamie.

"Sure," he said. "Why?"

"I want to run a check on something."

Blaine pulled out her private mobile device, and clicked open a Google screen. She keyed in NATURAL DISASTERS and then typed in the three dates from the email. 9/25, 9/28, 9/30.

2:39 P.M.

The assassin watched from the next block as his target emerged from the suburban apartment building and rolled a medium-sized suitcase to his car, a blue Camry parked at the curb.

He loaded the suitcase into the trunk and turned, surveying the street, his eyes seeming to linger on the assassin's Range Rover for a moment—although, of course, he could see nothing through the tinted glass.

This was unexpected: the journalist leaving early, attempting an escape, without knowing who or what was coming for him.

Ultimately, it does not matter, the assassin thought. *It just hastens the process.*

The journalist, whose name was Jon Mallory, pulled quickly from the curb, driving away in the opposite direction.

The assassin followed at a careful distance, feeling a charge of adrenaline. He was fully engaged now, on the other side of the partition. The assassin existed for only a few hours at a time—and in the end he didn't really exist at all; in the end, he was an unknown soldier, a man whose purpose was to protect the mission. This was a containment exercise; a pre-empt. *Protect the mission.* Jon Mallory knew things that he shouldn't know, and the cost of that knowledge was going to be very expensive for him.

THREE

AS THE LANDING GEAR unfolded below the C-20F Gulfstream IV, Blaine realized that they were not coming in to Reagan National Airport as scheduled. She saw instead a familiar rectangular runway. Then barracks. Hangars. Military vehicles.

Andrews.

She looked at Jamie, who mirrored her frown.

They were landing at Joint Base Andrews—what used to be known as Andrews Air Force Base—eight miles outside of D.C. in Prince Georges County, Maryland. The forty-five-acre base was home to some twenty thousand active duty military people, civilian employees, and family members. Home base, too, for the VC-25A aircraft known as Air Force One. If there were ever an attack on Washington, the responding US combat air patrols would lift off from here.

Blaine shook her head in reply to Jamie's unspoken question. Before she had a chance to say anything, her secure cell phone vibrated.

"Catherine Blaine."

"Madam Secretary. It's Gabriel Herring."

The White House chief of staff.

"Yes."

"Secret Service has requested a change in venue for security purposes. I will be meeting you on the air field as soon as you de-plane."

"Okay. What's going on?"

"You will be briefed here on the base."

He clicked off. Blaine stared out the window. The plane was taxiing toward a cluster of vehicles—two black Suburbans, a Lincoln limousine, a half dozen military SUVs with blue lights flashing over the wet pavement—forming a semicircular barrier around the nose of the plane. She recognized the light blue berets of the Air Force Security forces, men standing at attention in the drizzle, armed with M-4 carbine rifles and M-4 pistols.

Walking down the landing steps, Blaine also noticed several Secret Service men hovering on the edges.

An Air Force security officer waited on the tarmac with an open umbrella for her. Beside him was Gabriel Herring, who stepped toward her stiffly and extended his hand.

"Madam Secretary."

"Thanks for the hero's welcome," she said to Herring as he escorted them to the open rear door of a military SUV.

Blaine turned and motioned for Jamie and Lila to follow.

But Jamie was looking at Herring and getting a different message.

"The president requests that it be just you," Herring said.

"Oh." She looked at her chief of staff. "Okay, I'll call."

She nodded to the military guards standing by the open door, ducked her head and climbed in the back seat. Herring scooted in beside her. The door closed.

Swirling blue lights shone in arcs off the pavement as the vehicles started to move.

"So," she said, trying a smile. "Can you tell me what the hell's going on?"

The chief of staff stared straight ahead. Gabriel Herring was known to have an easy, collegiate sense of humor. Blaine had seen him do spot-on impressions of Harry Reid, Mitt Romney, and Joe Biden. But during times of crisis, he sometimes shut down and resembled a mannequin.

Blaine watched him, saw him blink once.

Finally, he said, "The president has requested your presence at a meeting." His voice sounded metallic. "We're going to an on-base SCIF. You'll be briefed there."

"Oh," Blaine said. "Okay."

SCIF, or Sensitive Compartmented Information Facility, was a term that had emerged in the wake of 9/11. They were secured enclosures where sensitive classified information could be processed and confidential conversations could take place. Strict criteria had been

established for SCIFs through a 2002 CIA directive: separate heating and ventilation systems, walls reinforced with steel plates, single
entrances, no Internet ports, everything protected by sound-masking
materials.

"And you're not going to tell me what it's about?"

"No. I'm sorry," he said. "I can't."

He looked slightly seasick to Blaine.

"Why not?"

"Because I haven't been told."

THEY RODE IN silence the rest of the way, a five-car motorcade,
headlights full on, roof lights flashing, curving along a base road and
then stopping behind a nondescript five-story office building. Herring got out first, all business. Two military vehicles had blocked off
the drive on the other side, she saw. Armed Air Force guards stood
beside the entrance.

Inside, Blaine followed Herring into the elevator. He pressed 5.

"Women's apparel, please," Blaine said.

Herring watched the numbers change. He didn't blink.

In a hallway on the fifth floor, two Air Force guards stood on either
side of an unmarked door with a cipher lock. Blaine didn't have to
be told to leave her cell phones in the tray on the table outside. The
White House chief of staff typed in a code on the cipher lock pad,
then pressed a release and the door clicked open. Blaine held the
knob, waiting. But Herring was not coming in with her.

"No eavesdropping," she said, as the door began to close. It shut
with a surprisingly loud thud.

The narrow rectangular room was lit by a single lamp on a
mahogany table. A sparse, functional space. Metal walls, four pad-
ded leather chairs. SCIFs came in all sizes and configurations, and
were used for many purposes. This one was for conversations among
a small group of people.

In this case, three.

Blaine looked at the two men sitting catty-cornered at the end of
the table who now stood to greet her.

"Hello," she said, a little startled.

The larger of the two men nodded for her to sit.

"Secretary Blaine."

The man at the end of the table was Clark Easton, the Secretary of Defense. The other was Harold DeVries, Director of National Intelligence, whom she had spoken with fifty-three minutes earlier.

Easton was something of a political force of nature in Washington, a veteran of five administrations. A former major general who had served as special presidential adviser, as CIA assistant director, assistant Secretary of State, national security adviser and now as top man at the Pentagon. In his mid-sixties, he was large and thick-chested, with hard blue eyes and a lopsided grin, a giant bald head rimmed with white hair. Easton was surprisingly soft-spoken, but enormously influential in the administration—too much so, some thought.

DeVries was in some ways his opposite. Thin and rangy, he had a sly, knowing smile that seemed to hint at things others couldn't imagine. He spoke six or seven languages and understood the complexities and nuances of world affairs better than anyone Blaine knew. He was also the first African American to head up the United States' intelligence community. The Director of National Intelligence, known as the DNI, was in effect the CEO of all seventeen American intelligence branches. It was a position, like hers, that hadn't existed fifteen years ago.

Blaine felt a kinship with DeVries, a man who seemed at times frustrated, as she was, by the layers of bureaucracy and the duplication of efforts within the intelligence community.

The men's dress was casual—DeVries wore a dark blazer and an open royal blue shirt, Easton a short-sleeved white shirt—but their manner wasn't.

Easton seemed to be studying her, which caused Blaine to look away. That was when she noticed the folder on the table in front of him, marked TOP SECRET. Beside it was a small, single sheet of notepaper, the top third covered with tiny, neatly scrawled writing.

"Welcome."

Blaine nodded hello.

Easton made a face, something akin to a grimace, which was, in fact, how he greeted people. The Secretary of Defense inhaled dramatically. "Secretary Blaine. We need to bring you up to speed on a national security threat. I will provide a summary review and then outline the protocol and the directives that have been established by the president. He'll be meeting with you later this evening."

"All right."

"Because of the extraordinary nature of this threat, it has to be dealt with in a very deliberate and prescribed manner." He narrowed his eyes at her. "Naturally, this is information that cannot be shared on any level."

Blaine nodded once, feeling suddenly ill at ease, weighed down by the gravitas in his tone.

"It is essential that those who are directly affected—and that now includes you"—he raised his eyebrows slightly, held her gaze— "understand the significance of these directives. There are some very specific parameters, in other words, that we must stay within."

"Go ahead." *Can't we do this in English?* she thought.

"The message you received this afternoon on your mobile SME-PED is part of an ongoing pattern, which began ten days ago. We are still in the process of evaluating exactly what it means. We are unable to say with certainty at this time who is responsible or what the motive is behind these threats."

"The breach, you mean," Blaine said.

Easton raised one eyebrow. The lamplight glinted for a moment in his left eye, catching the deep blue pigment.

"The *breach* is part of a pattern," Blaine said.

"Well, yes. But more importantly, the message."

"I don't understand."

"That's why you're here." Watching her, Easton took a prolonged breath. He was known for using silence as an assertive tactic, to underline a point. "Do you have any idea why you might have been singled out as the recipient of this email, Secretary Blaine?"

Blaine looked to DeVries. "Well, let's see. I suppose being the Secretary of Homeland Security may have had something to do with it."

"This was made to look as if it came from your son," Easton said.

"Yes."

"I assume your son does not have your classified address?"

"You assume correctly."

"What does this mean? 'ES'?"

"Eastern Shore. We're planning to go to the Eastern Shore together this weekend. He was reminding me."

He continued looking at her as if she hadn't spoken, and Blaine felt a current of apprehension course through her, thinking about Kevin again, the fact that the perpetrator knew his abbreviations.

She told him the rest of it, the meanings of the other abbreviations, and she answered his questions about when and how often she used her mobile device, feeling as if she were being interrogated by a schoolteacher who suspected her of cheating on a homework assignment.

"Are you familiar with the name Janus, Secretary Blaine?"

"Vaguely, yes."

"Are you aware of the significance of the three dates listed in the message?"

"I am now. I looked them up on the way here. Three natural disasters. In Bangladesh, Uruguay and Fiji. Tsunami, hurricane, and earthquakes."

"Correct."

"Of course, anyone could have Googled those dates the same way I did."

Easton stared at her blankly, as if he'd forgotten who she was.

Blaine said, "I'm assuming the concern here is that our internal classified communications network was compromised, right? Not the message itself, which I'm assuming is a prank." She looked at Easton, then DeVries, neither of whom revealed anything. "Right?"

"That would be a reasonable assumption," Easton said. Sliding his palms against each other. "Based on what you know."

"Okay."

Blaine felt something shift in the room.

"Based on the available evidence, however, I'm afraid we're not able to treat it that way."

DeVries seemed to sense her restlessness. "We're going to explain all this, Cate," he said. "That's why we're here."

Easton cleared his throat. "As I said, the message you received is part of a pattern."

"Ongoing, you said."

"Correct. Similar messages were sent to my classified email account. To Director DeVries'. And to the President's."

FOUR

CLARK EASTON OPENED THE folder in front of him. His thick arms, with their dense curlicues of gray and white hair, cast shadows on the walls of the rectangular room.

There were several sheets of paper in the folder, she saw. He lifted the top one, turned it around and slid it across the mahogany table to Blaine.

"The president has authorized me to share these with you."

"All right."

Blaine felt a little numb all of a sudden, straightening the sheet of paper in front of her. It was a printout of an email dated September 29. Last Thursday. Three days ago. A message sent to the secure inbox of the man sitting opposite her—Harold DeVries, the Director of National Intelligence.

The sender was identified as RET: Robert Ellis Thompkins, the Director of the CIA.

The subject line: CATCHING UP. The two men were, almost by the nature of their job descriptions, frequently at odds with one another.

But clearly, this wasn't a note from the head of central intelligence. Blaine read the message:

Dear Mr. Director,

On 9/25 & 9/28, two so-called natural disasters occurred, the first in Bangladesh, the second in Uruguay. You undoubtedly read about them. Neither of them, in fact, was natural. The next ones will take place in the South Pacific Ocean tomorrow.

You have the ability to stop this pattern. If you choose not to do so, a similar event will soon devastate the United States.

Details will follow, but only if this communiqué is kept within the circle of you and the recipients of my previous messages. If this message is reported by the media, or shared with anyone else in the administration, including the FBI, the United States will suffer severe consequences.

—Janus 94S75Y38W86.

Blaine looked up.

Her eyes went from DeVries to Easton. Then back to DeVries.

The South Pacific Ocean. The next ones. On Friday, two days ago, more than a dozen earthquakes had rocked the South Pacific Ocean between Fiji and New Zealand, a region known as the Pacific Rim of Fire. The chain of earthquakes and subsequent tsunamis had killed at least two hundred people in Fiji, Tonga, and Samoa, while causing dozens of injuries and massive structural damage in New Zealand.

Easton watched her with his unblinking blue eyes as she handed the paper back.

"You said 'messages.'"

"Yes. Two others."

He slid a copy of the next printout across the table.

Blaine looked down, better understanding Gabriel Herring's reaction now.

This message had been sent to the President of the United States. An email address known by fewer than fifteen people.

The sender was Vice President Bill Stanton.

The subject line: NEED TO TALK.

This one was dated September 26. Last Monday.

But it wasn't from the Vice President.

Dear Mr. President,

Yesterday, a deadly "natural disaster" caused massive destruction in the Bay of Bengal, in Eastern Asia. As you will soon begin to understand, the disaster was not, in fact, natural.

This was the first in a series of such events. The second will occur in two days in South America.

You have the ability to stop this pattern. If you choose not to do

so, or if you decide to share the contents of this message with the media, or with any agency or individual within your government, including the FBI, an event will occur very soon that will irreversibly damage the United States. Details will follow, but only if this communication is kept within the circle of those who have received my previous messages.
  —Janus 3L38P93G676

Blaine read through the note again, and handed it back. "The next one was Uruguay," she said.

"Correct," said Easton.

"Last Wednesday's hurricane."

"That is correct."

A rare South Atlantic Ocean hurricane, the first ever reported on the shores of Uruguay. A wobbly offshore storm system that had suddenly become organized, gathering speed and strength, slamming the coastline east of Montevideo. Dozens of homes and apartment buildings were destroyed by the 90 mph winds and flooding, at least 120 people killed.

Easton pushed the third message toward her, exchanging it for the second.

This one had been sent to him on his secure mobile device, she saw, dated September 23. Two days before the Bay of Bengal tsunami.

The sender was DebE@aol.com. Deborah Easton. The subject line: BETTER COME HOME EARLY.

But the message was not from Easton's wife.

Blaine read the text:

Mr. Secretary,

In two days, an event will occur in Eastern Asia. It will be reported in the media as a "natural disaster," although its cause will not be natural.

A pattern of these "natural" disasters will continue for about twelve days. You have the ability to stop this pattern. But if this warning is reported in the media or is shared at any time with other countries, or with any agencies or individuals within the federal government, you will forfeit that privilege and the United States will

*itself be struck by a crippling event. At this point, you're instructed
to simply wait for further details.*
    —Janus 73X54K8439P

"Last Sunday. The deadly tsunami in the Bay of Bengal."
"Correct."
More than three thousand people confirmed dead.

Blaine read through it again, twice, searching for unusual phrases or
word choices that might contain hidden meanings. Then she handed
the paper back to Easton. The air in the room felt too warm all of a
sudden. So *these* were the breaches that the media had reported on
earlier in the day—without knowing any of the actual details. Just
knowing the White House was on high alert about something.

If it had happened four times, the infiltrations showed a vulnerability that the President apparently couldn't get his head around.
Somehow, someone had managed to repeatedly break in to the government's most secure communications network. A closed private
network separate from the Internet. But something about that didn't
feel right to her. Shouldn't this have gone to cyber command nine
days ago—and, if so, shouldn't she have been briefed?

Blaine waited, aware that she was the last one in this club. The
incredulity she felt was a stage the others had probably already passed
through, and, she suspected, all of her questions had already been
asked.

"As you indicated, there are two issues here," Easton said. He
closed the folder on the memos and clasped his hands on top of it.
"The first is the breach of our classified communications network.
The second issue is this series of messages and the implications for
national security. Obviously, both issues are of deep concern to us."

Easton drew a breath. His huge head was tilted slightly to the
right, his blue eyes steady on her.

"The natural inclination is to be more concerned by the first issue
and to react with disbelief to the latter," Easton said. "And, initially,
that's what we did. Clearly, we're dealing with a very sophisticated
hacker, who has been able to bypass our safeguards and protections.
We've altered encryption codes, isolated all possible points of infiltration, changed passwords, replaced the actual devices. But he seems
to be able to anticipate each move and come right back to us."

Easton narrowed his eyes and leaned back, a signal for DeVries to pick up where he left off.

"Cate, at first we treated this as essentially a high-level IT issue," the intelligence director said. Blaine glanced again at Easton. *Has he kept this information from me deliberately?* "But as you can see, the threats themselves have supplanted that. Until we have more definitive information, the President would like us to keep this inside a closed circle, as the perpetrators have requested."

Blaine averted her eyes, recognizing the larger issue. If the threat was real, it represented something the government was woefully unprepared for. It was, in fact, what she had warned about in her sometimes-maligned *Foreign Affairs* magazine article, "Anticipating Unforeseen Threats." A threat the country could not see coming, that it had no effective defenses to fend off. One of the most disturbing features of the new technological landscape, she had written, was that it was becoming possible to attack another country without engaging the military at all. New technologies could make militaries virtually obsolete. They could undermine nations that hadn't kept pace, automatically stripping them of their advantages and abilities to retaliate.

Checkmate.

But that assumed this threat was real.

Which Blaine did not believe.

"Thoughts?"

She considered how to respond. "Still processing."

"You've been a champion of this sort of research, haven't you?" Easton said. "Weather modification. Geo-engineering."

"Um. No," she said, forcing a smile. "Not a champion." He was pushing her buttons, Blaine knew, as he sometimes did. Easton employed an old-fashioned, unassuming brand of guile. One of his most effective tools was the deliberate but seemingly innocent distortion of other people's points of view, forcing them to correct him and in the process explain themselves. "I've endorsed the idea of exploring new technologies, yes."

There was no change in Easton's expression. "And imagining potential new forms of warfare?"

She shrugged.

"Including weather modification. And exploring geo-physical technologies."

"Not to any great extent, no."

He frowned at his sheet of notes, which were scrawled in tiny print. "You've written that we're, quote, 'lagging behind China in weather and climate research.' And you have urged that the military consider re-establishing a research program for quote 'climatology studies.'"

Blaine felt her heartbeat accelerating. "Urged" was the wrong word. She'd simply pointed out what was being done in other countries.

"Well," she said, "as you know, China *does* have a weather modification bureau, which employs about forty thousand people and spends over a hundred million dollars a year. We don't. We've had bills on the table for years to create one, but there hasn't been sufficient interest for them to go anywhere. Senator Kay Bailey Hutchison introduced legislation in 2005 that would have created a weather modification research bureau but it never came to a vote. It's not a high priority concern, as you know." She folded her hands and sighed. "But that's all a matter of record."

In the protracted silence that followed, Blaine heard the ticking of Easton's wristwatch.

"As you also know," she went on, "there are at least sixty countries engaged in weather modification projects right now. And a lot of activity in the private sector. Tens of thousands of weather modification patents have been filed. A lot of them are crackpot ideas, granted. Some aren't. Bill Gates recently filed five patents, for instance, to explore hurricane mitigation technology."

Easton inhaled very slowly. "And what has China's weather modification office accomplished, in your estimation?"

"You've seen the same reports I have," Blaine said. "They claim they're capable of producing rain and snow on demand. The Chinese news agency reported recently that they had created two hundred and fifty metric tons of artificial rain over the past few years. They claim they *prevented* rain during the opening ceremonies of the 2008 Olympics in Beijing. All of which is arguable. They've set a five-year goal of reducing losses caused by weather disasters from three percent of gross domestic product to one percent." She added, "Of course, there have also been reports that China is engaged in weather research they *aren't* talking about."

"For potential military use," said DeVries.

Blaine nodded.

"Russia, as well," he added.

"Yes."

There *had* been intelligence reports that China and Russia were exploring, if not developing, weather technologies for military use. But it wasn't anything new. The American military had committed more than thirty million dollars during the Vietnam war to an operation called Popeye, which seeded clouds with silver iodide to artificially extend monsoon season along the Ho Chi Minh trail in Laos, impeding the movement of enemy troops.

"In your estimation, is China even remotely capable of something like *this?*" Easton asked, lifting the folder.

"No. I really don't think so." Her eyes caught those of the intelligence director. "Is it theoretically possible that one day someone could cause these kinds of events? Probably. As you know, there have been countless computer simulations exploring storm activity and climate modification. But I haven't seen any credible evidence that anyone has successfully taken the leap from model to actual implementation. I think that's a long ways off. In large part, for practical reasons. It would require enormous funding. And our government decided long ago not to make climate research a national priority."

"But then we don't know everything that China and Russia's militaries are doing," DeVries said.

"No. We don't."

Silence expanded into the room again.

"I realize I'm coming to this late," Blaine said. "But I'm not sure I would rule out this being an elaborate hoax. I mean, it's a fact that on average a natural disaster occurs somewhere in the world almost every day."

"We considered that," said DeVries.

"And rejected it," Easton said.

"Why?"

"Study each message, Secretary Blaine. And each subsequent event. In every case, the warning was validated by the event. It's too precise to be coincidental. The President has determined that we have no choice but to take this as a legitimate and very dire threat."

After another silence, Blaine said, "Where do these breaches originate? Have we been able to determine?"

Easton rubbed his palms together. DeVries said, "Two of the four messages have been traced to servers in China. But, of course, we can't take that to mean that Beijing is involved. They could have been bounced off servers there as a diversion. A third goes to Eastern Europe. Stiles's cyber team at Fort Meade has been looking at that around the clock. But, frankly, we may never be able to determine exactly where they originated."

"It's odd that they haven't given any indication of what they want," Blaine said, still skeptical. "What the endgame might be."

"Actually, not so odd," Easton said. One edge of his mouth twitched. "It seems fairly clear: Their initial strategy is to establish credibility. That's exactly what they're doing. Once they've achieved this primary objective, we expect they will use that advantage as a bargaining chip. For what, we don't know."

"Are there any preliminary theories?" she asked, trying to read DeVries. "I suppose you've been around the table with this a few times already."

"We have some ideas, of course," DeVries said, his tone surprisingly guarded. "We're taking a close look at China. And elements within China. We'll get to some of that later. But, again, Cate, the bottom line is, we don't know. And because of that, we are proceeding in a cautious but purposeful manner." He looked at Easton.

Blaine saw from the Secretary of Defense's body language—the way he hunched forward and placed his notes on top of the folder—that he was about to close this meeting.

"Do I get a copy of those?" she said.

He gazed down and grimaced. "For now, the President does not want any additional copies made. He'll explain that to you later." *So that's the reason for the air-tight security around this building.* "We have a directive, until we receive additional information: to go after the known to find the unknown."

"And the known at this point is what—Janus?"

"Correct."

"That's where we're going now, Cate," DeVries said. "For a briefing on Janus."

Easton stood. "There's a car waiting outside," the Secretary of Defense said. "I will be returning downtown to the White House. There will be an additional briefing afterward."

Blaine nodded. As they walked down the corridor to the elevator, three pairs of footsteps echoing on the tiles, she recalled the last line in the message she had received and felt chills. *If you choose not to stop this pattern, the events that occur after Monday will devastate your country.*

FIVE

THERE ARE ANY NUMBER of reasons that people become politicians. Some start on grade school student councils and discover they have a natural bent for civic discourse and debate. Others are seduced by a specific cause that sparks their imaginations. Or a historic figure who inspires them. Motives may be selfless or self-serving, practical or presumptuous; usually, they are complicated combinations of the above. Many people excel first in other disciplines, coming to politics from business, law, sports, or entertainment. Whatever their starting points, politicians get mixed into the same pot once they arrive in Washington, a town that requires thick skin, uncommon patience and a tolerance for platitudes. Unlike chess masters, physicists, athletes and rock stars, politicians tend to peak in middle age or later. The average age of a member of the House of Representatives today is fifty-six years old, the average age of a US senator sixty. The median age of Cabinet members is typically between fifty-five and sixty-four.

When Catherine Blaine began her tenure as Secretary of Homeland Security, the age range of the presidential Cabinet was thirty-nine to sixty-eight. That put her at the low end—one notch up from the youngest. She felt privileged to serve with accomplished, experienced men such as Clark Easton and Harold DeVries; yet at the same time she'd been raised to find her own way through complicated issues. That was the internal tug of war—between her own instincts and the experienced counsel of her colleagues—that she felt now, walking with Herring and DeVries—three abreast—toward the back of a waiting limo as a soft chill hung in the air.

Only DeVries and Blaine got in the car.

They rode in silence at first, part of a six-car motorcade, speeding along the Capital Beltway toward Virginia, blue lights sweeping the black pavement.

"You okay?" DeVries said, pulling her from her thoughts.

"Sure. Still assimilating, I guess."

"I know," he said. "We all went through the same thing, Cate."

"Did you?" She watched his face in the flickering light—the high forehead, thin nose, firm set of his mouth; his observant eyes seemed reassuring to her, but expectant.

"He wasn't comfortable with that, was he?" she said at last. "With me."

"How do you mean?"

"Clark Easton. He wasn't comfortable bringing me into that room."

"Oh." He turned toward the window and she sensed that he was smiling. "Very perceptive," he said. "Yes, there was a discussion with the President beforehand. About bringing you in now or bringing you in later. Secretary Easton wanted to wait."

"For what?"

DeVries hesitated a beat before answering. "He's just a careful man. An old soldier, who likes to keep things close to the vest."

"I know he is. But I should have been briefed on the cyber breach."

"It's nothing personal, Cate. It's just a principle: the fewer people in the circle, the less chance there is that anything will get out."

"I understand that," she said, trying to stay even-tempered. "And how about you? What do you think?"

"Me? I'm with the President."

"So I'm in now because of the President?"

"No. You're in now because of the message you received. Period. The President thinks it's not our decision. That everyone who has been contacted directly has been contacted for a reason, and we need to respond as we've been instructed. I concur. For now."

"We're playing this by Janus's rules, in other words."

Cate glanced at the flashing lights of the military police vehicles sweeping across the four lanes of the Beltway as they whisked past slower traffic.

"Only until we can determine who Janus is," he said. "Do you have any other suggestion? Because if you do, I'm sure the President would be glad to hear it."

"No," she said. "Not at this point."

"Nor do I." He looked out at the rain, letting silence settle for a moment. "The President is very cognizant of the enormous risks here, Cate. It's a personal test for him. If he doesn't pass, this becomes his legacy. Either way, it'll be with him the rest of his life. He hasn't slept properly for days. He hasn't told his wife. I know he respects you and is going to want your input."

Blaine sighed. "I don't know that I'm really qualified to add much."

"Well, *he* does. I'm sure he'll value your participation."

She soaked that in as the motorcade passed through a long dark stretch of rolling countryside, part of the twenty-two miles of I-495 that passed through Virginia.

"You believe this," she said, studying his face.

DeVries was silent for a moment. "Yes, I do," he said. "You will too, Cate. Just be patient. You said yourself it's possible."

"Possible. But I also said it's contingent on funding. It would take a fortune to make something like that operational."

"Let's not get ahead of ourselves, okay?" DeVries said. The motorcade was slowing down, she saw, coming to the turnoff for Liberty Crossing. "A lot of what you're wondering will be answered at the next meeting. I'm glad you're part of this, Cate."

There was something in his tone that sounded rehearsed and unfamiliar. Not really him. It was eerie. He sounded a little too officious, as if he were playing a Cabinet member in a stage play rather than actually being one. That's what she was thinking as the procession of cars passed through the gates of the government's intelligence headquarters in McLean, Virginia.

THE ASSASSIN FOLLOWED Jon Mallory at a distance to the Grosvenor Metro station parking garage—the same route they had taken the day before. He parked his black Range Rover one level above where Mallory parked, and watched from the fourth level as he crossed the street to the subway station.

He had visualized how this would go—the look of surprise turning to panic after Mallory saw him—although he'd expected to have another day of surveillance before taking action.

The assassin had learned the other man's patterns: Mallory did not take his car downtown; he always parked here and rode the Metro; probably he was going to the *Weekly American* offices again; most likely he would be back within two hours.

He had already intercepted the encryption code from Mallory's car fob, creating a master key that enabled him to hack open his door lock with the press of a button. When Mallory returned, the assassin would be in the back seat, waiting for him.

Certain images from the last assignment played like loops of film in his mind now as he waited: the woman stretching in the shade, wearing a pink, long-sleeved zip-up jacket, navy leggings, New Balance trainers. Walking down the gravel path with a slight bounce; crossing the aqueduct to the towpath, where she checked her watch just before starting to jog; her short blonde hair flapping, incandescent for a moment in a sudden shaft of sunlight.

He had waited patiently for her. Choosing the moment judiciously. Startling her as she opened her car door. Tapping her arm, and then showing her the back of his wrist; asking his innocuous question: "Do you have the time?"

There had been an instant of hesitation, her face damp and mottled from running. And then a long moment of fear, as Dr. Keri Westlake's eyes went again to his hand and saw the cloth glove. Followed by the heat of anger. He had pulled the soaked rag from his jacket pocket and shoved it into her face, forcing her to breathe the sweet-smelling isoflurane while he pushed her head down into the seat. He moved in on top of her, his knee stabbing her belly and groin. He had seen the sudden swell of anger in her cornflower blue eyes; the hard downward tug of her mouth, as if she were trying to lift something that was too heavy. Felt her bony fingers clutching desperately at him. He had watched as her pupils dilated and her breathing became slower and ragged. And, finally, her eyes shut. Pre-empt completed.

He had wanted her to stay alive a little longer. But he had kept her in the farmhouse for more than twenty-four hours anyway, returning to her twice before putting her in the ground. That had been his secret; a fringe benefit, unknown to his commander. It was the first time he had made love to a dead woman. Just thinking about it now sent a charge through him. *Yes, I'd like to try that again*, he thought.

But he reminded himself that he needed to stay in the moment, focused on the current assignment. To protect the mission.

Slumped in the back seat, he watched a woman walk past through the tinted windshield of Mallory's car, dressed in a charcoal-gray business suit, carrying a briefcase. Then two men, in three-piece suits.

It wouldn't be much longer. He could just imagine it.

JON MALLORY TURNED right out of the Foggy Bottom Metro station and walked along I Street toward the offices of the *Weekly American* magazine. It was a crisp afternoon in Washington, the sky a hard blue, the leaves shedding.

He scanned the pedestrian traffic, alert for anyone who might be watching, and the street, for a dark SUV perhaps. He'd walked this same course the day before, seeing it all with different eyes; indifferent eyes. There had been a reversal since then: the story he'd been chasing was suddenly chasing him.

Jon rode the elevator to Roger Church's corner office on the second floor. He sat in the familiar burgundy guest chair across the desk from his longtime editor.

"I need to leave this with you," he said, handing Church an envelope. "I'm hoping my brother will come for it shortly. But I also want you to know about this."

Church opened the envelope. He unfolded the paper inside and looked at the list of seven names. Church was a tall, thoughtful man with a mop of silver hair and a highly attuned sense of curiosity. Before taking over the *Weekly American*, he'd earned an international reputation as a reporter, writing for the *Times* of London and for *The Economist*.

"Okay," he said, looking up at Jon. "Who are they?"

"Men and women who knew too much, evidently."

"About the same thing?"

Jon shrugged.

"What links them, then?"

"That's the story," he said. "I don't have it yet. What I know is that all seven are gone. Four dead. Three missing. Going back about nine years."

Church looked again at the list. Jon told him the rest, leaving out the parts that he wanted to tell only his brother, the parts that he carried on a flash drive in his pants pocket. Mallory was a veteran journalist, good at asking questions and telling stories. Occasionally, he became part of his own stories; he wasn't so good at that.

"And where did this come from?" Church said.

At the bottom of the list were three initials. DKW. Dr. Keri Westlake.

"That's the woman who gave it to me," he said. "She's a physicist, professor of environmental sciences at the University of Maryland. A proponent of weather modification and geo-engineering research."

Jon had had an appointment to meet Keri Westlake again on Friday, September 30. But when he arrived at her office in College Park, her door had been closed and locked. No explanation left behind.

"Until this morning, I thought it was just information," Jon said. "Which may or may not have added up to anything. But this morning I learned that her home was broken into and her computers were accessed. Files and emails copied and erased. Some of which would probably tie her to me."

"Learned how?"

"Police sources."

"And her whereabouts?"

"She's a missing person."

"Hmm." Church tugged at his sleeve, processing what Jon was telling him. "So you feel you're a part of this chain now?"

"I do. I don't think I should stay at my apartment. So I'm going to disappear for a few days. Try to figure things out."

"Can I find you a place to stay?"

"No. I don't want to get you involved."

Church watched him. "Have you told police about the list?"

Jon nodded, knowing that it was probably too complicated, too dispersed in space and time, for police to get their hands around it, at least for a while. What he really wanted was to talk with his brother Charles, a former CIA case officer and private intelligence contractor. Dr. Westlake had even suggested that he contact Charlie. But Jon had left a series of messages for him over several days and received no reply. It was possible, he knew, that the messages hadn't been received. His brother had disappeared, too, in his own way, on his own terms, years earlier.

"Have you told anyone else?"

"No."

"Not Melanie Cross?"

Jon shook his head, felt his face flush, and smiled. "No."

"Good."

Jon's on-again, off-again relationship with Melanie Cross was off again, following a brief, ill-fated recent attempt to live together. Melanie was also a reporter, a smart, disturbingly attractive woman with an unhealthy competitive streak.

"I'm seriously thinking about getting a dog," Jon added.

Church allowed a rare smile. He looked at the names again. "So where will you go?"

"I'm going to play it by ear until I hear from my brother. I'll contact you by email. Try to send a first installment of the story in a few days."

"Based on . . . ?"

"Police sources. Research. Some notes Dr. Westlake gave me that I haven't figured out yet."

Church studied him. "Want to talk about it before you go?"

Jon looked out at the street and felt anxious, thinking about Keri Westlake's warning. *There's a story here, and it must be told soon.* The sun was going down among the buildings of Foggy Bottom. The outside seemed unwelcoming all of a sudden; the inside a cage, safe.

But Jon knew he needed to get on the road. *Simplify.* His brother's mantra.

"Not yet," he said.

Church frowned. Jon knew that if he stayed and talked, his editor would try to convince him to come up with a different plan. Instead, Jon stood.

"Be careful," Church said.

"I will."

Outside, Jon blended in with the flow of pedestrian traffic. Students, faculty, state department employees. He thought ahead to his next steps. He'd retrieve his car from the Grosvenor station, drive onto the Beltway, head south into the night, hook up with I-95, turn in late at a highway motel.

At G Street, a car stopped incongruously in the crosswalk, blocking his way.

"Jon Mallory!"

A woman's voice, behind him. He turned.

The rear door opened.

A man on the sidewalk flashed a handgun and pushed against him.

Minutes later, Jon was sitting in the back seat of the car, watching the city through tinted windows.

SIX

6:41 P.M., McLean, Virginia

THROUGH A BULLET- AND blast-proof conference room window on the fifth floor of the X-shaped building that houses the National Counterterrorism Center, Thomas Rorbach watched the motorcade as it flanked off the Capital Beltway, high beams on, police lights flashing. Two Cadillac Sevilles and four armored Chevy Suburbans snaked onto the Dulles Access Road and through the hydraulic steel gates at 1500 Liberty Crossing. Then Rorbach, who had worked here for the past six and a half months, turned and walked down the antiseptic white hallway to the elevators.

Set behind tall, sloping berms and chain fences fronted by signs reading US GOVERNMENT CONTROLLED PROPERTY NO TRESPASSING, the Liberty Crossing site did not carry the cultural cachet of Langley, longtime headquarters of the Central Intelligence Agency. But the Liberty Crossing complex was now the nerve center for American intelligence, housing the National Counterterrorism Center and the ODNI, or the Office of the Director of National Intelligence, which Harold DeVries oversaw.

Liberty Crossing embodied the government's efforts to centralize and streamline its sprawling intelligence services after the 9/11 attacks. Here, dozens of analysts from the CIA, FBI, NSA, and various other agencies worked together sharing information and tracking potential threats twenty-four hours a day.

Rorbach, a stocky, pock-faced man in his late forties with wispy blond hair and unusual dark eyes, was deputy defense director for military intelligence, a recently created hybrid position. A former Special Forces soldier, Rorbach had served in two previous administrations—on the staff of the Assistant Secretary of Defense for international security and as National Security Council liaison for counter-insurgency. He had spent years, too, as a military contractor in the private sector. Twenty-seven hours earlier, he had been asked to become operations director of what was now informally called the "Janus Task Force."

HAROLD DEVRIES WALKED a pace ahead of Catherine Blaine down the second-floor corridor, their shoes echoing on the shiny tiles. DeVries was a lean, agile man who looked younger than his fifty-two years. He stopped before an electro-magnetic-locked SCIF, where he punched in a code on the keypad and then pushed open the door.

This SCIF was larger and more high-tech than the one at Andrews. Mounted on the encased metal walls were four fifty-six-inch plasma screens. Smaller desk monitors were at each of the twelve settings around the oblong cherry-wood table. The blue briefing booklets in front of the nine people in the room were identical except for the name stamped on the bottom right corner of each.

Blaine took her designated seat in the middle, nodding to several of the familiar faces. The gathering was a who's who of top-level intelligence officials, including the director of the CIA, the head of the National Security Agency, the White House cyber czar and several deputy intelligence directors. Sitting opposite her, at the center of the table, was Vice President Bill Stanton.

Moments after she sat, Stanton flashed his toothpaste smile and glanced at the notepad beside his desk monitor. "Ladies. Gentlemen. Welcome," he said. "We're here for an emergency meeting of the Janus Task Force. And before we get started," he added, nodding across the table, "we'd like to welcome Secretary Blaine into the room for this evening's meeting."

Blaine smiled politely at the Vice President. He was a big, cordial man with thinning white hair, an easy smile and an informality that she liked. No one ever called him William Stanton. Mr. Vice President seemed too formal. He was Bill, a folksy Washington veteran, prone to using colorful, idiomatic language and occasional malapropisms, which sometimes caused people to underestimate him.

"As you now know, folks, we've had another breach attributed to our friend Janus," he said, and held up his blue briefing book. "We've also received some new intelligence over the past eight hours suggesting that an unspecified attack within our borders may be in the advanced planning stages. An attack related to, uh, these breaches. Harry will give us more specific details on that."

Blaine opened her briefing book and scanned the details. There was an element of theater to having this meeting here, she knew. To show that Liberty Crossing was now where the nation's seventeen intelligence agencies came together and solved problems.

"The purpose of this meeting," Stanton added, "is to mobilize all resources, with an objective of locating Janus within five days. That's the President's directive." He slowly made eye contact with several of those in the room, including Blaine. "This means we make it a twenty-four/seven priority. We pull out all our guns and cancel everything else. Clean the slates." He made a strange sound in his throat. "I will head the task force and we're making Thomas Rorbach the point man in charge of operations."

Blaine looked quickly at Rorbach, who seemed slightly ill at ease being singled out but feigned a smile.

She skimmed through the pages of her briefing book: Background on Janus. Summary of his suspected whereabouts over the past decade. Chronology of the received emails, by date.

It didn't take long for Blaine to recognize what was missing. They had left out the specific threats. There was no mention of the "natural disaster" warnings, of the actual subject matter in Janus's emails.

The President's directive.

This had been orchestrated to go after a more narrow objective. *Why?*

"For the benefit of Secretary Blaine, we will start with a brief overview. Harold?"

The ten desk screens lit up and a grainy black-and-white image appeared in the center of each: a man wearing a dark overcoat, walking along what seemed to be an empty train or subway platform. DeVries, who was seated to the right of the Vice President, began: "Janus is Xiao-Ping Chen," he said. "He's forty-one years old. 'Janus' was a code name created in Beijing about ten years ago."

A second photo of Janus came on the screens. Then a third. In the first, he looked boyish and slender. In the next, his face had filled out and he wore rectangular, wire-rim glasses. In the third, his hairline had receded considerably. *They almost seem like photos of three different men,* Blaine thought.

"He was born in Shandong province in Eastern China," DeVries continued, speaking in his clear, steady tone. "His father was a diplomat. The family moved to India and Russia during his childhood. The father was apparently something of a taskmaster. And, a heavy drinker. He ended up a suicide when the boy was twelve."

DeVries pressed a button on his desktop and the screens went dark.

"Chen joined the Chinese military at age seventeen. He studied computer science and eventually earned an elite post. At a young age, he became an accomplished hacker. Computer hacking is, of course, a different game there than it is here. The Chinese government employs about fifty thousand hackers as part of its military operations."

DeVries glanced at his notes as if he'd momentarily lost his place.

"Chen apparently had some issues with authority within the Chinese military. He moved to Germany in 2004 or 2005 and began to work independently, we believe. He became a private contractor, in effect, but still sold his services to Beijing."

"Please. Explain what that means," Robert Thompkins, the director of Central Intelligence, said from the other end of the table, holding up his reading glasses. Thompkins and DeVries had several times crossed swords in recent months over jurisdictional boundaries.

"In other words," DeVries said, not looking at the CIA director, "he would initiate an operation on his own, but the operation would yield information that was of value to a third party. Say Beijing, or Pyangpong. He would then approach a representative of the third party with this information and broker a deal. Creating a buffer, in effect."

"To avoid the appearance that the government was directly involved."

"That's right. What's known as the problem of attribution."

"Chicken or the egg," said Stanton, incongruously.

DeVries typed several numbers on his desktop keypad. "It's convenient, of course, for governments or corporations to learn secrets about other governments, or other corporations, while avoiding the appearance of initiating those inquiries."

The screens glowed and another photo came up: a blurry image of two men walking along a path in a park.

"The intelligence on Janus indicates that he's not a man of great national loyalty. Or any other sort of loyalty," DeVries went on. "We have reports that he did some high-level hacking for Moscow. We also believe that he may have played a role in setting up the Ghost-Net operation. At least as a consultant." He paused, looking around the table. "GhostNet, as most of you know, infiltrated political, economic and media targets in more than a hundred countries, including the inner workings of the Dalai Lama's organization. Before we shut it down in 2009."

Blaine was beginning to remember something else she had heard about Janus: a portion of which had gone public. But she sensed that it was out of bounds at this meeting, so she said nothing.

"Nevertheless, this is the most recent photo we have," DeVries said. "It was taken in Munich over the summer. Chen, we believe, is on the left. The man he's talking with is a high-ranking member of the MSS."

China's Ministry of State Security. Counterpart to the US's CIA and FBI.

"Which would indicate that his client is now Chinese intelligence?" the CIA chief said.

The Vice President made a coughing sound. "Possibly, yes. At the least, we think Beijing is probably aware of this man's activities, if not directly involved. And we believe, based on the most recent intelligence, that Chen is currently in Munich." The Vice President waited, then added, "Now I'm going to let Dean Stiles have the floor."

Stiles, a gruff, wide-shouldered man with a shaved head and a long chin, was the new White House cyber czar. He cleared his throat, a deep raspy sound, then began to describe the technical details of the breaches, reading from notes written in longhand on three-by-five cards. Blaine noticed the suppressed yawns and restless shifting around the table as he described the adjustments of stopgaps and encryption safeguards.

It was essentially a cat and mouse game, Stiles explained. You install counter-measures and the other side finds a way around them. Back and forth. Blaine had been told by a cyber crime analyst at the National Security Agency once that only about two hundred people in the world fully understood the hacking game at its highest level, and she doubted if any of those two hundred were in this room today, with the possible exception of Stiles.

Afterward, a slightly awkward silence filled the chamber as the Vice President paged through papers in his folder, as if searching for something.

"Wasn't Janus also a US asset at one time?" said Kyle McCormack, the CIA's head of counter-terrorism, raising the question Blaine had decided not to ask. Stiles frowned and turned his eyes to the Vice President.

"That's right," Stanton said. "We discussed that at our initial meeting. He identified a series of computer science centers in China being used by the Chinese military to hack into American networks. This was five, five and a half years ago."

The CIA counter-terrorism chief nodded, watching him with hooded eyes.

"But the information was deemed unreliable, wasn't it?" said McCormack.

In fact, there was something else about the episode, Blaine recalled, something damaging or embarrassing, some of which had gone public, but she couldn't remember exactly what it was.

"Of course, we don't believe that one person is behind this threat," Thom Rorbach said, changing the subject. "It's more likely that Janus has been retained as an independent contractor to hack into our systems and deliver these threats. That may be the extent of his involvement."

"Do we even know that he's really involved?" Blaine said. "Couldn't it be someone simply using the name, as a way to get our attention?"

"Possible," Rorbach said. "But not likely." Blaine glanced at him, then looked back at her booklet. He had strange eyes—wet and virtually black, as if there was no center to them, no pupils. "A very specific code has been used in all of his communications. Four variations of eleven numbers and letters. They were the same classified codes Chen used in his dealings with us six years ago. A signature, in effect."

Blaine nodded. But she was remembering something else. A man who had written a report about Janus years ago. A former intelligence field officer named Charles Mallory.

"At any rate," the Vice President said, "the feeling is we're flying into something of a fertilizer storm here. The President's directive is that we mobilize all of our resources. He would like a preliminary working plan tomorrow morning by ten, involving all pertinent agencies. Data searches. Signals intelligence. Banking transactions. Everything that we can pull together. Thom Rorbach will coordinate."

Rorbach, Blaine noticed, seemed to still be looking at her. In fact, his head hadn't turned away from her since she had asked her question.

As Blaine stood, Gabriel Herring touched her arm. "One more meeting," he said. "After that, you can go home."

"Good." She turned toward the doorway without looking back.

"This one," Herring said, "will be on Pennsylvania Avenue."

SEVEN

CHARLES MALLORY DROVE THE twisting, two-lane road as golden sunlight gleamed through the pines and spruces, back-lighting the darkening pods of cumulous clouds. A quarter mile past the second of the MOOSE CROSSING signs, he hooked a left onto an unmarked gravel drive and followed it to its dead end at Thunder Hill Quarry.

He had lived in this remote harbor town for close to two years now, but he had yet to see a moose, let alone encounter one crossing the road. The signs, he suspected, were mostly for the summer tourists.

He parked his truck on the neck above the quarry and breathed the cool air, the shifting, subtle scents of water, tree bark, and pine sap. Then he stripped off his jacket and T-shirt, his shoes and trousers. He walked to the edge of the rocky outcrop, took a breath and dove in, swooshing in a long arc down through the frigid, sixty-three-degree water and coming up to the surface.

He caught his breath in the chill air and backstroked across the quarry, watching the fading light through the webs of pine branches.

By the time Mallory had climbed up to the rock ledge and was sitting at the top, his body temperature had dropped from ninety-seven to ninety-five degrees and he was shivering.

The late sunlight felt good on his skin, until the clouds moved across it. He sat there for several minutes, listening to the birds and the occasional creak of branches in the breeze. The birds were congregated on the wires along the road, he had noticed. A pressure system was moving through. Something was coming, probably a big offshore storm. *Clement would know.*

Several times a week, Mallory came here to swim before sunset.

The icy rush of the water was about the most invigorating feeling he knew these days. Sometimes he thought he did this as a substitute for something else; for what he had given up, perhaps, in deciding to move to this distant outpost.

He lived the life of someone else here, a man whose name and personal history he had invented. A life he'd created out of necessity. Thirty-one months earlier, Mallory had turned over D.M.A. Associates, his private intelligence contracting firm, to Joseph Chaplin, the chief of operations, with the idea that he would be free to disappear into a more normal life. At first, he had traveled, backpacking in South America and Europe, riding one-way buses and trains, living in unfamiliar rooms. But eventually he began to crave a routine again. Two years ago, he and a woman named Anna Vostrak had driven into this harbor town and decided to invent a life here. Mallory leased a store, Anna opened an art gallery. They rented an old fisherman's cottage on the point and moved in.

For most of their time here, it had been a good life, if a duplicitous one. Two weeks earlier, Anna had left to visit her family in Switzerland. Living a life of invention had begun to wear on her and he suspected that she wouldn't return, at least not for a while. He didn't blame her, although he missed her more than he had imagined he would.

Mallory dressed and walked to the pickup, still shivering, and began to drive the winding road back toward the harbor.

Several miles on, he saw an older model pickup parked in a clearing. He pumped his brakes, scanning the eyes and hands of the two men seated in the bed. Then, recognizing them, he waved and accelerated. He still did that—fell back into the observational habits from his years as an intelligence agent. It was no longer necessary when choosing a table in a restaurant to make certain that he could see who was coming in the door, but he did. Or to scan parked cars to make sure no one was sitting in them, but he did. Spy work was devil's work. To understand the enemy, you needed to think like the enemy; to defeat the enemy, sometimes you needed to become the enemy. Here, though, there was no enemy.

He pulled up in front of the store, parking next to two pickups he recognized as Clement Caldwell's and Harvey Spellman's.

The wooden screen door squeaked and Spellman came out

carrying a twelve-pack of Natural Light. The two men exchanged familiar greetings.

Mallory's store sold a little of everything—milk, beer, soda, toothpaste, chips, bread, used books, local art, bait, ball caps. He called it Harbor Store because that was how people named things here. There was a Harbor Tackle, Harbor Inn, Harbor Books, Harbor Fish Market, and Harbor Real Estate.

He'd run the store himself for most of the first year. Then one day Clem had walked in, asking for a job. Mallory hired him to work the register three nights a week. But Clem had his own ideas and began taking on extra hours whether he was paid for them or not. Before long, he was calling himself the store "manager." It seemed to give him an identity and Mallory didn't mind the free time.

Clement was seated behind the counter as he came in, wearing his knit cap and dark, tattered flannel jacket. He only shaved every few days; this wasn't one of them.

"Don't tell me you've been swimming again."

Mallory suppressed a smile. The store smelled of old pinewood and microwave popcorn. He stood in front of the space heater, watching the brightening harbor lights.

Clement had come from elsewhere, too, but he didn't talk about it. Occasionally, he mentioned a wife, Adele, who had died some years ago. But he preferred to talk on other topics, the weather and fishing, mostly.

"What's it looking like?" Mallory asked.

"She's coming. See how the birds're flying? When the birds fly that low, the pressure's down, she's coming. See the rainclouds? They're swollen with tomorrow already."

"How long?"

"Oh, I'd say we're good for another twelve, fourteen."

"Then what?"

"Then she'll come in hard. You can see it in the way the sky's bending." He pointed out the window. "Way out there to the northeast."

"How bad?"

"Hard to tell. You can see her already in the outer squibs. See that out there?"

Mallory looked and nodded. Clem had an instinctive understanding of coastal weather patterns and he had taught Mallory a few things about pressure systems and reading the clouds. Clem had spent much of his life on the water as a lobsterman, observing the sky and the sea for days on end. He had learned by looking, as Mallory had learned by watching people's behaviors. Clem had developed his own vocabulary along the way, using words like "bends" and "squibs" as if they were real terms.

"You better get out in that shower now, you're going to catch pneumonia, freeze yourself to death. We're not in summer any more, young man."

Mallory came out from the shower minutes later wearing faded jeans, a flannel shirt, and work boots, no longer shivering. Clement handed him a bottle of local-brewed beer, and they sat out back on rusty metal chairs watching the water breeze up and the last of the daylight fade, smelling the brine, the char-grilled seafood and the gasoline. Lights in windows were brightening on the small hillsides around the harbor.

"Oh, I almost forgot. Your girlfriend come in, asking for you."

"I don't have a girlfriend anymore, Clem."

"*She* thinks you do."

She being Monica Tinsley, the woman who ran the historical museum. She'd become solicitous toward Mallory in recent days—ever since Anna left—and apparently Clement didn't see anything wrong with playing cupid, although Mallory wasn't interested.

"I'm serious," Clem said.

"Don't be." Mallory took a pull on his beer.

"You're chomping a little bit again, aren't you?" Clem finally said.

"Maybe."

"I can tell."

Mallory looked out at the dark, featureless horizon and felt old yearnings. "You know what it is, Clement? It's like that storm you were just talking about. Sometimes I feel there's something out there I should be aware of. I don't know what it is yet, exactly, but I can feel it. You know?"

"Sure."

Minutes later, Mallory was finished with his beer and standing.

"You just be careful now," Clem said, pointing the neck of his beer at him.

Mallory winked, but his mind was elsewhere. "She's not going to be bothering me at home, is she?"

"Never know." This time, Clement winked.

"I'll be careful. Take care, Clem."

IT WAS A hilly road to the house that Charles Mallory rented on the point, a rocky arrow of land that jutted into an inlet on the Atlantic Ocean. He parked in the drive beside the house and sat for several minutes breathing the night air, listening to the waves on the rocks. Across the inlet, fog drifted past slowly, dimming the glows of the motel and the lobster restaurant along Main Street. Maybe he *was* chomping. But not to go back to Washington. Or Langley. There were too many unresolved memories there, still. Maybe it was some-thing else.

A couple of weeks ago, Charles Mallory had received two emails from his old employer, the United States government, asking him to contact them. Mallory had no intention of responding, but the messages had triggered something; ever since, he'd had idle moments of curiosity, as if a familiar voice from his past were trying to say something to him.

Sometimes, now, he went days and even weeks without checking messages, in part to avoid those voices. He had found himself, liter-ally, in a safe harbor here, separate from all that had gone before. The past didn't exist in this place and that was how he liked it. But the past still existed in his head, and there were parts of it he couldn't excise. Mallory's father had been killed four years earlier, hunted sur-reptitiously because of what he knew about an undercover govern-ment operation. Mallory had helped bring the truth to light. But only some of it; the rest would probably remain in the shadows forever. Most of the time, he was at peace with that; there was no percentage in wrestling with it. But tonight, he felt the past seeping in again. Maybe it was the way Clement had talked about the storm. Or what he had seen in the news on television over lunch.

Inside, he fired up his computer for the first time in days. He typed in two seven-letter encryption codes, then called up emails that had been routed to him through his old secure and encrypted account, forwarded to an address he had set up anonymously.

He saw that there were five new messages he had missed.

Three were from his brother.

Going back six days.

The first two emails carried the same subject line: PCNTT.

There was no text in the message windows. It was a simple code they had established years earlier: *Please Call. Need To Talk.*

The third message, which had landed in his inbox thirty-one hours and twenty-seven minutes ago, contained an additional letter. U, meaning "urgent."

Then he saw that there were two encoded messages from Joseph Chaplin, who ran his old intelligence business from an unmarked office in Northwest Washington, D.C. Each with the same subject line: PC.

He felt an anxious shiver, thinking of his brother's dark, vulnerable eyes. In his closet, Mallory had stashed a half dozen untraceable, disposable cell phones. Some habits were hard to break.

Chaplin had given him a number that he could call in cases of emergency, but he had never used it. Until now. The wind whipped across the water as he punched the number into a new phone.

After four rings, he heard a click on the other end. "Greetings." Chaplin's lilting African accent.

"You've been trying to reach me."

"Well, yes. Someone has," he said. Chaplin, one of the most trustworthy men Mallory had ever known, still looked out for him.

"Do you know what it's about?"

"I do. But you'll need to visit Cleveland, sir, first. Mr. Green will meet with you next week. Room 789. Then to St. Louis in the afternoon. He'll have more."

"You're sure."

"Yes."

Charles Mallory sighed. "Okay, then. Goodnight."

"Goodnight."

Mallory walked out onto the back deck to decipher what he had just been told. Chaplin wanted him to come back again. He had told him so with a simple verbal code that was written nowhere but in their heads. Words substituting for other words. Cleveland meaning Washington. Next week meaning tomorrow. Mr. Green was National Car Rental, and Room 789 a hotel in the Maryland suburbs.

Just like that. Mallory felt a deep-rooted mixture of apprehension and curiosity. Chaplin was summoning him back. But it was really his brother reaching out to him. Jon was the "someone." And that was the only reason he would even consider doing what he had sworn he would never do again. Mallory felt a fine mist of rain in the breeze and he thought about what might be coming. Storms he'd never imagined.

EIGHT

8:45 P.M. Oval Office, Washington, D.C.

"HELLO, CATE."

Catherine Blaine reached across the famous Resolute desk to shake hands with Aaron Lincoln Hall, the President of the United States.

"And welcome. Our circle has five members now."

Blaine smiled politely. The President's face seemed tired, belying his upbeat tone. He was a tall, striking man with inviting brown eyes and a classic senatorial profile—strong chin, narrow, slightly curved nose, swept back silver hair. In meetings, journalists had said, his assurance and charisma seemed to "suck the oxygen from the room." Blaine had been struck by the difference between how self-assured he could be in person, though, and how self-conscious and wooden he occasionally came off in television interviews. When you separated Aaron Lincoln Hall from the contact sport of politics, he was a sharp-witted man, and a brilliant speechmaker, even though his enemies had diligently branded him otherwise—he'd been called everything from a milquetoast to a Muslim terrorist sympathizer. For Blaine, the only criticisms that carried any weight were the claims that he could be too cerebral and that he depended too much on the counsel of his advisers, particularly in military matters.

"I'm sure this has been a lot to absorb in a short period of time," he said, looking at her as if they were the only two in the room.

"It has."

"Naturally, I'm curious what your impressions are. I respect your background and what you can bring to this."

Blaine blinked self-consciously. She glanced at Harold DeVries, her former mentor, who was seated in the rosewood chair to her left. To her right was Clark Easton. These were the two advisers the President relied on most.

"I know you've been given the outlines of what's happened, Cate. I want you to understand we're doing all that we can diplomatically. Which isn't much. The Secretary of State has opened channels with Beijing. That's not yielding much, unfortunately. We're really in something of a holding pattern right now."

She nodded. "You said five members."

"Yes. The Vice President has been briefed on all of this. He's the fourth, you're the fifth. We're a circle of five." His smile faded so quickly that Blaine wondered if it had been there at all. The President was a man of big ideas and she could sense that he was already mulling over the possible outcomes of this crisis. "The Secretary of State has a limited knowledge but has not been privy to the actual contents of the emails. Nor has anyone else. We're now honoring the request to keep those threats within a tight circle."

"What about at the IT level? Isn't someone aware of this at NSA?"

"Dean Stiles, yes, of course. It started there, as a cyber threat. The email incursions are being thoroughly analyzed by a special unit at Fort Meade, but the messages themselves have been scrambled or removed. As I say, we're honoring the specific request to keep this within our group."

Blaine stiffened, slightly intimidated for a moment, as she often was, by her surroundings. The white marble mantle. The presidential seal on the rug and the presidential medallion on the ceiling. The two flags behind the desk—the US flag and the President's flag. The Resolute desk, made of timbers from the HMS Resolute, presented to President Rutherford B. Hayes in 1880 by Britain's Queen Victoria.

"As Secretary Easton told you earlier, we consider these messages a credible and urgent threat to national security," the President went on. "And we are responding accordingly. The details, needless to say, cannot be divulged to family or staff. We have already communicated this to your chief of staff. Until this issue is resolved, Cate, DHS will be run by Deputy Secretary Laine Wells."

"Oh," Blaine said, surprised.

"You can set up office across the street in the EEOB." Eisenhower Executive Office Building, the ornate 553-room slate and granite building that served as offices for the White House staff, the

Vice President, Cabinet members, and various other government officials. "We need you on this full-time, Cate." Then he took a slightly warmer tone. "We've set up a separate, secure room in the Eisenhower building, which is in effect the command center for this. We're calling it the Data Visualization Center, which is serving as a portal to the NASA Center for Climate Simulation in Greenbelt. It's been outfitted to monitor all available incoming storm data, from NASA, NOAA, the Space Station, as well as aircraft reconnaissance data, satellite, land-based radar data, buoy sensors, and computer models." He slid a blank white rectangular badge across the desk, glancing at Defense Secretary Easton. "This will grant you access. We're monitoring any and all geo-physical activity around the world that has the potential to become a threat to this country. From here forward, all of our meetings will be held either there, in the Cabinet Room or downstairs in the Situation Room. Okay?"

"All right." Blaine felt numb, thinking about the others in the "circle of five"—men, older than her; married, parents. She thought of her father, what he would think of her being here; it made her self-conscious.

The President pushed a sheet of paper across the desk to her. "We've also set up a climate science advisory committee, which we will call upon as needed. Dr. James Wu is heading it up."

"Okay." Blaine scanned the list quickly, looking for one particular name. Not finding it. The dozen names were all well-known climate scientists and meteorologists, most of whom she considered "policy" scientists. Men and women friendly to the administration's views on climate change, global warming, and various other issues. The science of weather had become increasingly politicized in recent years and Blaine's favorite source, Rubin Sanchez, once one of NASA's most innovative researchers, had become marginalized because of his unorthodox views and even more unorthodox public presentations. It did not surprise her that he'd been left off the advisory board. Dr. Wu, the President's chief science adviser, was a well-known professor of atmospheric science who'd been a pioneer in the field of storm forecasting, although he had taken an increasingly conservative stand on global warming and other weather issues.

"You bring a valuable perspective to this, Cate," the President said. "I'm looking forward to hearing your thoughts and questions."

"Thank you." She tried a smile. "With all due respect, sir, being the last one in this 'circle,' I think I'd rather hear what you've already found before I venture any opinions."

"Understood. Let's go through the latest, then."

DeVries summarized the efforts that had been made to track the source or sources of both the email threats and the geo-physical events. His report lasted just over nine minutes, mostly repeating what she'd been told earlier. Easton then explained how the United States had responded quickly and diligently to each of the natural disasters, extending aid to the devastated countries. Two former US presidents had established a relief fund to assist the ravaged Bay of Bengal region.

Blaine nodded periodically, trying to be diplomatic, although Easton's presentation rubbed her wrong. Finally, he straightened his notes and sat back, elbows on the arms of the chair.

"Questions?"

"A few, actually," she said, "although this is probably territory you've already covered. So, please, if you'll just indulge me." The President blinked his assent, waiting. "The first, I suppose, is an obvious one: how could things have gotten to this point without our intelligence services picking up what was happening?"

President Hall exchanged a look with DeVries, then with Easton. "Harold?"

"Priorities," DeVries said. "As you noted earlier, Cate, Russia and China have increasingly devoted time and financial resources to this branch of research. We simply haven't considered it a national priority."

The President lifted his right hand, a motion that reminded her of a conductor readying the orchestra to come in. "Cate, do you know how many countries have landed a man on the moon?"

Blaine studied the President's face, his warm brown eyes, wondering what he was getting at. "We're the only one, aren't we?"

"That's right. Twelve times. Twelve men have walked on the moon, all between the years 1969 and 1973. Why? Because we decided to make it a national priority. After Kennedy's speech in 1961, we pulled together in a concerted effort to prove we could do it. And we did. But priorities change. Attention spans shrink. We elect new leaders more often than most countries. And every time we do, continuity is lost, priorities shift. It's one of the weaknesses in our system."

"Although, of course, there's a difference between going to the moon and controlling the weather, isn't there?" Blaine said.

"Yes and no. The point is, our objectives don't always have time to germinate properly. In recent years, our priorities have been more immediate. The wars in Afghanistan and Iraq, for example. But what if somebody focused on this one objective over a period of a decade, say, or two decades, while we weren't particularly paying attention? The fact is, as you've said yourself, it's probably doable."

"Yes. But the costs would be unfathomable."

He nodded very slightly. "Yes, the same as with our space program. But we had an imaginative rationale to get that done and we did. The same with the military's role in creating the Internet. For years, private industry didn't consider developing the Internet to be feasible. So the government took charge and helped create it. And the same goes for computers. For ten years, before the costs came down, NASA was the only buyer of large computers. The point is, the government has traditionally supported emerging technologies and in many cases has been responsible for their existence. We could do that with weather technology but there just isn't the same enthusiasm, or imaginative rationale, that we've seen with these other projects."

"Okay," she said. "Point taken. But I still wonder why our intelligence wouldn't have been able to pick up what was happening."

Easton, she noticed, was watching her. His gaze felt like a dark blue wall.

"We all asked that after 9/11, didn't we, Secretary Blaine?" he said. "This is, obviously, something that has occurred under our radar. We're not here to point fingers."

"Of course not," she said. "I'm certainly not doing that."

The President gave her a reassuring nod. "Other questions," he said.

"Just one, and I'm sure you've discussed this at length, as well." She felt nervous asking it, sensing Easton's disapproval. "If you've determined that this is credible and that thousands of innocent people may have already lost their lives, why aren't we reaching out more to the international community?"

"We are," Easton said. He leaned forward in his chair, glancing at her.

The President's eyes closed for a moment. She could sense that it was a question they'd already discussed.

"I just mean, isn't there a moral obligation—I mean, couldn't a warning mitigate what's going to happen by drawing attention to the threat?" She looked to DeVries for support, but didn't find it. "Mobilizing the world community against it?"

"Or perhaps have the opposite effect," said Easton. "The fact is, we don't know enough yet to make that sort of judgment, Secretary Blaine. Or to take that sort of risk."

"Cate, I understand your question," the President said. "The main reason we aren't doing this more transparently is that, until we learn exactly who we're dealing with, we can't afford to. We've been asked very pointedly not to let this information out of our small circle. The implication is that there will be catastrophic consequences if we do. That leaves me with a very difficult choice. After much deliberation, I've decided to heed that warning until we know more. Remember, this is day ten for us, Cate, and day one for you."

DeVries added, "And if you look at the case of the most recent threat, there was no specific location given. Just 'Western Europe.' The first one was 'Eastern Asia.' I think information of that sort is essentially useless, anyway."

Blaine nodded. "And we don't have the ability—I mean, our satellites aren't able to detect how this is being done?"

It was Easton who answered. "If we knew where they were, Secretary Blaine, we'd have ordered bombing runs ten days ago."

"Sorry," she said. "I guess I'm just playing devil's advocate."

"Understandable," the President said.

"Although, in this case, the devil doesn't need an advocate, Secretary Blaine," Easton said, showing what might have been a smile.

"Cate, let me just reiterate," the President said. "We've all asked these same questions. We're looking at everything very closely. Changes in the atmosphere, ionospheric irregularities. Any anomaly that might offer some pertinent information about where these events originate. We do have a game plan."

"Of course."

"If we play by their rules, at some point—very soon—they're going to make a demand. At that point, we'll learn who they are, and we'll learn what their motive is. Then we will respond accordingly."

Blaine was silent, absorbing what they were saying: *So the rest of the Cabinet has no idea this crisis is happening. Nor does anyone in Congress.* It was not how Blaine would have handled it. But she understood the stakes, and the unstated concerns that the President was balancing. This was the sort of crisis that could define Aaron Lincoln Hall's presidency—or sink it.

"What about the media? How concerned are we about something leaking?"

"Another reason for keeping the circle tight," Easton said.

"They've already gotten hold of the wrong story, as you know," DeVries said.

"I do."

"Here's what I'd like to think, Cate," President Hall said. He leaned back and lifted his chin, giving her a stern, unfamiliar look. "And what I'd like all of us to think: that whatever this is, there's still a possibility it can be resolved behind closed doors. Without any public crisis. Without any catastrophic event visiting our shores."

Blaine watched the President's measured smile, suspecting that this was actually Clark Easton's idea. It wasn't quite the way the President talked, or thought. Easton had come up through military intelligence, and he held old-school ideas about secrecy and protection of information.

"It's just hard to fathom," Blaine said. "What would China—or anyone—gain by such an attack? I mean, it doesn't seem to make sense."

After a long silence, the President said, "We suspect they would prefer a negotiation to any sort of attack. But, again, we'll learn all that soon enough."

"All right," Blaine said. She took a deep breath, not wanting to be at odds with these men. *We're all parts of a team,* she reminded herself, thinking of her father. "And so what's the next step?"

"The next step is for *them* to take, not us," the President said.

Right, she thought. Tomorrow was Monday.

The President held up a forefinger and raised his eyebrows as Blaine stood, a familiar directive, indicating he wanted her to remain in the room. She sat back in the rosewood chair and waited for DeVries and Easton to exit.

NINE

"I JUST WANT YOU to know that what you refer to as the 'moral obligation' is something I take very seriously, Cate." The President was leaning forward on the desk, watching her. "And will continue to do so."

"I'm sorry, sir, if I spoke out of place."

"No. I just want us to be clear with each other. I also don't want us to be second-guessing ourselves." He closed his eyes, as if he were disappearing inside some private thought, then opened them again. He could do that: go somewhere else, like he was playing an entirely different chess game in his head. "If you have a concern, or a question, feel free to bring it to me. All right? Even outside of the group, if you'd like. *Especially* outside of the group."

"All right."

Blaine considered what he was really saying.

"Also," he said, his face brightening, "I just want to say that I'm glad you're on board."

"Thank you, sir."

He scooted his chair back. Then, one at a time, he lifted his long legs and settled his feet on a corner of the desk. She could see that he was trying to forge a bond of informality between them. "Heading into October, Cate, I thought I'd be dealing with a couple of routine budget issues and getting away with Mrs. Hall for a few weekends to watch the leaves turn up at Camp David."

"I know."

"But it doesn't look like that'll be happening."

"No, sir."

"Anyway." He fixed her with a look, and winked. "I'm hearing some good reports about DHS. The handling of the floods, in particular. We're getting some very good marks for that. So, thank you. And I understand you're bringing a lot of fresh ideas into play over there. Just what I was hoping."

"Thank you, Mr. President. It's an ongoing process."

He looked away, his brow furrowing. "Although I'm told that you sometimes play a little hide and seek with the Secret Service."

"Me?"

This time the President didn't smile. He knew her father slightly and sometimes took a paternal tone that made Blaine uneasy.

"Not often," she said. "I sometimes just want to be alone with my son. It makes him very uncomfortable having security people around all the time."

"I'm only concerned about your safety, Cate. And your son's safety, for that matter."

"I appreciate it, sir."

"Anyway. I want you to know that I value your perspective on this. No one else in our circle is as well versed on these subjects as you are. If you see something I'm missing, at any time, I want you to come to me. Okay?"

Blaine nodded.

He watched her, letting his look linger. "What's your gut feeling at this point?"

"About the threats?"

"Mmm hmm."

"To be honest?" she said. "I guess I'm still not fully convinced that it's real."

"Oh, it's real, Cate," he said, his eyes showing a sudden steel. "You said it yourself earlier. This *is* possible."

"Well, yes. Hypothetically."

"It's a paradox, though, isn't it? The public hasn't shown the support for exploring this type of technology, nor has Congress. But on the other hand, if someone beats us to it, the public would be outraged that we let it happen. They'd hammer us."

Blaine knew that he was right; she had been thinking the same.

"And that concerns me."

"Of course," she said. "It concerns me, as well."

The President re-crossed his ankles on the desk, placing his right foot on top. "Did you know, Cate, that China is about to surpass us in the amount of scientific research they publish each year?"

"Yes," she said, "I do."

"That's an area we led for the entire twentieth century."

"I know."

"Do you know where the tallest building in the world is today, Cate?"

"Dubai, isn't it?"

"That's right. Dubai. During the twentieth century, up until 1996, I believe it was, or '97, the tallest building in the world was always in the United States. Did you know that? Seven or eight separate buildings, beginning with the Park Row building in 1900. On through the Empire State Building and the Twin Trade Towers."

"Yes," Blaine said. "I read that article the other day, too."

"It's only a symbol, granted," he said. "But symbols matter. Coupled with other declines, in education and patent applications, for instance, there is a very real perception that this country is falling behind. Now I'm an optimist by nature," he added, turning his eyes to hers again, "but I want to be realistic, too. I can see that this technology has the potential to bury us. I want to keep focused on the larger picture here until we can see what we're really up against." He looked off, showing her his famous profile. "I'm sorry. I'm probably being more dramatic than I ought to be. Anyway, Cate." He turned to her. "Live and breathe this thing for me, if you can, okay?"

"I will."

"And we'll see what happens tomorrow."

"Yes."

Several minutes later, Blaine walked across West Executive Drive to a waiting limousine that would take her home. Before scooting in, she glanced at the blinking red light atop the Washington Monument and felt the unfamiliar undertow of things she wasn't being told.

TEN

THE REPUBLIC OF CAPE Verde is an archipelago of ten islands and five islets about three hundred and fifty miles off the coast of Senegal, West Africa. Settled by the Portuguese in the mid-fifteenth century, Cape Verde later became a way station for African slaves bound for North America. Many of the people living there today are these slaves' descendents.

In late September, the equatorial sun beats down on the calm seas surrounding Cape Verde, causing water to evaporate and form warm waves of unstable air. As these waves come into contact with low pressure systems, they expand, beginning a cycle of rain and further evaporation. When conditions are right, these atmospheric disturbances feed on one another, growing in size, eventually spinning in a counter-clockwise pattern, fueled by the warm seas and the westerly trade winds.

Each year, several hundred atmospheric disturbances occur in the Cape Verde Islands, dozens of which develop into tropical storm systems. On average, nine of these storms become hurricanes. Exactly what causes an atmospheric disturbance to transform into a hurricane is a mysterious process, each resulting from a complex series of interacting weather patterns; no two hurricanes are alike. It generally takes a week to ten days for a Cape Verde hurricane to reach the United States. Most of the Atlantic Ocean hurricanes that impact the Eastern Seaboard begin as atmospheric events east of the Cape Verde islands.

On the morning of October 2, a band of rain showers to the southeast of the lower Cape Verde islands merged with a low pressure system and began to spin in a chaotic motion, dumping heavy rains on the islands and the seas to the south. By early afternoon, it had begun to organize around a well-defined center, absorbing several other storms as it moved west.

Minutes before 3 P.M., it became a tropical depression, meaning its top wind speeds were greater than thirty miles per hour. Four hours later, Cape Verde Island government officials in Praia, Santiago, issued a Tropical Storm Watch for the region. A TSW meant that winds of 39 to 73 miles per hour were expected within the next twenty-four hours.

But it did not take twenty-four hours for this system to reach Tropical Storm strength. Less than two hours later, satellite and buoy sensors were tracking speeds in excess of 50 mph. At 9:15 P.M., what had begun as a series of routine disturbances in the sky above Senegal became Tropical Storm Alexander, the second named storm of the Atlantic hurricane season.

ELEVEN

CATHERINE BLAINE'S DRIVER LET her out in front of her two-story brick townhouse in Cleveland Park, a residential neighborhood between Wisconsin and Connecticut avenues in Northwest D.C. She lived on a quiet street of Victorian-style houses with old trees and cracked sidewalks.

Her driver waited as she unlocked the townhouse door from inside the garage. Then she waved and went inside.

The words from the President were still reverberating in her head as Blaine climbed the stairs to her galley kitchen and poured herself a glass of white wine. There was a subtext to what he had told her, but she wasn't sure yet just what it meant. As she twisted the wand of her window blinds she saw the familiar dark Suburban parked across the street. Secret Service. The government provided a security detail, which watched her house through the night. The White House preferred that she use a government car and driver and on most days she did. But she still insisted on driving herself to work several times a month. And occasionally she *did* play hide and seek with the Secret Service.

She called down to the man seated behind the wheel of the Suburban, a genial agent named Ralph, to say that she was in for the night.

"Let us know if you need anything."

"I will. Thanks, Ralph."

"Have a good night."

"You too."

Blaine twisted the blinds closed and pulled off her suit jacket. The day had begun for her in the drizzle of West Virginia, where she had gone for a routine tour of a flooded valley, and it was winding down with a crisis she still couldn't fully fathom—or believe. She was anxious to take out her contacts and to trade her suit for soft clothes.

Her townhouse was tidy, appointed with warm colors, artworks from her travels, books, and various photos of her son, Kevin. Only her study revealed her other, less organized side. Before switching on her computer, Blaine tried to reach Kevin, but had to leave a voice mail. She tried to remember if he was working tonight; or maybe he was out with his new girlfriend, Amanda.

After a long, hot shower, Blaine pulled on sweats and socks and poured another glass of wine. She sat in front of her computer, trying to recreate each of the email threats she had read that evening. Afterward, she innocuously titled the file "Recipes," and began to surf the Internet, giving herself a quick refresher course on climatology.

The modern history of weather modification had begun in the 1940s when researchers at General Electric in New York discovered that silver-iodide smoke transformed cloud droplets to ice, a process that could lead to rain formation. By the late 1940s, the Soviet Union, Britain, and the United States were all experimenting with cloud seeding projects. In one infamous incident from August of 1952, a British cloud-seeding experiment over the town of Lynmouth, England, supposedly caused wild flash flooding that killed thirty-five people. During the more hubristic 1960s, the United States launched Project Popeye, a military weather modification operation used in Vietnam and Laos. The US military also oversaw Project Stormfury, which sprayed silver iodide into the sky to weaken hurricanes. The program claimed several modest successes, including Hurricane Debbie in 1969. But many scientists were skeptical, calling the experiments inconclusive, arguing that it was impossible to isolate the effects of cloud seeding from other natural processes acting on hurricanes.

Weather modification research had, for a time, been part of the Cold War, like the space race and the nuclear arms and chemical/biological weapons races. But the United States seemed to lose interest in the late 1970s. In 1977, a United Nations treaty banned the use of weather modification for military purposes.

Research continued, though, in other countries, particularly China and the Soviet Union. Blaine found several dozen accounts in the *Wall Street Journal*, the *New York Times*, and elsewhere of weather modification programs in China, Russia and the private sector over the last two decades, but little in the United States.

Why had the US lost interest? Blaine wondered. A cynic might say failure of imagination, she supposed. But there was also the question of priorities, as the President and Secretary DeVries had said. After Stormfury, the United States had decided to spend time trying to first *understand* hurricanes rather than stop them.

Blaine finally shut down her computer, still bothered by what the President had said, and what he hadn't said. What Blaine needed was a sounding board outside the circle to answer some hypothetical questions that were nagging her.

It was 11:14.

She decided to try her friend Dr. Rubin Sanchez at his office, leaving a message for him to call. She knew he wouldn't get it until the morning. Sanchez was a former professor at Columbia's Earth Institute and a onetime assistant director of NASA's Goddard Institute for Space Studies; he now worked for a private research lab near Baltimore. He was one of the scientists who'd brought global warming to the world's attention, testifying to Congress often on climate issues. But he had become increasingly eccentric of late, in both his pronouncements and his appearance, growing an unruly white beard and wearing his shoulder-length hair in a ponytail. Detractors called him Professor Rubin Santa Claus.

Blaine felt a little funny calling him, as if doing so were a species of disloyalty. She lay in bed and thought about it, and about all that had happened that day. She should have been tired, but wasn't. She lay awake for several hours, and her thoughts became like paths through a thick woods that somehow always returned to the same clearing, and the same thought. *It was already Monday in Western Europe.*

TWELVE

Monday, October 3, 7:23 A.M.

RONALD REAGAN NATIONAL AIRPORT is located on 733 acres of land in Arlington, Virginia, just over the Potomac River from Washington, D.C. It serves about five thousand passengers each day. Charles Mallory was one of the first of those five thousand on Monday morning. He felt a pleasant surge as he stepped out of the terminal building after arriving on a JetBlue flight. It was eleven degrees warmer in Washington than it had been in Maine and the sky was painted a crisp, hard blue that reminded him of the past. Early football season weather.

Mallory claimed his rental car at the National counter, where he was also handed a sealed, letter-sized envelope that had been left for him. He opened it before pulling out of the parking garage.

It was a series of letters printed in twelve point on a single sheet of paper: RFCROFAUTLFOATHRHOOORUCCG. A message that he knew was from his brother. Typical Jon. He was in some sort of trouble, Mallory suspected, although he couldn't yet imagine what it might be. His brother saw things that others didn't see; he saw stories where Mallory might just see information.

He drove the Ford Taurus along the G.W. Parkway beside the Potomac, catching glimpses of all of the famous landmarks: Washington Monument, Lincoln Memorial, Jefferson Memorial, Kennedy Center, Watergate. The hotel was on the river in Maryland, an eighteen-story, two-thousand-room monstrosity with a giant glass atrium. Chaplin had made the arrangements; instructions about his next hotel would be in the room.

Mallory liked large, anonymous hotels where he could disappear and think for hours at a time. He intended to use this one as his base for a couple of days, as Chaplin made plans for him to meet with his brother.

As he walked to the check-in counter, he noticed that some sort of IT conference had taken over much of the hotel. A Tessitura conference.

Upstairs, he unpacked in less than two minutes, then sat in an armchair and looked at the message again:

RFCROFAUTLFOATHRHOOORUCCG

The first part, he knew. *RFC* identified the code: "Rail Fence Cipher." The second *R* meant "reverse." As in "reverse order." It was a simple system they'd worked out as kids. In recent decades, Charles and Jon Mallory had been distant acquaintances, kept separate by their very different careers and temperaments. But several years ago, in a remote part of Africa, Jon had saved his life, and they'd connected in ways they never had before. If he was in some sort of trouble now, or ever, Mallory would do whatever he could to help.

He stared at the letters and reversed their order in his mind. So, instead of OFAUTLFOATHRHOOORWCCG, the actual cipher became those letters in reverse order:

GCCWROOOHRHTAOFLTUAFO

Mallory worked out the rail fence cipher grid on a sheet of paper, plugging in the letters left to right.

Three levels:

```
G...C...C...W...R...O
.O.O.H.R.H.T.A.O.F.L.
...T...U...A...F...O.
```

Then, reading diagonally, again left to right, the message became: GO TO CHURCH AT WA FOR FOLO.

He tore the sheet of paper into tiny pieces and flushed them down the toilet.

There was a gym on the first floor of the hotel, and Mallory went down for twenty minutes of upper body weights followed by twenty on the treadmill. Afterward, feeling pleasantly tired, he walked out to the poolside atrium restaurant for an early lunch. He took his club sandwich and fruit juice to the only empty table he saw, surveying the computer people as he ate. A slow song by ABBA played fuzzily on the PA.

GO TO CHURCH AT WA FOR FOLO.

After several minutes, a pony-tailed woman in her thirties showed up with a cup of beer. She stood beside him, as if at attention, smiling as he looked up.

"Did I lose my spot?"

"I don't know. Did you?"

She nodded to a pair of sunglasses on one of the other chairs.

"Oh," he said. "Discreet, but valid. Sorry. Didn't realize anyone was sitting here."

Mallory gathered his plate and cup. But the woman touched his wrist.

"No, please. Stay right there. It's all right," she said, her voice conspiratorially husky.

He glanced again. A slender, nice-looking woman, dressed in khaki slacks and a loose gray T-shirt. She had intelligent blue eyes, he saw, and a slight but interesting smile.

They both sat.

"So. Are you part of the conference?"

"Me? Not really," he said.

She sipped her beer, glancing at the pool activity.

"You?"

She exaggerated a shrug. "Guilty."

"Somehow you don't strike me as the geek type."

"Oh. Thank you," she said, grinning as if he had said it with great irony. "You know what it is. Ninety-nine percent of geeks give the rest of us a bad name."

Now Mallory smiled.

"No, my company sends me to these things," she went on. Sipped. "I'm a tech. In addition to doing these seminars, we're expected to network a little. That's the part I'm not so keen about. I'm really not much of a mixer."

"No? Me neither." He could tell the woman wanted a conversation, and he wasn't in the mood.

"I mean, you're expected to sort of play a role, right? Be the rep for your company and all that kind of crap. I can't do it. I mean, I *can*, right? If I wanted to. But that's the point: I don't want to." She sipped again. When she lowered the cup, a trace of foam rimmed her upper lip. "I prefer to just be myself. You know?"

"I do." Mallory nodded. "Which is a good thing, because, as they say, all the others are taken."

It took her a moment, but when she got it, she laughed, a big, happy laugh, showing a surprising alignment of teeth. The reason for her tight smile, maybe.

Mallory looked across the pool and saw a man with *The Economist*. It suddenly reminded him of a different magazine.

WA.

Weekly American.

CHURCH.

Roger Church, the magazine's editor.

"What?" the woman asked.

"Nothing. I was just remembering something."

Mallory stood. For a moment, her face sank, then she managed to restore the tight, interesting smile.

"Are you leaving?"

"I'm sorry. I need to make a call."

"My name's Gwen, by the way." She reached to shake his hand.

"Fernando."

"Really?"

He shrugged.

"Well. If you'd like to have a drink or something later, Fernando, I'll probably just be hanging in the lounge."

"I'll look for you."

THIRTEEN

MALLORY DROVE BACK ALONG the George Washington Parkway and across Memorial Bridge into the city. Snaked through the late morning traffic and found a public parking garage near the State Department in Foggy Bottom. He walked seven blocks to the *Weekly American* offices, skirting the campus of George Washington University, which was busy with students. It was a brisk day, sixty degrees. Bright cloud towers hung in the sky; rain was coming.

Jon had been a contributing editor to the *Weekly American* for more than ten years, turning out news features and profiles from around the world. His editor, Roger Church, was once considered among Britain's top investigative reporters. For most of the past decade, he had run the *Weekly American* in Washington, giving it, despite its moniker, an international following.

A bas relief map of the world covered much of one lobby wall. There was also a ceiling-tall trophy case and poster-size blowups of past magazine covers.

"To see Roger Church, please," Mallory said to the receptionist.

"Do you have an appointment?"

Exactly the question he had expected.

"I don't."

She crinkled her face. "And your name?"

He told her.

"And this is in reference to . . . ?"

"It's not in reference to anything."

"Okay." He gazed at a magazine cover showing Bill Clinton and Boris Yeltsin at a joint press conference. 1998. Another, more recent one: Vladimir Putin with Barack Obama, sharing a Russian breakfast.

The receptionist buzzed Church. Minutes later, a tall, thin man with a mop of silvery hair strode into the lobby and extended his hand. His tie was loosened several inches, his shirt sleeves turned up unevenly.

"Well, well," he said. "A mystery come to life."

"A pleasure."

"Likewise. Please. Come on back." Church dipped his head graciously and led Mallory into the corridor, taking loping, long-legged steps, past a series of small offices to his own large, immaculate corner space. He closed the door and nodded at the burgundy leather chair in front of his desk. Mallory took in the view—office buildings, the State Department, the tip of the Washington Monument.

"Been expecting you," Church said.

"Sorry I took so long."

"Have a seat. Here, let me get something for you."

Church had the restless energy of a twenty-five-year-old and the weathered, lined face of an old man, just as his brother had once described him. When Mallory finally sat, Church crouched down behind his desk. Mallory leaned forward to see what he was doing: opening his wall safe.

He extracted a nine-by-twelve envelope, closed the safe, and passed it over the desktop.

"For you."

"From my brother."

He nodded and sat, resting his right thumb and forefinger on the handle of his steaming coffee cup.

"Where *is* Jon?" Mallory asked. "Do you know?"

"No idea. He told me he was going to disappear for a while. He has, evidently." He nodded at the envelope. "Have a look."

Mallory opened it. Inside was a single sheet of paper with a typed, numbered list of names. Nothing else. He studied it: seven names, none of whom he recognized.

1. *Steven Loomis*
2. *Dr. Susan Beaumont*
3. *Deborah Piper*

4. *David Worth*
5. *Michael Dunlopen*
6. *Dr. Frank Johnson*
7. *Dr. Atul Pradhan*

Beneath the list, written in blue ink, were the initials *DKW*. Mallory recognized the handwriting as his brother's.

"Who are they?"

Church touched his coffee cup handle. "At least four of the people on the list are dead."

"The other three?"

"Unknown."

"So . . . ? What ties them together?"

"Don't know. I've run a couple hours of data searches. Checked with police agencies. Four were scientists involved in weather research. That's the closest I've found to any sort of link. But the projects they worked on had no apparent connection. All in different parts of the country. Number five was a newspaper reporter. He's one of the confirmed dead."

"What happened?"

"Shot. A remote wooded region of Alaska."

"Unsolved?"

"Unsolved."

"And the others?"

"Susan Beaumont was murdered in a motel room near Caspar, Wyoming. Dr. Atul Pradhan died in the tsunami in the Bay of Bengal."

"Last week?"

"Yes. September twenty-fifth."

"What about this weather research? What specifically were they working on?"

"Very different arenas, as I say. Steven Loomis, to start at the top, was involved with the Defense Department from the 1960s through the 1970s. He worked for a time on Project Stormfury."

"The hurricane mitigation project," Mallory said. "Now largely discredited."

"Yes. About ten years ago, he signed on as a consultant for a private industry weather mapping project in California. He also worked for a company called Energy and Atmospheric Research Systems, or EARS, which was a big government contractor for a while."

Mallory nodded. He knew a little about them.

"Dr. Beaumont was a forensic meteorologist. She was a researcher at MIT. Frank Johnson was a physicist who created weather tracking computer models. Died of a heart attack, apparently. No connection between the two, though. At least none that I've been able to find. Deborah Piper, I'm not sure. Not much on her yet."

Mallory glanced at the names. "And their paths never crossed? None of the seven?"

"Not that I've been able to determine."

"Who were the other confirmed dead?"

"The confirmed dead are numbers two, five, six, and seven."

He glanced at the four names. "And the three disappearances. Any signs of violence?"

"In one case, yes. Number four. There were signs of a struggle at his home," Church said. "In three of the deaths, interestingly, DNA was found at the scene which was not that of the victim and could not otherwise be identified. Not spouses or anyone else who was considered a possible suspect."

"And not part of the FBI's DNA database."

"Exactly."

"Any connection among those DNA samples? Indicating it could have been the same person?"

Church pressed his lips together, showing the faintest trace of a smile. "I actually planted that idea with one of the detectives. Said I'd received an anonymous tip that the cases might be connected."

"And?"

"He followed up. The DNA doesn't match. In one case, it belonged to a woman."

Mallory was forming an idea.

"It's possible, of course, that they're *not* related," Church added. "That this is some kind of elaborate ruse. Or a mistake."

Mallory glanced at the paper again. "And these initials at the bottom?"

DKW.

Church sighed. "She's the one your brother was talking with for his story. Dr. Keri Westlake. Based in College Park. Now officially a missing person."

"She's the one who gave him this list?"

"Evidently. I wish I had asked him more, in a way. He was very reluctant to discuss any of this with me. It was very dangerous information, he said. Which is probably true. But he seemed quite determined that you get this list. He said he had tried to reach you for several days. Unsuccessfully. Almost a week, I think."

"Yes, I know." Mallory looked away.

"He said if anyone could figure this out, you could."

"Well. He sometimes overestimates me." Mallory read through the names again, feeling guilty that it had taken him so long to pick up the messages, wondering: Was Jon in the same situation their father had been in—pursued for what he knew? Had something happened to him?

"Why was he talking with this Dr. Westlake, anyway?"

"He'd been doing preliminary research for a story on the geo-engineering industry. He didn't talk a lot about it, although he did tell me something quite interesting. He said, 'She answered a question I didn't ask.'"

"Without saying what it was."

"Right."

Mallory watched Church, the way he nervously fidgeted with his sleeves. "Why geo-engineering?"

"Not sure." He shrugged. "I just know it interested him. He thought geo-engineering was going to be a major growth industry eventually, and he wanted to explore how legitimate it really was. How viable it will be."

"Thinks."

"Pardon?"

"Thinks, not thought."

"Of course. Sorry."

Church's long hairless arm reached for his coffee cup, then he seemed to change his mind and pulled his hand back. "It's a controversial subject, of course," he said, exhaling audibly. "The viability of the industry is really down to whether or not you accept the premise of quote unquote climate change, or global warming. We talked about that a few times."

"And?"

"He said that if you accept the premise of global warming, then there are really only two options for how you deal with it: you reduce carbon dioxide emissions, which, of course, is what everyone talks about. Or else you mitigate the effects of those emissions."

"Through geo-engineering."

"Yes. For the first option to really work—to reverse the effects of climate change—would require reducing carbon emissions by eighty percent. Which isn't feasible." Church tugged at his left sleeve. "Did you know that Exxon Mobil has spent thirty million dollars over the past decade to discredit the idea of man-made global warming?"

"Okay," Mallory said. "So, option one, cut the CO_2 by eighty percent, isn't going to happen, you're saying."

"Not likely, no. It's messy and it's political. Mitigating the climate, on the other hand, isn't. It just isn't taken very seriously yet."

"I don't follow politics much anymore," Mallory said. "Tell me about it. How does it work?"

"Well." Mallory waited while Church deliberately sipped his coffee, his eyes blinking rapidly. "The idea that gets the most currency these days is you pump sulfur into the upper atmosphere to create a sun shield. It actually wouldn't take much. Block one to two percent of the sunlight and you've offset the doubling of the CO_2 levels." He smiled, his face becoming an old man's. "It sounds a little kooky, I suppose. But at the same time, there's something very American about that idea, isn't there?"

"You mean that we can solve our problems through innovative science rather than through conservation."

"Exactly, yes. American ingenuity." They shared a look. "That's what your brother thought. From our few conversations on the subject, I think he believed there was something inevitable about the geo-engineering industry."

"Believes."

"Right. Sorry."

"Why?"

"Why? Because when you get down to it, the costs of geo-engineering would be relatively trivial compared to the costs of cutting carbon. Not to mention the practicalities of it."

Mallory looked again at the names. "And so, while he was doing preliminary research for this story, he came to talk with Dr. Westlake. And she gave him this list. Telling him that these seven people were somehow connected."

"That's right. By something I haven't yet discovered."

"And who's this most recent name? Number seven?"

"Dr. Atul Pradhan? A well-respected climate scientist. Originally from India. Died in the tsunami of September twenty-fifth, as I said. He was sent to Bangladesh as a consultant by a California-based firm, supposedly."

"Why?"

"Studying the effects of climate change on nomadic populations on the char islands, evidently. He was quite outspoken on issues of climate control."

Mallory waited for him to say more. When he didn't, he asked, "And how about Dr. Westlake? What happened to her?"

"Unknown. She told a colleague at the university that she was going out running Friday afternoon on the C & O canal and never returned. Her car's still missing. She was reported as a missing person by her estranged husband three nights ago."

"Has it made the news yet?"

"No. I expect it will any time." He smiled ambiguously, his face fissuring into a grid of lines.

Mallory said, "Have you shown this list to the police?"

"Not yet." Church looked away. "Jon did. As I say, at this point I don't know that the list really means anything."

"What are you going to do with it?"

"Wait." Church moved his fingers on the handle of the coffee cup. "If there are connections I'm not seeing, it may eventually become a story."

"Can I call you if I think of anything?"

"Please. Any time." Church pulled a business card from the top drawer of his desk. Scribbled a number on the back. "That's my home. I'm a night owl. Call up until midnight if you want."

"Thanks, I will." Mallory pulled a blank business card from his pocket and wrote out the number to one of his disposable cells.

He stood. The two men shook hands and Church walked him back through the lobby. The receptionist glanced up and smiled this time.

Mallory winked. He walked outside and stared for a while at the sky, which was darkening with stratus clouds.

HE HAD BROUGHT five disposable cell phones with him in his gym bag. One of them vibrated as he drove away from Foggy Bottom. He recognized the caller ID: it was Joseph Chaplin. *Good.* If Mallory didn't return the call, it meant he was agreeing to meet Chaplin in St. Louis, per his message the night before.

"St. Louis" was a reference to the Smithsonian's Air & Space Museum on the National Mall, where Charles Lindbergh's forty-five-foot-wide "Spirit of St. Louis" single-engine plane—the plane he'd flown solo from New York to Paris in 1927—hung from the ceiling above the entrance lobby.

Mallory found Chaplin on the second floor, studying a placard in front of the Wright Brothers' flyer in an adjacent gallery. He was dressed in a dark, tailored pin-stripe suit, a purple kerchief puffed out of his pocket. Not particularly inconspicuous, but in keeping with Chaplin's new Washington persona. Chaplin loved Washington and made a point of exploring its wealth of history and culture on an almost daily basis. Seeing his eyes turn and recognition light his familiar face—the sculpted features and hard, sincere set of his mouth—gave Mallory a sense that, for a brief moment at least, all was right with the world.

"Greetings," Chaplin said in his lilting African accent, without looking at him.

"Greetings."

"Your brother, you'll be pleased to know, is fine." He was pretending to read the placard about the Wright Brothers.

"Do you know where he is?"

"I've got him, yes."

Mallory felt a rush of relief.

"I had to make an executive decision. As you Americans like to say."

Chaplin moved to another exhibition, this one showing a diagram of the Wright Brothers' plan for "Wing-Warping." Mallory went with him. "What sort of decision?"

"To assist him. He had been trying to reach you, as you know. Failing that, he seemed determined to disappear. I attempted to talk to him about that, but he had made up his mind. He only wanted to speak with you. Unfortunately, your brother is not as adept at disappearing as you are."

"No."

"Not many people are."

"So you made an executive decision and assisted him."

"Affirmative. I don't know that he fully understands the nature of his adversary."

"Probably not," Mallory said. "Do you?"

"Not entirely. Better, perhaps, than he does."

He handed Mallory an envelope, and turned to study the next exhibition. Mallory pulled out a blurry glossy photo of a Range Rover, parked on a residential street. Another of a bearded man wearing a flak jacket, a ball cap and blue jeans, standing in what seemed to be a parking garage.

"That's the fellow who was staking out his apartment," Chaplin said. "He was there this morning when he left. And at the Metro stop waiting for him to return to his car. Your brother was planning to drive away from the parking garage and disappear. He probably wouldn't have made it."

Mallory studied the photos, then slipped them back in the envelope.

"What happened?"

"We lost him, unfortunately." Chaplin sighed. "You understand, of course, I don't do this sort of work any more. I have a very small staff these days, and I'm not set up for it. Otherwise, we might have attempted to stop him."

"I understand, and will compensate you very well, Joseph. Thank you," Mallory said. He felt a chill of apprehension, thinking how close the bearded man in the photo had probably come to killing his brother.

After buying Mallory's consulting firm, Chaplin had let most of the staff go and shifted the emphasis from intelligence contracting to data mining. He ran the company now out of a two-room office in Georgetown, although the heart of the business was a Maryland warehouse computer cluster. In the old days, sleuthing involved lots of what was often called "shoe leather" work. Now, it was largely about computing power.

"No idea who this man is?"

"Not really. Clearly, he's disguised. Something of an escape artist, too."

"What about the license plate?"

"It's an expired tag with a current registration sticker. The tag was registered to a Virginia man who died three years ago."

Chaplin walked toward the railing and gazed down at John Glenn's Mercury Friendship 7 capsule. Mallory stood several yards away, looking toward the Lindbergh plane. "But my brother is safe," he said.

"He is fine, yes. And he'd like to see you."

"I'd like to see him." Mallory reached into his pocket and pulled out a sheet of paper, folded in quarters. "In the meantime, I have something for you to check for me."

"Okay."

Mallory turned, did a quick scan of the gallery, and handed Chaplin the list of seven names. He then summarized in four sentences what Church had told him. "I need you to find out everything you can about those seven people. In particular, what ties them together."

"Where does this come from?"

"It's from a woman named Dr. Keri Westlake. University of Maryland. She's the eighth name on the list. The initials at the bottom."

"Okay." Chaplin re-folded the paper and pushed it into a trouser pocket.

"How soon before I can talk with my brother?"

"Tonight."

"Okay." *Good*, Mallory thought.

"As I say, this is not the sort of thing I do anymore. But considering the circumstances . . ."

He was walking toward the planetarium now. Mallory watched the crowds of tourists and school groups as he walked just behind Chaplin.

"Where are you going?" he said.

He nodded toward the Albert Einstein Theater. "I have 12:45 tickets for this."

"Oh." Mallory looked up at the planetarium time board. "Okay. So what do I do?"

They stopped as Chaplin pulled out his ticket. "You just need to be at the bus shelter on Connecticut and Teagarden at 6:17 this evening. Okay? A car will pull to the curb and pick you up. A white car. A Honda."

FOURTEEN

DR. JAMES WU SAT before a row of computer monitors in the Data Visualization Center at the Eisenhower Executive Office Building, watching the infrared, color-enhanced spirals of Tropical Storm Alexander as he waited for Chief of Staff Gabriel Herring, who was already seven minutes late. Normally, Herring was easygoing and punctual. But he did not handle stress well, and there had been plenty of that in the Oval Office these past few days—for reasons Dr. Wu did not understand.

Suddenly, the President seemed to be on high alert over the weather, of all things. In his sixteen months as presidential science adviser, Wu had never known him to show more than a passing interest in science of any sort, let alone the weather.

The night before, Dr. Wu had informed the Oval Office about two anomalies in the development of Tropical Storm Alexander off the Cape Verde Islands. Today, he was seeing what he thought might be a third. But this one he wasn't ready to talk about. Not yet.

Dr. Wu was considered one of the pioneering scientists in the field of tropical storm methodology. Twenty years earlier, he had co-created a program for forecasting hurricanes and cyclones that was now widely used around the world. Dr. Wu was a prudent man with two daughters in college and a vibrant, attractive wife who taught meteorology at the University of Chicago. Although he stood barely five feet tall, Dr. Wu had become a looming figure in the world of climate science, by virtue of his almost surreally calm manner and his ability to explain complicated weather issues clearly and in layman's terms. Dr. Wu had been adopted by the media as a voice of reason and reliable information, whenever a major hurricane threatened.

His fascination with storms could be traced to a single event from childhood. In 1960, at the age of five, Wu had witnessed firsthand the fury of Hurricane Donna when it tore apart his family's home and left their Miami neighborhood a pile of rubble. Donna had instilled in him a reverence for the power of nature, not just to destroy what mankind had built but also to reduce men and women to primitive versions of themselves. He'd returned to South Florida after Andrew in 1992 and seen it all over again: people thrust for weeks into a world without electricity or air conditioning, queuing up for limited rations of food and water, relieving themselves in the open.

Dr. Wu's parents had immigrated to the United States shortly before he was born and his family still ran the same corner grocery in North Miami Beach. His brothers and sisters had all stayed close to home, working at the store. But he had been driven by something else, something intangible, an urge to learn and better understand the natural world. He had made the weather his life's work, leaving Florida to study meteorology at the University of Chicago, and geophysical science at the University of Colorado, where he had met Alison, his wife. Over the past three decades, Dr. Wu had flown into the eyes of more than two hundred hurricanes and written three books and countless articles on the subject. The weather had been his own peculiar route to the heart of the American Dream.

Dr. Wu used to believe that one day the terrible destruction wrought by events such as Donna and Andrew might be preventable. But he had grown more skeptical and practical as he had aged, avoiding personal stands on controversial subjects in the increasingly political realm of weather and climate science. In his current job, he preferred to accommodate the President rather than to draw attention to himself.

The shift at the Oval Office over the past week, though, had left him baffled, and he suspected that he was not being told the whole story. He felt it again now as Gabriel Herring finally strode into the room, a strange tilt of urgency in his face.

"Dr. Wu," he said. "Sorry, I've been with the President." Dr. Wu nodded graciously. 12:46. Twenty-one minutes late.

"I'm told you've picked up something unusual that we should be aware of? Two anomalies?"

"Yes." In fact, the system known as Alexander was behaving in ways that no computer models would have predicted for a Cape Verde storm. "Please," he said. "Let me show you."

Dr. Wu led him to one of the computer stations; three monitors were set up side by side. He pointed to the first, at the color-enhanced swirls of Alexander, which was churning away from the Cape Verde Islands into open sea. Herring stood behind him, his hands on his hips, looking. "These images come from a Geostationary Operational Environmental Satellite, or GOES," Dr. Wu explained. "This is Alexander, approximately twenty-five minutes ago. An infrared, color-enhanced image. Infrared images, as you know, record invisible radiation emitted directly by cloud tops, land surfaces, or ocean surfaces."

"Okay. So what do the colors indicate?"

"Heat. The warmer an object is, the more intensely it emits radiation." He pointed to the rows of numbers on the middle monitor.

Wu's steadiness only seemed to annoy Herring. "And so why do you call this unusual?"

"Well. There are two characteristics of this storm that strike me as anomalies. Let me show you this larger image, to give this some perspective."

He hit several keys, calling another image up onto a four-foot wall monitor. It showed the cloud tops of the storm. "This was taken from the International Space Station. As you can see, the cloud cover now stretches across more than three hundred miles and is steadily expanding."

"Uh huh. Okay," Herring said. "And what does that mean?"

Dr. Wu smiled, patiently. "That's your first anomaly."

"The size."

"That is correct, the size. Frankly, I have never seen a North Atlantic storm system so large at this early stage of its development."

Herring, watching the screen, crossed his arms.

"Now, let me take you below the cloud cover, if I may." Dr. Wu switched the monitor image. A different view of colored bands. "These are taken from NASA's QuikScat and Tropical Rainfall Measuring Mission satellites. They carry microwave sensors that can in effect 'see' through the clouds and give us a better sense of conditions inside the storm—rainfall, wind, water temperature. A few years ago, we didn't have the technology to do this."

"All right, so what are we looking at?"

Dr. Wu felt a reciprocal impatience with Herring. *I should be talking directly to the President about this,* he thought. *Surely my message will only become garbled in translation.*

But he managed to smile, forcing the feeling to pass. Emotions were like storm systems, he sometimes thought; if you fed them, they only grew worse.

"This image, as you can see, gives us a snapshot of the speed and direction of ocean surface winds—"

"You said two anomalies."

"That is correct, two anomalies. The first is the size, as we just discussed. And now, I am showing you the second one: water temperature," Dr. Wu said, maintaining his calm demeanor. "A hurricane is a little like a steam engine, you see. Heat is what drives a hurricane and the spinning motion is what keeps that heat in the center of the storm."

"And the bottom line?"

He clicked several keys, calling up new rows of numbers on the middle desk monitor. "These are temperature readings. From both buoy sensors and satellite microwave beams. We're getting readings with this storm system that are quite unusual."

"Why?"

"In general terms, to fuel a hurricane so that it keeps growing, the water temperature would need to be about eighty degrees Fahrenheit to a depth of, say, a hundred to a hundred and fifty feet."

"And . . . ?"

"We're getting consistent readings in that range right now, but also considerably higher. We're getting eighty-three and eighty-four degrees on the western edge of this system with some hot pockets at eighty-five and eighty-six."

"And that's unusual."

"It's unprecedented. I've never seen it before."

Herring stared at the infrared images as if he knew what he was looking at.

"Here's another interesting detail," Dr. Wu said, calling up a new image on the wall monitor. "When we track temperatures ninety miles to the west of the storm's outer bands we see a difference of as much as seven degrees."

"Cooler?"

"Cooler, yes. It's almost like there's a wall of warm water running interference, driving this thing west."

They stared in silence at the large screen.

"But . . . that doesn't make sense, does it?" Herring finally said.

"No, it doesn't. Of course, you must keep one thing in mind: weather does not always follow predictable or logical patterns. The elements that make up global climate are essentially non-linear. We often see hurricanes take sudden turns that defy all of our computer models. In August of 2004, to give you just one example, Hurricane Charley took a sudden, quite disastrous northeast turn that no one had predicted, devastating several communities on the west coast of Florida. There are countless weather factors interacting with one another in a storm system. And they are capable of transforming from one state of organization to another at a moment's notice."

"So. How alarmed should we be?"

"Alarmed?" Dr. Wu considered for a moment. "Oh, I don't think there is any cause for alarm. All we can do is pay attention. Although I would be remiss not to mention that further strengthening is likely."

Herring's brow drew up. "How do you mean?"

"I mean that over the past twelve hours, the wind shear has decreased from twenty-five to ten. At the same time, we're seeing some enormous convection activity around the eye wall." He pointed to the large screen. "And it's moving very rapidly into what are typically warmer waters."

"Meaning . . . ?"

"The predictors tell us that we will see a rapid strengthening over the next twelve to twenty-four hours," Dr. Wu said, speaking in a deliberately slow cadence. "In speed and, probably, in size. I wouldn't expect the system to continue like this for long, though," he added. "It really can't. It's too large. Most likely it will run into wind shear and change course. Or it will collide with a low pressure system or a cold front and break up."

"But if it did . . . if this continued in a westerly direction, when and where would it become a threat to the United States? Give me a time frame. Best guess."

"I would say it could be anywhere from five to nine days."

Herring mouthed the last four words, his arms still crossed.

But Dr. Wu was thinking again about the third anomaly. He didn't want to say anything yet. Not until he was sure. And not to Herring. The next time, he wanted to talk directly to the President. He wanted the President to know. And he also wanted to be a part of whatever it was that was happening. Whatever it was they were keeping from him.

As she dressed for lunch with her son, Blaine kept her eye on the silent television screen on her bedroom mantle, watching for any developments. It was late afternoon now in Western Europe.

CNN showed the swirl of Tropical Storm Alexander. Blaine punched up the sound. "Weather officials continue to keep a close watch on Tropical Storm Alexander, an unusually large system off the coast of Africa that is expected to become a hurricane within twenty-four hours."

At 12:47, Blaine's landline phone rang, startling her.

"Cate?"

"Yes."

"It's Rube."

"Excuse me?"

"Rube."

Dr. Rubin Sanchez. "Oh." She had all but forgotten about calling him the night before. Blaine listened to his heavy breathing on the other end.

"I got your message."

"Sorry I called so late."

"No worries. It's funny because I was just thinking of calling *you* yesterday."

"Oh? Why?"

"Well. It's a rather interesting coincidence. But you go first. What might your humble servant do for you today?"

"I have a question," Blaine said. "Just something hypothetical."

"Please."

"I'd love to sit down with you and pick your brain for a few minutes."

"Have at me."

"Actually, I'm getting ready to go out now," she said. "And anyway, I'd prefer to talk in person."

"All right. When?"

"Whenever you're free."

"Tomorrow?"

"Okay."

"Tell me what it's about."

Blaine told him briefly, only the basics, mentioning four recent natural disasters and asking him a hypothetical question.

"Very interesting," he said, imitating Artie Johnson from *Laugh-In*. "Come by in the morning. I'll have answers for you."

"What time?"

"I'm in the office at five thirty."

"Can we make it a little later?"

"Seven?"

"Eight?"

"Eight it is."

Then she called Jamie Griffith, her chief of staff, and asked him for a favor. Before leaving, she looked in her old Rolodex and found a number for Charles Mallory. She wondered if she might be able to reach him.

FIFTEEN

CATHERINE BLAINE PARKED ON a Georgetown side street of old bare trees and brick townhouses. She walked down the hill to one of her favorite M Street bistros, enjoying the cold breeze and the brief freedom she had to spend time with her son.

It was 1:33 when she entered the restaurant, an old-fashioned brass-rail sandwich place with comfortable booths, fern plants, lots of privacy.

Kevin worked as a waiter in an Italian restaurant down the street, while studying business at George Washington University. Eventually, he wanted to open his own restaurant. He was independent-minded, sometimes to a fault. She had offered to let him stay with her, but he didn't want that. He lived in the city with a roommate and had begun dating a girl from school. She was proud of how he had changed his life.

He was always early; this time was no different. He gazed up from his mobile device as she approached and said, matter-of-factly, "Hi Mom," then looked down again and finished texting.

Blaine slid in the booth, all the way across, and reached out to hold his hand. She glanced around, surprised and pleased that no one had noticed her.

"Honey, you look good."

He winced, finally shutting off his phone.

"Sorry. You don't want me to say that."

"It's all right." Kevin looked at her appraisingly. He had his father's mouth and it still sometimes spooked her, seeing him smile, those full lips conjuring his dad's handsome features. Their split had been his idea, not hers. He had found someone less career-oriented than Blaine, not to mention nine years younger. He'd moved back to California, where he opened a fusion restaurant, and quickly remarried. He had a whole different life now, and very little communication with Kevin. But Kevin admired his dad from afar. Going into the restaurant business had been a way of staying connected with him.

Kevin was tall and tied his dark hair back, with an uneven part down the middle. He had a deep voice and large green eyes. He wore a small hoop earring in his left ear. As she normally did, Blaine let him talk, pleased to observe his enthusiasm as he ran through his eclectic interests, relaying the events in his life as if reciting a school report. His girlfriend, Amanda, was going to Wisconsin for Thanksgiving and he was thinking of traveling with her (although he obviously wasn't ready for his mom to meet her yet). He was playing stand-up bass again in a jazz combo, still looking for their first paying gig. Amanda was into acrylics. They both liked Charlie Rose and *Frontline* and occasionally even *The X Factor*. But he couldn't stand *Dancing with the Stars*, which he called "cheesy exploitation." When his level of enthusiasm accelerated past a certain point, Kevin occasionally called her "dude," which almost made Blaine smile. She enjoyed his energy, and tried to stay with him, although she was still plugged in to the events in Washington that had dominated the past twenty-four hours. And to the knowledge that it was evening in Western Europe.

Blaine had her standard lunch—salad with iced tea—and Kevin had his—a Coke, cheeseburger, and fries, which he squirted with zigzags of both ketchup and mustard. When Catherine Blaine lost focus on what he was saying, he stopped, mid-bite, and narrowed his eyes.

"So," he said. "There was something you wanted to tell me?"

"Yes. There is, actually." She dabbed a napkin at a corner of her mouth. "No big deal. It's just that there's been a change of plans. It looks as if I'm going to have to postpone our trip this weekend."

"Oh?" The look of vulnerability that she had known since he was a little boy suffused his face, reminding her of his first day at grade school. "You mean we're not going to the Shore?"

"I'm sorry, not this weekend. But we'll do a rain check."

Kevin's eyes slid to the left; his mouth parted as if he were about to cry. He became hurt easily, but got over stuff just as quickly.

"I'm sorry. It's work, honey."

"But I thought you said you *weren't* working."

"No. I wasn't, that's right. But things come up with this job. We'll do it, I just need to postpone it a week or so."

"A week or *so?* That's pretty vague, Mom." Kevin made an exasperated face, exaggerating his displeasure. Outrage, then acceptance. Then not caring. It could be a charming transformation; she imagined his girlfriend found it rather endearing.

Blaine looked at her watch and felt a rush of adrenaline. It was 6:52 there now. "We'll make up for it, honey. I promise. We'll try for next week."

Kevin was looking toward the television above the bar, not wanting to make eye contact anymore.

"Is it something serious?" he said. "I mean, like terrorism or something?"

"You know I can't talk about that."

"Okay. Fine." He decided to concentrate on his food for a while. "I just hope you were serious about wanting to quit in a couple of years," he added, still refusing to look at her.

Blaine felt a sharp anger. She looked quickly around the restaurant. "What did you just say?"

Kevin shrugged. "You told me once that you only expected to do this job for a couple of years."

"No, I didn't," she said, her pulse racing, trying to force him to look at her. "Or if I did, I shouldn't have."

"But you *did say it.*" A look of outrage rose to his face. "Right? Are you denying that you even *said* it?"

"Honey, no, of course not." She lowered her voice, and took a deep breath. "The point is, whatever is said about my work is very sensitive, and it needs to remain strictly between us." She leaned closer. "Honey. To be honest, I don't know how long I'll do it. Okay? I'm serving the President and he decides how long I work for him, not me. I hope you can respect that."

"There's that word again."

Blaine smiled, remembering how she'd felt when her parents had spoken to her the same way.

"What's funny?"

"Nothing."

He concentrated on his food, devouring the rest of the hamburger in two bites.

"That's just how your grandfather brought me up," she said. "If you're asked to serve, especially at this level, you do it. You consider it a responsibility and an honor."

"Yeah, yeah." He was taking each of his fries in two bites, eating with a detached self-consciousness, his right leg beating time to some unheard music. He finally broke the silence, as he often did, with an unrelated question.

"Mom, have you ever heard of Thomas Merton?"

"Sure," she said. "Why do you ask?"

He shrugged, looking intently up at the television news. "Do you like him?"

"Like him? I haven't read him in years. But, yeah, sure, I thought he was very interesting. Why?"

Kevin just shook his head, and focused on his fries, adding a final zig-zag of ketchup. Apparently this was an acceptable style of conversing for him.

Blaine paid the bill and went to the ladies' room to check her makeup. Calm again. She saw the Secret Service detail standing on the sidewalk now. Despite Kevin's reaction to the postponement of their trip, he was doing well, and she enjoyed knowing that.

As Blaine returned to the booth, her secure cell phone vibrated in her purse.

Kevin, she noticed, was no longer at the table. *Where was he?*

"Mom!"

He was standing by the bar, signaling her with an urgent wave. For a moment, she didn't recognize him. He looked like an older man, not her son. She walked toward him. Stopped.

"What is it?"

"Look."

A BREAKING NEWS banner stretched across the bottom of the television screen. She heard her secure phone vibrating again and knew: she was being summoned back to the White House.

It had happened. There had been another one.

That's when Blaine felt chills race down her back, and for the first time, realized with absolute certainty what the others in the circle had already accepted. *This was real.*

SIXTEEN

Picardy, Northeastern France

THE NAME OF THE valley where Louise Fournier had grown up meant "tranquility," although the stories she had heard about the Somme Valley as a girl were not about tranquility, they were mostly about war. In the summer of 1916, her grandfather had lost his life in a wide-open meadow that was now home to market gardeners, country cottages, and dairy cattle.

More than one and a half million Allied and German soldiers had died along the Somme River that year. The valley was visited by war again in 1944, when she had lost an aunt and an uncle in a bombing raid just miles from where she now lived. These days, people came to the Somme Valley from around the world to see the gothic cathedrals and the numerous cemeteries, to wander through the quiet fields, thinking about those long-ago battles. But for people who lived here, war was not just history; it was real; it was something that had changed their lives.

Louise was reminded of that today as she glanced up and saw something very strange crossing the open meadow. Something like she had never seen before—dark and V-shaped, a giant funnel, skipping over the land, raising up dense swirls each time it touched down. Then behind it, a second funnel, just as large.

Beyond the picket fence she saw Paul Martin next door, pointing frantically toward the sky and shouting something to her, his hair blowing wildly in a gust of wind. But he was too far away and Louise could not hear what he was saying. She looked back and became hypnotized by the otherworldly colors suddenly streaking the sky—odd shades of greens and browns and oranges—and by the dance of the peculiar twin funnels: touching down, lifting up, kissing the earth, skipping back into the sky. It was almost like watching a life-size silent movie.

But then she began to hear the sound of it—a low roar of wind, like an approaching airplane—and she realized that the dark swirling funnels carried the wreckage of homes and trees; that it was chewing up the countryside like a giant lawnmower.

Her heart began to pound furiously as she breathed the cool, potent currents of wind. Paul was running toward her now. "*Depechez-vous! Entrez dans le sous-sol!*"

He grabbed her arm and led her across the yard and inside her house. Pulled her down into the cellar and bolted the door. Breathless, they huddled together in a corner of the concrete room, listening. Waiting.

Minutes later, she felt the tornadoes moving overhead. The house shook with terrible violence, what she imagined were the windows exploding, then the walls blowing apart. The roar seeming to hover above them for a full minute or more. Then the cellar doorway tore open and briefly the beast was visible again, hurling shredded debris down the steps toward them.

Paul moved in front of her in a protective crouch. A brave, fatal mistake; in the next instant, he was knocked back by a shaft of wood.

Louise huddled against the wall in the corner, shaking. She listened to the vortex of wind moving away from them. Waited. Eyes closed.

And then, all at once, there was silence.

She crawled to Paul and touched his forehead. His eyes were wide open, but he could no longer see anything. A spear of wood had gone through his chest. Blood was still oozing out, staining the front of his white shirt.

Louise pushed the broken wood out of her way as she made a path up the steps, knowing before she reached the top that none of her house remained. It was only a pile of wood and stone now, her belongings all gone. She stood at the top of the steps in what had been her living room, and peered out over the valley. All of it was gone. No one, nothing, moved. In every direction, destruction. But somehow, *she* had been spared.

What had been cottages and houses a few minutes before were

heaps of wood and stone. Cars were overturned and crumpled. Among the piles of wreckage, she began to see pieces of human debris—a man in his undershorts, his head and torso terribly crushed; an old woman she did not recognize literally torn in pieces, one of her legs against a pile of stones; a decapitated body on its back in a field; a child impaled on a tree branch. And in the valley, she saw cattle torn open, their limbs ripped off and scattered.

She felt a cold sweat ripple over her skin. "Help!" She turned and tried to scream. But nothing came out. No one was there to console her. *Why? Why had this happened?*

The worst part was the silence. The lack of answers. There was not even a wind anymore, just stagnant air that was beginning to smell like death. Louise walked on into the shredded valley, trying to scream. Listening for a human sound but hearing only the silence. Imagining that she was the last person left alive on Earth.

SEVENTEEN

CATHERINE BLAINE FELT NUMB as she pulled through the White House gates near Fifteenth Street and parked in one of the VIP spaces. She checked in at the security booth, and was escorted inside by a Secret Service officer and through the French doors into the Cabinet Room. Name plates for each of the Cabinet members were on the backs of the chairs. The President's chair, centered on the east side of the table, stood two inches taller than those of the Cabinet secretaries. Outside, a light rain blurred the Rose Garden.

Blaine felt the weight of history as she took her seat at the large mahogany table that dominated the room, a gift from President Nixon in 1970, beneath three pendant lights. This was the room where President Kennedy had deliberated about the Bay of Pigs. Where the Bush 43 Cabinet had convened the day after 9/11.

And now they had *their* crisis.

The "circle" shared a sober silence before the President signaled the start with a sigh. "This is clearly the event we were warned about," he said. "We don't have a lot of information in yet. But Harold will first share what we do know."

DeVries recited the grim details. A series of three deadly tornadoes had ripped through the Picardy region of France, near the border with Belgium. "We're still receiving damage assessments and there are some contradictory reports. The latest number we have is eighty-nine confirmed fatalities. That number will certainly go up." DeVries glanced at Blaine with his dark sober eyes. "The deadliest tornado in French history occurred in 1845, killing approximately one hundred. The reports we are getting from the ground in Picardy are putting this disaster at probably two to three times that, with a huge loss of property."

Blaine was thinking something else, though. Something she'd thought earlier.

"The words 'Western Europe'," she said, to fill the silence. "That's a little odd, isn't it? It's a geographical area, but not often used in that context; it also has a political connotation, from the Cold War, doesn't it? Eastern Europe. Western Europe."

DeVries nodded. "Yeah," he said. "I thought of that. Good observation."

"Needless to say, we will be offering our aid to them," the President said, switching subjects. "I've already talked with the French president and we are issuing a joint statement later this afternoon."

Blaine sensed the underlying frustration in his tone. There was a routine to this now and a sense of helplessness. She had to find out more on her own. This was a president who thought big, and she suddenly sensed that he might even have a parallel agenda that he wasn't sharing.

Clark Easton was uncharacteristically quiet, his arms on the table. Several times he glanced at Blaine.

"Looking at patterns," DeVries said, "two of the three follow-up messages came within twenty-four hours of the events."

"So we'll be back here again in a few hours," Blaine said.

"Probably. And I hope we'll have a clearer direction then," said the President. "Any thoughts? Questions?"

There was a deadly silence in the room. Even the rain seemed to go quiet.

"Okay. Two additional items, then," President Hall said. "We've had a report from the Janus Task Force that I'd like to share with you. The Vice President just brought this to my attention. They've picked up some additional electronic surveillance linking Janus to Chinese intelligence. As recently as last week. I don't know if that will help us much, but I just want everyone to be up to speed. We'll all receive briefings on it this afternoon. There's a feeling that we may be closing in on him, anyway."

Blaine saw DeVries lower his eyes and shake his head, as if momentarily disgusted. Easton rubbed the palms of his hands together.

"And secondly, as you know, we've got a storm out there in the

North Atlantic right now that we need to be watching very closely. This thing's come out of nowhere and is developing in ways we haven't seen before."

Blaine watched the President as he relayed the news that Dr. Wu had shared with the Oval Office earlier about Tropical Storm Alexander, feeling a shared tension.

Two anomalies.

And then it was over and they stood to return to their lives. *Until the next message. The next meeting.*

As they were leaving the Cabinet Room, DeVries caught her eye. Blaine lingered for a moment beside her chair, timing it so they would be at the doorway together.

"Talk for a minute?"

"Sure."

"Come on up. I'm heading to my office."

THE AFTERNOON AIR had turned crisp and the leaves were falling in the Virginia suburbs. Charles Mallory felt the delicious autumn breeze through the screen of his third-story hotel room as he ran Internet searches on the seven names, fighting off a nostalgic urge to daydream—growing up nearby, playing football every autumn; the way that life used to narrow down to a single, clear objective each fall as the team got better and the season's end grew more tangible.

He had, in fact, found two more connections among the seven names, although they were not necessarily important ones. Two of the seven had worked for the National Oceanic and Atmospheric Administration, the government organization that studied hurricanes, and both had been involved in a computer analysis operation known as Project Cloudcover, though in different parts of the country.

The reason that this particularly interested Mallory was that he knew a former CIA analyst who had also been involved in Cloudcover—a woman named Patricia Hanratty. Whether she would talk with him was a different matter. But Mallory found a number for her and left a message.

Then he closed up his computer and walked out into the afternoon breeze, so that he could meet his ride at the Connecticut Avenue bus shelter at 6:17, to take him to his brother.

EIGHTEEN

HAROLD DEVRIES LED BLAINE through the steel and concrete tunnel from the White House back into the Eisenhower Executive Office Building. Originally known as the State, War, and Navy Building, the EEOB was one of Washington's most historic buildings, a stunning example of French Second Empire architecture, which had taken seventeen years to build. Not everyone had been taken by its ornamental façade, though. Harry Truman called it "the greatest monstrosity in America."

They walked up the granite stairs to the intelligence director's satellite office on the second floor. The marble echoed with their footfalls as they approached his office down an empty hallway. The cavernous space felt a little eerie to Blaine.

DeVries was in his early fifties now but retained the alert expression of a much younger man, as if life were a puzzle that he was perpetually on the verge of solving.

"Pardon the mess," he said, closing his office door. "I'm not used to conducting meetings here. Try to make yourself at home."

Blaine looked around and smiled. It was a functional office. Small, cluttered, only slightly larger than the one she'd been given on the fourth floor. Computer, phone, file cabinets, boxes. Nothing like his high-tech office at Liberty Crossing. She sat in the old leather armchair.

"So." DeVries leaned back in his swivel chair behind the desk and watched her. "I take it you're on board now."

"You can still read me pretty well, can't you?"

"I guess I can. I didn't completely believe it at first, either. I don't know that any of us did. I think we're hard-wired to think there has to be some other explanation. Coincidence. Hoax."

Blaine nodded. "I'm sorry I questioned the intelligence earlier. I didn't mean to put you on the spot."

"No, no offense, Cate." He chuckled. "Believe me, I've envisioned the headlines. 'Eighty billion dollar intelligence community misses global threat.' 'Massive intelligence blunder cited.' I'm cognizant that it ultimately comes back on me."

"What do you think?"

"What do *I* think?"

"Yeah. What do you really think it is?"

He made a face, and swiveled to one side. "I don't know, Cate," he said, his voice softening. "I've been around and around about that. I think we're engaged in a new sort of warfare. But I hate to speculate beyond that. I think it's what the President said earlier. If someone cared about weather science as much as the United States did about sending a man to the moon in the 1960s, and they had the funding and the smarts, and I suppose the ruthlessness, they could probably make this happen."

"Some*one*?"

He shrugged. "A country."

"China?"

"Maybe. Or a sophisticated business consortium of some kind, maybe connected with the Chinese government." He frowned at her. "You said yesterday it's theoretically possible. It *could* happen."

"If the funding were there, yes, it probably could. Although not all scientists would agree."

He let his gaze linger ambiguously. It reminded Blaine of how he used to flirt with her, years before. And how sometimes she had responded, always pulling back before it led anywhere. DeVries and his wife Faye had been married for twenty-seven years and as far as she knew it was a good marriage, with two grown children, a son and daughter, both of whom were Washington attorneys.

"And we really don't have the ingenuity to figure this out?" she said. "I mean, how they're doing it." She flashed again to the grainy images she had just seen of the mutilated corpses strewn across the French countryside and felt sick.

"We're working on it around the clock, Cate. With each event, there have been physical clues. Changes in air pressure, changes in the atmosphere, physical alterations in the sky. But we haven't been able to isolate a location or locations yet."

"Is it Janus?"

"I don't know. Maybe yes, maybe no."

Blaine turned her eyes away, feeling frustrated. "And you're comfortable that we're handling this right?"

"I think we have an obligation to be as thorough as we can," he said. "But also to be united. To follow the President's lead."

"It doesn't bother you that we're keeping it so reined in, before this small group?"

He was frowning as if he didn't understand. "No, that's how you handle a crisis, Cate. You don't do it out in the open." He showed his cagey smile, but it seemed misplaced this time, as if he were being disingenuous. "Let's wait for the next message. I have a feeling we'll be getting something else tomorrow. Be patient. Go along with it, Cate. Don't question too much unless it's necessary."

"Really?"

"Really."

As she walked to the stairway, Blaine thought about the system she was a part of, reminding herself that it operated as it did for a reason—that decades of wisdom and trial and error had gone into its making. So why did it seem so flawed and inefficient at times? She'd been at odds with her father over that question. "Rules exist for a reason," he used to tell her. "Individual commitment to a group effort is what makes society work." *Maybe*. She still sometimes wondered about that.

The early evening sky was thick with dark rainclouds, the cool air breezing up. Blaine added the numbers again as she walked along West Executive Drive to her car in the light rain, and came up with 3,700. The approximate number of people who had died in the "unnatural" disasters since the email warnings began.

NINETEEN

A WHITE HONDA PULLED to the curb in front of the Connecticut Avenue bus shelter, its emergency lights blinking as it slowed to a stop. Charles Mallory stepped forward and opened the back door. He slid inside. The driver was a man Mallory didn't recognize.

Two switches followed, both deep inside parking garages in the city, before he came to a third garage beneath a Howard Johnson's hotel downtown, where Mallory stepped out of the back seat of a gray Camry and saw Joseph Chaplin standing by the stairwell. He wore an all-black suit and tie, and looked like an undertaker.

"Greetings," Chaplin said.

"Greetings."

The set-up was the kind Chaplin had arranged countless times. It assumed there were watchers. And maybe watchers watching the watchers. It was designed to find the watchers and also to elude them, although Mallory didn't think anyone was following him in Washington. Not yet.

Chaplin entered the stairwell first, leading him to a room on the third floor. He knocked twice. Then inserted a key card. He held the door open, as Charlie stepped in. The door closed, Chaplin still in the hall.

Charlie saw his brother walk toward him across the unlit room, wearing old jeans and an oversized Georgetown sweat shirt. He reached out to shake, tentatively at first, then more firmly. Jon's hair was much longer than he remembered.

People who saw Jon and Charles together were often surprised to learn that they were brothers. Charlie was taller, blond, fair-skinned and sharper featured, with slate-blue eyes. Jon's eyes and hair were dark. He lacked the agile movements and physical dexterity of his older brother, possessing a slight awkwardness of manner that had actually worked to his advantage sometimes as a reporter. They seemed the products of two different families, if not nationalities.

The Mallorys had been opposites in their trades, as well. Jon was an outsider, a keeper of stories, who used journalism as his passport into the realm of international issues. Charlie had been on the inside for years, working as a government intelligence operative before starting his own contracting business and, eventually, retiring. Only rarely had the two crossed paths in recent years.

"So," Charlie said. "How has my man Chaplin been treating you?"

Jon shrugged.

"Okay?"

"Other than kidnapping me from a crowded street corner, I have no complaints."

Charlie smiled. "He says it was for your own good, though."

Jon clucked his tongue.

"Anyway, he apologized, right?"

"He did."

Charlie sat on the easy chair by the desk and took in the room: king-size bed with duvet covers, bedside tables, wall mirror, tan cloth sofa, chest of drawers. The drapes were drawn. A laptop was open on the bed, newspaper sections strewn on the floor, a medium-sized suitcase beside the bed, unzipped. On the chest were several magazines, paperbacks by Michael Connelly and John LeCarre, and his beat-up old *Complete Shakespeare* from college. *Casablanca* played silently on the television. Chaplin had set out a silver tray with bottles of water and orange juice on the desk, along with a plate of cheeses and vegetables. Typical Chaplin.

"So," Charlie said, seeing the wariness in his brother's face. "How have you been, anyway?"

"Me? Good."

"Good."

"*You?* You look good."

"Thanks. Early retirement was treating me well."

Jon frowned.

"I meant it sort of ironically," Charlie added.

"Oh."

Jon coughed, standing stiffly. "So? I mean, have you been able to figure any of this out?"

"Not much. Please. Have a seat," Charlie said, indicating the sofa. He reached over for a carrot, ate it in two bites.

Jon finally sat, and leaned back. Then, as if reconsidering, he hunched forward. "You talked with Church."

"I did. He gave me your list. I was hoping you could tell me a little bit about this story. About what Dr. Westlake told you."

Jon nodded. When he didn't say anything else, Charlie said, "How did all this come about? How do you know about this list? How do you know Dr. Westlake?"

"I don't know her. I mean—I interviewed her. We emailed back and forth a few times." Jon looked at him sideways and, for a moment, Charlie saw their mother's dark eyes gazing back at him. "Our common interest was geo-engineering. She was concerned about a certain research project based in California that was happening under the radar, so to speak. She reached out to *me*, actually, telling me this. I was supposed to meet with her last Friday."

"But she went missing."

"Yes. That's right."

Charlie held out the vegetable tray for his brother, who shook his head. "She answered a question you didn't ask."

"Right."

"We've gone through the list you left," Charlie said. "Chaplin and I ran some data searches on the names, as you probably have. Church did, too. There are a few loose connections we're following up on. But, unfortunately, there's no clear intersection among them yet. No sense that their paths ever crossed."

"I know."

"But Dr. Westlake thought that there *was* something tying these people together."

"Yes. She *knew* there was," Jon said.

"Okay."

"It's just that it's very difficult to prove."

"All right." Charlie ate another carrot, waiting for Jon to say more. "And she considered herself the last name on the list."

"Yes." Jon leaned back again. "When she went missing, I realized I was probably part of this list, too. If Dr. Westlake was number eight, I was number nine."

"Because of what she told you."

"Right." There was another silence. "Also, she suggested I contact you."

"*She* did?"

"Yes."

That was odd. Charles Mallory had never met Dr. Keri West-lake. Had never even *heard* of her until the day before. His brother watched him, reminding Charlie of how he used to occasionally stare when they were kids; when he'd done something wrong and expected his older brother to help him fix it.

"How did she put it, exactly?"

"Pardon?"

"How did she put it? Dr. Westlake."

"She said I should share this with someone who can do something about it. 'Maybe you can pass this to your brother.'"

Charles Mallory thought about that, trying to make sense of it. He couldn't. "And what about the other thing?" he said. "The answer to the question you didn't ask."

Jon leaned forward again and clasped his hands. He took a deliberate breath. "Okay," he said. "This was practically the last thing she told me. That each of the people on this list had learned something. Through their work. Something he or she had found disturbing."

"Okay."

"And each of them . . . had begun to ask questions about it. And what they were asking questions about was, in effect, the same thing."

"Really."

Jon nodded.

"Even though their careers and their lives didn't seem to intersect."

"Right. That's what she said. I can't tell you how she came to that conclusion, exactly. But she obviously believes it. That each of them had become suspicious about something. Someone, actually."

"Some*one*."

"Yes. Someone who has been working very quietly for a number of years, apparently, consolidating research firms, R&D, doing it under various names, different foundations, corporations, and front groups. So that it wasn't clear who it was or what exactly was happening. There was an intricate effort, in other words, to conceal patterns."

"But these seven people somehow saw those patterns."

"Yes, right."

"And threatened to expose them."

"Or had the ability to do so. That was the implication."

"Okay. And? This person didn't want to be exposed because—why? There's something illegal about what he was doing?"

"Presumably."

Charlie ran through the seven names again in his head, and the sketchy details he had learned about each. "So she knows *about* this person, without knowing who he is."

Jon cleared his throat and sat forward. "No," he said, "she does."

"She does. But she didn't have a chance to tell you."

Jon's dark eyes moistened. There was something in his face that Charlie had never seen before. "No, that's the thing," he said. "She *did* tell me."

"Oh." Charlie tilted his head, looking at his brother with incredulity. "So you *know* who this person is."

"Yeah. That's why I called you. That's why I needed to disappear."

TWENTY

CHARLIE SAW THE FLUSH of fear and urgency in Jon's face.

With privileged knowledge comes heightened responsibility. Words their father had said to him days before he died. Words that had failed to save his life.

"She *told you?* You know his name."

"Yes. I know his name."

Charlie waited. "Okay."

Jon took a breath. His eyes widened and moved quickly around the room, from the doorway to the television to the drapes. Then he said, "His name is Vladimir Volkov."

"Okay." The name meant nothing to Charlie. "Who is he?"

"I have only a sketchy background. He's a second-generation Russian oligarch, supposedly. A mysterious billionaire who made his fortune in oil and banking during the 1990s. Operating largely through intermediaries and shell companies. For years, he's been investing in climate and weather research." Jon paused. "He learns that someone is developing computer simulation models that might result in better weather tracking, or that a patent has been issued for an artificial rain process, then he learns all he can about it. If it's viable and it's for sale, he buys it. If not, he starts his own company and tries to produce the same results."

"Volkov."

"Vladimir Volkov."

"Spell it."

Jon did. "There's one man in particular who does much of Volkov's bidding in the United States, supposedly. His name is Victor Zorn. Mr. Zorn. He's an investor and a venture capitalist."

Mallory made a mental note of both names. "And Dr. Westlake told you all of this? Where did she get the names?"

"I think it came to her from someone on the list. I don't know who, although, from what she said, I think it might have been the last person."

"Dr. Atul Pradhan."

"Yes."

"This Victor Zorn," Charlie said. "He's American?"

"Yes. Based in California. Also very low profile and secretive. Dr. Westlake had been trying to learn more about Victor Zorn. She had attempted to contact him."

"Okay." Charlie nodded. "And what's wrong with someone doing what he's doing?"

"Pardon?"

"I mean, buying up companies, supporting R&D. If he didn't want to be so private about it, wouldn't *Time* magazine put him on their cover and call him a visionary?"

"Well, there's the list, for one thing. The chain."

"Dr. Westlake thinks Volkov is responsible for those disappearances?"

"Yes. And she was also told that his business is not all necessarily above board. Supposedly, he has used intimidation tactics and industrial espionage to close some of his deals." Jon sat forward, glanced at the door.

"And what kind of person is *she?* I mean, does she think LBJ was in on the Kennedy assassination, for example?"

Jon showed his first real smile. "No. No, I've known a few conspiracy nuts over the years. She's not like that. But she's genuinely afraid. I think she received a threat just before she gave me this list."

Charlie thought about that. "Okay. And what else did she say about him?"

"Volkov? She said that he is a very brilliant man who tends to get what he wants. He's ahead of the game because no one else is playing at the level he is. Or even able to recognize it."

"But somehow these seven people did?"

"Or some part of it. That's what she thinks. I don't know. I haven't been able to figure out what it might be."

"Why didn't Dr. Westlake tell anybody else about this?"

"She did. Including police."

"Okay." Charlie absently chomped on a carrot, thinking. "So, if something happened to these people, it's because they became a threat to Volkov's operation. Or because they threatened to draw attention to it."

"Presumably." Jon watched his brother as if expecting him to solve a difficult puzzle for him.

"And what else does Dr. Westlake know about Volkov? Where does he live, for instance?"

Jon shrugged. "He has a home in Russia, but supposedly lives there only a few weeks, or months, of the year. Only when the weather is pleasant. She thinks he has a very cultured exterior, but is quite ruthless underneath. Also, he supposedly carries some weight at the Kremlin."

"With the government."

"Yes."

"Anything else?"

"Mmm, no. Not really."

Charlie nodded. "Well, it's a big story, isn't it? Maybe we can work on it together."

Jon nodded, lifted his eyebrows. *I'll do whatever I can to help,* Charlie thought. *But, more importantly, to keep Jon safe.*

"Let Chaplin provide security for you. You can reach me through him. But just lie low for a while. Okay?" He stood and pressed Chaplin's number on his cell phone, letting it ring once. "You've handled this in the right way," Charlie added.

Jon shruged and nodded.

"You been okay, otherwise?"

"Until this, fine."

"Good," he said. "How's Melanie?"

"Oh."

Charlie smiled. He reached to shake his brother's hand. "Take care," he said. He turned and glanced around the room, taking in the newspapers, the vegetables, Humphrey Bogart and Claude Rains on the television. Two knocks on the door broke the slightly awkward silence.

Chaplin began to accompany Charlie back to the stairway. Mallory stopped.

"I'll be okay," he said. "Look out for my brother. Stay with him. And please find out all you can on these two names." He handed him a card. He had written on it *Vladimir Volkov* and *Victor Zorn*. "I need it ASAP."

Chaplin frowned at the card.

"All right?"

"Yes. But I'd advise against you going back outside yourself without any cover," he said, reverting to the formal business tone he used with clients. "We have arranged a ride for you."

Mallory smiled. He shook Chaplin's hand and walked to the elevator. Took it down to the lobby, without looking back, and walked out into the blustery Washington night until he found a taxi cab.

11:24 P.M.

The 14-ton freighter ship MS *Kassel* plowed through the churning North Atlantic sea at a steady 18 knots. The ocean had been rough for the first four days of their nine-day crossing, with ten-foot waves and miles of white water, but the winds had died down over the past twenty-four hours and the journey ahead promised to be much smoother. The 705-foot-long German ship was more than halfway across its ocean passage now, with a final destination of Savannah, Georgia. On board was a cargo of 780 forty-foot shipping containers, filled with industrial machinery, steel, furniture and Fiat automobiles. It was still well ahead of Tropical Storm Alexander, the monster storm that seemed to be chasing it from afar.

Dieter Gerhard had captained this ship for eleven years; before that, he had crossed the ocean hundreds of times on various other freighters. Life on the water had become the norm for Dieter and the sea now felt like his home; the roots he'd planted on land had all been pulled up long ago—his marriage dissolved, his children gone. It was at times like this, alone in the pilothouse late at night, with the seemingly infinite expanse of ocean surrounding him, its swells reflecting the muted lights from the sky and moon, that he felt alive, connected to the wild, sublime elemental realities that most people never experienced—or could understand.

He stepped onto the deck for several minutes wearing his yellow raincoat, under the shelter of the pilothouse overhang, and smoked a Davidoff cigarette, watching the water. Looking out at the rain slanting in the moonlight. Thinking about nothing in particular. Being here was empowering and humbling, both at the same time:

the constant motion, the subtle shifts, the sheer size—70 percent of Earth was covered by ocean, going as deep as seven miles below the sea's surface. This distance they were traveling now—from Germany to Savannah—was more than double the distance across the United States. Those were the kinds of spaces that humbled Dieter and gave him perspective, that made most of what people thought and worried about seem trivial. They had become his version of religion.

Dieter was back in the pilothouse making a routine check of GPS coordinates when he happened to glance up and saw something that shouldn't have been there—what looked at first to be a giant white mountain rising up out of the ocean.

But it couldn't be.

No. Of course not. There was no land around for hundreds of miles. And certainly no icebergs this far south.

But there it was. To the starboard side of the ship's bow. *What the hell is it?*

He flicked on the rows of deck lights and squinted through the glass, stunned by what he saw. It was a giant wave of water, rising up out of what had been a relatively calm night sea. No, it couldn't be. It didn't make sense. He had seen freak waves over the years, clashing systems of deep ocean currents and sudden mighty winds. But he had never heard of a rogue wave this large.

He lifted his radio and accessed the marine band channel, then the marine VHF radio frequency. "Mayday, Mayday. This is *MS Kassel*," he shouted, speaking in German, and then gave his coordinates. He knew he was in serious danger; that his ship was going to be severely damaged by this. Part of him even knew it wasn't going to survive. Dieter was still speaking into the radio when the wave came over the *Kassel* broadside, blowing out the windows of the pilothouse, and then collapsing over the deck, splitting the ship into the trough of another wave as if it were a toy.

IN WASHINGTON, DR. Wu was thinking about his wife, Alison, and their two daughters—Kim, who had just begun her senior year of college at Princeton, and Melinda, who was a sophomore at the University of Maryland—when he received an electronic alert that two more distress calls had been picked up in the North Atlantic Sea, one from air traffic control frequencies, the other from the Coast

Guard. Dr. Wu added them to the four from the day before, knowing what it was. *The third anomaly.*

Rogue waves—giant, spontaneous ocean waves that sprang up out of the deep seas, reaching heights topping a hundred feet—were once thought to be nothing more than legends related by wily sea captains, akin to reports of sea serpents. But they were now widely accepted as real, even if their origins were not well understood.

Over the past twenty years, about two hundred super cargo ships had been lost at sea, some of them to freak waves. Now, in just the past day—since Tropical Storm Alexander had formed in the North Atlantic Sea—there had been six reports of cargo ships lost in the deep ocean.

Dr. Wu typed a subject line on his handheld monitor: THIRD ANOMALY. He began to address his note to Gabriel Herring but then thought better of it, remembering his promise to himself. Instead, he called Herring. This time, he wanted to brief the President personally. But more importantly, he wanted to ask the President what was really going on.

TWENTY-ONE

Tuesday, October 4, 7:01 A.M.

CATHERINE BLAINE UNLOCKED HER fourth-story office in a non-descript building on K Street downtown. She twisted open the blinds a crack, then sat at her desk and glanced through the morning's *Washington Post*, seeing that the tornadoes in France were at the bottom of page one. She flipped through the "A" section. Found a story on page fourteen about the Cape Verde storm: MONSTER STORM FORMS IN ATLANTIC.

Nine minutes later, she walked down the stairway and came out in the lower level of the parking garage, where Jamie Griffith had left a rental car for her. A silver Ford Focus. The keys were underneath the mat.

She *was* playing hide and seek again with the Secret Service, but on occasions like this it felt justified. The issue was freedom, she had decided. The need to find information on her own. She drove to the Beltway, then took 95 north toward Baltimore, getting off in the suburb of Towson, following the directions she'd printed out for the Environmental Physics Research Laboratories, where Dr. Sanchez worked.

At this hour, there were only three other cars in the lot of the single-story, beige-brick building. She recognized one of them—a beat-up old brown Toyota Corolla that looked as if it hadn't been washed for a year. Blaine smiled to herself as she walked to the entrance, wondering if she should write "Wash Me" with her finger on the back window.

It was two minutes after 8 A.M. and the office didn't open for another hour, so Blaine banged on the front doors until she saw him coming, walking with his intense and slightly prissy swagger. He was wearing a loose-fitting dashiki and flip-flops.

"My god. How'd you get loose?" he said, holding the door for her. He poked his head outside and looked one direction then the other. "I mean, where's your entourage? Bodyguards and all that?"

"Gave them the slip."

"Goodness," he said, and engulfed her in a hug. "Come on back. Please. Your questions have got me thinking. Tea?"

"Sure." His office was large but impossibly cluttered, with tottering piles of books and magazines, precariously balanced boxes, scattered folders, and a variety of antique musical instruments. Among his many interests, Dr. Sanchez collected antique string instruments, many of which he had learned to play. Charts, memos, emails, and newspaper clippings were tacked on the wood-paneled walls, most of them yellowed, along with maps of various sizes and locales. Three computer monitors were lined up on a work station and a much larger monitor stood on a table beside it.

"I've been working on your questions since five thirty. I have to say, they interest me a great deal."

Blaine smiled. Dr. Sanchez was still one of the smartest weather scientists anywhere, although he didn't do politics too well. He was in some ways the opposite of Dr. Wu, who had a skill for sounding reasonable and for saying the right thing. Dr. Sanchez had worked for NASA, NOAA, and Lawrence Livermore labs, and, for one year, had been a professor of atmospheric science at Columbia's Earth Institute. But he didn't get along well with other people, and each job had involved some degree of confrontation with his employers and co-workers. As he grew older, Sanchez seemed to divide people into two categories—those he liked and those he didn't like. Blaine was one of the privileged few who still resided in the former category.

"Have a seat. Just clear that off there," he said, flapping a hand at the sofa. For a moment his head jerked to the side, as if he were trying to shake water from his ear. It was a tic he had, which occurred every few minutes.

Blaine set down her briefcase, and pushed aside papers and a crusty old beach towel, clearing a spot to sit. Sanchez poured them each green tea in plastic tea cups and then sat on a creaky wooden swivel chair and kicked off his flip flops.

"Science begins with questions, yes?" he said, smiling. His personal appearance—full beard, long white hair tied back in a ponytail—and surprising childlike enthusiasms only seemed to accentuate his eccentricity. "And you've asked some interesting ones."

"All hypothetical, of course."

"Of course, of course." He winked. "And when we're finished, I'd like to tell *you* something hypothetical, a theory that may or may not be relevant to what you're asking me."

Blaine sipped her tea as he walked to the computer station and sat.

"Now. First things first," he said, typing on the keyboard in front of him. "You asked me to look at four geo-physical events and determine if any of them could, hypothetically, have been man-made."

"Yes." She waited, as if she were in his classroom.

"My answer would be no."

"Really."

"Yes." He nodded gravely, swiveling the chair to face her, his lips pursed. It was not the answer she had expected. Then the messages *were* hoaxes? The events coincidences?

"So," she said, "even hypothetically speaking. It's not, in your judgment, feasible that—"

He held up his right hand to stop her. "I'm responding to the question as phrased," he said. "The term you used was 'man-made.'"

Blaine saw a twinkle in his dark eyes. Although he didn't show it much anymore, Dr. Sanchez had a winning smile that seemed to transform him into a child. "And to that question, the answer is no. If you had used a different term, I might have responded with a different answer."

He was waiting for her to ask him. "What term?"

"Man-induced, let's say. Or man-manipulated."

"And then what would your answer be?"

"Then I would have said yes."

"To which event?"

"All four." He clicked open a slide show on the large monitor and stood. She recognized the first image as an aerial view of eastern India and Bangladesh, with the wedge of the Bay of Bengal between them.

"Take the first example. A tsunami in the Bay of Bengal. Next," he said, as if instructing someone to change the image, although he was holding the remote control himself. He zoomed in on the horseshoe-shaped upper bay.

"As you know, the Bay of Bengal is one of the most vulnerable spots on the planet. You won't get a lot of disagreement about that. The reasons are well-documented: it's low-lying and heavily populated, prone to deadly floods. Okay? Each year, thousands of people lose their lives during the monsoon season." He changed the image—this one an aerial of floodwaters encroaching on the land. The borders seemed to have drawn in, the water redefining the shape of the coast. "Projections show the country may lose seventeen percent of its total land mass over the next thirty years. Which, needless to say, will have severe consequences, considering the population density. Next."

He clicked to another slide, a diagram showing layers of the earth's crust. It reminded her of something from a college geology class. "The vulnerability that you *don't* hear about so much has to do with the plates in the earth *beneath* the Bay of Bengal," he said. "An earthquake, in fact, has been overdue there for decades. An undersea earthquake, in turn, could trigger a tsunami, which is what we now know happened on September twenty-fifth."

She watched him as he enlarged the image, pacing in front of the big screen like a teacher. "As you know, of course, earthquakes occur when the tectonic plates of the earth's crust suddenly shift."

Blaine nodded.

"Now, we aren't, as of yet, able to determine just *when* earthquakes will occur, in the sense that we can predict thunderstorms or hurricanes or low-pressure systems. But we are able to predict where, on long-term models, earthquakes are *likely* to occur. We know, from magnetic geophysical surveys, for instance, where fault lines lie."

"Okay."

"But what triggers the shifting of these plates, and causes these vulnerabilities to actually become disasters? Let's separate it into two general categories: the triggers that are natural and those that are not natural."

"We're still talking hypothetically here."

He stopped pacing. "No," he said, "not hypothetically. We can say with a degree of certainty that some earthquakes clearly have man-made triggers. It's what's called induced seismicity."

"For example . . . ?"

"Yes. Next," he said, changing the image to an aerial view of an earthquake's aftermath.

"May 12, 2008," he said. "At two twenty-eight in the afternoon, a magnitude 8.0 earthquake struck the Great Sichuan region in Western China. Okay? More than seventy thousand people died as a result. Five million were left homeless. Many prominent scientists consider this an induced seismic event. Possibly the worst man-induced disaster in history."

Blaine watched as he clicked through two more images: rescuers wearing masks, standing on the rubble of a fallen city. Limbs of dead bodies jutting from concrete slabs of collapsed buildings.

"But I don't understand. What man-induced trigger would have caused an earthquake that killed seventy thousand people?"

He changed the image to a bright clear aerial of a mammoth reservoir and hydroelectric dam. "In this case, the Zipingpu Reservoir, which was built four years earlier, near a major fault line." He zoomed in on the water pen. "This reservoir held three hundred and twenty tons of water, which placed enormous pressures on the fault line. The scientists who believe this was induced seismicity believe the pressure of the reservoir caused the plates on the fault line to shift and rupture."

Blaine absorbed that for a moment. "Do you believe it?"

"I think it's well within the realm of possibility, yes."

"There are other examples?"

"Many, yes. Next: a 6.3-magnitude earthquake occurred in Maharashtra, India in 1967, for instance. The epicenter and aftershocks were all located near or under the Konya Dam reservoir. One hundred and eighty people died and fifteen hundred were injured. Closer to home, a magnitude 6.1 earthquake in California in the mid 1970s was attributed to a massive earth-fill dam and reservoir there."

"And, presumably, there can be other causes besides dams?"

"Any number, yes. Mining explosions. Nuclear tests. Extraction of fossil fuel and groundwater. Well-drilling. In Colorado in 1961, the United States Army drilled a twelve-thousand-foot disposal well at its Rocky Mountain Arsenal, where waste fluids were dumped. It caused two hundred earthquakes in one year."

"Because of the drilling?"

He briefly showed his fetching smile. "No, because of the fluids. What was happening was that they were lubricating the rock layers and making them prone to slip, causing a series of very small earthquakes."

"So you're saying it would be possible to exploit existing vulnerabilities to create a 'natural' disaster such as an earthquake."

He nodded.

"And what about these other disasters? The examples I gave you?"

He reached down for a sip of tea, as if composing himself for the next presentation.

"It's interesting." He set his tea cup down. "On the face of it, each of these four events seems unprecedented. In terms of severity, certainly, each one is. But the events themselves are actually not unprecedented at all. In fact, each region, it turns out, is particularly vulnerable to a man-induced event of exactly this nature. I'll show you why."

"Please."

TWENTY-TWO

CATHERINE BLAINE WATCHED THE large monitor as Dr. Sanchez called up a new image. A scene of coastal devastation: collapsed condominium buildings, windows blasted out, twisted steel and shattered glass, house roofs torn off and deposited in the road, cars overturned, signs blown apart, gashes in a highway where the pavement had buckled.

"Let me take you quickly through your other three questions," he said. "Beginning with the hurricane off the coast of Uruguay. September twenty-eighth. 'Unprecedented' is, again, the word the media kept using."

"Yes."

He frowned and his right hand wavered. "Technically, that may be true. Okay? There had never before been a recorded hurricane strike on the coast of Uruguay. The common wisdom is that sea temperatures in the South Atlantic are too low and wind shear too great for these kinds of storms to form.

"But, in fact, severe storms have been occurring with increasing regularity in the South Atlantic. In 2004, for the first time that we know of, a hurricane hit the coast of Brazil, five hundred miles south of Rio. Which, I might add, is only about two hundred miles north of Uruguay."

"So it's not as unusual as it seems."

"No."

"Okay. How about the tornados in France yesterday? As far as I can tell, there's never been a disaster like that before."

He pursed his lips. "Actually," he said, "events 'like that' happen all the time over there. France has more tornadoes than any country in Europe. And this particular region—Picardy, near the border with Belgium—has more than anywhere else. So, in fact, we're again dealing with an existing vulnerability. The same is true of the series of earthquakes in the Pacific."

Blaine considered that. "All right. Next question, then: *could* these have been man-manipulated? In other words, are there existing technologies that could create or enhance a tornado, for example?"

"Well." He typed in a new prompt on his computer keyboard, waited a moment, and typed in a number sequence. "Let me just show you something." He called up a video file on the large monitor. An animated black-and-white image that she began to recognize as a tornado funnel. But as the camera pulled back, she saw that the tornado was swirling inside a giant enclosed space. "This is, in fact, a man-made tornado," he said. "It was created by what's called an atmospheric vortex engine. Invented by a Canadian petroleum engineer more than ten years ago."

"For what purpose?"

"Energy. Scientists have investigated man-made tornadoes as a source of electricity for many years. This, as you can see, was done in an enclosed environment." He ran the image again, this time in slow motion. "Air carrying waste heat is blown in from vents on the sides of these walls, spinning into a vortex that mimics the formation of a naturally occurring tornado. Once started, the vortex draws in more hot air from vents in the wall, spinning it through turbines and generating electricity. This tornado measures about fifty meters in diameter."

He clicked the remote to produce a new image, a printed document with the famous Mercedes-Benz logo on the top. "This is a press release issued in 2009," Dr. Sanchez said, "from the Mercedes-Benz company in Germany, claiming it had created the largest man-made tornado. It's in the *Guinness Book of World Records* now, in fact. I have it on good authority, though, that it really isn't. Larger ones have been created more discreetly by researchers in both China and in Canada."

Blaine skimmed through the press release, then looked up at Dr. Sanchez.

"How about hurricanes?" she said. "How could they be manipulated?"

"That's slightly more problematic, because of their size, but the objective would be similar. The power generated by a Category 2 hurricane, if we were able to convert it to electricity, would satisfy the United States' energy needs for three years, Cate. So, again, there are scientists studying this. Models of artificial hurricanes were, in fact, created in the wake of Hurricane Andrew in 1992, part of an attempt to learn more about how to prevent building failures."

"And, staying hypothetical: What about the earthquakes in the South Pacific Sea? How would they have been man-induced? There's no dam there."

"No." His eyes twinkled and he sat back in his wooden chair. "But essentially, all you need to do is apply a force that would cause the plates of the Earth's crust to rub against one another. Okay? There are any number of ways that might happen. An underwater explosion could do it. There are other processes that have been researched and eventually, I believe, will be viable. Ground radio tomography, for one."

"Ground radio—?"

"You bounce a wave of energy into the ionosphere and it comes back to earth. On a small scale, this has been used to look for oil reserves in Alaska. It's the same principle as a CT scan or an X-ray."

Blaine thought of something, then brought forward a question she had wanted to ask in the meeting at the White House: "If, hypothetically, a disturbance could be created in the atmosphere, would there be any visible sign of that disturbance? That might even determine the source of it?"

"Maybe yes, maybe no."

"Take yes," she said, watching him intently. "Would there be any way of tracing it?"

He shrugged. "That would depend on the process. You could say that the energy bouncing back from the ionosphere should be detectable, yes. The radio field devices that the government is using experimentally in Alaska right now often light up the sky." His head twitched as he thought about it. "Yes, I see what you're getting at, Cate. It's most interesting. Let me look into that a little and I'll get back to you."

Blaine nodded. "But you believe this is feasible."

"Feasible? Of course. I don't know that the technology currently exists on the scale you're talking about. But it's being studied. There's one firm in particular that has been aggressively purchasing companies and research labs to advance this technology. I think it will eventually either go bankrupt or become a leader in an emerging industry. And that, I must say, worries me." He sat back, looking sad all of a sudden.

"Why?"

"Do you know what natural disasters are, Cate? They're adjustments. They're not isolated occurrences that come out of nowhere. The weather is a big interrelated process, with no national borders. Hurricanes transport heat out of the tropics, helping to balance the planet's heat budget. If you strengthen or weaken them, you're going to affect weather elsewhere. If you artificially create monsoons in one part of the world, you may create drought in another. I'm just afraid if this happens, there'll be serious side effects.

"And the fact that natural disasters are becoming more prevalent worries me a great deal." He opened his desk drawer, pulled out a wrinkled sheet of paper and scooted toward her, leaving the drawer open. "This crossed my desk the other day," he said, planting his feet widely apart and handing her the paper. She glanced at the headline. "It's from the World Health Organization. From 2000 to 2009, it says there was an increase in natural disasters of two hundred and thirty-three percent as compared to 1980 to 1989."

"So—you're saying we might be solving one problem and creating another."

"Or many others. And it's entirely possible that these new problems will be infinitely worse than what we had before."

TWENTY-THREE

11:37 A.M.

VICE PRESIDENT BILL STANTON bounded up the steps of the Queen Anne-style turreted mansion that he reluctantly called home, anxious to get in the kitchen and make his favorite sandwich: bologna, mustard, and Swiss cheese on wheat toast with lettuce, tomato, and crumbles of Ruffles potato chips.

As a congressman, Stanton had been known as a "man of the people." He'd frequently taken the Amtrak train from his home in Pennsylvania to Washington and prided himself on being accessible. But the Secret Service detail made it difficult for him to be a man of the people in Washington anymore, as did living in this Victorian mansion.

Number One Observatory Circle, the official vice presidential residence, sat on fifteen acres of land at the US Naval Observatory along Embassy Row. Stanton described it to friends and family members as "something else." Known as Admiral's House, the Victorian-style home was built in 1893 for the superintendent of the US Naval Observatory. It became the official vice presidential residence in the mid-1970s.

For Stanton, who had lived much of his adult life in a two-bedroom Philadelphia-area house he'd purchased in 1978, calling this place "home" felt silly—thirty-three rooms, ten thousand square feet of floor space. The place looked like a museum, with rare artworks, polished wood floors, couches and chairs upholstered in gold, windows draped floor-to-ceiling with silk taffeta.

He ate his sandwich slowly in the shade of the back porch, sitting on the steps and watching the squirrels. He gazed at the grounds of the National Cathedral, and, to his left, across Canal Road, the north bank of the Potomac River and the Georgetown University campus. Sometimes Stanton would sit on these steps and tell himself, "Hey, Billy, you know something, you're the Vice President of the United States now, so you better start acting like it," and then he would laugh.

He enjoyed the chill in the air and the falling russet oak leaves, and tried not to think much about his afternoon meetings. Particularly the one with Thom Rorbach and Dean Stiles on the Janus Task Force. This Janus thing was "something else," too, Stanton thought. A *different kind of something else.*

As he took another bite of sandwich, Stanton felt his phone vibrate in a pocket of his pants. He didn't check it right away, though. He slowly finished his lunch instead, enjoying the crunch of the Ruffles chips. Finally he set down the plate, pulled out his SME-PED mobile device and looked.

"What the—?"

A message from the POTUS. President of the United States.

Golf tomorrow?

For a moment, Stanton smiled. This was the same message Aaron Hall used to send Bill Stanton during the early weeks of the campaign, when the two former presidential rivals were just getting to know one another socially.

But then he realized what was wrong with it: President Hall had quit golfing months ago.

CATHERINE BLAINE WAS back in her office on K Street, typing out notes, sifting through what Dr. Sanchez had told her. *Induced seismicity. Man-made tornadoes. Harnessing the energy of hurricanes. Atmospheric disturbances. Balancing the planet's heat budget.* Concepts she hadn't thought much about before. The meeting had reinforced her suspicion that they were accepting the threats too easily. Sanchez, for all his quirks, had given her ideas, and raised questions that hadn't been raised in the White House. She wondered, for instance, if the group's scientific panel had fully considered the atmospheric changes that occurred during and immediately after each event. One summary had called them "untraceable."

The vibration of her mobile device pulled Blaine out of her reverie. It was Gabriel Herring. The President's chief of staff was calling an emergency meeting. His message was the acronym they had all been given for meetings of those in the circle: *YARI*.

Your attendance requested immediately.

Twenty-seven minutes later, Blaine was driven through the southwest gate of the White House onto West Executive Drive. The others were seated around the conference table in the Data Visualization Center when she entered. There was one difference, though. There weren't three of them this time, there were four.

Vice President Stanton, the newcomer in the room, stood and greeted her as "Secretary Blaine," the only one to say her name.

Blaine sat. She liked Bill Stanton, found his informality refreshing. Supposedly, his geniality masked burning ambition—he had run for President himself twice—although she had never seen that side of him. He seemed to her ideally suited for his current job.

The others nodded curtly, although it was clear they'd been waiting for her. A mood of tension hung in the room, an irritation, maybe, that she occasionally went off the radar.

Blaine looked across the table, saw the EYES ONLY folder in front of the President.

"Cate," he said. "We have received two more messages."

TWENTY-FOUR

THE CONFERENCE ROOM IN the Eisenhower Executive Office Building had an old, welcoming smell. Musty, ancient wood. The smell of history. But it was also intimidating: Blaine felt it as she took her seat at the table, and the President silently distributed copies of the latest email.

Blaine read:

Dear Mr. Vice President,

Yesterday a deadly weather event occurred in northern France. This was the fourth in a series of "natural disasters." I trust that you now accept the legitimacy of this process. There will be no further preliminaries.

The next two events will be on American soil. The first will reach fruition within five days. The second event, if you allow it to occur, will devastate your country, killing at least one-third of the population. It will occur within ten days.

Your government has the ability to stop these events. But only if this communication is kept within the circle of you and the recipients of my previous messages. If you or anyone else chooses not to follow these instructions, you will have the blood of tens of millions of Americans on your hands.

—Janus 5D909G648F6

P.S. Don't forget your umbrellas for the rest of the week.

"So we have a clear time frame now," DeVries said, still studying his copy.

"We do," said the President.

"We're past the preliminaries," said the Vice President.

"I just hope we really are," said Easton.

The President collected the emails and closed the folder. Then he opened a second folder, underneath. "This came through twenty-one minutes later," he said.

The second message was also addressed to the Vice President of the United States, from the President. The subject line was GOLF? Blaine read:

Mr. Vice President: you now have your opportunity, which may prove beneficial to all involved. If you choose to play, you must send a signal to a third party indicating your willingness. This is the manner in which it must be done: tonight, the Lincoln Memorial will go dark from 9:07 P.M. until 9:14 P.M.

Respectfully, Janus 258B0976R83

There were subtle reactions around the table: DeVries shifting in his seat, Stanton breathing out through his nostrils. *Send a signal to a third party.* It was almost as if Janus, or whoever was responsible for these messages, was bowing out now, Blaine sensed.

"This is as mad as a bag of hammers," said Stanton. "I mean, what if they come back tomorrow and ask us to shut down Washington for a month, do we do that, too?" The Vice President incongruously showed his engaging white smile.

"Harry?" the President said, no humor in his voice.

DeVries, too, was all business. "Our position on this all along has been one of strategic compliance. We do what they ask—as long as what they ask is essentially nothing—until we find out who they are and what their motive is. But we will continue to monitor all communications. Also, as I've discussed privately with the President, we are drawing up a strategic operations plan for when we do actually make physical contact with this group, which would involve extensive ground and air surveillance."

The Vice President leaned back in his chair and glanced at the ceiling, Blaine noticed.

Easton said, "I understand what Bill is saying. But, I mean, turning the lights out at the Lincoln Memorial? I don't see that as a big deal."

"It isn't," the President said.

"I wonder what this five-day window is about," DeVries said.

Blaine had been thinking the same thing. "The length of time it will take for Hurricane Alexander to reach the East Coast of the United States, perhaps," she said.

"Perhaps."

"Is it a hurricane already?" asked Easton.

"It's just become one, yes," Blaine said.

"How would we even do it?" the Vice President asked.

Blaine smiled. Stanton was still thinking about the Lincoln Memorial.

"I guess I'd call the Director of Parks and ask her. Say we need it done on the QT," President Hall said. "We're only talking seven minutes."

The Vice President nodded. The eyes in the room were avoiding one another all of a sudden, she noticed.

"Cate?" the President said.

Blaine sighed, feeling the tension again. "I understand the need to move forward," she said. "I just want to make sure that we're doing all we can to understand this. Maybe because I'm the last one in the club, I still have some questions. I'm thinking in particular about the atmospheric changes that might accompany these events. I was doing some research independently. I have one scientist in mind who's worked on this sort of thing—"

"That's why we have our scientific review panel, Cate," the President said, curtly.

DeVries surprised her by nodding. "The problem with measuring atmospheric changes, Cate, is that there're so many variables in play. We're addressing that issue very thoroughly but so far the results have been inconclusive."

Blaine saw his unblinking and suddenly unfamiliar dark eyes watching her. Again, it was as if he was someone else, not the man who had once been her mentor, who had spent hours with her talking openly about foreign affairs.

"And let's just be clear," the President said. "Agreeing to turn off the lights for seven minutes isn't the same thing as agreeing to their terms. It's just getting us a step closer to finding out who they are."

"Correct," Easton said. He adjusted his hands on the table, then showed his crooked smile. "Look, folks, at this point I don't care if a dozen scientists come in this room and tell me they don't believe this thing is technically possible. It *is* technically possible. It's *happening.* Now, whether this group can really impact a third of our population—which, if my math is correct, would come to a little more than one hundred million people—or if their capabilities are somewhat less, I think it doesn't make a whole hoot of a difference."

A heavy silence followed. Easton's remarks were a non-sequitur, addressing a point that no one had made. But they were clearly aimed at Blaine—at her reservations, and her question about bringing in an outside scientist.

Five people in a room could convince themselves of nearly anything, she thought. *Somehow, I have to preserve my own perspective, whether I express it here or not.*

"Okay," the President said. "So we move forward with this. Any objections?"

No one in the room said anything. Blaine heard the ticking of Easton's wristwatch again. She looked out and noticed that it had begun to rain.

TWENTY-FIVE

IN HIS NORTHERN VIRGINIA motel room, Charles Mallory studied the list of seven names and the brief biographical sketches that he had added after each. The bios combined the report Chaplin had provided him with his own research. They had established a few tenuous connections, but Mallory still didn't know what linked these seven people. Or what might tie any of them to Vladimir Volkov.

1. Steven Loomis. US Navy commander. Briefly an administrator of the Hurricane Research Division of the National Oceanographic and Atmospheric Administration in the 1970s, based in Miami. An assistant coordinator of Project Stormfury, the government hurricane mitigation program. Later went into the private sector. Became a consultant in 1993. Started his own firm, Loomis Consultants, in Northern California in 2001. In 2003, he was hired by a company called EARS, or Environmental Atmospheric Research Systems. Reported as a missing person in San Mateo, California, in May 2005. Never found. 71 years old at time of disappearance.

2. Dr. Susan Beaumont. Graduate of MIT. Worked as a climate studies scientist for the Lawrence Livermore National Laboratory in California. Later worked at the National Geo-Spatial Intelligence Agency in St. Louis. May have worked on Project Cloudcover there. Left St. Louis in 2005 and returned to her native Wyoming. Did at least one consulting job for the NGA there. Lived alone, never married. Found dead in a motel room in rural Wyoming on August 21, 2006. Shot in the head during a possible sexual assault/robbery. DNA evidence found in the room and in her car was never identified. Case remains unsolved. 43 years old.

3. *Dr. Deborah Piper. An imagery scientist who developed atmospheric models at the National Imagery and Mapping Agency, based in Bethesda, Maryland. Earlier worked at NASA's Goddard Space Flight Center in Greenbelt, Maryland. Involved with Project Cloudcover, a joint intelligence/defense project, and later an operation called FAST. Lived in Gaithersburg, Maryland. Husband worked for the Department of Defense. Two teenage daughters. Published at least two letters to the editor about wasteful government spending. Had been outspoken about alleged misappropriations in the space program. Left work in Greenbelt on January 11, 2007 and was never heard from again. 44 years old at time of disappearance.*

4. *David Worth. An attorney and journalist turned lobbyist. Worked with several prominent politicians and contractors who had ties to the intelligence and defense departments of the US government, including EARS and Raytheon. EARS canceled his contract in October 2006 for undisclosed reasons. Disappeared four months later, while at his second home in Carmel, California. 39 years old.*

5. *Michael Dunlopen. Environmental reporter, Anchorage Daily News. Freelanced for Rolling Stone and The New York Times magazine. Lived all of his life in Alaska. Wrote often about oil drilling, land-use conflicts, and global warming. Was hiking alone in Kenai Fjords National Park on June 17, 2007, when he disappeared. Found two days later, shot in the chest with a bullet from a hunting rifle. 31 years old.*

6. *Dr. Frank Johnson. Canadian cloud physicist. Worked as a research professor at Colorado State University. Contracted with the National Center for Atmospheric Research in Colorado. Died suddenly on February 9, 2010 near his home in Vail, Colorado. Death ruled heart attack. 53 years old.*

7. *Dr. Atul Pradhan. One of India's leading climatologists, Pradhan earned a PhD from the Indian Institute of Technology in Delhi, where*

*he later taught. He wrote extensively on global warming and global
"dimming." A provocative and controversial speaker who appeared at
several American universities, including the University of Maryland, in
recent months. May have met Dr. Keri Westlake there. Disappeared in
the Bay of Bengal tsunami in late September. 64 years old.*

Seven people who lived, and died—or disappeared—under very
different circumstances. Very different locales. Five of the seven had
been involved in some form of climate science, but their work was
unrelated. There was no evident overlap or any indication—with
one possible exception—that the seven had known one another or
even met.

Still, there was one connection in particular that Charles Mallory
wanted to explore: two of the seven had apparently been involved
with a government project known as Cloudcover, although in different cities and while employed by separate agencies. Mallory had
worked with a slightly kooky—but in her own way brilliant—woman
named Patricia Hanratty. A cultured contrarian who'd been an analyst on Cloudcover. She would have an opinion on this, he was sure.

He tried her again, leaving another message.

Less than two minutes later, one of his cell phones rang. But it
wasn't Pat Hanratty. It was Joseph Chaplin.

"Greetings. I'm finding a little about your Victor Zorn," he said.
"That's Viktor with a *k*, by the way, although some years ago he
changed it to a *c*. I will have a list for you of the companies he's
involved with." There was a silence, then he said, "I should tell you
I'm missing Placido Domingo at Kennedy Center tonight because of
this. But I can tell it's important to you."

"I'm sorry."

"No, I was able to swap my ticket for Sunday, but just to let you
know."

"Appreciate it."

"That's not why I'm calling. I have received a message that I've
been asked to relay to you," Chaplin said, slipping into his formal
tone.

"Oh?"

"Yes."

"Go ahead."

"Catherine Blaine. The Secretary of Homeland Security?"

"Yes. I know who she is."

"She called your old company office number. Twice. Said it was on a business card you gave her six or seven years ago. Does that sound right? The second time, she left a message. I spoke with her. She says she would like to meet with you. As soon as possible."

"Really." *Strange.* Mallory conjured an image of the attractive Homeland Security Secretary. He had met her only once.

"Why?"

"The Secretary provided no further information."

"How does she know I'm here?"

"She doesn't. As I say, she was using your old number. I told her I would probably be in touch with you, but that I could make no guarantees." He cleared his throat. "She can meet as soon as the morning."

"As in tomorrow morning?"

"Yes, that's the one. What should I tell her?"

"Tell her yes."

"All right. Eight o'clock, then. Be dressed to work out."

AT THE WESTERN end of the National Mall, intricate webs of lightning silently lit up the sky behind the Greek temple-like Lincoln Memorial. It was a blustery evening with the smell of rain in the air. Only a handful of people were strolling nearby when the Memorial went dark at precisely 9:07 P.M.

AT HIS MODEST, sparsely furnished office in a three-building complex set behind thick brush and trees on Sand Hill Road in Menlo Park, California, Morgan Garland reached for his encrypted BlackBerry. It was 6:09.

"Please hold for Mr. Zorn," came the familiar female voice. Curt, inflectionless, almost as if it were machine-generated.

Always the same greeting. Never *Victor* Zorn. Always Mr. Zorn. And always a lengthy wait before Zorn's voice actually came on the line.

It was okay. Morgan Garland accepted such quirks, because Mr. Zorn was easily the most interesting and charismatic client he had ever worked with. Garland had had face time with Zorn on just three

THE LEVIATHAN EFFECT   135

occasions, but each meeting had been more extraordinary than the one before. It wasn't only that Victor Zorn had developed a product that Garland believed would change world markets, not to mention technology and science; it was also that he had managed to create a team and a strategic vision that would generate instant credibility for that product.

Garland was among the best-known and most successful venture capitalists in the country—one of the few so-called celebrity venture capitalists, who had famously backed several dark horse California start-ups that today were Internet icons. He was adept at forecasting trends, and at keeping pace with the sort of high-stakes games Mr. Zorn played.

Secrecy and eccentricity were not unusual among his clients, who had made fortunes in emerging technologies. "New business models," he called them. But Mr. Zorn played at a higher level than any client he had known, revealing himself, and his endgame, a move at a time. His latest revelation—the woman and two men who would be traveling to Washington with them—had again taken Morgan Garland by surprise.

It was 6:21 before Garland actually heard Mr. Zorn's voice in his ear.

"Morgan."

"Mr. Zorn."

"Okay, just to inform you: we've received a positive response. You will be joining us tomorrow?"

"I will."

"A driver will come by your office to pick you up in the morning. Eight o'clock. All travel arrangements have been made. We'll discuss presentation on the plane. It's imperative, of course, that you not tell anyone where you're going."

"Understood."

"Plan to be away for three nights."

"Fine."

"Thank you, Morgan."

"Thank you, Mr. Zorn."

TWENTY-SIX

THE LOCKHEED WP-3D ORION turbo-prop airplane lifted off from Amilcar Cabral International Airport on Sal Island in Cape Verde shortly after 2 A.M., climbing into the night sky at two thousand feet per minute. The plane, which belonged to the fleet of the United States' National Oceanic and Atmospheric Administration, or NOAA, was headed due west, toward Hurricane Alexander, which it was scheduled to penetrate and pass through four separate times—a quickly organized government mission to better understand this highly unusual Atlantic storm. The crew would measure the hurricane's winds, temperatures, and air pressure; create atmospheric and thermodynamic profiles; and look for any visual cues that might help scientists make sense of the storm's inner workings.

The plane's pilot, David Quinn, had flown through almost three hundred hurricanes over the past twenty-six years, piloting Orion planes and the larger DC-8 NASA flying labs. Quinn's co-pilot on this mission was a newbie named Kristen Landy, an energetic, blond-haired south Floridian who had trained as a Navy pilot before joining the NOAA Corps last year. This was only her third flight into a hurricane and she was eager to learn what they would experience inside "the bad boy," as she called Alexander. Quinn found her invigorating; she reminded him of the daughter he never had.

The crew on board included a navigator, flight engineer, aerial reconnaissance officer, two meteorologists, and two dropsonde operators. Dropsondes were fifteen-inch-long electronic cylinders that would be released from the belly of the plane once they were inside the hurricane's eye; each contained a GPS receiver and an array of other sensors that would deliver a steady stream of data to computer stations in the back of the plane and, via satellite, to the National Hurricane Center in Miami and other NOAA agencies. The satellite feed would also be transmitted to Dr. James Wu, who was monitoring the flight in real time from the Eisenhower Executive Office Building across the street from the White House.

The first time an airplane intentionally flew into a hurricane was in July 1943, when an Army Air Corps two-seater penetrated what became known as the Surprise Hurricane near Galveston, Texas. Despite the evolution of sophisticated hurricane tracking technology since then, the government still routinely sent "hurricane hunter" planes into the hearts of monster storms to learn what radar and satellites couldn't tell them.

"You ready for this?" Quinn said as the plane began to cut across a band of severe thunderstorms. His eyes darted to the color-enhanced radar screen, which was morphing from yellow—moderate rains—to red and magenta, heavy rains.

"Ten-four," said his co-pilot. In a calm moment, she added, "Bring on the bad boy."

David Quinn smiled to himself. "He'll be a teddy bear once we get under his skin."

At 6:27, the sky was beginning to lighten. But it was dark ahead as they flew at a steady 200 knots into Alexander's "skin"—the hurricane's eye wall, a protective ring of violent convective clouds that surrounded the center of the storm.

Quinn watched the monitor as the wind speeds ticked up: 43 knots . . . 67 . . . Suddenly the 116-foot plane was shaking violently, riding updrafts and downdrafts, rocking side to side. Then falling suddenly, causing a brief sensation of weightlessness. Mock screams came from the back of the plane. Landy let out several whoops and smiled once at the pilot. But David Quinn knew she was overcompensating.

"Ever been on the Cyclone at Coney Island?" he asked when it momentarily calmed down.

"What?"

He repeated himself.

"What, is that a roller coaster or something?"

"One of the best. It was named for one of those guys," he said, gesturing at the storm outside. "I have a feeling Alexander will be a much wilder ride."

He glanced over and saw that she was grinning distractedly. But not for long. The turbulence continued for another hour—bumps, sudden drops, and slow, rough rises. It *was* a bit like being on a roller coaster. A roller coaster ride that never seemed to end.

But then, at last, it did. Wind speeds throttled down rapidly as they began to emerge from the eye wall, just as the winds had accelerated going in—66 knots, then 42, 31, 12. Then nothing. They pulled away from the convection-charged turbulence and everything changed. The air was suddenly perfectly calm. The sky was robin's egg blue, the wind almost non-existent. Cottony clouds seemed to spread forever above them. It was as if they had flown into a perfect New England afternoon. A hundred miles of bliss lay ahead.

"I think we may have just entered heaven," Landy said.

"Yeah. Something, isn't it?" Quinn said, marveling at the calm skies outside the plane, as crew members prepared to release the electronic-packed dropsonde cylinders. The eye of a hurricane was a stunning oasis that still thrilled him even after all these missions. It felt as if they were floating through the sky, no longer propelled by engines. Only the distant surrounding black bands reminded him where they really were. Quinn looked up. *Beautiful. Perfect blue-white sky.*

Then he looked down. And what he saw wasn't so beautiful.

"Oh my god," he said.

For several minutes, the pilot and co-pilot didn't speak. The eye of a hurricane had always seemed like a wonderland to Quinn, the reward for the long tedious flight to the storm, and the turbulent, Mr. Toad's wild ride through the surrounding winds and eye wall. Calm, surrounded by chaos.

But this storm was clearly different; somehow the turbulence ahead looked far worse than what they had just come through.

Quinn glanced down again. The sea appeared to be a violent cauldron of giant, colliding waves, which suggested the spewing lava from an erupting volcano.

"Ever read Dante's *Inferno?*" Quinn said to his co-pilot.

"I don't think so," Landy said. "Who's it by?"

"Fellow named Dante."

"No. Why?"

"If you want the *CliffsNotes* version, just look down."

But Quinn no longer wanted to look himself. The sight was starting to spook him a little. He'd never seen anything like it before. The raging turbulence of the waves was only growing worse, the water reaching higher, as if each wave were trying to break free of the holds that bound it to the sea. *Weird.* Then, as they began to near the outer eye wall, a sudden downdraft shuddered the plane, tilting it on its side.

"Going to try to get us to a new altitude," Quinn said, his voice sounding thin and unfamiliar to himself.

He pulled back on the yoke and the nose of the plane rose at a forty-degree angle, then leveled out. They flew uneventfully for another twenty minutes, before hitting the first strong bands of rain and convection.

The plane was jolted again as it entered the outer eye wall, and vibrated with a hard, steady side-to-side motion. Quinn watched the wind speed ratchet up again, from dead calm right back to hurricane strength. This wall was different, though. The air wasn't just turbulent, it seemed charged, too, in all directions, with wild veins of kinetic electricity.

Quinn glanced at the radar, steering to avoid the magenta splotches. But the plane jerked downward, inexplicably, then to the right and to the other side. Quinn glanced out, saw what appeared to be a giant wave of ocean water wallop the left wing and engine of the plane. But, of course, it couldn't have been water. It must have just been a heavy gust of wind and rain. They weren't anywhere near the ocean surface. Were they? He gazed down again and saw angry waves seeming to rise up just beneath them, bathed now in a dark, eerie green light, what almost looked to be giant translucent tentacles reaching up. Then he felt the plane shaking and saw another glowing wave of water, this time crashing over the nose of the plane.

"What the hell's happening?" Landy said, her voice shaking.

"Hold on."

Another. And then a succession of waves— bursts of raging water, each crashing across the front of their plane, shaking the cockpit violently each time. *No,* Quinn thought. *This isn't possible.* Were they really that close to the ocean surface? *We can't be.* Quinn checked the altimeter again, saw that they were below the set limit of one thousand feet, but still nowhere near the surface. *What in God's name is happening?* Were the instruments malfunctioning?

He pulled back steeply on the yoke, but the force of the winds acted as a counter-balance, keeping the plane on a shuddering, slightly downward course. "Hold on," he said again. Suddenly, a hive of lightning seemed to engulf the plane and Quinn saw sparks spitting from the right engine. The nose dipped sharply and began to plunge. The plane jerked side to side. He pulled back hard on the yoke. No change. One of the P-3's four engines was suddenly coughing fire; Quinn tried vainly to pull them to higher altitude.

"What's happening?" Landy screamed. "What the fuck's happening?"

Quinn said nothing. He didn't know. The plane was toppling and spinning, losing altitude, hammered by the winds, unresponsive to anything he tried to do in the cockpit.

It was morning, but they were lost in a pitch-dark sky, falling through a vicious band of vertical clouds lit by wildly ricocheting veins of lightning. Several times the explosions of light stunned his eyes, like giant, too-bright bulbs. Then, for a moment, Quinn was able to regain control and pull the aircraft up . . . for a moment . . . before losing it again . . . because something was pulling them down, toward the water, toppling them upside down . . . strange, clashing forces of wind and rain and ocean currents . . .

Quinn saw Kristen's face in a burst of light and he didn't recognize her. *It's not her.* She was gone. The life had drained from her skin and she looked to him exactly like a corpse. A fury of new lightning burst over the front of the plane and then Quinn saw another face—out there, emerging from the webs of light. Then again. A giant bearded man, who appeared to be observing them through the glass. Quinn turned his eyes away, shaking his head. But each time the sky lit up, he saw it, saw the figure's hand reaching toward them, its index finger touching the glass of the cockpit. Then he felt a whomp of water beating over the plane, slamming it downward again, toward the rising troughs of raging sea. The lightning was everywhere suddenly, a strobe light show, and right before he went blind, Quinn began to see other faces and figures and features—the water becoming hands, reaching up and grabbing the plane's wings, shaking it like a toy. Preying vines of water coiling around the plane, bouncing it down into the waves. *I'm hallucinating now.* He had to be. He glanced at the corpse in the co-pilot's seat, then looked through the cockpit glass, his heart pounding—and saw the bearded man, walking on the water, stepping backwards now, moon-walking away from him; and a succession of enormous, undulating figures following him, women in a conga line. Then darkness again engulfed the plane, which was twisting and plummeting toward the sea.

Quinn managed to speak into the microphone as the water prepared to receive them: "Caught in a tornadic downdraft . . . not sure what we're seeing . . . faces . . . figures . . . structural failure . . . something huge . . . waves . . . not getting out of this."

DR. JAMES WU listened to the final transmission from Captain David Quinn and he felt his arms break out in goose bumps. He'd been monitoring the stream of data coming in from the hurricane hunter plane every thirty seconds and had no idea what might have gone wrong.

Dr. Wu knew and admired David Quinn. He had worked with him for two years at the University of Colorado. Later, he had flown with Quinn into two North Atlantic hurricanes. He'd felt comfortable calling him to ask a question or to share a story. Had even visited Quinn and his family at their home in North Carolina's Outer Banks once for a weekend. Dr. Wu did not much believe in religion. But sometimes, he prayed anyway. This was one of those times.

Afterward, Dr. Wu picked up his phone and called the Oval Office. "I need to talk to the President," he said to Gabriel Herring. "Directly," he added. "And as soon as possible. I'm sure he'll want to hear what I have to say."

TWENTY-SEVEN

Wednesday, October 5, 7:34 A.M.

PRETENDING NOT TO BE doing so, Charles Mallory took a quick inventory of Catherine Blaine as he approached the treadmills: hair up, clasped in back; high cheekbones; determined eyes; long legs in black tights.

She turned, caught his eye and gave him a slow smile. Mallory waved. He was dressed in the only set of workout clothes he'd brought: cutoff sweat pants, a wrinkled charcoal gray T-shirt, and basketball shoes.

"Taken?"

"Nope."

He stepped onto the treadmill next to hers and began running. It took him a few strides to figure it out and a few more to find his rhythm.

"I met you years ago, didn't I?" she said.

"You did."

"You remember."

"Of course."

Mallory looked at her again. He knew a little about Blaine. Her dad had been a military man, a general, her mother a teacher of some kind. She was not someone he imagined would ever want the job she now held. Not in a million years. She was smart, tough and self-protective, he could tell, driven by an altruistic sense of purpose—although he wondered what that purpose was, exactly.

He noticed one other thing: she was in good shape, better than he was.

Blaine's Achilles heel, supposedly, was loyalty. Her father had been a three-star general who was retired now, living on the beach in South Carolina. Maybe North Carolina. She had set high standards for herself, but also nurtured a stubborn rebellious streak.

Was it a coincidence that she would be contacting him now? Possibly. But Mallory had always been suspicious of coincidences.

"You were part of a committee on cyber security," he said. "You came to Langley to question a group of us. We were in a conference room on the sixth floor. It was 2006, I think. Our group was not terribly receptive. I was working for Richard Franklin then. Special Projects."

"Yes."

"He's in prison now."

"I know. You had something to do with that."

"Mmm hmm. You talked with me afterward."

"I did." Blaine looked at him quickly. Occasionally, her green eyes took on a wild, impatient look, which he kind of liked.

"I could tell you weren't happy with your committee."

She said nothing.

"Or with us."

"I wasn't."

They ran for a while in silence, then Mallory said, "Why here, by the way?"

"What?"

"Why meet here?"

"Oh." Blaine laughed to herself. "I made a request when I took this job. I didn't want security people with me around the clock. I asked that I be allowed two instances when I'm not watched—when I work out in the mornings and when I meet with my son. It makes him very nervous. To my surprise, they agreed."

"They're outside, though."

"Oh, I'm sure. They park on the street outside my house, too, at night. All night long. It's okay." She looked at her distance on the monitor. "Thanks for agreeing to meet with me."

"I think I need the workout, actually."

Blaine glanced over. "Aren't you curious why I called?"

"I guess I should be." He waited, then said, "Am I supposed to ask a question now?"

Blaine ran several beats in silence. "Any conversation we have has to be in confidence, though."

"What conversation?"

She smiled and ran through another silence, Mallory trying to keep pace. "I guess I'm just sort of looking for an opinion on something at this point," she said finally.

"Okay," he said. "Should I give you one now, or do you want to suggest a topic first?"

"A topic," she said. "A matter has come to my attention that I thought you might know something about."

"All right," he said. "I'm leery, though, about getting involved in any conversation that contains the phrase 'a matter has come to my attention.'"

Blaine didn't respond. She looked straight ahead, and seemed to run a little harder. "Sorry," he said.

"We're trying to find someone."

"Okay. Someone I know?"

"Someone you know about. Or *knew* about."

"Okay."

"A former Chinese military officer named Xiao-ping Chen."

"Oh." He felt her looking at him. "Janus," he said.

"Yes."

Mallory slowed his pace slightly. "Why would you want to find him now?"

"Well, I can't really go into details. But, hypothetically, based on what you know, where would you look if you wanted to find him?"

"Where would I look?" Mallory gazed across the gym at the television monitor: a bumper-to-bumper stream of traffic leaving a barrier island somewhere ahead of Hurricane Alexander. "I wouldn't," he said.

"No? Why?"

"I mean, there'd be no reason. He's been inactive for many years, as you probably know." He glanced at her, saw the steady expression. Added, "You're implying he's not inactive anymore?"

"Would that surprise you?"

"It would."

"Why?"

"Because. He wouldn't have any reason to get back in it."

"Isn't that what people do? They come back?"

"Some do. The wiser ones move on. They find something else."

"And you'd put him in that category."

"I would." For a while, Mallory thought that he *had* known Xiao-ping Chen. A man who had betrayed the American intelligence community. One of the government's mistakes, long since covered up. He had warned Richard Franklin about Janus and his boss had largely disregarded him. The Agency had been *betting* on Janus. Franklin in particular.

"In the comic books," Mallory added, "the bad guys always make comebacks. But not in real life. He's a computer hacker, not a serial killer."

"What if he needed money?"

"Not likely."

"You seem pretty certain."

"I am. I'm not thinking about what he did, I'm thinking about who he is. Frugal and socially uneasy. A man who did what he did because he planned to fade away. And to do so on his own terms. I kind of understand that, actually."

"He's not someone who would have any interest in retaliation? Who might hold a vendetta against the United States government, let's say?"

"No."

"Or who might work for someone who did?"

"No, not likely. But I'll tell you what: I could give you much better information, and help you a lot more, if you told me why you're asking about him."

"I'm sure you could," Blaine said. A faint glaze of sweat shone on her face. "I wish I was able to tell you everything. But, unfortunately, I can't."

"That's too bad."

Mallory knew that it would be a challenge getting her to open up. Blaine was loyal and careful. He decided not to say anything for a while. Besides, he was getting tired, and talking had become increasingly difficult.

Afterward, they sat on a green, paint-chipped wooden bench against the cinderblock wall. Mallory watched a young, heavyset woman lifting weights across the room. He counted seven other people working out.

"You do realize that something's wrong with what you're telling me, though," he said. "I mean, I hope you realize that."

"But I'm not telling you anything." Blaine looked at him and laughed quickly. "I'm asking questions."

"No, you're telling me a lot, actually. You're telling me that the government has been receiving threats of some sort from Janus, or, more likely, someone claiming to be Janus." He glanced at her, saw her raise her eyebrows subtly, the equivalent of a nod, it seemed. "Meanwhile, there have been vague reports in the media over the last couple of days that someone's been hacking into secret government websites and/or computer networks. Possibly threatening an attack on the nation's SCADA network. The power grid." Blaine's eyes were watching his in the mirror now, he saw. "We both know that's not likely. So the stories are probably false. Or incomplete. But they must have some basis in truth. Right? Therefore, there must be some sort of high-level hacking going on. But different from what's being reported."

Mallory took a deep breath, and glanced at his own reflection. "Using the name Janus would surely get your attention. I'm just guessing here, but if I were to speculate, I'd imagine that the threat you're dealing with has something to do with the weather. And I sense it's something fairly substantial."

He finally looked at her reflection. She was suppressing a smile, he was pretty sure. Seeing him notice, she began to stretch out her right calf, then her left.

"And why would you think that?" she said.

"Is that a yes?"

"To which question?"

"All of the above."

Blaine inhaled slowly. "I just wish I could comment."

"Me, too," he said. "The problem with Janus," he went on, "is that this isn't his MO. He wouldn't be doing it this way. Also, there's a distinct possibility that Janus is no longer alive."

"Really," she said, a new interest rising in her tone. She stopped stretching.

"Really. But inserting Janus into this—whatever 'this' is—would serve a purpose. It shifts attention to China. And to the Chinese military."

"Yes, I know. But from where?"

Now Mallory smiled. *Shrewd.* "That's the question, isn't it?"

"Do you have a guess?"

"Not now. But if you were to provide me with just a little more information, I could probably give you a reasonably educated one."

"Let me think on that."

"Sure." Mallory stood. He could tell that Blaine *was* thinking on it. Uncomfortable with the set-up and probably wanting an ally, as she had years before. But she was also beholden to protocol and law. It was probably something she wrestled with every day.

"It's funny about this conversation, isn't it?" Mallory said.

"Is it?"

"Mmm hmm."

"Why is it funny?"

"We're doing exactly what the United States' intelligence community does, aren't we? We're demonstrating its weakest link."

"How so?"

They were walking toward the locker rooms now.

"This conversation we're having. This sort-of conversation. I know something you want to know. And I suspect you know something I want to know. But neither of us is going to tell the other. Because of territorial concerns, on your part. On my part, I guess, just because of pure stubbornness." Blaine creased her brow. "That's been the story of US intelligence for the past thirty or forty years, hasn't it? Then when someone recognizes that a problem exists, rather than try to fix it by opening up channels of communication, they enlarge the problem, creating a new agency to coordinate the other agencies. Like yours."

She laughed a genuine laugh—easy, robust, surprising—which Mallory immediately considered a small victory. But she quickly turned serious again as they came to the entrance. "The trouble is, I'm bound by law from divulging classified information."

"I know. A shame."

"Yes, it is. I just wanted to hear your thoughts. If you'd like to share any others, though, I'd be glad to talk again."

Mallory said nothing. He sensed that there were other ways in, just not today.

"Anyway, I'm going to hit the showers," Blaine said. She reached to shake.

"Just keep your options open." He pulled the business card

he'd brought from his pocket, a little worse for wear. "Here's my number."

"Okay." She smiled. "And I will."

THE FACT WAS, Charles Mallory had begun to sense that something was going on even before Chaplin had contacted him. Sensed it like a subtle, irrevocable shift in the weather; unusual patterns beginning to interact in ways that he could feel without having any idea what they meant, where they came from, what they might become. There had been the unanswered messages from Langley. The media reports about cyber-security breaches. Then the emails from his brother. The list of names, and now Blaine contacting him. Converging forces, not yet forming a coherent pattern. But they would.

It wasn't his business, of course, nor was it his responsibility, to try to figure out any of this. Except that it now involved his brother; that changed everything. So Mallory had begun working the puzzle in his head, knowing that he needed more information before it began to make sense. He thought of people who might be able to help him. People like his friend Patricia Hanratty, the former intel analyst who had worked on Project Cloudcover. In part it was a game, like working a crossword. Something he kept going back to, finding that each new combination made the earlier clues easier to figure. Blaine had just given him a lot more. As he pulled out his cell phone to call Chaplin, walking across the parking lot, he noticed that he had missed a call. And when he saw who it was, he sensed that he was about to learn another important piece. Patricia Hanratty had called back.

CATHERINE BLAINE SAW the Suburban pull out behind her as she drove onto Wisconsin Avenue from the gym parking lot. Secret Service detail. Rain was still steaming off the pavement from the morning's downpour and the air smelled of soaked lawns.

The Suburban followed her as she drove toward her office on K Street, keeping a distance, but taking all of the turns she took. Even when she deliberately went the wrong way.

As Blaine came to Pennsylvania Avenue, her phone vibrated and she saw that she wouldn't be going to her office this morning, after all. There had been another message. She was being summoned to the White House: *YARI.*

TWENTY-EIGHT

9:12 A.M.

FOUR OF THE FIVE members of the circle were already seated around the mahogany conference table in the Cabinet Room when Catherine Blaine entered.

Clark Easton gave her a look. Sideways, steady. Impossible to tell what it meant. Stanton, the Vice President, rose and shook her hand, as usual.

Blaine saw the now-familiar setup. Five of them gathered around one end of the conference table. Four men: husbands, fathers, grandfathers. Shirtsleeves. Secretary Easton, with his tiny scribble pad, his hard blue eyes silently managing the proceedings.

The President told her the news. Another message had been delivered.

"We gave them our assent last night," he said. "We received their response this morning. The final one, apparently."

The President passed copies to each of the people in the room. This one had been sent to the President's email address.

The subject line read, FAREWELL.

Blaine read the message:

Hello. This ends my involvement in this business. Soon, one of you will most likely be approached by representatives of a third party. What happens after that is entirely up to you. Keep in mind that this group will know nothing about our email communications or about me. This is a separate relationship. I do not anticipate the need for any further communication. Thank you.
—Janus 58D39J675T9

No one spoke for a while. Blaine read through the message several times, noting the word choices; the tone, this time, seemed slightly different from the earlier ones. She looked at Easton, then at the President, feeling claustrophobic all of a sudden. Charles Mallory had been fresher air; she wished she'd been able to open up more with him.

"Well," Vice President Stanton said, breaking the spell. "That's it, then. This is what we've been waiting to hear."

Easton grimaced ambiguously.

"So we're going forward with this," DeVries said. Part statement, part question.

"I don't see that we have much choice," said the President.

"I just can't help feeling there's something nasty in the woodshed here that we're not looking at," said Stanton.

"There is," the President said. "Of course, there is. But meeting with them doesn't mean we're capitulating to anything. It just means we finally sit down face to face and see who the hell they are. That's been the objective of our strategy all along."

DeVries nodded.

"I don't like it," the Vice President said.

"Cate?" the President said.

Blaine nodded. Showing she was on board.

"Okay." The President sighed and collected the messages. "Now," he said. "Second item: this storm in the Atlantic. Alexander. It's about to become a Category Two hurricane. It's a huge system that's stretching across more than four hundred miles and growing. We lost a weather plane in it overnight, with eight people on board." He paused, looking down at a summary from his morning intelligence briefing. "They were flying a fairly routine mission into the eye and the plane disappeared. That's the first time we've lost a plane in a hurricane since 1955. All communications lost, no trace of her. We're not making that announcement until we have more details, but obviously this is a matter of grave concern. We're also fielding reports of communications lost with several ships in the Atlantic. Six ships in two or three days. Four of them freighters, two fishing vessels. I've been briefed by Jim Wu, who tells me that this storm is developing in ways that are very unusual." He glanced down at his briefing paper. "Alexander is behaving more like a Pacific Ocean hurricane than an Atlantic storm."

"That's it, then, isn't it?" asked the Vice President, turning and pointing toward the windows.

Blaine nodded absently, trying to make eye contact with DeVries.

"Possibly," the President said. "Let's not jump to conclusions. Let's just say, we'll be watching the system very carefully."

For a long time, though, no one said anything. They just listened to the rain on the windows.

CATHERINE BLAINE WALKED up the steps to her townhouse, thinking about Janus's final message. And Charles Mallory's warning that this *wasn't* Janus. That it wasn't his MO.

What *was* it, then?

In the kitchen, she poured a glass of diet soda and noticed that her message light was blinking. She hit the retrieve button, hoping to hear Kevin. Instead, she heard the gruff but friendly voice of her mother, calling from North Carolina.

Dear, we're about to leave the beach here and drive to Tennessee. Your father's out loading the car right now. This storm sounds just awful! They're asking everyone to leave, so we're not going to chance it. We'll be staying with your Uncle Pete and Aunt Carol in Pigeon Forge for a few days, okay? So I know you'll be busy and hard to reach but you call Uncle Pete's if you want to talk with us, okay? You just be safe, sweetie. Give Kevin our love. Bye, dear. We love you.

Blaine felt a bittersweet twinge as the message clicked off. She was disappointed—though not surprised—that her father hadn't left a message. Increasingly, he let her mother handle communications between them, as if he were expanding his retirement to include family affairs, too. He had been a taskmaster during Blaine's childhood; now, he often seemed a quiet, aloof stranger, only marginally interested in her career.

The storm was making her feel a little blue, she realized. She tried calling Kevin, who answered after five rings.

"Hi, Mom. Amanda's here," he said right away. "We're getting ready to go out for pizza. But I can talk for a minute."

"All right," she said. "Are you okay?"

"Of course," he said. "Why wouldn't I be?" Then he told her he was worried that Alexander might force them to postpone their trip to the Eastern Shore *another* week. Blaine said they'd just have to wait and see.

"Amanda's parents have a place on the beach in, like, Dewey? So I may end up going with them."

"Not if the storm's coming, honey."

He quickly changed the subject, asking if she had seen Letterman last night.

"No, honey, I normally don't watch that," she said.

"Well, you should have seen it last night. It was a classic." He then told her all about it, reciting almost word for word Letterman's exchange with Seth Rogen.

Afterward, Blaine turned on her television and switched among the cable news networks. She was surprised to see that the hurricane had already begun to impact the East Coast. She left it on CNN and watched:

At this hour, the outer bands of Hurricane Alexander are buffeting the coasts of Florida, Georgia, South Carolina and North Carolina with high tides and gale-force winds. Officials in North Carolina have issued mandatory evacuation orders and more are expected elsewhere along the coast over the next 24 hours.

Alexander is now a Category Two hurricane on the Saffir-Simpson scale with maximum sustained winds of 107 miles per hour and gusts topping 130. The storm, moving west-northwest at 12 miles per hour, is projected to strengthen into a Category Three storm overnight with landfall projected near Virginia Beach, Virginia early Sunday morning.

The effects of the hurricane are already causing property damage and flooding in several coastal communities. In Savannah, Georgia, wind gusts up to 65 miles an hour have downed trees and power lines. Heavy surf and drenching rains in the Outer Banks of North Carolina have flooded roads and strong winds have reportedly blown the roofs off of several beachfront properties.

FEMA crews have been deployed up and down the coast to work with state and local emergency management agencies. Meanwhile, ten thousand National Guard troops and scores of Red Cross teams are being mobilized to deal with the aftermath of Hurricane Alexander.

But federal officials stress that the most important thing right now is for people to take this storm seriously and prepare for it properly—and in many cases, they're saying, the best preparation is simply to get out of its way.

The scene shifted to FEMA Director Shauna Brewster, standing behind a lectern at FEMA headquarters on C Street.

Anyone who lives in a coastal county should be prepared to leave. For the sake of yourself and your families, we implore you to act responsibly.

Brewster's normally animated expression was flat and sober, Blaine noted.

Blaine surfed channels for another several minutes, and found something else that got her attention, this time on FOX News: Dr. Keri Westlake, physicist at the University of Maryland, had gone missing several days earlier.

Blaine knew Keri Westlake. Not well, but she had worked with her several times when Blaine was in Congress. A bright woman, with lots of ideas and enthusiasm. She'd advocated a federal initiative for climate research, as Blaine had done, and supported Senator Hutchison's bill to create a weather modification bureau.

She was thinking about Keri Westlake, staring at the rain puddles in the street, when her cell phone rang.

"Cate, Rube."

It was Dr. Sanchez.

"Oh, hello."

"I've got some more information for you. Can we talk?"

"Sure. Please. Go ahead."

"No. It's something I'd like to show you. In the morning again?"

"Sure. All right."

"Same Bat time, same Bat station?"

"Yes. Sure," she said. "Works for me."

DMITRY PETRENKO DROVE slowly through the rolling Virginia hill country, surveying the sloping entrance and exit ramps to the underground facility, well hidden behind a wall of stone and a dense cluster of trees, on property Victor Zorn had purchased with funding from Volkov.

Petrenko had arrived two nights earlier on a private jet, with five members of his security detail, to move the mobile Command and Control Center into the facility and to make it operational. An additional four men would be arriving early tomorrow morning on two separate commercial flights. Three had already driven across country in two cargo trucks, bringing the communications equipment that could not be transported by plane.

Petrenko had been prepping this meeting for weeks, although many of the specific details had only been provided to him over the past two days. He had arranged for the hotel rooms, the decoy vehicles, the drivers. His most important task, though, would be securing Mr. Zorn. Clearly, the Americans would want to learn all that they could about him, to take advantage of the small window of vulnerability that he would be giving them. And naturally they would use everything at their command to do so: satellites, planes, digital audio and visual sensors, high-tech security cameras. Petrenko's job was to thwart those efforts. To shield Mr. Zorn as much as possible. They had war-gamed their tactics for weeks, and he was certain that he could protect Mr. Zorn from close scrutiny. What worried him was something else.

The other part of Petrenko's job was simply to observe. To make certain that Mr. Zorn was doing what he said he was doing—and to report the results of his observations to their boss, Vladimir Volkov.

TWENTY-NINE

CLARK EASTON'S PENTAGON OFFICE was in Room 3E-880—part of the same suite of offices that had been used by every Secretary of Defense since just after World War II. On the wall behind his desk were more than a dozen photos, most of them showing Easton with important men he'd worked with and worked for—presidents, congressmen, generals, soldiers, business leaders.

The rooms of the world's largest office building were identified by floor, ring, corridor, and room numbers. Easton's was on the third floor of the outermost, E-ring. His office looked out on the Potomac River and the US Capitol, through windows that had been tinted years earlier as a precaution against outside surveillance. Room 3E-880 was about a thousand feet from where American Airlines Flight 77 had ended its journey on the morning of September 11, 2001. Easton still thought about that tragedy every day. When he looked across the river, he frequently considered the fourth plane, too; a plane that might have destroyed Washington's most potent symbol, the US Capitol, if it hadn't been brought down in that field in Shanksville, Pennsylvania.

Secretary Easton typically worked at his Pentagon office until at least 6:30 P.M. each night. His long working days were well known. The person calling his Pentagon office on the afternoon of October 5 would have known he'd probably be at his desk.

At 5:13, Easton was informed that he had a call from a representative for something called the Weathervane Group.

"Okay," he said.

Easton pressed a button to take the call and then another to activate the digital recorder so that he could replay the conversation to the members of the "circle."

"This is Easton," he said.

"Secretary Easton. This is Mr. Zorn." A deliberate voice, gravely, confident. Metallic.

ONE HOUR AND thirty-nine minutes later, Catherine Blaine was sitting in the Cabinet Room, preparing to listen to the playback. Rain washed down the windows and low thunder rumbled occasionally in the distance. It bothered her a little that the President, Easton and DeVries had clearly already met to discuss details of the conversation.

"All right?" Easton said. He pressed the PLAY button on the digital recorder and the audio began. Vice President Stanton caught Blaine's eye as they began to listen:

"This is Easton."

"Secretary Easton. This is Mr. Zorn. I think you are expecting my call."

"Yes. Go ahead."

"I represent an international consortium known as the Weathervane Group. We represent twenty-seven individual science research concerns. I believe we have been referred to you by a third party?"

They listened to a protracted silence. Blaine glanced at Harold DeVries to see his reaction, but he showed nothing.

"We would like to arrange a meeting with your group for tomorrow afternoon, if that is feasible."

"All right. Give me the details."

"We would like to meet in the Cabinet Room at the White House, at one P.M."

Easton's breathing was audible on the recording.

"Who would we be meeting?"

"We will bring a four-person team . . . Dr. Jared Clayton, Dr. Susan Romfo, Mr. Morgan Garland, and myself."

Blaine heard Easton's slow intake of breath on the recording. In the Cabinet Room, he slid his palms against each other.

"We will arrive at the southwest gate of the White House at twelve forty P.M. *Will that be acceptable?"*
"Yes."
"Who will meet us there?"
"The White House Chief of Staff, Gabriel Herring. Along with the Secret Service."

Zorn's voice was an interesting blend of accents, Blaine thought, both American and something vaguely European.

"We will have to run background checks on all four parties before you are allowed to enter."
"I'm afraid that will not be not possible. You may do your standard security and identification checks, of course. Unfortunately, we will not have time for any sort of background checks other than what you're able to do on your own between now and then. Will you be coordinating your group for this meeting?
"Yes."
"And who will be representing your group?"

Easton gave him the five names.

"Good. Thank you, sir."
"How can we get back in touch with you?"
"That will be explained tomorrow. We will be at the gate at twelve forty, ready for our security check. Is that acceptable?"
"All right."
"We are looking forward to this meeting."

Easton clicked off the recording.
"So. That's it," said Vice President Bill Stanton. He scooted back his chair and began to shake his head. "I don't get it, though. How could they have gotten those people on board?"
"Yes, an interesting question," the President said.
It *did* instantly change the calculus, Blaine realized. *Morgan Garland.*

Dr. Jared Clayton, Dr. Susan Romfo. All three names were familiar to her; household names, in certain households. Morgan Garland was the country's most successful venture capitalist. Jared Clayton was a Nobel Prize-winning physicist. Susan Romfo was a climate researcher well known for her sometimes provocative television interviews on global warming. Three nationally known and well-respected figures.

The President turned to DeVries, who had a folder of notes in front of him. "Tell us what you have on this group, Harold."

DeVries provided an overview. Weathervane Energies, or the Weathervane Group, was a for-profit "foundation" that had incorporated just five weeks earlier. It represented a consortium of cutting-edge companies in the fields of energy, weather tracking, climate research, and geo-engineering, including companies based in China, Russia, Europe, Canada, Africa and the United States.

"How about this man in charge?" Blaine asked. "Victor Zorn. Who is he?"

"An investor and entrepreneur who has financed and directed a number of research firms during the past decade. Very deep pockets, evidently, although his background is a little murky. He's invested heavily in emerging technologies, particularly in the fields of energy and weather. He's American but evidently spent many years in Europe. Low profile. A very persuasive and charming man, supposedly. I'll have more on him by tomorrow."

The Vice President was shaking his head again, half-grinning at something, Blaine noticed. "Sorry," he said, "but I don't think I can get behind this, folks. This just doesn't add up to me. After the threats, it seems hard to believe they'd be sending someone to meet with us like this. I'm sorry, this just does not compute."

"But remember what the last message was," Easton said, his mouth twitching slightly. "The group that will be contacting us has no knowledge of the email communications. Presumably, this is not the person who sent the emails."

"Or that's what we were led to believe, anyway," said DeVries.

The President said, "I don't know that we'd have grounds to arrest a Nobel Prize physicist or the world's most prominent venture capitalist, would we?" He looked at the Vice President, then at DeVries, the intelligence director. "But we can certainly monitor them closely. In particular, this Mr. Zorn."

DeVries's face was expressionless. "We'll implement all security precautions," he said, "as well as electronic, satellite, and ground surveillance."

The President nodded. "All right. Let's get everything we can between now and one P.M. tomorrow, then. Work around the clock. Data mine this thing to death. I want to be armed with everything that's out there. I don't want any of this to be a surprise tomorrow. We've had enough surprises."

"Agreed," said Easton.

DeVries nodded.

"Just remember what our objective has been all along," said the President, turning his gaze to Blaine. "We want this to have a face, so that we really know what we're dealing with. And when we do," he added, "we're going to bring them down. In a big way."

JON MALLORY GAZED out at the sheets of rain in the rolling countryside and remembered a very different afternoon, five months earlier. Remembered cool winds blowing through a pine-scented forest and the faint smell of water just before they came over a rise and saw the sparkles of a lake through the trees. Remembered resting on a rock in the shade after a long hike through the woods and hearing the stillness of early afternoon, the creak of tree branches, water splashing on stones. Remembered feeling very fortunate that he had the day with Melanie, far from everything that had ever gotten between them; fortunate knowing that they loved each other and that even if it didn't last, they had it then, and it felt as good to him as anything he knew.

It was Jon's second day now in this room, on a gated, guarded property more than fifty miles from his home. He could live in a cage here, comforting or torturing himself with memories, or he could live in the story. His better instincts told him that he had enough pieces now to begin writing it; but he also knew it wasn't that simple.

Jon looked at what he had started two days earlier:

Scientist's Disappearance Linked to Others
    Four days before she disappeared, Dr. Keri Westlake, a professor of meteorology at the University of Maryland, talked about a story that she said "needs to be told soon."

It was a story about groundbreaking scientific research into the field of weather modification, Dr. Westlake said, some of it involving the federal government. But it was also a darker tale of suppression and murder, she believed.

Dr. Westlake produced a list of seven names—seven people who had died or disappeared over the past nine years. The people on the list, five of them scientists who had worked on climate research, knew at least part of the story that Westlake said needed to be told—enough perhaps to have gotten them killed.

It was Dr. Atul Pradhan, the seventh name on the list, who told her about the others. Pradhan, an Indian climatologist who met with Dr. Westlake earlier this year, died September 25 in the Bay of Bengal tsunami.

Several days later, Dr. Westlake herself went missing. Police say her home had been burglarized and her computer accessed.

No, he thought. That wasn't the way to tell the story—not only because it felt incomplete; but because it felt wrong. Dr. Westlake had forwarded Jon an email containing notes and documents: two memos from Frank Johnson, name number six on the list, from 2004 and early 2005; four documents about an energy consulting firm known as Energy and Atmospheric Research Systems, or EARS; and a seemingly disjointed series of notes, some attributed to the initials S. L. It was in those documents that the real story would be found; if he just spent enough time with them, the information he had would eventually take the shape of a story.

Jon did not always enjoy the process. But it was what he did and what he was good at and he had to keep faith that the end result would justify the often tedious work in getting there.

He pulled the blinds closed and went back to his computer.

Here we go, he told himself. *Let's figure this out.*

FORTY-THREE MILES away, the assassin was preparing for his new assignment. It would be considerably easier than the last one, his prey unaware of any danger; still, it felt unsettling to receive another job so soon.

As he drove away from the farmhouse in the rain, a Cole Porter song stuck in his head, the assassin received an alert on his handheld computer. He switched to the GPS tracking app and saw a flashing signal, indicating that the reporter's cell phone had been re-activated. He pulled over onto the gravel shoulder of the two-lane rural road. Within seconds, he had the latitude and longitude and a map location. A motel off of Interstate 95 in Virginia.

That was strange. For the past two days, Jon's cell phone had been turned off and undetectable. Now, the assassin had a track on him again; or, at least, on his phone. Except the timing was wrong. The timing was all wrong.

He had to focus on this new assignment first. *Protect the mission.* Someone else knew too much, and was planning to talk about it with a newspaper reporter. This one had to be headed off quickly.

THIRTY

Patricia Hanratty agreed to meet Charles Mallory for dinner at Café Ole in Tenleytown on Wisconsin Avenue. It was a cozy Mediterranean bistro, a few blocks from the National Cathedral, known for its extensive menu of mezze dishes.

Retired now—forced out, really—Hanratty remained an outspoken critic of the government she had worked for most of her life. Her name still popped up in letters-to-the-editor columns, where she lambasted government pork-barrel spending or misguided military projects. Some regarded her as a cranky old lady and conspiracy freak. Mallory considered her a friend, and a valuable source with a photographic memory. She *did* see conspiracies a little too easily and always had; but the thing was, sometimes she was right.

Hanratty was already seated at a small wooden table for two, wearing her trademark red beret and navy cape, her hands cradling a vodka and tonic. She looked the same to him, with thin, brittle white hair and her wide, slightly crooked smile, generous amounts of rouge on her powdered cheeks.

"Hello, dear, marvelous to see you again," she said, extending her hand without getting up. "This city just gets stranger all the time, doesn't it?"

Mallory kissed the top of her hand and sat.

"Oh, it's been such a dreadful spring," she said, speaking in her slightly affected accent. "So much rain! Where have you been, anyway?"

"Away," Mallory said. "I moved to a land far, far away."

She blurted out a single-syllable laugh. "And so what brings you back? Business?"

"Afraid so." He noticed the crescent of lipstick on her glass.

"I heard somewhere that you had become a private intelligence contractor."

"Mmm hmm."

"What on earth *is* that, exactly? You have your own intelligence agency?"

"More or less. Less, these days. I'm here on kind of a special case."

She let out a surprising, bawdy laugh that caused more than one diner to turn.

"Well, you're lucky you caught me," she said. "I'm flying to Scotland in three days. Although I hear we're getting a doozy of a storm, aren't we?"

"We are."

"After that, I'm supposed to be on a cruise for two weeks. I have some dear friends in Greece that I haven't seen in ages. It should be great fun." Looking down, she said, "I love the lamb stew shepherd's pie mezze here—quite delicious. I think I'll have that."

Mallory realized then that the waiter was standing beside their table. He quickly scanned the menu, settling on a Bastila mezze— brick pastry dough stuffed with Moroccan couscous, chicken, almonds, and spicy yogurt.

"The couscous here is quite good, too," she said, winking at him.

She talked animatedly for the next twenty minutes about her travels. Pat Hanratty traveled alone and had a gift for making friends out of strangers. This year, she said, she had already toured northern Africa and the Middle East and spent two weeks in Austria over the summer. In 2011, she'd been in Marrakech, just blocks from the Argana Café when it was bombed by terrorists. "It was dreadful. Just absolutely dreadful. Those poor, poor people. They were targeting tourists, you know. Dreadful business. But, you know, you can't live in fear over that sort of thing. I never have."

Mallory listened and nodded at appropriate intervals. He waited until their second order of mezze arrived before broaching his topic.

"I wanted to ask you about something," he said as she sipped on a fresh vodka and tonic. "A project you worked on several years ago."

Hanratty's shoulders began to shake convulsively.

"What?" he asked.

"Somehow I didn't think you'd asked me to dinner to hear about my trip to Austria," she said. "All right. What is it you want to know?"

"A project you worked on. Cloudcover."

"Oh, God, *that*." She squinted at him, then held up her drink and studied it. "A dreadful project. I'm amazed I survived it."

"What was it, exactly?"

"Data," she said. "That's all. Data collection. Absolutely horrendous amounts of data."

"Data about what?" He smiled unassumingly, poking at his food.

"*Everything*. You name it." She stirred the ice in her glass with her pinkie finger. "That's a big part of what NOAA does, you know. They collect data and they store data. Sea levels. Sea surface temperatures. Wind currents. Air temperatures. *Chlorophyll* concentrations in sea water, for heaven's sake. Ad infinitum."

"Storm data?"

"All sorts of data, dear. Absolutely horrendous amounts of it." She sipped her drink and seemed to become more thoughtful. "What happens is, NOAA's supercomputers run climate-forecasting models twenty-four/seven. Sixty or seventy terabytes of data a day we used to process. God knows what it is now. Marvelous machines, though. And of course, the computing capacity keeps getting stronger . . ."

"So what was the purpose behind Cloudcover?" he said. "Why did it exist? I seem to recall you got in some sort of trouble because of it?"

"Oh, God, yes." She laughed. "It was pure madness, really. I still don't know what the fuss was about. Actually, I think it started because of that Chinese thing."

"What Chinese thing?"

"Project 86. That's what they called it, anyway. NSA supposedly intercepted signals intelligence about it and launched Cloudcover in response."

"What was Project 86?"

"Computer simulations of weather patterns. 'Project 86' just referred to China's country calling code. Not very clever, as project names go, was it? Anyway, the feeling was that maybe they had an advantage there, and so we decided we needed to catch up."

"There was a researcher involved in Cloudcover named Deborah Piper," he said. "Did you know her?"

"Of course, I knew her," she said. "I mean, not well. I liked her. She was a very bright woman. Later, of course, she became something of a thorn in their side. For a while, she used to call me late at night and ramble on about this and that. And people think *I'm* kooky. Anyway."

Mallory made a mental note to ask her more later about Deborah Piper. For whatever reason, she wasn't comfortable talking about her. "Tell me about Cloudcover, then," he said. "What was it? When did it start?"

"Cloudcover? It began in, oh, I don't know, 1999, I guess. As I say, dear, there were rumors about China that lit a small fire here in Washington. Although, frankly, I was never convinced that Project 86 was real."

"What do you mean?"

She frowned into her vodka for a moment. "It's not exactly a secret that sometimes they will manufacture something to help justify spending millions of dollars for a new project."

"Is that what happened?"

"Well, I could never prove it, but, I mean, it seemed fairly obvious to me."

"Who was driving it?"

"It was a joint Defense Department–intelligence project. But a lot of it was actually carried out by the private sector. A lot of overlap."

"Did it ever involve the NGA—the National Geospatial-Intelligence Agency—or the NIMA—the National Imagery and Mapping Agency—by any chance?"

Hanratty laughed explosively. Mallory noticed three heads turn to look, almost simultaneously.

"What," he said, ducking down slightly.

"You might as well ask me about the National Photographic Interpretation Center, too."

"I could," he said. "Why? Why is that funny?"

"It's funny because they're all the same agency."

"Ah."

She went to her drink, which was just ice now. "Yes, it was called the NPIC when Eisenhower started it in 1961. It was absorbed by the National Imagery and Mapping Agency sometime in the mid-nineties and was renamed NGA, I don't know, seven or eight years ago."

So two of the people had worked for the same agency.

"And it's based, where, in Bethesda?"

"It was, yes. Now in Virginia. With facilities in St. Louis, I believe."

"Tell me what you did. What *was* Cloudcover, exactly?"

"Oh, heavens." She waved for the waiter first. Catching his eye, she held up her glass. "We did computer simulations of weather patterns, as I said. Storms. And then with the data, we built models on these supercomputers. This was very precise data, about all aspects of the storm."

"What did the models do?"

"They're what are called dynamical models and dynamical-statistical models. You take all the data you have about previous storms, and factor in the physics of the atmosphere. Then you vary one element of the storm. Say you introduce a low pressure system as the storm is beginning to form, for example. Okay? Or you make a slight variation in wind speed or air pressure within the eye of a hurricane. If you adjust one factor, particularly early in the storm's evolution, all the other variables are affected."

"For example."

"Okay, for example: we changed air pressure inside the eye of Hurricane Andrew and as a result it veered to sea and never made landfall in Florida."

"These were computer simulations."

"That's right."

"So Cloudcover was a computer simulation project."

She assented by lowering her head. Mallory sensed, as he often had in the past, that Hanratty possessed remarkable knowledge in her head, although not all of it had been parsed into useful portions.

"That's all?" he said.

"What else did you want it to be, dear?"

"I don't know. And so what happened to it? What became of Cloudcover?"

"Well, 9/11 happened. After that, it was scaled back. People didn't care so much about what China was doing."

The waiter brought her a third vodka and tonic. She carefully squeezed juice from the slice of lime, then took a generous sip. "Mmm," she said. "That's good."

"Could it have changed in some way after that? Mutated into something else?"

"Lots of things could have happened, dear. Lord knows, they didn't share everything with me."

"Because, the thing is, Dr. Piper continued to work for the government on another project. Something called FAST."

"Well, I wouldn't know about that. I mean, I could probably make a call or two and find out."

"Could you?"

"Is it important?"

He nodded.

"Then I guess I could."

"Good." Mallory looked across the restaurant and made eye contact with the waiter. He held up his beer bottle, ordering a second. She still had most of her third vodka and tonic to go and he had a feeling the conversation would soon turn to her coming trip to Greece.

8:23 P.M.

The assassin worked in darkness, wearing black clothing and deck shoes so that he blended with the shadows of the suburban neighborhood. The air was wet and breezy, carrying the stray scents of suppers cooking. He hopped the chain-link fence in a single scissoring motion and came at the house from the rear, darting among the shadows cast by elm and oak trees.

Entry would be a simple, five-step maneuver: pulling off the window screen, punching a hole in the lower pane of the top window, reaching in and unlatching the window, lifting up the lower window and then climbing in the residence.

The prospective victim did not imagine that this sort of an attack was even possible. He lived alone and his home had no alarms; sometimes, he left his car doors unlocked and his house windows unlatched. He was a brilliant man but not a particularly practical or prudent one. All of which made the assassin's task easier.

This was another pre-emptive mission, the objective to eliminate a threat and also to remove potential evidence. Thinking momentarily about what had happened with the last assignment filled the assassin with dark emotions; for the first time, he had been outmaneuvered. He wanted badly to go after Jon Mallory again, to hunt him down. But he had to wait on that.

He felt his way through the darkness of a hallway and into the living room, where he clicked on a standing lamp. He let his eyes adjust. Then moved into the study and drew the blinds. Clicked on the desk lamp. It took him less than two minutes to find the flash drives in a desk drawer. He pulled out the other drawers and then dumped the files from his file cabinet. He plugged a reader into a port of the man's computer, first copying and then erasing all of the files from his hard drive and then eliminating the recovery wall.

After that, he turned off the lights. Now it was just a matter of waiting.

THIRTY-ONE

CHARLES MALLORY LAY ON the motel bed thinking, occasionally sipping from a bottle of beer, trying to construct bridges between the known and unknown. He thought of several follow-up questions he wanted to ask Patricia Hanratty but decided to wait for her to call him first.

His cell rang at 9:03. Chaplin.

"I promised I'd get back to you on Mr. Zorn," he said.

"Yes. You did."

"I'm afraid there isn't much."

"Okay." Mallory hadn't thought there would be.

"Victor Zorn has been making deals on behalf of what's now called the Weathervane Group for at least a year and a half, it looks like. Many business interests before that, some of which were absorbed into the consortium. A lot of dealing, all fairly legit. He's a slick character, apparently. A salesman of the highest degree."

"Okay."

"What's unusual, though, is that everything dries up on him nine years ago. Before that, it's just on paper. There are no confirmable records. It appears to be a carefully constructed legend."

An invented past.

"Also," Chaplin said, "I found a motor vehicle record showing he was Canadian by birth, not American. That has since been covered up, apparently."

"The old Soviet gambit?"

"Maybe." Traditionally, it was easier to get counterfeit documentation in Canada than in the United States and easier to move undercover there. Until 2008, anyone could cross the Canadian border simply by making an oral declaration of citizenship. "There are some sizeable gaps in the bio," Chaplin continued. "He had ties in the early 2000s to a Russian energy firm. I can't confirm this yet but there's a Russian businessman named Viktor Zaystev. That may be who he really is. If so, he worked for Volkov in the late 1990s."

"Would US intelligence not know something like that?"

"They should. But they'd have to know what to look for. He's been careful to invent a past and keep quiet."

"What about Volkov?"

"Harder. Everything well covered. He is listed on several boards but no real information about his activities ever seems to come up. His businesses are mostly owned by shell companies. Also, I've found some interesting information going back years about a connection with someone named Dmitry Petrenko."

"Who is he?"

"He runs a security consulting firm based in Moscow. But going back I've found organized crime ties dating to the mid-1990s. At one point, he was accused of running a passport forgery operation. Charges didn't stick."

"Okay."

"That's all I've got right now. I'll call you back when I know more."

Mallory thanked him. He lay back on the sofa and turned up the sound on the television. Chris Matthews was on MSNBC, talking about the storm:

Isn't this going back to that old saw from the Nixon era—that we can put a man on the moon but we can't win the war on poverty here on Earth? Isn't this the same thing? We can go to the moon but we can't stop a storm from beating up our coastline? Or what's the old Pogo line? I've seen the enemy and the enemy is us? Isn't this a case of I've seen the enemy and we're our own enemy?

THE ASSASSIN WATCHED the headlights sweep through the front windows, lighting up the walls of the living room, gleaming off the glass vases and picture frames. He stood in the hallway several feet from the door, waiting. Rehearsing how this had to go.

He listened as the key went in the lock and twisted, a click of metal. Heard the doorknob turn, the hinges squeak, and pictured the man's hand going to the light switch.

As soon as the light came on and he closed the door, the assassin stepped forward. The victim made a startled gasp.

The next sound was the thud of his hand colliding with the right side of the man's face. Then his body falling in the hallway. And the muffled sound of the .22-caliber handgun, firing an inch from the man's ear.

The assassin crouched down and emptied the man's pockets. Then extracted the DNA evidence from his own jacket pocket and carefully placed it on the man's shirt and fingers. Fibers, hair and saliva samples.

He waited a moment, then, listening, and finally let himself out the back door. Walked through the drizzle in the night shadows along the edge of the yard, climbing back over the fence, crossing the yard of another house. Strode toward the sidewalk.

But then something happened that shouldn't have happened.

"Hey!"

The assassin turned. Someone shouting at him as he came across the yard. He froze. A man standing in the grass by the sidewalk with a dog on a leash. A sudden, panicked shout. Someone seeing something wrong, not knowing what to do about it.

The assassin assessed his options. Both of them. He walked toward the man slowly, expecting that he might turn and run. But he didn't. Instead, he stood motionless. The assassin became a soldier again. Recognizing the threat, confronting the enemy.

He scanned the street to see if anyone else was out. When he was nine feet away from his target, the assassin lifted his .22 and shot the man in the face. Then he shot the man's dog in the head. The assassin lowered the gun and surveyed the street once more. Then he ran through the drizzle across another residential yard. Four blocks away, he tucked the gun under his seat and began the drive back to Washington.

CATHERINE BLAINE NEEDED to unwind. She poured a bourbon over ice and sat before the computer monitor in her cluttered study. She tried to call Kevin, but his phone went to voice mail again. She left him a message. The drink felt good and she began to work, running searches on each of the people they would be meeting with the next afternoon. There would be an intelligence briefing in the morning, but she wanted to know as much as she could before she entered the room.

Dr. Susan Romfo. Dr. Jared Clayton. Morgan Garland. All three were considered visionaries, leaders in their fields. *What would make them become involved with Victor Zorn?*

She was reading an interview with Morgan Garland, the venture capitalist, when her phone rang.

10:21.

Odd that someone would be calling so late.

Even odder who it was.

"Yes."

"Cate, Harold DeVries."

"Yes," she said. She listened to the rain on the roof, feeling her heart rate accelerate.

"Do you have the news on, by any chance?"

"No. Why?"

"Did you hear about this thing in Baltimore tonight?"

"What? No, what thing?"

The Director of National Intelligence sighed. "Put on Channel five, Cate. They've got it on right now."

"What thing?"

"Put it on."

She walked into the living room and clicked on her television. Turned up the sound. There was a "Breaking News" story, she saw, about a shooting. Two men had been shot to death in the suburbs of Baltimore. A teary neighbor was standing on the sidewalk in the rain, police lights flashing across her face. Saying, "This kind of thing doesn't happen here. We don't even lock our doors. *We don't even lock our doors.*"

"What is it?" Blaine said.

"A scientist was killed. It was a home invasion, supposedly. Senseless thing."

"Who was it?"

"You knew him."

"What are you talking about?"

Blaine punched up the sound some more.

Stared at the set.

Then her blood went cold.

"Oh my God. No."

THIRTY-TWO

CHARLES MALLORY HAD FINALLY drifted to sleep on the dusty-smelling motel sofa. He was not ready to call it a night yet but was unable to keep his eyes open. In his dream, he was seated in a plush, state-of-the-art conference room with Catherine Blaine and Roger Church; his brother Jon and Patricia Hanratty were outside and Hanratty kept banging on the walls, screaming "Open the door, dear! Pull it open!" But Blaine and Church could not find any doors or windows to open. A wild wind was driving the rain against the conference room walls. Then a telephone began to ring.

Mallory sat up. He stared at the thick curtains, the shadow of rain cast from a parking lot light, the swirl of Hurricane Alexander on the silent television screen. One of his phones was still ringing. He reached for the one closest to him, realized it was the wrong one. Then he picked up the Hanratty phone. But it wasn't her, either. It was a muted sound. One of the phones buried in his bag.

He unzipped the bag and reached for it. It was the number he had given to Blaine.

"Hello." He parted the drapes, saw rain slanting hard against the streetlights.

"Hi," she said. "I'm sorry to call so late. Did I wake you?"

"No, not at all." Mallory glanced at the clock on the bed-stand. 10:56. He was glad to hear her voice, actually, although it didn't quite sound like her. "Go ahead."

"I decided I'd like to talk with you again."

"Okay. Good."

"Tomorrow morning?"

"Fine." He listened to her silence. "Want to talk now first?"

"Nope."

"Tell me what it's about?"

"Not right now."

"Are you okay?"

"Not really. I'll see you tomorrow."

Now Mallory was wide awake. He sat in the armchair and thought about the thing that had been bothering him about the list—a clue that Roger Church had inadvertently provided.

He poured a cup of coffee and thought about it some more. *I'm a night owl. You can call until midnight.*

He found the card the *Weekly American* editor had given him and pushed the numbers for Church's home.

On the second ring, he answered. "Church."

"You're up."

"Yes. Ah, hello," he said, apparently recognizing Mallory's voice.

"Can I just ask you a quick question? Something I should have asked Monday."

"Sure, if you'd like."

"You told me you had talked to the detectives in a couple of these disappearances."

"That's right, I did."

"You mentioned that DNA was found in a couple of the cases that was never matched to anyone?"

"Three, actually."

"Three of the cases."

"That's right."

"Do you know what it was?"

"What do you mean?"

"I mean, do you know what the DNA was that they found?"

"Oh. Yes, of course. Why?"

"Not sure. It's just an interesting detail that might mean something."

"Saliva on a cardboard coffee cup, in one case. From McDonald's. Hairs and skin tissue in the second case. The third was hairs, semen, and fingerprints."

"Who was the third?"

"Susan Beaumont. Trace amounts of semen were found on a chair in her motel room. Hair, skin, and fingerprints in her car."

"What about the other DNA? Coffee cup and hair samples?"

"Hair in both cases was female. Saliva on the cup was male. Fingerprints were on the cup, too. But nothing in the NSIC database. Why?"

"I'm not sure yet. I'll let you know when I am."

"Let me ask *you* something, then."

"All right."

"Did you meet with Jon?"

"Yes, I did."

"And? How is he?"

"He's fine. He's in a safe location, working on the story. With a little luck, he'll have something for you in a day or two."

"You sound optimistic."

"I have to be. I'm collaborating with him."

"Keep me posted?"

"I will."

Mallory signed off and slipped open the drapes. He stood by the window for a long time, watching the rain, thinking about what Church had just told him.

JAMES WU COULD not get the voice of David Quinn's final transmission out of his head. *"Don't know what I'm seeing . . . Faces . . ."* Quinn's words echoed in his head like a dark refrain as he walked through the tunnel back to the White House and the President.

All day, he had waited for President Hall to respond to his calls and emails, but had heard nothing in reply. He was beginning to imagine that he would have to wait through the night—and maybe indefinitely—when Gabriel Herring appeared at the entrance to the Data Visualization Center with a pair of White House police officers. "The President would like to see you now," he said in a flat voice, his face drawn and pale.

It was six minutes after eleven when Dr. Wu entered the Oval Office, past a posted Marine guard. He was tired and feeling vulnerable, thinking very strange and turbulent thoughts.

The President, dressed in khakis and a wrinkled blue oxford dress shirt, nodded a wary greeting. "Dr. Wu," he said. "Welcome. I under-stand you've been wanting to see me."

"I have." The scientist cleared his throat, standing in front of the President's desk, his legs together. "Thank you, sir, for taking the time to meet with me. Normally I would not reach out in such a manner as this. But I have a concern I think you ought to hear."

"All right. Please. Have a seat."

Dr. Wu sat. He cleared his throat again, leaning forward in the rose-wood chair, the toes of his well-worn wingtips just reaching the floor. He felt nervous, and wasn't sure that he wanted to go through with this.

"In a sense," he began, "my work has largely been about predicting outcomes. Predictions based on the accumulated results of previous outcomes. That's what science does."

"Yes."

"I have studied storms for more than three decades, sir, as you know. I have flown into the eyes of more than two hundred hurri-canes. I know what causes a storm and I know what causes a storm to break apart. I know how storms behave and how they don't behave."

"All right." The President blinked rapidly; Dr. Wu sensed his rest-lessness.

"A hurricane, as you know, is the most powerful force on the planet. But it is nevertheless at the mercy of other forces. Clashing wind patterns, pressure systems, cold fronts, wind shear. Nature has built-in checks and balances that prevent hurricanes from growing past a certain size and a certain speed. As you know."

"All right. Yes, I do. And so . . . ?"

"And so. Something about this storm, Alexander, doesn't fit with any model that I—we—have ever plotted. Or imagined. Something about Alexander isn't right, sir." Dr. Wu cleared his throat a little too loudly; the President frowned.

"Okay, so what do you mean, exactly? What's on your mind, Jim?"

"I'm sorry, sir. What I mean is: this storm is not reacting to changes in the atmosphere the way a storm system should. Frankly, I think there's something unnatural about this storm." He cleared his throat again. "I can't explain what that means exactly, only that there are forces *inside this storm*, sir, that are simply not following the laws of physics, of science, or nature."

The President surprised him with a smile. "Okay, and so what do you imagine it is?"

"I don't know, sir." Dr. Wu paused. "I mean—I know this is probably going to sound . . ." He hesitated; he couldn't believe he was about to say it. "I think, sir, based on what I know, that it's possible this is *not* a natural storm system. I really don't know how else to explain it."

"What could it be, then?"

"Well, sir. I don't know, exactly." Dr. Wu tried to read the President, but his face was a mask. Part of him felt the President knew exactly what he was saying; part of him wasn't sure. "I was hoping perhaps you could tell *me* something. Help shed some light on it. I know you took an unusual interest right as Alexander was beginning to form."

The President seemed to be studying Wu all of a sudden. "Yes, that's right. You're observant."

Dr. Wu waited for the President to say more, seeing that he'd struck some sort of nerve. *But what could it be? What was the government concealing about this storm?*

Instead of responding, the President gestured for him to continue. "Go ahead, what else is on your mind?"

"Oh. Well." He took a deep breath. "Several years ago, sir, I paid a visit to a research lab in California. One of the scientists there was Dr. Susan Romfo. She was pursuing what seemed to me a rather esoteric idea. That of quote unquote altering a storm system, as she put it, using ideas associated with artificial intelligence." The President frowned. "This was strictly a computer simulation project," Dr. Wu went on. "But she speculated, to me and to several other scientists, that someday this sort of science might actually have practical applications. I am a skeptic by nature and did not take this idea seriously at all. But, frankly, sir? I have begun to re-think some of my assumptions, just in the past twenty-four hours. Simply because the laws of physics and nature cannot explain to me what is happening out there."

"Because of this storm."

"Yes. That's correct, sir. It's almost as if it has somehow been programmed *not* to respond to the impediments that nature places in its way. As crazy as it sounds, sir, it's behaving as if it has a will to survive, or even a collective intelligence. It almost reminds me of a distributed intelligence program. As if it were invested with memory and an ability to adapt."

Dr. Wu laughed awkwardly and looked down at the carpet, realizing how crazy he must sound. But he was desperate for the truth, to hear it from the President; whatever that truth might be. "I'm sorry, sir," he said. "As someone who's built his career on science, and on skepticism, I'm amazed that I'm actually saying those words."

"But you're saying them for a reason, aren't you?"

"I suppose I am." He realized then that he was reacting this way because of what had happened to David Quinn, and his crew. And the lost freighter ships. He *was* saying this for a reason, but he was also being overly emotional. Maybe even having some sort of breakdown. "I'm sorry, sir," he said. "I'm not saying that's what's literally happening. It *couldn't* be, of course. I know that. I'm just saying that's what it resembles."

"Or maybe it *could* be," the President said. "Go on. Tell me what you're really here for."

Dr. Wu took a deep breath, trying to regain his composure. "As I say, sir. It really goes back to my deep-rooted love of science. This is something—" He swallowed. "I just want to suggest, sir, that if you would like to bring me further into your confidence, I mean— I would, of course, abide by any confidentiality agreements you request. I think it falls under the purview of my role as science adviser to the President. And I also think I could help."

The President waited a long time. Finally he smiled and nodded. "At this point," he said, "I think I'm going to take you up on that, Jim."

THIRTY-THREE

Thursday, October 6, 7:23 A.M.

THE GYM WAS A different place Thursday morning. Two women were running, five treadmills apart. The only other person Mallory saw, as he paid his entrance fee, was Catherine Blaine, standing by the dumbbell racks, feet spread, leaning forward, torso rail-straight, stretching. Actually, it was odd that anyone was here, he thought, considering how the storm had taken over the news. "Alexander the Great," the media were all calling it now. He listened to the report on the Weather Channel.

> *Much of the East Coast of the United States is under a Hurricane Warning this morning as Alexander continues to barrel its way through the Atlantic Ocean. Alexander has been upgraded to a category three hurricane with sustained winds of 120 miles per hour. Landfall is now projected for late Saturday or early Sunday.*
>
> *The storm has been blamed for at least seven deaths in the Carolinas along with extensive property damage and flooding, which has rendered many roads impassable.*
>
> *President Hall has declared a state of emergency in North Carolina, Virginia, and Maryland.*

Mallory could see right away, in her eyes, that things had changed. *One day later. Everything different.*

"Thanks for coming," she said. "I've thought about what you said. I should have told you why I really called the other day."

"You mean it wasn't because of Janus."

"It was. But it was more than that. Weights?" she said.

"All right. Upper-body day?"

She forced a smile and pulled two dumbbells off the rack. Her green eyes glittered in the artificial light. Her hair was down and she wore no makeup today. It gave her a confident, no-nonsense look he liked.

"Under the circumstances, doesn't it seem a little frivolous to be spending the morning trying to enhance our physiques?" he said.

She shrugged. "Routines are what keep us sane. My dad used to say that a lot. Anyway, that's not really why we're here."

"No? Good." Mallory watched her reflection in the full-length mirror.

"I've changed my mind about something," she said. "I've decided that maybe we *can* share information, as you put it. On a limited basis."

"Okay. What changed your mind?"

"Something that happened last night."

"In Baltimore."

"Yeah."

Dr. Ruben Sanchez, murdered at his residence in the Baltimore suburbs. Mallory finished a set of curls with twenty pounds and set the weights down. He knew that she wanted to talk to him on her terms and sensed that if he waited, she'd open up. He also knew that she was taking a risk, breaking protocol and, maybe, the law.

"We're meeting with someone today," she said, speaking just above a whisper, as she lifted and then lowered a pair of ten-pound dumbbells.

"Okay. It's about that, isn't it?" He nodded at the televisions. *Alexander.*

"Mmm hmm."

Lift, lower. Inhale, exhale.

That was all he needed to hear, really. He could begin to figure other things now. *Cross clues.* "Can I take a guess who you're meeting with?"

"Okay."

Inhale, exhale.

"Victor Zorn?"

Her eyes slid to his in the mirror and he saw that wild look that he liked. "How would you know that?"

"Just a guess." He watched her set the weights back and shake out her arms. "And who else?"

"What?"

"Who else are you meeting with?"

"Why do you think there's anyone else?"

"Another guess. I'm thinking there must be two or three others for this to work."

"Why?"

"Because Zorn isn't a known quantity. He doesn't have the creds. But if he walks in with two or three or four legitimate people, it's a different ball game. Again, I'm just speculating."

She glanced at him in the mirror, rubbing her hands on a towel. "You're good. Three," she said. "Morgan Garland. Dr. Jared Clayton. Dr. Sue Romfo."

Mallory coughed, pretending not to be astounded. He adjusted the weight on a pulley machine and sat down at the workout bench for a series of overhead tricep extensions. The names answered one question, but immediately raised others.

"When's the meeting?"

"One o'clock."

She was lifting again, watching his eyes in the mirror.

"The four of them are going to be there?"

"Apparently."

Mallory pulled the overhead bar to chest level, then let it ease back up with the pile of weights. "But Vladimir Volkov won't be part of it."

"Pardon?"

He studied her reaction, letting the pulley bar return.

"Who is Vladimir Volkop?"

"Volkov," Mallory said. "Supposedly, Victor Zorn is Volkov's proxy. Volkov is a Russian billionaire. Second generation oligarch, I'm told. Made his fortune in oil and banking. Supposedly has some strong, but secretive, connections with the Kremlin."

"Volkov." She watched him in the mirror.

"Yes."

"And how would you know that? Or any of this?"

He shrugged, standing. "Well. I can't say, really. Only that it comes on pretty good authority."

"Who *is* Volkov? What's he done?"

Mallory sat on a bench and considered. He could tell her everything he knew or he could cherry-pick. He decided to tell her everything. It was going to be a trade. Plus, he kind of liked her and wanted to help.

"From what I understand, he's put together a consortium of research companies—geo-engineering, energy, weather—over the past ten, maybe fifteen years. He's established something of a monopoly on the serious end of the climate control industry."

"Are you saying this is really about Russia, then?"

"I don't know," Mallory said.

"We've been led to believe it's China."

"Yes, I know."

"How would Volkov have done all this without setting off alarm bells?"

"I guess very carefully. I don't know. A lot of the deals were evidently put together through Victor Zorn, using various shell companies and intermediaries. He took advantage of an industry that isn't carefully monitored. Scooped up individual scientists and research firms in very discreet ways."

"So who is Mr. Zorn?"

"Not clear. His bio says he's American, but I think he may be Russian. From what I've learned, he may have had connections with organized crime at one point. Have you heard of the Izmailovskaya syndicate?"

"Of course. One of Moscow's oldest mafias."

"Supposedly he was involved with them for a number of years."

She finished another set of curls, set down one dumbbell, then the other.

"Tell me about Dr. Sanchez," he said.

"Oh." She reached for a towel and rubbed it over her face. "He was a friend," she said, looking at herself now. Mallory saw her eyes moisten in the mirror. "A man I had enormous respect and affection for. I saw him two days ago." She sat, still catching her breath. "I don't want to get too paranoid but I think he was killed because of what he was going to do."

"Really."

"I think so."

"What was he going to do?"

"I think he was going to talk. He had a couple of contacts in the media and was about to share what he knew."

"Talk about what?"

"Something we had discussed two days ago. That was the first time I heard the name Victor Zorn, actually. We were supposed to meet again this morning."

"What did Dr. Sanchez say about Zorn?"

"He told me what you just told me. That he was consolidating research facilities involved with climate studies. That he was a very clever and charismatic man. Dr. Sanchez thought he was about to make a move of some sort."

"What kind of move?"

"I don't know. I guess maybe we'll find out today."

They were startled by a sudden rumbling. Thunder.

"I've been wrestling with going outside of the circle on this," Blaine said, speaking just above a whisper. "I shouldn't, but last night changed that. Something inside this circle isn't right. Someone. I can't figure out what, or who, exactly, but it scares hell out of me."

A man in a blue windbreaker walked in the door. It was the same person Mallory had seen the other morning. Black shoe-polish hair. Secret Service, probably.

"Want to stretch a little bit?"

As they stretched, she told him about the anonymous email threats, the warnings about "natural disasters" that weren't natural, speaking succinctly in a soft, even tone. *Trade completed.* If it had come from anyone else, Charles Mallory probably wouldn't have believed any of it. Coming from Blaine, he did.

"I know I shouldn't have said any of that," she told him afterward. "Before last night, I wouldn't have."

"It's good that you did."

She sighed. "How about you?"

"What do you mean?"

"Yesterday you said we're like two intelligence agencies that aren't willing to share information. So what else have you got for me? What aren't you sharing?"

"Oh." Mallory watched her steady green eyes. He decided to tell the rest of what he had learned. The seven names. There was no sense in holding anything back now. Afterward, he wrote them out for her on a scrap of paper.

"Okay," she said, tucking it in a pouch of her gym bag. She draped a towel around her neck. "And so? What do you think this is really about?"

Mallory didn't say anything for a while. He didn't want to speculate too much about that. He was formulating a theory, still, coming back to the details that didn't make sense, but would ultimately stitch it together.

They were sitting on benches in front of the mirror, watching reflections of each other. Sweating slightly.

"I think the endgame is about legitimacy," he said at last. "It's about someone who is very resourceful. Brilliant, wealthy, connected. Someone who has created a network that could probably revolutionize science and technology worldwide. But somehow this person has an Achilles heel. Something about his character, his past, is tainted. There is a reason he needs to stay in the background. He's come this far and now he needs a stamp of legitimacy. The US government could give him that. This President, in particular, seems responsive to grand gestures, to big symbolic ideas. And it sounds like they're about to hand him one."

"But if he doesn't have legitimacy," she said, "how was he able to get people like Garland, Romfo, and Clayton on board?"

"I know," Mallory said. "I'm still working on that part."

He sat up straighter, gazing at the entrance to the gym. Then he thought of another idea. "Let me ask you something," he said. "What doesn't seem right to you about all this?"

Blaine snorted. "Where do I begin?"

"Begin with the first thing that comes to mind. What doesn't fit? Three words or less."

She smiled, but he could see that she was thinking about it.

"The President," she said.

Mallory nodded, although he hadn't really imagined what she would say. "Why, what about him?"

"I don't know. Something just doesn't seem right. The President's career could be on the line over this crisis and he seems to be going along with everything too easily. I don't know, it just feels kind of reckless."

"Do you think the President is involved?"

"No," she said. "I don't."

"Okay." Mallory stretched out his legs. "And it bothers you because you like this President."

"No. Well, I mean, yes. But that's not why it bothers me. It bothers me because I don't understand it. It doesn't make sense. He's acting like the threats are a separate issue from the storm that's out there. They aren't."

Mallory watched her and he suddenly understood something else about the list. Something he'd missed.

"What are you doing after the meeting?"

"I don't know." She looked at him this time, not his mirror image. "Why?"

"Let me tell you my idea."

THIRTY-FOUR

Nice, France

VLADIMIR VOLKOV STOOD ON an edge of the pink marbled pool terrace gazing at the sequins of sunlight on the Mediterranean and thinking about fate, as Prokofiev's Fifth Symphony filtered through a dozen speakers concealed in the lush shrubbery. It was a perfect, calm afternoon in the south of France. The sky was nearly cloudless as far as he could see, even as storms were raging elsewhere. Rain was forecast here, too, by the weekend; but by then Volkov would be gone.

"You always find us the most beautiful places," Svetlana said, coming up beside him and kissing him carefully on the cheek.

Volkov glanced at his gold watch, and showed her a quick smile. His mistress came from where he had once dwelled, a life of few rewards, lots of desires.

"Yes, well, that's what I do, isn't it? Now, please, wait for me inside."

Volkov leaned on the railing and looked back toward the sea, wondering about the monster that was right now raging across the Atlantic.

As a side business, Volkov operated a string of luxury resorts, which allowed him to live in the most agreeable climates on the planet. One day, he would like to see a world in which the weather was hospitable everywhere. Because when the weather was bad, Volkov's mind became a haunted palace; a place he could not bear to live.

He was a tall, slightly jowly man, once strikingly handsome, who still often felt like the champion athlete that he had been decades earlier. This morning, he was headed into competition again, after years of secret training. A man in pursuit of a prize.

For Volkov, the championship was проект, or "The Project." A plan meticulously constructed over the course of many years, which would be executed now over the course of a few days.

He sat on a chaise beside the swimming pool and took out his encrypted mobile device. Checked his watch and waited. Only fourteen seconds late, the call came.

"Проект is about to go forward," Dmitry Petrenko said, speaking in his cultured, central-Russian accent.

"And how is he? Is he ready?"

"Victor?" Petrenko was careful not to hesitate, Volkov noticed. "He seems to be."

"Has he been honest? With himself?"

"So far, yes. I'd say yes."

There was a silence. "I don't want you involved, Dmitry, other than to provide security."

"I have no other intentions."

"I don't want you offering any assistance or any advice. Otherwise, we will never be able to say it was really him This is his project and he must rise or fall by it."

"I understand that. I have no issue with that."

"Good."

Volkov clicked off and gazed again at the azure sea. He closed his eyes and thought about his lieutenant, Victor Zorn, for several long moments. *Mr. Zorn.*

Volkov, raised in Russia during the Cold War, had never been to the States, although he expected to visit very soon. His second wife and their two children lived still in Russia, at a villa outside Moscow. But Volkov kept a boundary between work and family. The Project had been constructed that way. His family understood, without knowing what his real business was; they knew not to question him.

Volkov's rise had been swift and, it sometimes seemed, to him and others, divinely inspired. He had adopted an aggressive, Western-style approach to management and organization, using his inheritance to buy up oil fields, refineries and pipelines, coal companies and port facilities; winning a major oil company in a loans-for-shares auction before he was forty; and then engineering several highly leveraged takeovers, selling the acquisitions to strategic investors, at times to himself. For several years, Volkov had even sat as a deputy on the Russian Fuel and Energy Ministry. Everything had been built carefully, and much of it nearly invisibly.

Eight and half years ago, Volkov had merged his largest oil company, TNK, with the Russian oil interests. It was a ten billion dollar deal, and the last of the chess moves he needed to make before he could launch проект.

Volkov understood the failings of the "Western model" even as he had benefited enormously from it. After the fall of the Soviet Union in 1991, the United States had celebrated the prospect of a "new" democratic Russia—a true capitalist society in which industry, housing, and land would all be privatized; in which industrial ministries would be replaced by private, multi-national corporations.

The outside world had applauded his country's shift to the Western model; but Russia herself had only suffered because of it. The capitalist example created thirty-five billionaires in less than a decade and gave rise to the oligarchs. But Yeltsin had not been able to stand up to the oligarchs and they had looted his country blind. The "reforms" of the early 1990s had not only failed, they had supported and validated a criminal culture.

The Western model—Volkov preferred to think of it as "the American model"—purported to be about free markets and opportunity. But in actual practice it was about weakness and lawlessness. It was a travesty; the kind of "democratic" system the United States blithely thought it could impose around the world.

Now all of that was going to change—and within a few years Russia would regain her deserved claim to greatness. She would be a country that believed in the future—and also created that future. Vladimir Volkov had been one of the architects of this coming Russia, one of the believers who had helped Putin's efforts to overhaul the political system, to centralize power in the Kremlin once again, to begin eliminating the criminal culture.

In the dark days of the late 1990s, Volkov had come up with an agenda that would enable Russia to eventually stop playing by the Western rulebook. It was a project that went far beyond politics. A plan that would showcase the visionary muscle of Russia again, making her a world leader in science and technology. It was Putin who had named it проект, "The Project," on the first night they had discussed it, a balmy May weekend at his vacation villa on the Black Sea.

Unlike his father, Volkov felt driven by the call of destiny. He had taken on an elevated mission, one that would ultimately restore greatness to his homeland. Americans liked big ideas. This President, in particular, embraced them. And Volkov had come up with a very big idea, one that he was about to sell to the President. Victor Zorn had been meticulously groomed to be the general who would journey to America and lead the mission. He was a world-class salesman, with a personality that worked like a magic trick. He had surprised and impressed Volkov with his ability to sign up such a strong advisory board—all high-profile American figures.

But Mr. Zorn had acquired an American softness, as well, and Volkov worried about him. The latest problem with Victor was that he thought too much. When you think too much, you imagine too many outcomes.

So he considered Mr. Zorn's mission to the United States a trial, and if it did not succeed, he would replace him with Petrenko. Petrenko was not as smooth or as charming as Zorn, but he was just as adept at negotiations, and he was considerably tougher—a former KGB man who had once been a middleman for Izmailovskaya.

Volkov pushed a button on his telephone and he summoned Svetlana. She would finish his massage now.

He checked his watch again.

It was time. 6:45 P.M. in Southern France.

12:45 in Washington. Victor Zorn should be arriving at the gate of the White House. Проект was going to have its first major trial.

THIRTY-FIVE

CATHERINE BLAINE INSTANTLY RECOGNIZED three of the four members of the Weathervane team as they were led by Chief of Staff Gabriel Herring through the doors to the Cabinet Room: Jared Clayton, Morgan Garland, and Sue Romfo. Dr. Clayton was a Nobel Prize-winner known for his pioneering work in cloud physics. Morgan Garland was among the most successful venture capitalists in the country; she had recently viewed a segment about him on *60 Minutes*. Dr. Romfo was a well-known researcher on the effects of global warming on hurricane formation and frequency.

What could have convinced them to become involved in this project?

Blaine did not know the fourth representative of Weathervane, who introduced himself as "Mr. Zorn." He was tall and svelte, dressed in a black, double-breasted suit; there was something slightly exotic about him—the well-proportioned face and regal nose that suggested nobility, the easy smile, the indeterminate accent, the thick brushed-back dark hair, with stray loose strands and the welcoming but slightly elusive eyes.

As Blaine shook his hand, though, she was reminded of the death of her friend, Ruben Sanchez, and felt a rush of anger.

The President sat at the foot of the table. His Cabinet secretaries and the Vice President took the seats on the right side of the table, his three guests to the left.

Victor Zorn, though, did not sit. He opened a laptop computer and set it in the center of the table.

"Mr. President," he said. "Madam Secretary. Gentlemen. Thank you for agreeing to meet with us this afternoon." He glanced at them one at a time, with a deference that seemed to hold everyone's attention. "I want to assure you from the outset that we are all here today for the same purpose." His cheeks dimpled slightly as he smiled; he was actually pleasant to look at, Blaine thought. "Our interest, you will see, is the national interest."

Mr. Zorn snapped open his briefcase and extracted a stack of dark binders, which he passed around the table to each of the people in the room, including his team. Blaine noticed his neatly manicured nails. On the black cover were two letters in embossed gold print: WG.

"As you know," he said, "we represent a consortium known as the Weathervane Group. In front of you now is an overview of our organization and a summary of our proposal. Please take a moment to page through it."

Blaine looked through her booklet. Twelve pages, divided into sections: a paragraph description of the company; a list of advisers, some of whom she recognized; prominent weather scientists and physicists; a list of twenty-seven participating companies, foundations, and facilities. The last three pages explained the project they had come here to talk about. It was titled "Hurricane Alexander Mitigation."

Blaine went back to the first page. According to the description, WG had been built over nearly two decades and represented "the most advanced work in the fields of environmental and climate research, meteorology, geo-engineering, and natural disaster mitigation."

The consortium's twenty-seven partners included research labs, consulting firms, weather monitoring data centers, and a private satellite company.

"As you can see," Mr. Zorn said, "the consortium deals with a wide range of research and technology issues and solutions. Although I'm sure the most pressing question you have today is what can these technologies actually do for us—all of us—right now?" He nodded out the window, at the heavy slants of rain in the Rose Garden. "Can they avert this apparent crisis that we are all now facing together?"

"And your answer?" said the Vice President.

"The answer? Is unequivocally, yes." He smiled. "In fact, in a sense, this storm presents the perfect case for us to demonstrate how, and why, all of this works. It is not a single technology or entity that we represent, you see, but a *consortium* of companies working together to find solutions to complex international problems.

"I would like to make it clear, too, as Dr. Clayton will explain to you in a few moments, that there is nothing theoretical or hypothetical about our proposal. This technology began with algorithm-driven computer models, fine-tuned over a period of many years. But it has now been successfully implemented in real time to mitigate three hurricane-force storms in the Pacific Ocean."

There was an inaudible ripple of surprise around the table, Blaine sensed.

Mr. Zorn bowed his head. "Mr. Garland," he said, "would you like to introduce a video of the process?"

Morgan Garland, the venture capitalist, a slightly frail-looking man in his mid-fifties with pale skin, oversized tortoise-shell glasses, and tufts of silver-blond hair, leaned forward. "Yes, thank you, Mr. Zorn," he said. "Keep in mind, these are not computer-generated pictures you will be seeing. These are actual satellite images of cyclone systems in the Pacific Ocean."

He pressed a key on the laptop and sat down again. An animated image materialized. Mr. Zorn eased back behind the row of chairs as the others watched. The video purported to show three Pacific Ocean storm systems over the past year. Each time-lapse sequence displayed similar patterns—the storm gathering, intensifying and then dissipating. Each presentation took about three minutes, although the tracking actually evolved over several days, Garland explained. The third example was a typhoon that diminished in wind speed from 105 miles per an hour to 20 miles an hour in less than a day.

Blaine was aware of the three storms, and their rapid deteriorations. But the videos alone proved nothing.

"Dr. Clayton," Mr. Zorn said, nodding toward the Nobel Prize-winner.

"Thank you," Clayton said, clasping his hands on the table. He was tall and slightly stooped, with disheveled gray hair, intelligent eyes and a strikingly deep voice. "Just by way of introduction," he said, glancing at a page of notes. "My involvement in this began three years ago, when I was hired as a consultant for a new weather-modeling research center in northern California. That research center today houses the largest weather data assimilation project in the world. Last year, as you've just seen, we managed to mitigate these three full-fledged cyclones—"

"Just to clarify," said the Vice President, raising a hand. "What is the difference between a cyclone and a hurricane? Or is there a difference?"

Clayton seemed taken aback for a moment, and looked to Mr. Zorn. "No, actually," said Mr. Zorn. "Cyclones, typhoons, hurricanes are all the same thing. They carry different names in different parts of the world."

"So," the President said. "Let's cut to the chase. How does this so-called mitigation work? How did you do this?"

Mr. Zorn nodded for Clayton to go ahead. "There are four primary mitigation operations," Dr. Clayton said, "which have been developed and refined over the past two decades. They are all summarized in your booklets.

"The first we call Manipulated Eyewall Degradation, or MED. This is, in effect, a more sophisticated version of what the government attempted in the 1960s and 1970s. It was called Project Stormfury then. The idea was to inject silver iodide showers into the first rain bands outside the wall of clouds that surround a hurricane's eye. The heating that resulted caused the clouds to enlarge, creating what is known as 'invigorated convection,' which weakens the center of the system.

"The earlier model used silver iodide, released into the clouds by ten or a dozen Air Force planes. Since then, and in particular in the past five years, private industry has developed a more effective synthetic property, which is capable of disrupting the energy in the eye of the storm, causing it to, in effect, lose its energy source and unravel.

"Second is Solar Laser Technology. This involves solar-powered satellite laser beams, which can both disrupt the balance inside a storm's eye and also steer the storm by heating the air on either side of the eye wall. This technology is being developed by one private company in particular, which launched its first weather control satellite last year. A second is expected to go up this winter. So far, they have demonstrated an ability to steer storm systems into cooler waters or into low pressure systems. This same technology has been studied by NASA. But the private sector is considerably further along with it at this point.

"Third is Sub-Surface Tomography. A hurricane, you see, is basically fed by warm water. Cooler water slows it down. SST causes a disruption under the surface of the ocean floor, which pumps cooler water from the bottom of the sea up to the surface. The effect is similar to that of the proposed technology referred to as 'up-welling pumps.' SST uses radio frequency beams, which bounce off the atmosphere and return to the sea floor, in turn causing cold water to rise to the surface, weakening the hurricane.

"The fourth process is known as Synthetic Cloud Disassembly. It involves the injection of what is in effect a genetically engineered bacteria into the eye of a hurricane. This process is the most experimental of the four, but also, in some respects, the most promising. It actually stems from ideas developed in the field of artificial intelligence. A plane releases clouds of this substance into the eye of a hurricane and the artificial bacteria attaches to the inner wall of the hurricane, counteracting the convection process. The bacterial agents multiply rapidly, self-combining, forming larger clouds that cause the system to destabilize. These cloud agents have been programmed with what might be called a self-sustaining 'collective intelligence,' which in theory, at least, is more effective than the self-sustaining forces driving the hurricane. This technology is being developed through a California-based firm that Dr. Romfo has worked with very closely."

He cleared his throat and leaned back, indicating that he was finished. The President exchanged a long look with Blaine.

Moments later, Vice President Stanton began to chuckle. Everyone in the room turned to him.

"Sorry," he said. "But if you want my honest opinion—this all just sounds a little crackers to me."

Mr. Zorn stepped toward the table. Placed his hands calmly on the back of an empty chair, showing the creases of a smile in his cheeks. "Yes," he said. "Much as sending a man to the moon did five decades ago."

"That's true," said Dr. Romfo, speaking for the first time. She was a large woman with heavy features and long, kinky dark hair. "These ideas aren't new, actually. With the exception of the last one. The others have all been studied, discussed, dissected, written about and modeled for years."

The President glanced at the Vice President, whose smile was still fading.

"Which one of these processes, then, would you use in this case?" Harold DeVries asked. "With Hurricane Alexander? Which would be most effective?"

"All four, actually," said Dr. Romfo.

"All four."

"Mmm hmm," she said. "Yes, I liken it, in a sense, to cancer treatment. There was a time when the medical community was split, with some researchers advocating radiation and others chemotherapy. Now, of course, we use everything we can. There is often a complex but beneficial collaboration at play among different processes."

"Is that what was done in the Pacific?" the Vice President asked.

"Yes." Mr. Zorn's eyes fastened for a second on Blaine's, as if reading her skepticism. Then he turned to the President and smiled graciously.

"But is there any guarantee that this will work?" Stanton asked. "I mean, with a storm of this size?"

"In science," Dr. Clayton said, "we always hesitate to use the word guarantee. But, yes, I think you can be assured that there will be a dramatic alteration. I don't know that we can promise we will stop or destroy the storm entirely. But it will be severely diminished."

"Which," added Mr. Zorn, "put another way, translates into thousands of lives saved. Probably many more."

Blaine could see the wheels turning in the President's head. It was actually a brilliant strategy, she realized, getting these particular people on board. All three were "big ideas" people, known for backing speculative projects. But at the same time, this presentation reminded her of an optical illusion—two images sharing the same space; seen one way, it could be perceived as a humanitarian breakthrough; seen another, it felt devious and disingenuous. Clearly, they were taking advantage of a vulnerability; there *wasn't* sufficient interest in this field. Even within the Department of Homeland Security, there had been a series of false starts over the years—including Project HURRMIT, designed to model the most promising hurricane mitigation experiments, and "FutureTECH," which was supposed to develop hurricane mitigation research partnerships between the government and the private sector; but both projects had been scrapped years ago, before Blaine came on board.

"If you have the chance to save so many lives with your technology," the Vice President asked, "why bring this to us? Why not just do it?"

"A fair question," said Mr. Zorn, resting his hands on the chair-back again. "Mr. Garland has, as you know, created funding for many technologies that have changed the way we live our lives. I believe he's the person most qualified to answer that."

The venture capitalist nodded, sitting up straighter, scooting his elbows forward. "Thank you," he said. "Before I go to the question, let me first give you a number. Three hundred and twenty-six. Okay? That's how many proposals are submitted to our firm on an average week. And I have to say, at the outset, that this is easily the most exciting project we—I—have ever taken on.

"What makes it particularly exciting is, as Mr. Zorn mentioned, this is not something that is hypothetical. It's something that has already shown highly tangible results." Garland, unlike the other members of his team, seemed comfortable talking without making eye contact, Blaine noticed; mostly, he seemed to look between people. "But it's a complicated and enormously expensive process, or series of processes, actually," he said. "Which requires a substantial funding mechanism to exist and evolve, whether it be government or the private sector. Eventually, as the industry expands, costs will come down, of course. To date, we have backed its evolution with venture capital money. With the understanding that this consortium will eventually be sold."

"It's really the ground floor of a new industry," added Mr. Zorn. "The United States government, of course, has traditionally gotten behind important new technologies. Which is why we are here today. This is, as you can see, a very significant opportunity for your government."

Garland nodded. "At some point in the not-too-distant future, we would like to think that natural disasters such as Alexander will become obsolete. The only substantial obstacle to reaching that point is funding."

Blaine saw something subtle light President Hall's face and realized that they were hitting all the right notes. Playing to the President's weakness for "big ideas." She felt a new resentment gathering inside her.

"But *our* concern, if I may, is not the future," said the Vice President. "It's right now. It's *this* storm. That storm," he said pointing toward the Rose Garden.

"Yes. Exactly." Mr. Zorn nodded without looking at him. His eyes turned to Easton, who nodded once.

"And so, what if we don't—I mean, say we don't want to buy into the rest of it?" asked Stanton.

Mr. Zorn tilted his head, as if talking to a college freshman. "I'm afraid the consortium doesn't differentiate in quite that manner," he said, showing his dimples. "It's a complicated business and, as we've said, the processes are all inter-related. But I think I see what you're saying. And I think after this case, you will be convinced."

Silence followed. Everyone seemed to be waiting for the President to speak.

"So. What is it we'd be buying?" he finally said.

"You'd be buying the consortium, sir," Mr. Zorn said, comfortable with everyone watching him take charge. "You'd be buying the science and technology of twenty-seven leading research and development firms. On an exclusive basis. Once the mitigation of Alexander is carried out, that is."

The President glanced at the briefing book, then raised his eyes to Mr. Zorn. "Meaning . . . ? We would own it?"

"In effect, yes," Mr. Zorn replied. "Inevitably, out of necessity, this would be a worldwide partnership, of course, because, as you are well aware, the world's weather is all inter-related. But, yes, you would take the lead. You would control it."

"How would it work?" Blaine asked. "The mitigation, I mean. How soon would it begin?"

"Well. Assuming we reach a basic working agreement this afternoon? Mitigation could commence at the conclusion of this meeting."

Vice President Stanton was shaking his head. "I just think we'd all like a few more details here, fellas. I mean, I don't see what this booklet—" He held it up, then reconsidered and changed gears. "I mean, where are the major facilities *doing* this mitigation? How exactly does it operate? We need more than this, fellas."

Without missing a beat, Mr. Zorn replied, "There are sixty-three facilities owned and operated by the consortium, Mr. Vice President. Seven of them would be directly involved in this initial mitigation project, enacting the four primary processes. They are all identified in the booklet. They will be controlled by a mobile Command

Center. There is no central physical facility. Dr. Romfo is the chief acting scientist for the consortium."

Blaine looked directly at Mr. Zorn, incredulous that no one on her team was making a more vigilant inquiry. "From what I can see," she began, "you've gone out of your way not to publicize your operation or any of this research. You've in effect created a monopoly, out of sight of the public." He offered no response, so she went on. "That's what it looks like, anyway. Are you now proposing forming this partnership without public knowledge?"

"Ah, a very good question. Actually, no." He showed her his dimples. "The opposite. The publicity surrounding the mitigation of this hurricane would generate enormous public support for this new technology. In fact, we would ask that, upon the successful mitigation of Alexander, the President make an announcement trumpeting this new technology."

Blaine frowned. "So you would *want* this mitigation and this partnership to go public?"

"Why, yes. Certainly. We would prepare a statement. Together."

Of course, Blaine thought.

Garland was nodding now. "That's actually one of the more attractive elements of this. For *you*," he said. "Establishing the United States as a leader in this field."

"Which would also be one of the more attractive elements for *you*," said the President. But his tone was more collegiate than challenging.

"Perhaps," Mr. Zorn said seriously. "But, of course, the credit for pulling this together, harnessing all the existing technologies to stop this storm, would go to the United States. It would be quite a boost to your international standing."

The President frowned and glanced at the rain; Blaine could tell he liked the sound of that. This *was* very smart. They had tailored this to *him*. Her instincts were telling her to slow this down. *But how?* It was just what Charles Mallory had said. *The endgame is legitimacy.*

"Would we have the opportunity to inspect these facilities?" the Vice President asked. "To see the whole set-up."

"Why yes, of course," Zorn said, as if this were the most obvious point. "Although, as you can see, this is not a project that we want to deliberate over for too long at this stage. The mitigation would have to begin immediately. I think you would all agree with that."

Bill Stanton made a non-committal grunt. He looked at Blaine, who shook her head. "I think what we're all wrestling with here, sir—and excuse me if I'm speaking out of turn—but, I mean, could we do this on an incremental basis? Or, as a trial, so to speak."

"Yes. It *is* a trial." Mr. Zorn said.

He then let Garland provide a more proper reply. "I understand your concern, Mr. Vice President. As we said, because of the costs and the complexity of this consortium—the twenty-seven partners involved—this will, naturally, require a commitment. However, the agreement hinges first on what happens with Alexander."

Blaine saw the President nodding very slightly.

"I'm not clear on this term 'partnership,'" Blaine spoke up. "Who would maintain this technology? These sixty-three facilities? They'd become part of the government? I'm not clear how this would work."

Mr. Zorn lifted his head in a reflective manner. "Well. There are several ways of going forward, aren't there?" he said. "Probably the most sensible would be to create an agency, either an international agency or an office within the United States government, to oversee these operations. But that's for you to decide."

Romfo said, "Let me just add. The real potential here isn't deflecting one storm, it's the science of mitigating natural disasters. The World Bank and United Nations estimate the annual cost of natural disasters is in the neighborhood of ninety billion. Much of that could be avoided with a responsible investment in this technology."

Mr. Zorn added, curtly, "Yes, but, let's not get ahead of ourselves. The first step, remember, is Alexander."

Moments later, everyone looked up as a crack of thunder shook the room.

THIRTY-SIX

THE SHADOWS OF RAIN swam in a hazy oblong across the conference table. Catherine Blaine imagined that there were various legal ways of shutting this down—violations of free trade and monopolies law, if not more blatant criminal and terrorism charges. But the President wasn't thinking that, she could tell; the immediate concern *was* this storm, the monster hurricane churning across the North Atlantic.

"If I may just elaborate," Morgan Garland said. "What we're saying is that the consortium—the Weathervane Group—is offering this technology to you because we believe the United States would be the most responsible steward for it."

But you're bringing it to us at a stage when we have no alternative but to accept, Blaine thought.

Mr. Zorn made a conciliatory gesture to the President, showing the palms of his hands. "One way you might want to look at this is to consider two stark alternatives. In the first scenario, let's say we reach an agreement this afternoon. The United States adopts this technology and utilizes it to successfully mitigate the worst Atlantic hurricane on record. This event then becomes the catalyst for a worldwide awareness of weather management. And, also, I might add, for the establishment of international guidelines, which, in effect, will bring about a new field of science."

The President nodded. "And the second scenario?"

"Well. That is a scenario in which an agreement is *not* reached." Zorn displayed his practiced smile, which seemed suddenly inappropriate. "And the United States does *not* play a leadership role in this field. Which simply means that *someone else* does."

"Explain that, if you would," said the President.

"Certainly." Mr. Zorn waited a moment, his eyes taking in the people around the table one at a time before settling again on the President. "In other words, if the United States should, for whatever reason, decide it *doesn't* want to adopt this proposal, then, in all likelihood, it would, of necessity, go to another buyer."

"And who's on your waiting list?" Vice President Stanton asked.

"There is no waiting list, sir. That is our point. No one knows about or would have access to this technology except for the United States."

"So you're not threatening to open up bids to China or Iran, if we don't accept?" he said. "Or to Al-Qaeda?"

"Precisely the opposite," Mr. Zorn said. "We don't threaten. We are a scientific consortium. We're simply assuming that you will not deliberately allow this to fall into the wrong hands."

Clark Easton leaned forward, his bulk pushing against the table. He had been looking through the booklet for the past several minutes with a strange detachment. "You're hearing some concerns from our team and I've been mostly quiet here," he said. "But I just want to interject two points. First, in looking through this list, I can tell you that I'm familiar with several of these twenty-seven companies. The Pentagon has worked with these contractors and research firms and I can—and will—vouch for them. Second, there is another aspect of this proposal that you haven't fully addressed, Mr. Zorn, which at least bears mentioning. And that's the military component."

"Military," echoed the Vice President.

Mr. Zorn was nodding. "Yes, he's quite right. There is reason to believe that militarized weather technology is being developed presently by both China and Russia. I might add that there are even some rumors flying on the Internet that *this* storm might have been hatched by the government of China."

Easton exchanged a glance with the President. "You know," Easton said, "in the 1940s we failed to see the military potential of space flight and, consequently, we fell behind. The Soviets understood that before we did. I do think we need to be forward-looking with this."

"So what exactly are you proposing here?" Blaine said. "What are the terms?"

As the room went silent, the rain seemed to fall louder against the windows.

"Because of the nature of the threat, we would simply ask for you to sign a letter of intent this afternoon, establishing our partnership," Mr. Zorn said, looking not at her but at the President. "Mitigation would then commence immediately. We will give you status reports beginning this evening at nine P.M. and continuing every two hours starting at eight A.M. tomorrow."

"A letter of intent with an initial payment?" the President said.

"Yes, that is correct. We would need to establish an account, which would become the initial funding mechanism for this. Our consortium members have recommended that the successful mitigation of this storm begin a five-year partnership. But, again, details wouldn't need to be negotiated until after this storm is mitigated."

"So what would you need today?"

"Just the agreement, and the initial funding."

"And what is this 'initial funding'?"

Mr. Zorn's brow furrowed dramatically. "The consortium has suggested that within four hours of signing this agreement, you create a fund to authorize and support the use of this consortium's full resources. The initial balance in that fund would be five billion dollars. That would cover costs and preparations for the mitigation. After that, we would meet again and establish a budget. All we would need now, however, is your signature."

Mr. Zorn extracted a single sheet of paper from his briefcase and handed it to the President.

This is crazy, Blaine thought. Why was the President letting this go so easily? Blaine wondered. Why wasn't Easton questioning it?

"If you wish, we will, of course, give you time to discuss this among yourselves. If you would like, I can call you one hour after we adjourn this meeting." He glanced at Blaine, his cheeks dimpling. "But it's imperative, as you know, considering the nature of the storm, that you give us as much time as possible to begin this mitigation."

The Vice President was looking pointedly at the President and then at Easton, neither of whom would look at him. He lowered his head and began to chuckle.

"Sorry," he said. "I hate to be the wet blanket in the boardroom, folks, but I'm afraid this is not going to work on your timetable, Mr.

Zorn. I mean, I guess you aren't familiar with the way Washington works." He grinned broadly. "We would have to go marching down to the other end of Pennsylvania Avenue this afternoon with tin cups in our hands for this thing to fly. Then, before even thinking about signing anything, we'd have to open it up to the bidding process. So, I mean—"

"No. Actually, we wouldn't," Easton said, speaking softly but firmly.

Blaine watched the Vice President's smile fade in the silence.

"He's correct," said Harold DeVries, the Director of National Intelligence. "Under normal circumstances, yes, there would have to be an open bidding process. And congressional approval. But we have an emergency provision excluding that. Which would certainly be within our rights to invoke if we decided to move forward."

The President was nodding soberly. Blaine knew he was right and saw Stanton frown to mask his embarrassment that he'd forgotten the process. She listened as DeVries explained it to the Vice President. In times of emergency, when national security was threatened, the White House could bypass the legally established expenditure procedures and award contracts to a company without competitive bidding. After the invasion of Iraq in 2003, the US gave a no-bid contract to Halliburton, which it later renewed several times.

Garland nodded. "As I recall, Halliburton was at the time considered the only company in the world capable of doing that work."

"Yes, and the comparison is apt, in at least that respect," said Mr. Zorn. "This is the only firm—or group of firms, I should say—that can do this."

Blaine saw an impatience creeping into the President's expression. "All right," he said. "I will sign a letter of intent now. And then we will let you know for certain in one hour. Okay? Let's move forward on this."

Blaine stared at the President, but he wouldn't look at her now and there was nothing else she could do. She looked out at the rain and wanted to cry.

THERE WAS ALSO a fifth process, Victor Zorn knew, as he walked out from under the West Wing awning into the rain on West Executive Drive. But it was not one that he could mention. It was, in fact, the process most likely to stop the giant hurricane that was raging across the North Atlantic Ocean. It was simply to turn off the laser-powered heaters and allow Alexander to die a natural death.

As the Town Car limousine came through the gates onto Fifteenth Street, three unmarked government-owned cars pulled out behind it. Two blocks away, Joseph Chaplin's SUV emerged from a parking space and followed at a distance behind the government vehicles. There was also surveillance by satellite and airplane, as well as a homing device that had been placed under the car on the White House grounds.

The limousine traveled down Pennsylvania Avenue, then made a hard left onto G Street. Four blocks later, it entered a parking garage in Foggy Bottom.

That was when the surveillance became more problematic. Five minutes after the car entered the garage, a nearly identical Town Car emerged, followed four minutes later by another and then a third, all of them displaying the same Washington, D.C. license plate numbers.

The car that had left the White House with the homing device under its carriage remained in the garage for several more minutes. When it at last re-entered the street, it carried none of the original passengers, nor was it driven by the same man who had taken it through the White House gates. Two additional cars, carrying Dr. Romfo and Mr. Zorn, respectively, came out several minutes later.

By the time Dr. Clayton was delivered to the Taft Hotel and Morgan Garland was let out in front of the Four Seasons, surveillance was no longer tracking them.

And when Victor Zorn arrived in the Virginia countryside that afternoon, he was not on anyone's radar. Dmitry Petrenko was there, waiting near the entrance to the underground bunker, along with a security detail of four men. They greeted Mr. Zorn warmly, all of them speaking in Russian.

THIRTY-SEVEN

A STEADY AFTERNOON RAIN beat against the windows, glistening in the bare trees and on the circular drive of the South Lawn. Blaine glanced at the four men in the room and felt the silent tension moving like electricity among them; team members, bound to one another by the need to make a joint decision. Five people sharing a raw, undefined sense of history. She thought briefly about these men's personal lives, their families and ambitions, about what had brought them together to this room, stealing quick glances: Stanton with his open, honest face. DeVries with his sly, knowing look. Easton gazing down gravely at the Weathervane binder, avoiding her. The President of the United States looking absently at the rain. Blaine watched the purple spirals of the storm on the television screen behind Stanton's shoulder.

"Well." The President sighed deeply. He suddenly seemed ten years older. "Whatever reservations I have at this point are largely intellectual ones," he said. "But let's take it around the table." He looked at the Secretary of Defense. "Secretary Easton."

"I don't see that we have a choice."

"Harold?"

"Concur."

"Bill?"

The Vice President cleared his throat unnecessarily. "Um. I must say, I have some reservations. Five billion dollars, for one thing. With no guarantee it's going to work? I mean, come on—"

The President turned his eyes back to Easton. "Clark? Give that some context, in terms of the Defense budget. What is five billion dollars?"

He shrugged, pushing forward against the table. "It's what we've been spending every two weeks on the war in Afghanistan."

The President nodded, looking hard at Stanton. "Okay?" he said. "Let's not get stuck on that right now."

The Vice President cleared his throat again and moved his hands on the table. "My thought, then, would be, shouldn't we be focusing more on evacuation management, that kind of thing?" He looked at Blaine, who nodded. "I mean, in case this doesn't work as well as they're forecasting."

"We are," the President said. "We've got ten thousand National Guard troops mobilized. Evacuations are under way in eight states. FEMA has deployed teams up and down the coast. Working with emergency management in ten states. We're on top of this."

President Hall seemed annoyed for a moment—the details of the storm management had been in their briefing packet this morning—but then Blaine saw a subtle transformation in his face. What she thought of as "inspiration gathering"—a flicker of some noble idea, charging him with adrenaline. She saw that same look during speeches, between sentences, subtly telegraphing the spirit of what was to come.

"You know," he said, "I mentioned this the other day, but I think it bears repeating. I've been thinking about 1961 recently. May 25, 1961. When President Kennedy made his speech about landing a man on the moon by the end of the decade. We set a goal there and we went after that goal and we accomplished it. And it wasn't an easy goal. People didn't think it was possible. It was a remarkable achievement, really—and a remarkably hopeful time for this nation. We don't set goals like that anymore. And it's a damn shame.

"I think we could turn this into that kind of moment, if we handled it right. I really do. Taking the lead on a new global frontier. Showing that we can do something thought unimaginable a generation ago." He looked at each of them in turn. "And it could be a moment that, I might add, is more clearly useful than a man in a space suit planting an American flag in the Sea of Tranquility. We're talking about a whole new science here."

"Not to mention potentially millions of jobs," said Easton.

"Right."

"And saving millions of lives in potential future disasters."

There was subtle assent around the table.

"Looking at this in the long term," the President continued, "I also see it as an opportunity for us to get into the green energy business. In a big way. Particularly with this geo-engineering thing." He turned his eyes to Blaine, who fought the urge to nod. "If we don't, I'm afraid we're going to be beholden to China, India, and Japan the same way we are now to Saudi Arabia for our oil."

Blaine felt the consensus gathering in the room, the idea that this move could lift the administration to greatness.

"Cate? Thoughts?"

She locked eyes for a moment with President Hall, not sure how to begin. Or if she should. She glanced down at the folder provided by the Weathervane Group, then looked at him again. "I wonder if I could meet with you privately for a few minutes," she said, surprised at the sound of her own voice. "I do have some thoughts and concerns."

"What concerns do you have?" Secretary of Defense Easton asked.

"Well." Blaine realized that the President wasn't going to give her an out. "I mean, at the risk of stating the obvious: I'm not comfortable with how quickly we've lost sight of the email threats and warnings. Which are, after all, what led us to this meeting."

The Vice President nodded several times, but said nothing. His fingers moved nervously, straightening his booklet on the table.

Easton inhaled dramatically. "No one's lost sight of them, Secretary Blaine. I think we're talking about two separate things. I mean, I don't think this consortium was behind the email threats."

"But it's be*cause* of the email threats that we're *here*, isn't it?" Blaine said. She heard in her voice a shrill undercurrent. "I think it's absolutely absurd that we're just blithely going forward with this."

The President looked away again, not wanting to engage her. And Blaine suddenly sensed that for whatever reasons, the deal had been set before she entered the room. She felt a wild current of anger race through her. *How is this any different from doing business with terrorists?* she wondered.

"Cate, I understand your concern," the President said. "Although, frankly, I don't know how relevant it is. We *don't* know for certain that the email breaches weren't just sophisticated hoaxes—as you yourself suggested at the outset of this."

Of course we do, Blaine thought.

Easton nodded. "For all we know, the emails *were* from the Chinese to steer us from this. Harry, do you agree?"

DeVries looked down. He didn't respond.

"Except we wouldn't be meeting with them if it weren't for those email breaches," Blaine said. "They were what *set this up*."

Easton breathed slowly through his nose in exasperation. "Well," he said. "I disagree. I respectfully but categorically disagree."

Blaine glanced at DeVries; he wouldn't look at her now. Her heart was still racing. She told herself to calm down.

"Okay." *Deep breath. Think logically.* "I will concede that it's unlikely that Dr. Clayton, Dr. Romfo, or Mr. Garland have any knowledge of the email threats," she said. "But I don't necessarily feel that way about Mr. Zorn."

The President looked to DeVries. "We've vetted Zorn, though, haven't we?"

"As much as we can in eighteen hours. It's ongoing."

"Okay," Blaine said. "And I've done some checking, too, actually. Would it matter to anyone if I found some discrepancies in his biography?"

"For example," said the President.

"I've found, for instance, evidence that he was not born in this country, as his official biography states. In fact, he has business ties to Russia going back perhaps a dozen years or more. That he might even be a front for a Russian business consortium that we *haven't* vetted. And that he may have organized crime ties."

To Blaine's surprise, Easton leaned back and laughed, a series of short, nasally guffaws. DeVries gazed at the table. Blaine felt her face flushing.

"Have you found anything like that?" the President asked DeVries, with feigned innocence.

"No."

"Are you pulling these allegations out of thin air, Cate? We're not finding any of this. Or is there some evidence you have that you'd like to share with us?"

"I'd need a little time to pull it together."

"Well," he said. "Unfortunately, as you know, we don't have that luxury right now."

"That's why I wanted to talk with you in private," Blaine said. She felt her voice shaking. The power in the room was overwhelming her.

Easton half turned his chair, and Blaine wondered if he was going to walk out.

"Look, Cate," the President said. "I do want to hear your piece. But I also want a united front here." His eyes held hers, and she could see, then, that there was no chance for a different outcome. *Why?* Surely he wasn't blind to what was at stake. *Is he?* No, for whatever reason, the President did not want her to push it anymore. He was saying that with his eyes. And with his silence. Her options were two: she could go along with him or she could resign her position.

Easton inhaled dramatically. "Even if Secretary Blaine's concerns were legitimate," he said, still not looking at her, "you don't damn the whole consortium because of quibbles about a man's birthplace." Easton's mouth went crooked. "Just for the record: Mr. Zorn is not why I would get behind this deal anyway. It's Jared Clayton and Dr. Romfo and Morgan Garland, and the scientists, contractors, and researchers involved."

"Cate," the President said, his tone suddenly condescending. "If we have legitimate concerns about this man, if there's a potential for embarrassment because of him, then of course we will address that accordingly, I assure you. But for now, I've got to go along with the intelligence. With what Harry's giving me. We're going to tell them yes."

There was silence around the table. After a moment, the President's eyes came back to her. "The immediate concern is that thing out there," he said and pointed at the multi-colored swirl of the approaching hurricane on the television monitor. "Even if you discount the opportunity that this opens up, for jobs and for emerging science and technologies, we still have one irrefutable problem. They know how to stop this, we don't. End of story."

"Okay." Blaine stood and turned away from them, her eyes misting. Knowing she had to let go. This wasn't her battle to fight. It was his. President Hall's. Blaine knew there was nothing she could do inside the circle anymore.

"Thank you," the President said. "When Mr. Zorn calls, I will tell him we are ready to move forward."

FOURTEEN MINUTES AFTER speaking with the President, Mr. Zorn pressed a button on his encrypted cell phone. He was feeling good, gazing out at the fast-moving Virginia countryside.

The presentation had gone even better than Zorn had expected. Within four hours, the down payment would be in their account, and Volkov could transfer it to his own account in Switzerland.

"The agreement has been accepted, as you know," said the man in Washington.

"Yes. And the discussion went smoothly?"

"Yes. Relatively."

Mr. Zorn heard something troubling in that word, however. A subtle inflection suggesting that something about the discussion, in fact, *hadn't* gone smoothly. He had expected the conversation to proceed one way, to be a quick affirmation. But he could tell that his associate was concealing something. Meaning this conversation would instead have to go another direction.

"Tell me about what happened," he said. "Tell me what was said."

THE SECRET SERVICE detail watched from across the street as the garage door lifted and Blaine's Lexus 250 pulled in.

It was raining heavily, pouring through the trees. The Secret Service officers were parked directly opposite Blaine's townhouse. Both men reflexively checked the license plate number and tried to make sure that no one seemed to be following.

Then they turned their eyes to the upstairs windows, observing a familiar pattern: the light going on in the hallway and Blaine moving across the living room, cracking open the blinds. Moments later, a cell phone rang in the car. The man in the driver's seat, a trim, forty-three-year-old man with a buzz-cut hair style, answered. "Hi, Ralph. It's Cate Blaine. I expect to be in for the afternoon and evening."

"Thank you," he said.

"Stay warm."

"I'll try. Have a good night."

"You too."

Blaine was not required to call the security detail when she arrived home but she usually did. She knew it would have a psychological effect: the officers could relax a little more now. Neither of them had any idea that the person who had entered Blaine's townhouse was not, in fact, Blaine. Or that the cell phone call had been placed from more than a mile away, not from upstairs in her townhouse.

THIRTY-EIGHT

THE NEXT PLACE JOSEPH Chaplin had found for them was an old rural Maryland motel with a red flickering sign that read PIKE MOTEL. For Charles Mallory, it had at least one advantage over a hotel—private outdoor entrances, so they could enter and leave discreetly. Mallory had Room 321. Blaine's room was downstairs, 217.

Chaplin had left both rooms unlocked, the keys beneath the bibles in the drawers of the bedside tables. In Mallory's room, he had also left a Beretta 9mm handgun under one of the pillows, as requested.

The rain had turned to a soft drizzle again and there was a fresh-laundry smell of ozone in the afternoon breeze, mixed with the acidic scent of the soil. Mallory carried up a mushroom and green pepper pizza, which Blaine had told him was her favorite, along with a bottle of merlot, sodas, paper plates, plastic silverware, and napkins.

In Room 321, he flipped open his computer and resumed searches on the seven names. He had begun to think about the case differently, coming at it from a new direction—considering who the perpetrator might be rather than who the victims had been.

At 5:22, one of his phones vibrated. Pat Hanratty.

"It was absolutely marvelous to see you again yesterday, dear," she said.

"Yes, it was fun."

"Although I think we may be in trouble now."

"How do you mean?" *Her voice isn't quite right*, Mallory thought. *Her words sounded slurred.*

"I called in a favor, as I said." She laughed. "I think I might have something for you."

"Okay." Mallory pushed aside the computer and opened his note-book. "Go ahead."

"I talked with my friend," she said. "And she reminded me of a couple of things I had forgotten. And then, I looked though my files. Some of what you wanted to know, I had right here at home. Are you ready, dear?"

"Please. Fire away."

"For starters, FAST was not a project, it was a private databank for storm information. It's one of the things Deborah Piper was always on about. That's what they used for these simulations. And you're right, dear, Cloudcover did change after 9/11. In the spring of 2002, it expanded. There were two research facilities associated with the project. One in Wyoming, the other in Alaska."

Mallory jotted notes in shorthand in his notebook.

"Buried in Project Cloudcover's budget was something else, though," she said. "Which actually became quite a bit larger. It had a separate name."

"Okay."

"It was called the Leviathan Project. Its objective was to, quote, create a storm and then take it apart. That part was classified."

"But we're talking computer simulations still, right?"

"No, dear, that's the thing. Beginning in 2002, it changed. They tried to turn the computer simulations into actual working models, altering elements of existing weather patterns or storms to bring about an intended result. That was Leviathan."

"To *literally* build a storm and take it apart?"

"Yes. That's right. That's what I'm told. Although, you see, it still went under the rubric of 'research.' The facilities in Wyoming and Alaska were both designed to manipulate storm systems in the same way the computer models predicted."

"Are you sure about this?"

"I have memos referencing it, dear. Which I'm sending to you."

"All right. And this was NOAA? What branch of govern-ment—?"

"A joint project, involving NOAA, the Defense Department, and the CIA. But which relied heavily on private sector contractors, from what I can see."

"The Defense Department?"

"That's right, dear. I found a document that Deb Piper sent me which includes the names of two of the companies involved. One of them was Raytheon. The other was called EARS, which stands for Energy and Atmospheric Research Systems."

Another connection. EARS was tied to two of the names on the list, Mallory recalled.

"Okay, so what happened to it?"

"Happened to what, dear?"

"This project, I mean. Leviathan. What happened to it?"

"Oh. Well." He heard the clinking of ice in a glass. "It became inactive in 2005, I'm told. The government's involvement in the Alaska project unofficially stopped at the end of December 2004. Although it remained funded for a number of months. The other part, in Wyoming, was phased out more gradually. Some of it was purchased and is now part of something called the Weathervane Group."

Mallory was scribbling frantically. "Okay. So there were two parts. Do you know what each one did? Specifically?"

"In general terms? Yes. The Alaska project involved ELFs."

"Elves?"

"Yes."

"Like Santa's helpers?"

"No. ELFs," she said, the slur in her voice accentuated by her attempt to be emphatic. "Extremely low frequency radio waves. Ionospheric radio signals. The Wyoming project experimented with lasers."

"What kinds of experiments are we talking about?"

"It's in the memos, dear."

"All right." Suddenly, the list was making a new kind of sense. "That's great, Pat. And where did these memos come from?"

"Deb."

"Pardon?"

"Piper. She sent them to me long ago and I haven't thought about them in years. But maybe you will find them useful. I'm in trouble, of course, if any of this gets out."

"I am, too," Mallory said. "Don't worry. Any chance of sending them to me electronically?"

"I just have, dear. As PDFs. Can you open those?"

"Yes," he said. "I'm eternally grateful."

"Eternity's a long time, dear. I'd be willing to settle for a year." After a pause, she laughed.

"Okay," he said. "Deal."

Less than two minutes later, Mallory was scrolling through the PDFs. Eleven memos. Three of them from Deborah Piper, vaguely questioning the motives behind the Wyoming Cloudcover facility. Four were from a "project administer" named Rajiv Gupta, full of technical details about satellite laser ranging, providing such insights as: "current measurements of the products of gravitational constants reveal that such measurements do not progress secularly;" and "the concurrent readings confirm an effective separation between altimeter system drift and long-term changes at the sub-cm level."

Nine of the memos provided nothing that seemed useful to Charles Mallory. But the other two were pay dirt.

THIRTY-NINE

MEMORANDUM FOR: *January 11, 2004*
FROM: *Frank Johnson, assistant administrator, Leviathan Project*
TO: *Roger Grimm, office of Clark Easton, Assistant Secretary of Defense*
SUBJECT: *Addendum to Leviathan Project Review*

This reiterates the concerns raised today in our conversation about the objectives of the Leviathan Project. The project administrator's report makes clear that this operation does in fact consist of two primary processes, both of which are expected to be tested on an experimental basis by the summer of 2005.

The objective of the first process is to develop the capability to create and then take apart a hurricane-force event in the Pacific Ocean. The foundation for this is more than four years of simulations modeled and compiled through Project Cloudcover.

The objective of the second process, as stated in the administrator's review, has only one part. It is to create a finite event that occurs very suddenly. In other words, an event that cannot be mitigated or taken apart because it gives no warning and is over within a few minutes.

Considering that the original objective of Leviathan was the first process and the first process alone, I would urge that we place an immediate hold on research into the second process until we have more thoroughly evaluated it and how it has been carried out.

Further, the initial purpose of the facility in Alaska was, according to a May 23, 2002, memo from the Secretary of Defense, to "measure and better understand tectonic plate convection in the Earth's mantle" and, *more generally, to "study Earth's interior processes." This original objective related to computer models showing the effects of cooler water being pumped to the ocean surface during a hurricane.*

The work going on there now has clearly strayed from this objective.

I strongly suggest shutting down the Alaska facility and implementing an internal review and audit of Environmental Atmospheric Research Systems, the contractor that has taken the lead there.

The feeling here is that not enough data exists regarding the second process and that more evaluation is needed before trials should go forward. I am also questioning exactly when, how, and why this process became part of the Leviathan Project.

MEMORANDUM FOR January 5, 2005
FROM: Frank Johnson, assistant administrator, Leviathan Project
TO: Clark Easton, Assistant Secretary of Defense
SUBJECT: Reassessment of Leviathan Project

As you know, the government's involvement in the Alaska portion of the Leviathan Project was shut down on December 27, 2004, in part because of concerns about the lead contractor, EARS. However, the project continues, and remains funded in large part at least through the current fiscal year by a Defense Department allocation.

On two prior occasions over the past year, I have expressed concerns to Roger Grimm, in your office, about the lack of oversight on this operation. I was particularly concerned that the project has gone far beyond its stated goal, which was to "measure and better understand tectonic plate convection in the Earth's mantle" and to study "Earth's interior processes." When and how did the "second process" of the Leviathan Project come about?

My feeling remains that it is in our interests to undertake a complete evaluation of the Alaska facility, its objectives and its project administrator. I do not think the withdrawal of the government's active participation is alone sufficient. I would be pleased to discuss my concerns with you at greater length.

Mallory re-read the memos, carefully considering what they told him—and what they didn't. Then he called up a search engine and entered a name. It took just three minutes to find a rudimentary

biography of Frank Johnson. Earlier, they had found detailed information about Frank Johnson, the Canadian physicist who had
worked for the National Center for Atmospheric Research in Colorado. Professional and personal data, including the fact that he had
died suddenly, in 2010, of a heart attack. Name number six on the
list provided by Keri Westlake. Except it had been the wrong Frank
Johnson. This Frank Johnson was an optical systems engineer, less
well-known. He had worked for Ball Aerospace and Technologies
Corporation for several years, then joined NASA. For much of 2003
and 2004, he worked on a government project called Leviathan, as a
liaison with EARS. He was found dead in a wooded region of central
North Carolina, with a single bullet wound to the head, on February 5, 2005—one month after writing a memo titled "Reassessment
of Leviathan Project." A newspaper account at the time speculated
that his death might have been "a hunting-related accident." The
case was never solved.

Mallory was startled from his thoughts by a rap on the motel
room door.

Three hard knocks.

He shut down the computer and lifted his Beretta from the table.

His heart was pounding as he stood to the side of the door, gun
raised.

He listened as the knock come again. Twice this time.

"Who is it?" he said.

IN THE CLEVELAND Park section of Washington, Blaine's chief of
staff, Jamie Griffith, got up from the sofa in his boss's living room to
fetch a bottle of iced tea from Blaine's refrigerator. Then he settled
on the sofa again and dove right back into David McCullough's biography of John Adams.

FORTY

CATHERINE BLAINE'S FACE WAS flushed, her blue nylon wind-breaker beaded with raindrops. She was standing under the concrete awning. Rain pounded the parking lot behind her.

"Come in," Mallory said.

She hung her jacket in the bathroom. She was wearing a beige tailored suit and a white shirt, a couple of buttons open. Rainwater dripped from her hair.

She stood near the center of the room and let her nose twitch. "Pizza?"

Mallory nodded. He pointed to the box on the counter. "You said mushroom and green peppers, right?"

Blaine smiled. "That's nice."

They sat at the wooden coffee table and pulled slices of pizza onto paper plates.

"I brought some merlot, too," he said. He lifted a bottle from the paper bag and examined the label. "Pretty good year, I'm told."

"I shouldn't."

"I know. But you'll join me anyway, for one glass, right? It'll help fortify us. See, I even brought some fancy wineglasses."

He reached into the bag again and produced two plastic stem glasses that he had purchased at Walgreens for $2.29 apiece.

"Well, half a glass wouldn't hurt."

Mallory poured the wine. They toasted and sipped.

"So," he said. "Tell me what happened?"

"Mm hmm." Blaine sighed and looked away, then sighed again. "It's a done deal," she said.

"How done?"

"All the way. The President's on board. They want him to go on television tomorrow, announcing the consortium, explaining the mitigation."

"Not good."

"No."

As they ate, Blaine told him the rest. The four mitigation procedures. The terms of the deal proposed by Mr. Zorn. The strange acquiescence from the President, Easton and DeVries.

"Harold DeVries knows something that he's not telling me," she said. "I can't figure out what it is."

"How about the others?"

"I don't know. I'm really disappointed in all of them, in how easily they're going along with this. I'm trying to see it from their point of view, but I can't."

She lifted the wineglass and took in the room for a moment. Looked at him and smiled. "Feels kind of funny being in a motel room like this," she said.

"Like what?"

Blaine shrugged. "Nothing. Never mind." She looked at his opened notepad on the desk. The dark computer monitor. "What are you doing?"

"Oh." He reached for another slice. "Figuring something. Two things, really."

"Yeah? Tell me about it."

"What did you mean about feeling funny being in a motel room?"

"I don't know." She shared a look with him. "I mean. It kind of feels like I'm playing hooky." She pointed her wine glass at his notebook. "Tell me what you're figuring."

"I'm figuring where this probably started," he said. "That's one of the things. Here, I want to show you something."

They wiped their hands using the pile of napkins that came with the pizza. Then he turned on the computer, and called up the two memos from Frank Johnson, and passed it to Blaine. He watched her eyes as she scrolled through the memos. Then went back to the top and read them again.

"Where did you get these?"

"I have a source, a whistleblower of sorts, who knew Deborah Piper," he said. "She worked as an intelligence analyst for years. She was often outraged by what she saw and heard. Some people think she's a crazy old lady, but she's not. She's smart as a whip. But so eccentric that people don't see it."

Blaine was carefully re-reading the memos, as if memorizing them, he saw.

"But there's still no connection with Volkov here, is there?" she said, at last. "Or Victor Zorn?"

"No. That's the second thing."

"What second thing?"

"The part I think I have wrong."

"Oh?"

"What you just told me, about the mitigation, helps explain it."

She was still frowning at him.

Mallory said, "They told you about four procedures for dismantling or mitigating a storm, right? But nothing about the technology to *create* a storm or a weather event."

"No," she said. "That's not what they're selling." Blaine drank the last of her wine and set the plastic glass down.

"That's it, then," he said. "That's how they pulled this off."

"What do you mean?"

"I mean, there are two completely separate components to this consortium. But they're only talking about one. They're only *selling* one. The prominent scientists have signed on to the concept of deconstructing a storm. Using weather technology to make the world a better place. To prevent droughts and heat waves. Slow down hurricanes, prevent tornadoes. I'm speculating here but it must have all been presented in a very attractive way, with lots of capital and plenty of hype behind it."

"Okay."

"Nothing was said about the offensive capability because those scientists weren't involved in that part. My guess is that Dr. Clayton doesn't know that the storm they are attempting to deconstruct may have in fact been artificially constructed."

Blaine nodded once, and looked away. "Yes, I thought about that."

"Which is why they're so adamant about keeping this within a very tight circle. They're doing both things simultaneously. If you hadn't stepped out of the circle, this may have all worked out on their terms."

"It still might."

"Yes, it might."

"But the ability to create a storm and the ability to mitigate a storm are two different things, right?"

"Yes," he said. "That's what's starting to worry me. Especially when I try to put myself inside their heads."

"Why?"

"I mean, how did they gain credibility with the President? Obviously, by accurately predicting these events. Showing they have this seemingly godlike power over nature. Therefore, it's reasonable to assume that, up until now, at least, they have placed a greater value on being able to *create* these events than on being able to mitigate them."

"But if they can't mitigate them, they can't do business."

"True. But we're talking percentages. Storm enhancement versus storm mitigation. Somehow, I don't think the emphasis, for them, has been fifty–fifty. Because, from what you just said, the storms they broke up in the Pacific were nothing on the scale of the event they're causing right now."

"What are you saying?"

"I mean, think about it."

"I am. That's not a very encouraging thought."

"No, it's not. On the other hand, it might work to our advantage. The scientists who are part of this are doing it because they're working on the defensive end, not the offensive end. They don't know that this storm is, in effect, an unprecedented act of terrorism. Terrorism disguised as a natural disaster."

"Right."

"So if we show them there *is* another side to it, maybe they can be persuaded to help us."

"Isn't it sort of late for that?"

"It may be. I'm trying not to think in those terms," Mallory said. "If my guy Chaplin can get a message to Dr. Clayton, for instance, with the recreated texts of the emails—to show them what's really going on—maybe we can even get him to help us. Can you do that?"

"I already have. I'll forward them to you." She stood, and surprised him, then, by cleaning up, with a sudden urgency, washing the plastic glasses in the bathroom sink. Setting their plates in the trash. "I better go," she said, turning to him. "I need to call my son and get my bearings for a few minutes. Thanks for dinner."

Mallory shrugged. "Just something I threw together."

He gave her the second room number, explaining about the key.

Blaine took her windbreaker from the bathroom and draped it over her right arm. Something seemed to hold her there, though. "What's the part you think you might have wrong?"

"Oh." He glanced at his notebook. In the next instant, one of his cell phones vibrated. Pat Hanratty. He decided not to take it.

"Volkov," he said. "That this was all about Volkov."

She frowned. "But you said you got that from a good source."

"A source who got it second-hand but didn't have the whole story yet. I'm afraid I've been looking too hard at the wrong thing."

"How so?"

"I've just assumed Volkov and his organization orchestrated the emails. I'm starting to think that he probably couldn't have."

"Why?"

"It's too far outside his realm of expertise. Or interest. Why target this so specifically to these particular Cabinet members? For one thing, it's difficult to do. This is an internal email system, not the Internet. But more than that, it's not the sort of thing he'd think of."

"Okay, so he hired Janus, or someone using his identity."

"He may have hired someone. Not Janus. Or else the idea came from someone else. Someone working *with* Volkov."

"On the emails."

"On everything. A more or less equal partner, let's say. Remember what you said when I asked you what surprised you most about all this? You said what surprised you most was the President."

"Yeah," Blaine said. "Because it feels reckless. It doesn't make sense."

Mallory nodded. "It *doesn't* make sense. He's a careful, highly intelligent, and rational person, right? Politically astute. Comfortable in the international arena. A good husband, family man."

"Yeah, all of that. That's *why* it doesn't make sense."

"Unless he's doing something other than what we think he's doing."

Blaine glanced at the silent television. Saw the color-enhanced radar spirals of Alexander's outer bands swirling counter-clockwise toward the East Coast of the United States. The storm was now the only news story in the country that mattered, it seemed. Blaine read the scroll at the bottom of the screen: ENTIRE EAST COAST UNDER HURRICANE WARNING.

"You mean, he may know what's really happening."

"Maybe."

"And he's deliberately letting it go forward?"

"It's possible."

"Why?"

Mallory found himself unable to meet her eyes. He was still thinking it through. "I don't know that part yet."

Her face flushed. "But you're implying that the partner is someone inside. That he's one of the people in the room with us, in other words?"

"I don't know. It's a possibility."

"Or the President himself."

"Probably not," he said. "But possible."

"There's just one problem with it," Blaine said.

"I know."

"Do you?"

"Yes. Motivation."

"Mmm hmm."

"I don't have that part yet. I'm working on it."

Blaine looked at the gusts of rain through the crack in the drapes. Mallory glanced at his phone, wondering where his brother was. What he was doing. Neither of them spoke for a while.

At last, Blaine said, "If it's true, then you know what that means?"

AT HIS HOME in Adams Morgan, the assassin answered his secure cell phone after the first ring. He wasn't the assassin this evening, though. He was on the other side of the partition again, watching the storm on the Weather Channel, and eating redskin peanuts from a can.

"We have two new security issues," his commander said.

He glanced at the clock on the wall of his kitchen, and the calendar beneath it. Scenes of Italy. A regatta on the Grand Canal. A place he intended to visit once this thing was finished.

"I have a track on Jon Mallory," he said. "I think I can get him before this storm hits."

He listened to the other man breathing on the other end.

"No, we've got something else, unfortunately. This will have to take priority. This needs to happen first."

Protect the mission.

"Go ahead."

"I know there are meetings ahead and that this is an awkward time, but it has to be—"

"There are no meetings," the assassin said, angry that he'd mention this.

"No, there aren't. Good."

The other man was controlling him, motivating him.

"Catherine Blaine has become a problem," he said. "She's going to try to poison the deal."

The assassin listened to the rain on the window. He was a soldier again, being summoned to a mission. "Can she do that?"

"No, not really. But she could after the fact. She's found out about Mr. Zorn's background. And, presumably, the rest of it."

"How?"

"That's the second problem."

"Okay."

He listened to the other man breathe.

"His name is Charles Mallory. He's a former CIA field agent and special ops man, and he's in town right now, digging into this."

"Because of his brother?"

"Because of his brother. He's apparently starting to go pretty deep."

The assassin took a long breath. "It can be done, but it's going to be delicate."

"Yes, I know, but we need it done. They'll have to be Jimmy Hoffas."

"How soon?"

"Tonight would be convenient."

"It's going to be delicate," the assassin said again, feeling the adrenaline kick in, a wicked potion sweeping through him.

"I understand. But in the context of the storm, maybe it won't be so delicate. There are going to be hundreds of casualties. These will just be two of them."

The assassin nodded to himself. Yes. The other man was in charge of strategy. And as strategies go, this was a pretty good one. No, it was an ingenious one.

THE LEVIATHAN EFFECT 225

"This, I think, could finally be the end of it."

"All right," he said, waiting. "Go ahead."

"Here's how it works: One will lead to the other. Blaine is with him now. I don't know where. She's got a decoy at her apartment. She's somewhere else."

"All right."

A few seconds later, the phone clicked off. The assassin looked out at the rain falling on Eighteenth Street in Adams Morgan. He got his jacket from the hall closet and prepared to drive to the farmhouse, where he stored his disguises in a large cedar closet.

FORTY-ONE

MALLORY STUDIED CATHERINE BLAINE'S intent gaze as she stood with one hand on the motel room doorknob, leg cocked.

"What does it mean?" he said.

"If it's true, if someone within the circle is involved, it means that I may have really just screwed up. *Big time*, as my son likes to say."

"How so?"

"By challenging him. By alluding to Volkov, questioning Victor Zorn's background in front of them. By calling the project into question."

"Maybe," he said. "Or maybe not."

"Or maybe not. Right." She pulled the door out several inches and glanced at the rain. "I need to call my son. Give me a few minutes, okay? I want to go to the other room and decompress."

"Sure. How long?"

"Twenty minutes."

Mallory looked at the clock. 5:43 P.M.

"Okay. Twenty minutes," he said. "Want me to walk you down?"

"I'm fine."

"Sure?"

Blaine smiled at him and turned. Rain streamed past the concrete overhang and he saw the red glow of the motel sign on the wet pavement. Felt the cold air seeping into the room.

"Be careful."

"Thanks," she said, "for the pizza and wine."

"Oh, it was nothing."

He watched through the window as she walked to the stairwell and disappeared. He pulled the drapes closed and clicked on his cell phone. Watched the storm on television for several minutes, and read through the memos again. Then he called Hanratty.

"Good heavens. What an intrigue you've pulled me into, dear." She sounded slurry again. "I'm just afraid I'm going to get into some bloody trouble over this, if it continues. But it's most intriguing. Any-way, this will have to be my last call."

"I don't want you to be in trouble."

"But I've found a few more details on your project, dear." He heard her rustling papers, breathing heavily. "It had two parts, I'm told. One was in Wyoming and the other in Alaska."

"Okay." Had she forgotten she'd already told him this?

"All right? Now. One was to create a disturbance with under-ground ELFs. That's what they were called. That part was in Alaska. It was a division of the Air Force, apparently, partnering with both Defense and private industry."

"Yes, you told me that. The project ran for three years."

"Three?" He heard a shuffling of papers again. "I don't know, let me see. It might have been three. Yes. No. Less, actually. Hold on. Let me look at my notes for a second. Okay. Let me just—are you still there?"

"I'm here."

"Okay. It was started in January of 2002. All right? The project became inactive, then, at the end of 2004. But the entire project was funded into 2005. Let's see, the Wyoming facility was then turned over in 2005 to a private research firm. And the government got out of both."

"What's the firm?"

"What?"

"What was the private research firm?"

"Oh. Well, I don't know that, dear."

"Who oversaw the two parts of the project? Were you able to find out who the project administrators were?"

"The project administrators? I've got that, yes. Let me just find it, dear. Okay. All right, the Wyoming facility was run by a Roger Grimm, of the Department of Defense. The Alaska facility was run by Thomas Rorbach, who was the director of a company called EARS. We already talked about that. He was the project administra-tor in Alaska."

Really. "And what do you know about Rorbach?"

"Rorbach? Nothing, dear."

Another silence. He said, "Look, I've got someone on my other line. I've got to go. I'm very grateful to you and I'll make it up."

"For one year, we agreed."

"Yes, although don't forget, I offered eternity."

Mallory let her go, feeling a jolt of adrenaline. He sat, called up the file of names on his computer again. Scrolled through them, studying his notes.

He was startled by a knock on the door. He reached for his gun and became completely still, listening.

Then he looked at his watch.

It was 6:04.

CATHERINE BLAINE SLID in the room and closed the door, bringing a cool scent of rain from her jacket and hair. Her first breath inside was vapor. Mallory saw that something had changed again.

"I'm going back to meet with him," she said.

"What do you mean? Who?"

"The President. I have to." Her eyes moved quickly, taking in the room. "I have to know if you're right. I have to know what he's really thinking."

Mallory watched her, his heart rate still returning to normal. A cold breath of outdoors seemed to linger around her. "Want me to go with you?"

"No. I just called him. I need to go alone." He saw the flecks of fluid gold around her green pupils and had a warm feeling toward her, admiring her sense of purpose; but worried for her, too.

"I just got one more piece of this thing," he said.

"Did you?"

"Yes. Something that sort of changes it again."

He told her about Hanratty's call. And then about Rorbach.

"Jesus!" she said. "Rorbach's the one heading up this Janus committee."

"I know."

"So do you understand the list now?"

"Better. More than I did."

"You still don't have the other part, though. Motivation."

"No. Not yet."

She twisted the knob, then turned to him. "I'll call you when we're finished, okay?" she said.

Mallory watched through the drapes again as she splashed across the lot to her Ford rental. The lights came on, the taillights reflecting off the pavement as she quickly backed up and pulled onto the Pike, disappearing in the rain. He felt guilty for several moments that he had let her go. Thinking about people he had lost. And almost lost.

He thought about the first time he had met Blaine, seven years earlier, on the sixth floor of CIA headquarters, in the woods of Langley, Virginia. He'd seen something then, as they had listened to a briefing on cyber-security, that had stuck with him. Something determined and restless. A subtle shade of dismissal and impatience in her eyes, as if she could not accept all the answers she was being given, but knew enough not to become argumentative. Diplomat and truth-seeker, trying to co-exist.

Eyes like that he didn't forget. They were eyes that saw things other people missed. Things that mattered. Usually, with time and the practicalities of getting older, the diplomat won out. But Blaine's eyes had not dulled in seven years. She still saw what wasn't quite there, the things that might be coming. And, when she looked at him, she sometimes seemed to see a potential ally. At least that's what he was beginning to think. To hope.

JON MALLORY LIFTED up the blinds and gazed at the storm—drenching rains, crackling veins of lightning above the rolling farm fields. He turned to the view on television—surge waves pummeling beaches in the Carolinas, submerging coastal roads. Two scenes, distant but related, parts of the same system. Then he got an idea; often that was how things worked for him—when he wasn't trying; when he'd turned off the thinking part of his brain.

He called up a file on his computer and sifted through the email Dr. Keri Westlake had sent. Bits and pieces of information, opinions, observations.

By the time Chaplin arrived with his dinner, Jon knew how he was going to tell this story.

"Greetings," Chaplin said.

"Greetings."

Jon watched him set their two deli sandwiches and sodas beside the television and hang his slicker in the bathroom. He wore a dark turtleneck and pinstripe trousers, wing-tip shoes. "So." Chaplin brushed his shoulders and placed his hands together as if praying. "How are you making out here, Jon?"

"Considering everything, not bad."

"Hungry?"

"Not terribly."

Chaplin looked quickly around the room, frowning at the clutter—soda cans, newspaper pages, magazines, paperback books. "We've been able to make use of your cell phone," he said.

"Oh?"

"Yes. I activated it. And moved your car. Both the car and your phone are now at the same location. Under surveillance."

"Where's that?"

"A motel off of Interstate 95 in Virginia. Days Inn. Perhaps where you would be now if we hadn't assisted you." He showed a grudging smile.

Jon winced. He still wasn't sure quite how to take Joseph Chaplin. "Is this something my brother authorized?"

He nodded ambiguously. "I made an executive decision," he said. He walked to the window and looked out at the rain in the darkening countryside. "We'll keep a watch on the location. Hopefully, he'll come to the trap and we'll at least learn who he is."

"He."

"The man who wanted to kill you." Chaplin turned to face him. Jon wondered how much he should tell Chaplin. But he knew he had to pass the story now to his brother; Chaplin was the conduit.

"Actually, I think I already know that," he said.

Chaplin's face went suddenly steely. "You do."

"Yeah, I think I know who was hunting me. The bearded man."

Chaplin looked at the window, the telephone, the computer.

"Did you call or email someone?"

"No, you asked me not to."

"How could you have figured it out locked in this room, then?"

"It's all right here," Jon said, touching the flash drive sticking out from his laptop. "And here," he added, tapping his right temple.

Chaplin's face tightened. "You're saying that you know who it is, the man who was pursuing you?"

"I think so. More importantly, I think I know why these people were killed. But I need to get that information to my brother."

Chaplin waited a beat, then adopted a more officious manner. "All right," he said, his posture straightening. "Let's get to it. Give it to me and I'll send him an encrypted email."

Jon sat at the desk and wrote down what he had discovered, pausing at one point to look at the rain. Feeling where he belonged at last: living in the story.

FORTY-TWO

CATHERINE BLAINE DROVE THROUGH the rain-soaked streets of downtown Washington to Fifteenth Street, where she pulled in through the southwest gates to the White House. She parked on Executive Drive, where a waiting security guard accompanied her to the gate house and a Secret Service agent signed her in.

A Jeep Liberty was parked four blocks from the entrance, at the curb along Fifteenth Street.

The man behind the wheel watched Blaine's car as it passed through the White House gates and came to a stop on the other side. The assassin leaned back and watched the rain. All he had to do now was wait.

PRESIDENT AARON LINCOLN Hall, dressed in shirtsleeves, gazed at her through the dim, rain-filtered light from the south windows. It was more than five hours since they had made the agreement. His eyes were bloodshot and puffy, but still alert.

"I've just had another briefing with Dr. Wu," he said. "The projections, I'm afraid, are terrifying. We've already suffered some big losses in the Carolinas."

Blaine thought about her parents, glad that they'd gotten out in time, headed to the mountains of Tennessee. She wondered if their house would survive. "It hasn't begun to diminish yet, in other words."

"No. I'm to have an update from Mr. Zorn in less than two hours. Then one in the morning at eight. And every two hours after that. The big change is supposed to happen overnight. But Jim Wu is telling me now he doesn't think this mitigation is going to work. Can't work, he says." She looked at the television monitor behind him, showing a feed from the Data Visualization Center across the street.

"You're surprised I told him."

"Yes," she said. "You said you wanted it to stay in our tight circle."

The President rubbed his temples, his hands hiding his eyes.

"I needed another expert opinion, Cate. An outside opinion."

"I can relate to that," she said.

"I'm told this thing is about to become larger than any North Atlantic storm system we've ever seen. Potentially twice as large. We're starting to get doomsday stuff all over the Internet. A preacher in Alabama is telling people that Alexander is God coming to collect our overdue debts. There's a professor in New Jersey who's saying New York City is going to be washed to sea. Another preacher wrote on his blog that two percent of the people on the East Coast are going to be raptured."

"What about the other ninety-eight percent?"

"They're going to drown." The President shook his head. "There are already lots of people saying this thing was created by the government. We'll be hearing plenty more of that."

"No doubt."

"I want this to work, Cate," he said, turning, showing the matinee idol profile. "I want to stop this."

"I think we all want that, sir."

The President lifted his coffee cup, sipped, and set it down. He seemed uncertain and, maybe, scared. Blaine had never seen him like this before.

"Jim Wu walked me through all the computer projections. Landfall is expected now in about—" He glanced quickly at the clock on his desk. "Fifty-one hours. Most of the spaghetti models have it hitting due east of us. Maybe a little to the north. Although one projection has the damn thing coming up the Chesapeake Bay and putting Washington under ten feet of water. Can you believe that? Making it uninhabitable. A lost city like Atlantis."

"What's happening with evacuations?" Blaine said.

He gave her a look. Evacuations were technically *her* territory, as head of Homeland Security; but he had taken away her authority.

"Everything's activated. Mandatory evacuations up and down the coast. We'll see what happens overnight. I don't think any of us will be sleeping much tonight." He forced a smile.

"Probably not, sir."

The President took another sip of coffee. "I've been getting a bit of a history lesson here," he went on. "I'm told this thing could be a Category Five when it makes landfall. Do you how many Cat Five storms have ever made landfall in the United States, Cate?"

"Three, I think."

"Three. That's right." He looked at her quickly. "The Labor Day hurricane in 1935 that hit Miami. Camille in 1969, which hit Louisiana, I believe. And Andrew, in 1992. Katrina was only a Three when it hit land."

"Yes, that's right."

"Do you know what was the world's deadliest hurricane ever, Cate?"

"Wasn't that the Bhola Cyclone in 1970?"

"Yes, right. Exactly."

"We've been reading the same article again, haven't we?"

He looked at his coffee cup and sighed. "Half a million people lost their lives in that thing. We have no frame of reference for a disaster of that magnitude. *Our* deadliest was Galveston in 1900. Eight thousand casualties, but that was mostly because we had no warning system then. Katrina was responsible for eighteen *hundred* deaths. They're telling me this could top Bhola, if it keeps on track. We've never had that kind of disaster, Cate. Nothing even remotely close. It's really beyond our ability to comprehend."

The President watched her expectantly.

"I know there's a reason you didn't want to have the conversation I initiated earlier," she told him. "I probably should have been with you one hundred percent. For what it's worth, I apologize."

"You were acting on what you thought was the best available information, Cate."

Blaine made a face. Had she been?

Then the President said the last thing she expected him to say. "Cate, we know about Vladimir Volkov." His eyes narrowed, watching her.

"What? You *know* about him?"

"Yes."

For a moment, Blaine was speechless. "How long?"

"Not long. A couple of weeks. I maybe should have made that clear to you earlier. I didn't know you were going to bring it up. I had no intention of making this deal, Cate. Of going through with it. Not on their terms."

Past tense.

"You *know* about Volkov."

"We don't know all the details. We don't know where he is or how exactly he pulled this off. But we know this is his project. And in a sense we have no choice but to accept his terms. For now."

So he was trying to lay a trap for Volkov. That was why he seemed so compliant.

"Our intelligence is continuing to provide useful information, just not fast enough. Most of it's needles-in-a-haystack stuff." He looked at her differently, as if making an assessment. Blaine nodded, staying with him. "I don't have to tell you, this is potentially an enormous setback for the country, Cate. And I'm just trying to do what I can to hold on."

Intelligence. Meaning DeVries.

"*How* do you know?"

"About Volkov? We have an informant. Someone who gave us a piece of information about him. About how he's doing it. It's a complicated game, Cate, and Volkov is obviously an ingenious adversary. I just can't afford to make a wrong move at this stage."

An elementary surveillance technique: observe the enemy's behavior until you're able to learn the identity and location of the enemy's leaders. That was the President's chess game.

"So that's why you kept moving forward."

"It was the only avenue to information. We didn't know enough. We still don't. We still don't know how and where it really operates. If we don't play by their rules, they beat us. They win a cold war that the public never saw. We can't afford that."

"No, I understand."

"Good."

"That's why you were so adamant about keeping it within this group."

"No." He leaned forward; for a moment, the rain shadows swam

ominously across his face. "No, the *other side* was adamant. If we'd
allowed it to go public or if we had in any way violated their terms,
he might have backed away and probably would have let the storm
do its damage. He may be doing that now, I don't know. I hope to
hell not."

"Did you transfer the down payment? Is that done?"

He nodded. "Of course. We've done our end. As I said earlier, five
billion dollars is the least of our worries. I assume we'll know more
in a couple hours."

Blaine considered that.

"We had Victor Zorn on the radar, too," the President continued.
He clasped his hands. "Before Volkov. We'd never been able to get
that close to him before, either. We were actually surprised that he
came in to do the negotiation himself."

That was why no one had pressed him. They wanted him to think
they had bought his illusion.

"There's another reason you didn't want dissension, though,
wasn't there?" Blaine said. "It's because you didn't want to raise the
suspicions of someone in the room with us."

She watched the President shift in his chair, turning away for a
moment. Finally, he nodded. "We've been carefully building a case.
Although I can't get into details."

Someone in the room. Theoretically, it could have been any of
them. Four men with strong, quiet ambitions. Stanton an affable
man, who desired the presidency. DeVries a brilliant international-
ist, who felt he deserved a larger role in US foreign policy. Easton a
loyal but forceful tactician, who wanted to pull the administration's
most important strings from backstage. The President a competent,
popular leader in search of a cause that could lift him to greatness.

But only one of the four really made sense.

"How did they get Garland? Clayton? The other scientists on
board? That's what I don't get."

"Venture capital at Garland's level depends largely on high-level
references," the President said. "If a heavyweight in the defense
industry recommends a contractor, it carries a lot of weight. If they
get one on board, it becomes easier to get two. It started there, with
a handful of defense contractors. Then they managed to recruit a
consultant or two. From there, it became a domino effect."

Only one of them had those connections, Blaine thought.

"So, Easton," she said.

He furrowed his brow, but didn't say anything.

"Why? Why would he do this? What would be his motivation?"

"I couldn't say, Cate." He looked off, at the television across the room, avoiding her eyes, and her question.

After a while, Blaine said, "I wonder, too, why they decided to bring me in to the mix."

The President was nodding. "I suspect because there was a degree of doubt somewhere. Maybe they felt that you would tip the scales; that, based on your background, you'd urge us to sign on with this emerging science. They also thought you'd be blindly loyal." He winked. "They were wrong on both counts. It's about the only mistake they've made so far."

He swiveled toward the South Lawn and the Washington Monument again. "We made the deal for two reasons, Cate. Most importantly, to stop that," he said, nodding toward the storm. "Secondly, to learn the rest of it. To get Zorn in the room was a bonus."

"Zorn is Volkov's proxy."

"Mmm." The President turned back to her, showing no expression. "Actually, he's more than that, Cate."

"What do you mean?"

His eyes flattened. "He's Volkov's son."

FORTY-THREE

CHARLES MALLORY RECEIVED THE encrypted email from Chaplin with his brother's message and immediately went back to the list of names, discerning patterns he hadn't recognized—the cross clues completing connections that hadn't made sense before. What emerged was a grid of intersecting points dating back nearly two decades. Two biographies intertwined in ways that had never drawn attention to themselves. Military. Government. Private sector. For eighteen years, Thom Rorbach had been Clark Easton's lieutenant, working for him behind the scenes, in some cases doing the difficult and dirty jobs that Easton couldn't do himself. Easton had hired his firm, EARS, to manage the Alaska arm of Leviathan, and he had made Rorbach the project administrator. Later, he had brought him back into government, first on the National Security Council staff and then creating a hybrid job for him in the Department of Defense, where he worked now.

But what would Rorbach be doing for him tonight? Mallory felt a current of apprehension rush through him as he realized the answer to his question.

"SO HAROLD DEVRIES knew, too," Blaine said, watching the President.

"Yes."

"But not the Vice President."

"No one else knows."

"Why didn't you bring me up to speed?"

He sighed. "We simply didn't see that it was necessary. We actually thought you'd be on board. Harold thought that. I thought that. We miscalculated."

"Mr. Zorn is Volkov's son."

"Yes." He smiled unexpectedly. "Volkov has two daughters by his wife. He wanted a son to carry on his business. To be his front man. Mr. Zorn was groomed for years to do what he did today, apparently."

"What happens now? What's the next move?"

He let out his breath. "I'm hoping everything goes forward per the agreement. I'm hoping your brief dissension isn't going to bring the spaceship down. On the other hand, I'm afraid they could walk away from it."

Blaine held his gaze. "Let the storm go ahead and tear up the East Coast?"

"Possibly. In which case, on top of everything else, I'd be the victim of a five billion dollar scam, wouldn't I?" His eyes went to the window for a moment. "I'd love to send in a SEAL Six Team and take out Volkov, Cate. But, unfortunately, we don't know where he is. And we don't know how they operate. It's like a foreign language no one has heard before. It's a new kind of warfare. And make no mistake, Cate, this is war."

"So, what can we do?"

"Nothing. Nothing but wait. And to be honest with you, I don't care about a lot right now. If I'm able to stop this storm, I will do whatever needs to be done. If I have to go on television and make that speech, I'll do it. If we have to become partners, we'll become partners. If they want another billion dollars tomorrow, they've got it. I don't want the world's worst disaster on my hands. Or in this country's history books."

"Why do we assume they can actually stop this, though?" Blaine asked. "This is much larger than the storms in the Pacific."

"Yes, I know." His mouth tightened. "That's what worries me. We don't know, Cate. We're into the realm of faith now, I'm afraid."

They both turned their gazes to the television, and the giant, counterclockwise bands of wind that were threatening an unprecedented collision with the East Coast of the United States.

THE FORD FOCUS'S headlights lit up the swirls of rain as Catherine

Blaine drove out of the southeast gate of the White House and turned south along Fifteenth Street, toward Constitution Avenue.

The assassin pulled from the curb in his Jeep Liberty, keeping a block and a half to two blocks between them. Blaine took a right turn onto Constitution Avenue, then crossed the Memorial Bridge into Virginia. She entered the stream of traffic on George Washington Parkway and picked up speed, headed toward Maryland and the Capital Beltway. The assassin kept his eyes trained on her taillights.

He followed her around the Beltway into Maryland, exiting a quarter mile behind her onto a rural highway. The traffic was sparse, the lights flashing yellow. About a mile later, her taillights flared and her turn signal begin to blink off the wet sheen of the street. A convenience store. She was stopping at a convenience store.

The assassin pulled into the parking lot of a business park and cut his lights. He waited beneath a canopy of dripping trees and watched. From there he had a clear view of the 7-Eleven. *A straight shot.* If he'd wanted to stop her with an M24 sniper rifle, it would have been a splendid location. But he couldn't do that with her. This one had to be a Jimmy Hoffa. *Without a trace.*

He was fully engaged now. Nothing mattered but the target. He watched as she came out the door, head down, swinging a plastic bag. Hurrying back to the car in the rain. She had made it easier for him, eluding her security detail the way she did. It would be her fatal flaw, although Blaine did not know that yet.

Her headlights went on again, the taillights brightening as she pulled out. The killer waited until she was back on the pike before he switched on his own lights. He followed her from a distance again on the rolling two-lane highway. The target drove another mile and three quarters and then he saw her turn signal blinking again, her brake lights pumping. The Pike Motel. The assassin slowed in the right lane and followed her car into the lot. She drove around the building, parking under an overhang of trees near the rear stairwell, again making things easier for him. He counted the cars in the lot. Seven.

He rolled past the office and edged his SUV toward the stairwell. The target came out of her car and splashed toward the overhang, head down, bag swinging in one hand, purse over her shoulder. Walking along the stucco wall out of the rain toward the elevators. The assassin suddenly accelerated his Liberty, startling her, then braked abruptly. He clicked off his lights. Parked. Opened the door.

DR. JARED CLAYTON walked toward the Bourbon Steak restaurant just off the lobby at the Four Seasons hotel, but he stopped before going in. He had been instructed to wait until he saw a man wearing a black carnation and to follow him. As he did, Clayton saw Zorn's man move to intercede. If he had had doubts about working for Mr. Zorn before, they were confirmed now. He followed the man with the carnation out the revolving front door to Pennsylvania Avenue, where two Homeland Security police officers emerged from the back of a Lincoln limousine to block Zorn's security man. Dr. Clayton slid in the open door, and one of the men closed it. The car began to move, up Pennsylvania Avenue toward the White House.

FORTY-FOUR

8:27 P.M.

CATHERINE BLAINE HAD PURCHASED a bottle of aspirin, a small carton of orange juice, and a six-pack of Heineken at the 7-Eleven. She had not slept well in weeks, and knew that this night was going to be an especially long one. As she walked through the rain from her rental car to the motel stairwell, she was surprised by the throttle of an engine and the bright flash of headlights in her eyes. An SUV, stopping by the elevators. She shielded her eyes but kept moving. For a moment, she debated taking the elevator, but decided to walk. The pavement was slippery and she stopped to test her footing. That's when she heard the SUV door close, and heard an urgent splash of footsteps coming around the back of the vehicle.

"Excuse me!"

Blaine turned. Saw a dark blur emerging out of the rain. A bearded man in a black plastic slicker. "Do you have the time?"

She froze, sensing right away that something was wrong. The man kept moving. Did not stop the way someone would have who actually wanted to know the time.

Then she saw his right arm lift, incongruously, as if he were reaching for something above him, and in the next instant she felt his fist smashing the side of her face. Blaine stumbled backward, falling into the wall, her bag slamming to the pavement, beer bottles shattering.

The man's arms went around her torso and he stumbled with her down to the concrete. His knee rammed her thigh, his right hand slapping at her face. She heard the shift points of his SUV engine idling in the rain behind them, a whine and drone of the windshield wipers, and felt herself about to pass out.

Blaine reached inside her jacket, grasping for a button on her cell phone. But the man noticed and violently jerked her arm out.

"No."

In the next instant, Blaine scooted back and kicked her knee into the man's groin, then scampered on hands and knees out into the parking lot, trying to gain her footing.

But the man was with her. She felt his full weight landing on top of her, her chest slamming the pavement. Felt his knee on her back, knocking the wind out of her. Holding her. And then he dragged her back to the stairwell, out of the rain, and turned her over. He punched the side of her head as she struggled beneath him. Then his right hand covered her nose and mouth and she felt herself beginning to smother.

THE ASSASSIN SAW Blaine reach into her jacket and he yanked her arm out, with the intention of breaking it. But his gloves slipped on the wet nylon of her jacket sleeve and then she caught him by surprise, ramming her knee just above his groin.

He recoiled for an instant, during which she got a good look at him, and managed to scramble away. Desperately, like a crab, crawling into the rain.

She didn't make it. The assassin lunged at her and pinned her to the pavement. Pulled her back under cover by the elevators.

"Okay?" he said. He lay her out again and sat on top.

Blaine watched him, breathing heavily, her eyes stunned. His hands traced a pattern on her face, as if he were a blind man reading Braille. *We're in a pretty good spot here*, he thought, *half-hidden behind the stairwell. I'm going to mold you now.* He moved his fingers delicately over her face and neck. He actually liked her; that was the sad part of this. In another life, they might have even been friends. But not now. That chance had been lost. He listened to the rain and the shifting of his engine and the drone of the wipers, straining to hear any other sounds. *No. No one would be out on a night like this.* He leaned down so his face was touching hers. "You want to try anything else?" he whispered, lightly licking her auricle, rubbing his beard against her cheek. She didn't respond. He sat up, watched her. Her face was mottled, eyes closed, her dark blond hair wet against her skin. She was breathing heavily. When she still wouldn't speak, the

man slapped his open right hand hard across Blaine's face, and he saw
her eyes open slowly. And then he studied the way her skin changed,
seeming to fill with blood. He liked that. He imagined what she'd be
like at the farmhouse, afterward.

He sat very still on top of her, feeling her heavy breathing underneath him. It wasn't unpleasant. "Okay?" he whispered, still catching
his own breath. A thin stream of blood trickled from one of her nostrils; the flesh around her right eye was already beginning to darken.
He gazed back at the parking lot, seeing the escape route she had
imagined for an instant. He smiled, but knew that he needed to move
quickly now, even though he felt protected here—out of the rain,
out of view from the road. He reached inside his left coat pocket and
extracted a rag that he had soaked with isoflurane and held it over her
face. Felt her breathing quicken under his hand, then slow. Watched
her eyes open once and close. Then the assassin replaced the rag in
his pocket and unzipped her jacket. He removed his right glove and
rubbed his hand over her chest several times, massaging the soft skin
of her breasts. "Okay?" he whispered.

Blaine said nothing. Eventually, he found what she had been
reaching for. It wasn't mace or a gun. It was just a cell phone.

The man stood, pulling on his glove, surveying the parking lot.
Nothing. He extracted the hinged cuffs from a rear pocket of his
jeans, and knelt on the concrete. Drew the backs of her wrists
together and double-locked the cuffs behind her. Then he lifted her
under the arms and dragged her across the pavement to the back seat
of his SUV. Yanked her inside; she was heavier than he had thought,
but it was not unpleasant lifting her, bending her legs inside the vehicle, one and then the other; rubbing the insides of her thighs. He was
out in plain sight again, though. Something he said he'd never do.

The assassin opened the driver's door and slid in behind the wheel.
He shifted to reverse, then drive. He pulled onto the highway, went
half a block and turned into the lot of a darkened office building.
Parked around the side, in a deep patch of shadow. He reached into
the back and went through her pockets and purse. Found a wallet
with twenty-seven dollars in paper money, several credit cards, and
a picture pouch with three photos of a young man—her son, no
doubt—car keys, a motel room key. He had to improvise now. To
finish it.

Room 217.

The assassin cut the engine and got out. He jogged back, splashing through the rain, coming at the motel parking lot from the rear, through a thatch of woods. Past the stairwell. As he reached the lot, he checked the Smith & Wesson .38 in his shoulder holster. Her shopping bag, he saw, was still lying by the stairs. He picked it up and pushed it through the slot in the trash can.

Then he walked up the stairs to the second floor, one step at a time, glancing out at the rain slanting across the empty highway, the blurred lights of apartment houses in the distance.

A lamplight glowed behind the curtain of 217. There was a thin crack for him to look through. *Nothing.*

He removed the safety catch on his gun and gripped it in his right hand. This would be delicate, yes.

He touched the knob, then inserted the key. When the latch turned, he kicked the door with his right foot, entering in a combat stance, ready to fire a succession of rounds into Charles Mallory. His second target.

But there was no one in the room.

Nothing.

He pushed the door closed behind him and stood straighter, though still ready, his heart thumping.

With his weapon extended in both hands, the assassin cleared the other spaces in the enclosure—a double closet; a bathroom. Nothing. All clear. The room was empty.

He kept the gun raised as he pulled the motel door open again, leaving it unlocked, alert for any sound or motion. But there was nothing. Site cleared. All he heard now was the rain. "Okay," he said. "Okay." He jogged back through the alley to the SUV, slipped inside behind the steering wheel, and drove back onto the pike, his prisoner of war lying motionless across the back seat.

FORTY-FIVE

CHARLES MALLORY TRIED TO call Blaine, and again his call went to voice mail. He shouldn't have allowed her to leave. He felt a rage tear through him, afraid he'd let her down. Afraid that some-one had followed her. Was she really off the grid of the government's surveillance? He didn't know. But he did know this: it had been his idea for her to come here, and she had been safe when they'd been together; but the game had changed as soon as she left alone.

Restless, Mallory stepped outside onto the ledge. He breathed the cold mist from the rain, looking past the red glow of the Pike Motel sign. Saw his breath become vapor as he exhaled. Beyond the awning, wind blew gusts of rain horizontally into the bare trees.

He counted the cars in the lot. Seven. Lights burned in the motel office, he noticed, but there was no one behind the check-in counter. Mallory saw a television screen through the office window in a corner of the room, and the familiar swirling color-enhanced bands of Alexander. Everyone's attention was riveted on the same thing. It took a disaster to do that.

Mallory looked up at the distant office buildings beyond the trees, dark silhouettes against the sky, and the dim glow of moonlight through the sheets of rain. He gazed down at the parking lot again and saw the incongruity. His heart began to race.

No.

He went back inside the room and grabbed his Beretta. Came out and looked again. The thing sat there in the corner of the lot without explanation, parked in the rain. A taunt. Something that shouldn't have been there: Blaine's Ford Focus, occupying the last space. But Blaine hadn't returned. She wasn't here. Was she?

He hurried to the stairwell and down to the second floor. Could she be in her room? Wouldn't she have called? He glanced at the bottom of the stairwell and saw something by the elevators that stopped him—a pool of orange liquid and broken glass. The liquid trailed across the pavement under the concrete awning, ending at a metal trash bin. Mallory hurried down. He tilted the cover of the trash can and looked. Saw a plastic bag, broken beer bottles, smashed orange juice container. Bottle of aspirin. *Hers.* "No!"

He ran back up the stairs to Room 217. There was light through the curtains. He squinted in and knocked, holding out his gun. Tried the door. It was unlocked. Mallory pushed it open and, gun drawn, stepped inside. Listened.

The room was vacant.

But then he noticed the wet shoeprints on the carpet. Someone had been inside, probably just minutes earlier. He stepped out and surveyed the lot. The walkway was too wet for clear indentations of shoeprints.

So where had he taken her?

He ran back to the third floor room and pressed a button on one of his cell phones. Chaplin answered after the third ring.

"Hello."

"I have an emergency," he said. "Do you still have tracking on Catherine Blaine?"

He heard opera music blaring in the background. *Rigoletto*, perhaps.

"Why, yes."

"Good." Chaplin turned down the music. "We need to follow her. Right away. Both of us. She's been abducted. Come on out. Be in touch with me."

After a pause, Chaplin said, "What should I bring?"

Mallory imagined where they would be going. He heard the soprano in the background hitting a high note, then Chaplin shutting the music off. "Bring night vision goggles and two telephone headsets, if you have them." He added, "And bring a gun."

Mallory clicked off, his heart racing. *Think like the enemy* was the mantra of intelligence field agents; but this was an enemy he didn't know. Not really.

There was also a GPS application on her phone, he knew. Walking down to his car, Mallory called up the zoomable vector-based map on his own phone and moments later found her—her location pulsing like a heartbeat, appearing to be moving back toward the Beltway. Only a couple of miles from the motel.

He got in his car and pulled out onto the pike. Floored the accelerator.

Several minutes later, he glanced down at the phone and saw that the locator had stopped blinking. The GPS was no longer transmitting. Whoever had her must have turned it off.

He kept driving toward the Beltway, though, trying to think like his enemy now. He was chasing a man who had done this before, and who had gotten away with it. Seven or eight times. Probably more. Someone who had a system. He'd be driving now toward a sequestered location, Mallory guessed, out of sight of accidental onlookers. A place where he could hide a car, perhaps. Or several cars. And maybe bury a body. *Where he took Dr. Keri Westlake.* A large plot of land. Rolling country out in the suburbs. A farm, maybe. That was part of his system. And it *was* a system. The MOs had all seemed different, but that was by design. To *seem* different. To mask their similarities. He understood that now.

But where? Which direction? How much time would he wait? Or had the abductor already done what he was going to do?

Minutes later, speeding along the two-lane highway toward the Beltway, Mallory glanced down at his phone and saw that the GPS app on Blaine's cell had been activated again. Had she managed to turn it on? Or was this a trap?

ONE FLOOR BELOW the Oval Office, four men sat in high-backed black leather chairs around a long wooden conference table in the Situation Room: the President, Vice President Bill Stanton, Intelligence Director Harold DeVries, and Dr. James Wu, the President's chief science adviser. At the President's directive, Dr. Wu had taken the lead on the White House's hurricane response. They were waiting for the first briefing from Mr. Zorn and the Weathervane Group. Starbucks coffee cups were in front of each of them, along with printed copies of the projections provided hours earlier by Mr. Zorn.

By eight the next morning, the storm was supposed to have begun breaking apart, according to those projections. Turning east into open sea. At this point, Alexander should have already slowed significantly, to less than 100 mph, according to Zorn's projections.

But Dr. Wu gave them the latest readings from the National Hurricane Center in Miami, and no such weakening had been detected. There had been a slight narrowing of the wind field and some slowing of the strongest winds over the past four hours, but it was much less substantial than predicted. The center of the system remained highly organized and Alexander was now a Category 3, with winds topping 127 mph. The National Weather Service had just issued a forecast that some coastal communities would be rendered "uninhabitable" after Alexander came through. FEMA had sent its Incident Management Assistance Teams to staging areas up and down the East Coast, deploying millions of liters of water and millions of meals, along with cots and blankets, and coordinating emergency plans with state and local officials. The National Guard and the Red Cross were also mobilizing, preparing for the aftermath.

"No signs yet of diminishing," Dr. Wu told the others, in summary, trying to sound unemotional. But inside, he felt sick. This was the worst storm system he had ever seen; the devastation would be unprecedented. "We're getting a lot of severe thunderstorm activity still in the Carolinas up into Virginia and Maryland. And some reports of violent and continuous cloud-to-cloud lightning storms."

"Let's just wait until we've heard what they have to say," the President said. A silence fell over the room. They all stared numbly at the four-foot monitor that conveyed the real-time storm coordinates and the monitor beside it showing a high-resolution satellite image of Alexander swirling toward the East Coast, its cloud cover and wind field stretching nearly from New England to Florida.

At 9 P.M., the digital speaker made a short chirping sound, indicating an incoming call. "Go ahead," the President said.

"This is Dr. Romfo, sir. Good evening."

Dr. Wu pictured the tall, husky, dark-haired scientist.

"Yes."

The President held eye contact with Wu. Waiting.

"Mr. Zorn and the rest of our team are here," she said, her voice thick and, it seemed, a little nervous.

"All right."

"This is our first update. I am pleased to report that the four mitigation operations are now fully active. The maximum sustained wind speed of the system has diminished from 135 miles per hour to 107. The wind field has also decreased significantly. We are seeing particularly strong results from the LRT process, which has, most significantly, begun to disrupt the storm's eye wall. This will produce results that won't be evident until the morning, however."

Dr. Romfo then recited a litany of readings from the past four hours, conveying variations and declines in wind speed, a steady decrease in the storm's vacuum dome, drops in barometric pressure, and increases in central pressure and wind shear. Her voice occasionally seemed to shift register.

When she finished, several minutes later, it was the Vice President who spoke first. "Uh, okay. And, so, let me just ask, then, if I may, in plain English: When will we see this thing actually break apart?"

"Sir?"

"When will this thing knock back down to a Category Two or One? Are we still on target to see that in the morning?"

"Yes, that's right," Dr. Romfo answered. But her voice sounded tentative. "Of course, I'm not able to make precise projections of that nature. But, yes, there should be continued weakening through the morning hours. Our projections, as you know, show it breaking up by late morning or afternoon and turning to sea. But there are still a number of variables at play with a system of this size. And those projections, as we have indicated, are nonlinear."

"A couple of questions," said Harold DeVries.

There was no reply. "This is simply an update," Dr. Romfo said. "Your next report will be at eight A.M."

"Yes," the President said.

Moments later, the line went to a dial tone.

The men in the room exchanged looks.

"Anyone having buyer's remorse here?" the Vice President finally said. No one smiled.

"Jim, do you see this thing tracking in any way with their projections?" the President asked.

Dr. Wu frowned, as if he hadn't considered that issue before. He didn't speak for a long time. "Honestly? No. Not really, sir," he said, eyeing the President earnestly. "It's—there *has* been some wind shear, which is having an effect on the outer bands. And the wind speeds *have* diminished. But the latest sustained wind-speed reading *we* have is 127."

"Not 107?"

"No, sir."

"So, what's happening?" the Vice President said. "Are they fudging?"

"We can't say that. It may be they're basing these readings on data that we simply don't have," said Dr. Wu, playing the diplomat. "They obviously have their own satellite-based technologies and their own measurements."

The Vice President looked to the President, who was staring at the computer monitors. Finally, the President glanced at Dr. Wu, the blue glow of the monitors coloring his face. "Is this consistent with a storm that may break apart or turn back to sea in the morning?"

Wu sighed, feeling the need to stay neutral. It was how he had operated for years. It was the reason he was here in this room with the President of the United States. "Yes and no, sir. It *has* slowed down very slightly, and, as Dr. Romfo just indicated, some of the outer bands do appear to be breaking apart. It's becoming a slightly smaller system, overall, in other words."

"But . . . ?"

"But it is still quite well organized at its center. And it's actually taken an odd turn over the past couple of hours. First to the south and then slightly to the northwest. Based on past models, that's often—I won't say usually, but often—a dangerous sign."

"Dangerous why?" the Vice President asked.

"Because it's introducing a new trajectory that threatens a larger piece of real estate. South-to-north as opposed to a more direct east-to-west hit at a single mid-Atlantic location, where the land would weaken it. The worst-case scenario now is that it will skirt the entire seaboard, bringing hurricane force effects along a thousand-mile stretch of coast."

"Jesus," said the Vice President.

"And what time frame are we looking at?"

"At this point? It looks like we'll be seeing significant effects tomorrow, with the first direct impact maybe forty-eight hours from now. But there's still a great deal of wiggle room. Depending on what other systems might come into play."

The President turned to Dr. Wu. "All right. We'll give them the benefit of the doubt and see what this looks like in the morning. People like to wake up to good news," he said, smiling weakly. "In the meantime, we'll continue to mobilize emergency efforts, anticipating a worst case."

"Yes, sir." Dr. Wu looked to the swirling color-enhanced image of Alexander. No one said anything.

10:21 P.M.

Dmitry Petrenko glanced from the bank of monitors along the wall of the underground facility to Victor Zorn's face in the blue glow of a computer monitor. His skin had taken on a waxen quality as it sometimes did when he was very tired, but he still had the confident swagger in his walk. He was confident by nature, not by circumstances. It was dangerous to fall under his spell, as Petrenko himself had done, long ago. He had a personality that worked like a magic trick, Volkov used to say. Now, though, for the first time in years, Petrenko was feeling a little sorry for Victor, knowing that he had worked all of his life for this evening and the next day. To be the leader of this operation. Knowing that Volkov had trusted him implicitly, giving him the reins. But also knowing that if he failed, Mr. Zorn, as he called himself, would never have another chance.

There were three workstations in the room, each with three computer screens lined up side by side. Wires and extension cords snaked across the floor. The facility felt temporary, which it was, part of a parcel of land that Mr. Zorn had purchased more than a year ago, with financing from Vladimir Volkov. It was only a hollowed space, the walls and ceiling made of rock, the floor an overlaid metal mesh.

Now, all at once, it seemed, there were serious problems with Mr. Zorn's operation, and Mr. Zorn was having difficulty handling them. "The true test of character is how we respond to troubles," Volkov liked to say. Mr. Zorn seemed to be auditioning a variety of responses, all the while keeping up his front. At first, he had been too nervous; now, it seemed, the opposite: nonchalant, showing his dimples as if everything were proceeding as projected.

But it wasn't.

The outcome of this operation was actually quite simple, Petrenko knew, like that of any sporting event. There were only ever two

possible results. If Mr. Zorn pulled this off, and the American president went on television to announce the partnership, then he won.
If anything else happened, he lost. The loss in this case would almost
certainly be permanent for him.

But Petrenko could see that Mr. Zorn was not thinking in those
terms. He wasn't made that way. There was too much at stake for
him to admit the possibility of a massive miscalculation. Yet it had
been more than eight hours now since they had turned off the laser
heaters and the mitigation was not following any of the projections
Mr. Zorn had prepared for the Americans—and for Volkov. Worse,
he was pretending that it did not matter, that they were simply in a
"transition phase."

No. There was something wrong with this storm. Something Mr.
Zorn hadn't prepared for. It was not responding as it should have. It
was almost as if the storm were somehow trying to undo all of their
efforts, trying to defeat them.

Already, Mr. Zorn had relayed manufactured figures to the White
House. He had done that with several of the investors, as well, Petrenko had noticed, during the buildup. "An American trick," he had
heard Mr. Zorn say once, in a hushed voice, to his chief scientist
Ivan Letkov. It was how corporations like Enron had appeased their
investors during rough patches, he said. They invented "fair value"
projections and "interim results" until the "weather turned." He was
playing this trick at a fairly safe level now; but if he was forced to
do it again, at the 8 A.M. briefing, the stakes would rise significantly.
And it would become increasingly difficult for Mr. Zorn to align his
numbers with reality. Soon, the group's credibility would be lost. And
Volkov would not be pleased.

The next report to the Americans would be at 8 A.M. By then, the
storm was supposed to have begun breaking apart.

Petrenko would be in the room well before then, doing his job. It
was a very simple job, but it was becoming a painful one. All he had
to do was observe. To watch and to listen. And report.

BLAINE COULDN'T MOVE. It was as if she were suspended between
consciousness and unconsciousness. Unable to open her eyes,
unaware of where she was. Then, gradually, the outside began to
seep in. She tasted the damp air. Heard rain thudding on a metal

covering. Felt metal bands squeezing her wrists. Recognized smells, earth scents—wet soil, minerals, rain. And then she heard a subtler, more distant sound of water; the rushing of a creek, perhaps. Finally she opened her eyes to the cold darkness.

When she tried to move, she felt a stab of pain in her shoulder; and then a duller ache around her right eye.

She was in the back seat of a car. The door was wide open to the night. It was cold and raining and her clothes were damp, stuck to her skin. She lay still and let her eyes adjust—trees, a slope of hillside, a wooden covering of some sort, which blocked the natural light of the sky. There was no artificial light in any direction here, but wild, occasional flashes of lightning that lit up the trees. She was deep in a sloping woods somewhere. Maybe a park.

Then she sensed movement—a shape shuffling beneath the wooden covering—and heard a scramble of footsteps on gravel in the rain and knew that the man was back.

She took a deliberate breath and closed her eyes, waiting for him. Trying to scoot back but feeling the sharp pain from her shoulder and the side of her head. She saw the man standing outside, wearing what looked like a flak jacket, not moving. Then the seat gave as the man moved on top of her and she felt his damp clothing against her skin and smelled the earthy scent of his jacket and the alcohol on his breath.

Whispering: "Okay? Are you awake yet?"

Blaine squinted: dark eyes looking at her, inches away.

"Speak?" he said, pushing something metal against her face. "Speak."

Blaine turned her head and felt herself shudder. "What?"

"Speak into this," he hissed. "Say you're okay."

Blaine felt the wet metal on her cheek again, then realized what it was.

A *telephone*. He was holding a cell phone next to her face.

"Okay?"

He pulled it back, pressed a number and then held it to her lips. "Speak."

"Help," she said, her voice sounding distant, like someone else's. "I'm in the back seat of a car in the woods."

She stared into the man's eyes.

"Where? Where are you? Give me a reference point."

Charles Mallory.

"In a park. Deep in the woods. You're right. It's east—"

The killer yanked the phone back and clicked it off.

"What were you going to say?"

Blaine went silent. She watched his eyes as he tried to flatten himself on top of her and felt a panic, realizing that he was probably going to torture and molest her before killing her.

"What were you going to say?"

"Nothing."

"Okay," he whispered. "Okay." He pushed the phone in his pocket and began to touch Blaine again, grunting crudely, his hand going up and down roughly between her legs. She struggled against him, lifting her knees as a buffer.

"Don't," she said. "Don't!"

Hearing her voice, he suddenly seemed to lose interest. He sat up. Backed away, stepped outside. Blaine listened to the rain, and heard the sound of a zipper. She breathed deeply, waiting, trying to sit up.

But she felt the give of the seat cushion again and smelled him as he climbed back on top of her. Then she felt something poking against her face and twisted her head away.

"No," she said.

"No?"

"No."

She felt him rubbing against her in the dark. She shifted her head and smelled him, the animal scent of his groin as he jerked himself against the side of her face, his knees moving awkwardly and a little desperately on top of her, as if he were trying to straddle her chest. He pulled back and leaned closer, and then she sensed that he was trying to kiss her, his fake beard bristling against her mouth. Dark eyes. Strange, like there was no center to them, no real pupil. As if he lacked the ability to focus.

He reached under her shirt again, massaging her breasts with his right hand, as if he were kneading bread, breathing heavily. She smelled the stench of him again as he scooted forward into her face and she gagged, catching herself before she vomited.

"If I put something in your mouth, you wouldn't bite it, would you?" he whispered. "You aren't going to bite me." He was straddling her shoulders now and she felt him rocking slightly, breathing deeply in and out. Suddenly, his open hand smacked the right side of her face. Blaine stung with pain. "You *would*, wouldn't you? That's why I'm not going to do it. I'm not going to give you that particular pleasure tonight. But I'll give you another one."

He slapped her again, and a moment later, apropos nothing, Catherine Blaine suddenly understood. *The other part. The motivation.* It all made sense to her. Just like that. She closed her eyes as he lifted himself up and ground his penis against the side of her face, her eyes and nose, grunting maniacally, his left hand jerking frantically, the fingertips of his right hand jabbing at her cheeks, squeezing her face until she hurt. Grunting. *Of course*, she thought. *Of course.*

She felt a warm liquid sliding down her neck and the man pulling himself off of her roughly, putting his full weight on her legs as he backed out awkwardly, breathing heavily like an athlete finished with competition.

With a dry rag he carefully wiped her off. Then he walked out into the rain, made the rag wet and came back in the car and wiped her off again. This time, as he lifted off of her, Blaine rose up and rammed her knee into his groin. The man let out a sharp yelp and recoiled.

"Mother*fucker!*" he said, doing a dance outside the opened car door. Blaine felt a momentary triumph and tried to rise to a sitting position. But the man came slamming in on top of her, punching her face wildly with both hands, jabbing her with his elbows. Blaine's panic turned to anger. She moved her head from side to side, missing most of it. "Bitch!" he said. "Fucking motherfucking bitch!"

Then it stopped. And suddenly, it seemed, the man was gone. He stood outside attentively, as if he had heard something approaching. And then he ran, half limping into the rain.

Blaine sat up, her face smarting, catching her breath. Listening. Seeing the shapes of bare trees in the darkness and puzzling through what she had just come to realize. Dates. Times. Motivation. Why Easton had done it.

Suddenly, she understood the whole thing.

FORTY-SIX

MALLORY HEARD BLAINE'S VOICE in his head as he waited in the rain for Chaplin: *In a park. Deep in the woods. You're right. It's east—*

He had followed the GPS indicator to a parking area by the Western Ridge Trail of Rock Creek Park. He had parked and walked out into the woods along the mouth of the trail, studying the darkened, sloping landscape of the parkland, which suddenly lit up with wild jags of cloud-to-cloud electricity that startled his eyes. He turned, his vision so stunned that he didn't see the headlights approaching until the car was right in front of him.

Chaplin parked his Cadillac Escalade next to Mallory's car. Mallory opened the passenger door and slid in.

"Sorry," Chaplin said. "Have you been waiting?"

"It's all right. She's in there, isn't she?"

"Looks like it." The only light was the glow of his computer screen on the front seat between them. Mallory noticed that Chaplin was dressed in a head-to-toe plastic covering.

"What's funny?"

"Nothing."

"Do you want an umbrella?"

"A little rain never hurt anyone," Mallory said. He watched the downpour through the trees. Saw a violent spray of lightning illuminate the tree tops.

"Jesus," Chaplin said.

"She just called me a few minutes ago," Mallory said. "I'm sure it's a trap, but I don't think we have a lot of alternatives right now. What do you have?"

Chaplin hit several keys, changing images on his laptop. "Both readings show she's in there." He turned his computer, giving Mallory the GPS readings from her phone and the homing device on a split screen.

"What's there, exactly?"

"Seems to be a covered picnic area. We're probably less than a quarter mile away."

"Okay."

Mallory could feel Chaplin looking at him.

"You're not thinking of going in there?" Chaplin asked. Mallory was silent. "I would strongly recommend against it if you are," he said, reverting to his formal tone.

"What would you recommend we do instead?"

"Notify the police. Have them execute a raid."

"No, can't do that. He sees police coming, he runs. Or worse, he might kill Catherine. Where exactly is your GPS signal showing she is? Can I see?"

He studied the satellite map, then enlarged it to show Mallory. "I did a map search of the area. This is a rain shelter, evidently. A picnic area. Two tables, a grill, looks like. There's an object there that appears to be a car or an SUV."

"Is it static?"

"Yes, both signals have remained static for twenty to twenty-five minutes."

"Okay." Mallory examined the set-up some more, then looked out at the slope of the hillside. Back and forth. He enlarged the area of the map image, opening it up to the north. "I'm guessing he might be in this area, up the hill, near the next picnic area. It would give him a fairly clean vantage point." He stared into the rain, figuring.

"For what?" Chaplin asked.

"For getting off a sniper round."

"How would you know that? And what makes you think it's just one person?"

"It's one person. I'm pretty sure."

"Why?"

"Because he's done this before."

Mallory again felt Chaplin looking at him. "How would you know?"

"The list I gave you," he said. "June seventeenth, 2007. A reporter named Michael Dunlopen was found in a remote wooded area with a gunshot wound to the head. The bullet was .243-caliber, from a hunting rifle. DNA was found in the man's car but never matched with anyone. August twenty-first, 2006, a woman was sexually assaulted at a motel in Wyoming and then shot once in the head. Hair, skin, fingerprints, and semen were found at the scene but never identified. Some of the DNA samples were female, some male. February fifth, 2005, the body of a man named Frank Johnson was found in the woods in central North Carolina, dead from a single shot to the head, again a hunting rifle, .243-caliber. I finally realized what connects these cases: the killer's MO. The DNA clues are obviously decoys. He finds a discarded coffee cup or a hair sample and leaves it behind. Also, he takes people out with shots to the head. They're all variations of a theme."

Chaplin was silent. Mallory took the safety off his Beretta. "We're talking about a military man," he continued, feeling a gathering of adrenaline. "Military people have hierarchal, ordered ways of doing things. They repeat what's worked before. But he's also an intelligence man. Intelligence people improvise. I think he's both. I'm guessing if he's luring me to a very specific spot, he's going to use a sniper rifle. And aim for the head."

Chaplin was breathing through his nose. "And what if he improvises?"

"Then I might be in trouble. But we have greater resources than he does."

"How do you mean?"

"I mean, there's two of us. And you've got night-vision goggles. Right?"

Chaplin took a deep nasal breath. "What are you suggesting?"

"You go up the hill wearing your night-vision gear. Try to find him or his car. I'll go down toward the target."

Chaplin fidgeted with what he'd brought. "I'd advise against that," he said.

"I know you would. But that's what we're going to do. Unless you want to stay here in the car and wait for me. If that's what you prefer, okay."

Chaplin looked out at the rain through the small round opening in his hood. He didn't say anything.

• • •

THERE WAS A car parked by the picnic area closest to the trail head. Wild, silent jags of lightning lit up the woods and Mallory saw it twice: a dark-colored SUV maybe an eighth of a mile down the trail. He walked sideways through the woods, several steps at a time, avoiding the trail. The ground was slippery with mud and leaves, and his shoes lost traction several times going downhill.

Chaplin maneuvered in a wide arc up the hillside behind him, wearing his night vision goggles. They both wore open phone headsets.

Mallory moved in a diagonal down the slope, scanning the woods for movement. He stopped and started. Listened. Waited. A single silent bolt of cloud-to-ground lightning lit up the woods and he saw that the back door of the SUV was open; saw the vehicle name on the back bumper—Ford Explorer—and three of the license plate numbers. Virginia plates. He was maybe thirty feet away now.

"There's nothing up here," Chaplin said in his ear. "No vehicle, no person."

"Keep looking." Mallory raised his Beretta, taking short steps among the narrow trees. Twenty-five feet away. Twenty.

"There's nothing here," Chaplin said.

A quick flash turned the sky to daylight, and Mallory froze, blinking. Realizing that he'd been mistaken. That his assumptions were all wrong. For an instant, everything became perfectly clear. The killer was standing twelve feet away, his dark eyes watching him through the trees.

FORTY-SEVEN

MALLORY FIRED TWICE AT the killer's after-image and ducked away into the shelter of thick brush, retreating frantically into darkness.

"He's here," he whispered into his headset, adrenaline pumping.

The other man fired once, the bullet cracking into a tree. Mallory scrambled sideways and slightly uphill, into deeper cover. He crouched behind the trunk of a thick oak and waited, catching his breath, listening. All he heard was the steady beat of the rain through the trees and a more distant sound of creek water rushing downhill.

The woods and sky lit up again, this time like a fireworks show. He saw no one—just dripping bark and the glitter of falling rain. The Explorer parked by the picnic spot, its back door open.

But the other man saw him. Two shots exploded the silence, one slamming into the oak tree, missing him by inches. Mallory rolled away and crawled to a new position. He heard a scrambling in the woods: footsteps, moving closer. He aimed his Beretta, steadying it with both hands. He heard the other man snap a tree branch, then stop. Quiet, just the rain. Mallory moved sideways. One step, two. One step. He crouched beside another tree and held his breath, picturing the man advancing stealthily, invisibly toward him. He waited, letting his senses sharpen. He was going to identify the other man's location through sound now, and wait until he was certain—or until the sky lit up one more time—before firing.

The rain poured through the trees, streaming down his neck, inside his shirt. He thought about Catherine Blaine. He was here because of her.

In a park. Deep in the woods. You're right. It's east—

Easton.

That's what she was telling him. *Easton.*

Another explosion of gunfire jerked him out of his thoughts. He crouched lower, intently listening. Then he heard a sharp intake of breath. He held his gun up, steadying it. The killer was ten feet away from Charles Mallory now. But this time the shots weren't his. No. This time the shots had come from a different direction.

Mallory froze, attentive to every sound, smell, movement. At first, nothing happened. Then he heard the killer tramping out of the woods onto the trail. Saw his dark shape in the rain, trying to run downhill, limping badly.

He heard another explosion and the man disappeared.

Nothing. He was gone.

Mallory held out his gun. A moment later, Chaplin's voice was in his ear: "Got him," he said.

Mallory walked down to the trail, Beretta raised. The sky lit up once more as he neared the killer, and he saw the dripping wound in the back of his head.

"Careful," Chaplin said in his ear. He was standing fifteen feet behind Mallory now, legs spread wide, dressed in plastic from head to toe. Rivulets of rain ran down the hillside.

"Good work," Mallory said, speaking softly. He kneeled and turned the killer over, recognizing Thomas Rorbach from years earlier. Thinking about the nine people he had probably killed. A list that would have included his brother, Cate, and him. Rorbach was the killer. But Rorbach wasn't Janus. And he wasn't the real enemy. He *worked* for the real enemy: for Easton and Zorn.

Mallory stood. Surveyed the woods. Chaplin kneeled down and went through Rorbach's pockets as Mallory walked toward the parked SUV, his gun aimed, adrenaline coursing through him.

He clicked on the dome switch and found Blaine's purse and phone on the floor in back. But no one was inside. The vehicle was empty.

Chaplin watched him from under the picnic cover as Mallory stepped outside and looked up at the trees, waiting for another flash of lightning. When Mallory caught his eye, he held up a cell phone and a narrow five-inch key with a double lock pin on one end.

"Handcuffs," he said.

Mallory scanned the woods. "There has to be another car."

"Why do you say that?"

"Because this was his decoy. He wanted to lure me here. But if something went wrong, he needed another way out."

"So the next park entrance, maybe."

"Yeah, maybe." *Down the hill, not up.* He had figured that wrong. They walked along the narrow, slippery trail, single file, Mallory in the lead, descending in the mud and leaves for another quarter mile or so, not speaking.

The clearing by the next parking area was flooded. No vehicle. Mallory continued walking, down through the trees toward the next trail entrance. He came to a wooden overhang, a picnic table. Then the sky burst with startling veins of lightning and he saw it: another SUV, parked on the edge of the woods.

Mallory approached it gun raised. A Jeep Liberty. The back door of this one was open, too, just like the first. He came around the side and saw something moving in the back seat.

He stepped closer, the rain pounding through the trees. He crouched, Chaplin covering him.

A figure was sitting up, facing them. Then the sky lit from several directions and he saw her green eyes, wide and alert, looking at him.

"Cate!"

"Hi," she said.

"My god."

CATHERINE BLAINE WINCED as she scooted sideways and leaned over the seat-back of the SUV, letting Chaplin unlock the handcuffs behind her back. Then she stepped out and shook her hands. Flexed her legs.

"Are you hurting?" Mallory said. "Do you need a hospital?"

"Yes to the first question, no to the second. I'll survive."

Chaplin, despite his head-to-toe plastic covering, moved under the awning, out of the rain. Only a small circle of his face showed.

"What do we do with the crime scene?" he asked, his voice almost lost in the rain.

Mallory saw what had happened. Her face was bruised and grotesquely swollen.

Chaplin asked his question again, louder.

"Leave it," he said. "Call the police and let them know."

"Is he dead?" Blaine asked.

"Yes." Mallory nodded to Chaplin. "Thanks to him."

She turned. "Thank you," she said. Then she closed her eyes and shuddered. Opened them and looked at Charles Mallory.

"Rorbach did that?" he said, pointing at her face.

"He did worse than that."

Mallory grimaced and felt a shiver of relief that she was alive, followed by a deep-rooted anger over what Rorbach might have done. A madman hiding in plain sight. "I wish it hadn't happened. I'm sorry," he said.

"I'll survive. How's the storm?"

"I don't know. Let's go find out." Mallory turned. He glanced at Chaplin. They began to walk up the trail, single-file.

"I wouldn't mind changing into some dry clothes," she said, halfway up.

"I'll second that," Mallory said.

Chaplin, walking behind them, said nothing.

They trudged up the muddy trail back through the woods to the parking lot, Chaplin's slicker making a whoosh-whoosh sound in the rain.

Friday, October 7, 6:47 A.M.

Dmitry Petrenko was already seated in a folding chair beside one of the workstations when Victor Zorn came through the heavy steel door that provided the only entrance and exit to the Command and Control Center. Petrenko nodded curtly and looked to Mr. Zorn's chief scientist, Letkov.

The other scientist, Dr. Romfo, had not yet arrived.

The night before, Mr. Zorn had seemed worn down, his eyes red and tired. This morning, his face exuded fresh confidence, the "magic" self-assurance that had driven this project so far. But nothing had happened overnight to justify that confidence, and the others in the room seemed to recognize that. In fact, the storm was no weaker now than it had been when Petrenko had left the compound shortly after midnight.

Petrenko saw Zorn huddling with Letkov, pretending at first that their conversation was casual and light-hearted. But the room was thoroughly miked and Petrenko heard every word they were saying through his ear buds.

He watched Mr. Zorn feign a smile and turn from his sight line. "But why?" he said, speaking softly, in Russian. "Why are these projections so far off? All these months you have been working on this, giving me your assurances, and now you present me this bad news?"

"I don't know, sir. I am sorry."

"*Sorry?*"

The scientist lowered his head, trying to appear contrite. *Bad acting*, Petrenko thought. "Except what I said before. That I'm afraid he may just be too large. Too chaotic. *Programmed* too large."

"How could that be?" Zorn said, still smiling.

"It's just—the models weren't based on actual storms of this size, as you know."

"Of *course* not. Since there never *has* been a storm of this size."

"No. You're right."

"So? What explanation do you have?"

"None, sir. Except—I think that maybe we've just pushed him too far."

"What do you mean '*him*'?"

"The storm. Alexander."

"*Don't call it him.*"

"I'm sorry, sir. It's just—I don't know. It's just—there's something about this storm. Something I don't know how to put—scary."

Petrenko listened to the silence, imagining the look in Vladimir Volkov's eyes when he heard about this.

"Come on, Letkov. Please. *Don't tell me that. Tell me something I can use*," Mr. Zorn said, his voice whispery but angry. And then, to Petrenko's great surprise, Zorn slapped Letkov.

Mr. Zorn looked sharply around the room, pretending to smile, embarrassed by his sudden loss of temper. Petrenko stared blankly in front of him, as if he were studying one of the computer models. Then Zorn said to Letkov "*What's the matter with you? We never speak that way in an open venue like this. We never express doubts like that.*"

"I'm sorry, sir. You are right."

Petrenko watched the two men as they turned away again and schemed, although he pretended to only be studying the animated images of Alexander on one of the desk monitors. He had not wished

Zorn ill, particularly, but if he was going to bully others while continuing to live out his illusion, the cost would be huge.

Petrenko had feared this, and he felt a strange mix of emotions
watching it actually unfold. Zorn's scientists were loyal and they were
certainly competent, but they were not as capable as the Americans.
He had used their expertise to create a monster, infinitely larger than
was necessary for "The Project" to go forward. And now, he had no
idea how to bring the monster down.

FORTY-EIGHT

FOR A LONG TIME, Mallory and Blaine rode in silence, Mallory
driving, both of them watching the rain on the twisting, unlit park
road as the wipers beat a steady rhythm. Thinking, replaying what
had happened. As they came into the Maryland suburbs, the day's
first light began to fill in the spaces between the trees.

"You know what I keep thinking?" Blaine finally said. "I keep
thinking about my father."

Mallory glanced at her. She was a mess, her face bruised, her hair
plastered and muddy, her clothes wet and torn. "The general."

"Yeah. I keep thinking how I'd like to tell him what happened
back there. How I'd like to explain the whole thing to him. Every
detail. How we did this. How I was a prisoner. How you rescued me."

"Why can't you?"

"Because we don't do that. We just don't," she said. For a moment,
her voice seemed choked with emotion. "I mean . . . because there's
a part of me that knows exactly how he'd respond if I tried. He'd
criticize me for letting myself get caught. For putting myself in that
position. And that would be it. We'd never get beyond that to have
the conversation I'd want to have."

"How long has this been going on?"

Blaine's sigh sounded like air leaking from a balloon. "Forever," she
said. "Grade school."

"Tough."

"Kind of. The cliché would be to say that he wanted a son."

"And like many clichés, it's actually true?"

She smiled, and Mallory thought of his own father. Lessons he had learned from him and lessons he was still learning. His father had been killed because of the information in his head. At least Blaine still had time to make things right; Mallory had lost that chance. "Maybe you could try again," he told her.

"I could. I have, actually. Many times, over the years." He realized that she was looking at him. "Maybe I will."

"You're an only child?"

"Yeah."

Mallory glanced over, saw her smiling at him again, in a way that he liked, despite her bruised features. When he looked back, she was turned away, watching the trees, but there was still the vestige of a smile on her face. "*You're* not," she said.

"No."

"Your brother's why you came back."

"Yeah. I'd decided I wasn't going to come back. For anything."

"The reluctant spy."

"I guess."

"I'm glad you did."

Mallory watched the road.

"What was he able to say that made you come back?"

"Nothing. He just asked me."

"And that was it."

"Yep."

They rode in silence for a while along the winding park road, the rain periodically thudding harder on the roof, then softening. Mallory thought about his brother. The story he'd be able to write, the parts still coalescing. The road was empty; traffic lights flashed yellow in the distance.

"It's Easton, you know," Blaine finally said.

Mallory came out of his thoughts. "Yes," he said. "I do."

"I think I figured out the rest of it, too," she said. "The last part."

"Which last part?"

"Motivation."

He glanced over, surprised.

"It was something you said right before I left the motel. Volkov needed someone on the inside. Or, someone capable of *being* on the inside."

"Yes," he said. "But Easton didn't want the job of Secretary of Defense. He said so publicly on several occasions."

"That's right. Then fourteen months ago he seemed to suddenly change his mind."

"So what happened fourteen months ago?"

"I think it happened earlier, actually," she said. "Maybe it was just fourteen months ago that Volkov confronted him with it—through Mr. Zorn, presumably—and it became leverage. You said that Volkov preys on weaknesses, right?"

"That's what I was told."

"So maybe he found one with Easton. Rorbach ran the facility in Alaska for the Leviathan Project. Isn't that what you said?"

"Yes."

"A project that conducted research into convections in the Earth's crust. Which at some point expanded to include ground radio tomography experiments. Then he was moved off of that. And the government quietly withdrew."

"It became inactive at the end of December 2004, supposedly."

"December twenty-seventh, to be exact," she said. "That was the date listed in the memo."

"All right. So?"

"So, I presume it was Easton who moved him off of it. He was the top level Defense Department liaison." Mallory waited. "The objective of Leviathan, the memo stated, was to study ways to build, and then dismantle, a massive storm system. Through computer models. And then in real time."

"Yes. Keep going."

"But there were actually two objectives, according to the memo Hanratty gave you. Two processes. The first was 'creating an event and taking it apart.'"

"A hurricane, presumably."

"Yes. That was the primary objective of Leviathan. The second process had only one part. That's because it was a finite event that happens very suddenly. That *couldn't* be mitigated because it gives no warning. It's over within a few minutes."

"An earthquake."

"Yes, exactly. That's why I think that date is significant."

Mallory frowned at her. "Okay."

"Suppose the real purpose of Leviathan was to explore a new sort of military weapon. An experimental technology, that was maybe pushed along after 9/11. Say it involved the use of high energy radio waves, bouncing energy off the stratosphere."

"For what purpose?"

"Say you wanted to create something that could be used militarily. A 'disturbance' that could pinpoint a strategic target. Where al Queda leaders were thought to be, let's say; where Osama bin Laden was hiding back when that was an issue. Something that was developed under the guise of Defense Department research. Easton bought into all that. Off-the-books secret defense allocations for selective covert ops projects."

"Okay."

"Rorbach was project manager but it was under Easton's watch. Hypothesis, then: suppose something orchestrated by Rorbach went wrong." Mallory watched the back and forth of the wipers. "Suppose it worked, in other words, but it worked too well."

"Okay."

"That's why I think that date may be significant."

"What's December twenty-seventh, 2004?"

"That's not the date."

"It isn't?"

"No. That's one day after the date."

"December twenty-sixth, 2004?"

"Yes."

Mallory watched the road through the glass. The wipers slicing out a moment of clarity, the rain stealing it away. Clear, opaque, back and forth. When he got it, he felt chills race up his spine. Amazed he had missed it.

"At this point, that's pure speculation, of course," she said. "I hope it's wrong."

Maybe. But then maybe not. Because it explained what they had been missing. *The motivation.*

Mallory closed his eyes for a moment.

December 27, 2004.

The day after one of the worst natural disasters in history: the Indian Ocean tsunami, caused by a magnitude 9.1 earthquake. The third-largest seismic event ever recorded, an undersea rupture that caused the entire planet to vibrate. The longest duration of faulting ever observed, lasting nearly ten minutes.

Two hundred and twenty-eight thousand people dead.

Mallory glanced to his right, saw the subdued intensity in her eyes, and the ghoulish dark circle where she had been beaten by Thomas Rorbach.

"No," he said. "It suddenly makes a perverse sort of sense. Easton was Assistant Secretary of Defense for strategic affairs at the time. I've learned about their history. Easton and Rorbach have had an unholy alliance going back almost twenty years. Rorbach looks out for him, in some cases does the dirty work for him. Easton promotes him to positions he doesn't deserve. Who knows what glue held them together all those years? Something in their past, that happened years earlier, presumably. It makes sense: Vladimir Volkov somehow learned what had really happened with Leviathan and he used it to coerce Easton to become involved."

"Or Zorn did."

"Yes."

"I'm hoping none of that's true," she said.

"Except it explains what can't be explained any other way. Something had to motivate Easton to do this. Why would a man with a seemingly sterling career become involved?"

"He wouldn't."

"No."

"So the only explanation is that he didn't have a choice."

Mallory thought about that for a while. "That would explain where it started," he said. "Projecting out from there—later, maybe, he came to *believe* in this technology. He became convinced that the United States needed to control it, that it could all be worked out behind closed doors, that it would ultimately benefit the world. He's a strong-willed man who rationalizes decisions having to do with Defense. Volkov knew the industry as well as anyone. So he would have known about Leviathan and maybe why it was shut down. And with some digging, he might have learned how Easton was involved. And Rorbach. It was all crafted in a way that the US would benefit. Easton would benefit. And Volkov would benefit."

"And if Easton didn't participate, he would be exposed."

"Yes. Responsible for a mistake that would cast him as one of the worst villains in American history."

"So Volkov offered him a way out."

Mallory nodded, still thinking it through.

"But then what were the email threats about?" Blaine asked.

"I don't know. That would be the other part of it," Mallory said. "There had to be someone inside, as we said. But maybe there were two."

"Why do you think that?"

"The set-up," he said. "It's odd that you were never required to *reply* to the email threats. How did he even know you were receiving them?"

Blaine's eyes were steady, watching him.

"Remember what you once said about computer hacking?" Mallory went on. "You said only two hundred people really understand the intricacies of hacking at its highest level."

"I was told that."

"It would be a perfect set-up to have one of them involved, wouldn't it?"

"*Stiles.*"

"Maybe."

"So Easton was orchestrating this from inside, and his lieutenants were Stiles and Rorbach."

"Maybe," he said. "If so, that's what I had all wrong. I'd been assuming the chain was about Volkov. But those seven names are all connected with Leviathan. They don't have anything to do with Volkov."

"So who was the informant?"

Mallory sighed. "I don't know that yet."

They rode in silence again through the slanting rain, thinking about it. As they came to the Pike Motel, Mallory clicked on his turn signal and glanced over at Blaine.

"He was running funny, you know," he said.

"How do you mean?"

"Rorbach. He was running funny before Joseph shot him."

"How do you mean, funny?"

"He was kind of hunched over and limping in a funny way. As if someone had given him a good kick between the legs."

"Oh." Blaine made a neutral sound. "Do you think that impaired his ability to get away at all?"

"It may have, sure." He added, "Might be something to mention to your father."

Mallory parked two spaces down from Blaine's Ford rental. They sat there for a while looking at the rain pouring through the trees.

"So what are we doing?" she said.

"I thought we could get into some dry clothes, as you suggested, and then maybe close our eyes for a few minutes."

"That sounds pretty nice. Then what?"

"Then maybe it's time to confront Easton."

7:50 A.M.

At the makeshift Command and Control Center in rural Virginia, Victor Zorn was flanked by his two lead scientists, studying the most recent satellite images and tracking coordinates of Hurricane Alexander. Weathervane's initial projections had shown that by 8 A.M. the storm's speed would have dropped to less than 90 mph and its eye would have begun to break apart. The whole system would be showing signs of a steep easterly jag, a return to sea. But the speed of the storm now hovered around 129 mph and its wind field stretched across more than seven hundred miles, making it about the same size it had been ten hours earlier.

Somehow, Victor Zorn seemed unfazed. "This is all still evolving," Victor said to Dr. Romfo, the tall, heavyset American. "It's a rather arbitrary—and awkward—time to give a summary, of course"

Petrenko watched from the corners of his eyes, behind the work-station. Mr. Zorn was turned away from Letkov, his chief scientist, whom he now blamed for the failure overnight, and was dealing instead with Dr. Romfo, who seemed to step right up her new role.

"Except we offered them assurances that we would," she told him, sounding disingenuously cheerful.

"Of course. And so we're going to have to provide fair value pro-jections in lieu of actuals. Until the project is fully engaged."

Dr. Romfo was holding a computer printout, something that Let-kov had handed her.

"Those are the composite numbers, which Ivan has prepared," Zorn told her. "We do not yet have true readings to provide for the eight o'clock report, although we expect to have them for the next reporting period. So what we provide are the composite numbers."

"Okay," she said, frowning now at the printout. "So, do I introduce these as 'composite numbers'? Will that mean anything to them?"

"Probably not, no. It's really just a technicality," Mr. Zorn said, his tone more firm. "These *are* the numbers. But it's a complex interaction taking place. It's so fluid, in other words, that it's not possible to give real numbers at this point and have them mean anything." Petrenko saw Zorn grab the printout from her hand. "In fact, let *me* give the report. *I'll* explain them." He summoned a quick smile. "You all seem so baffled by this."

Seated in his darkened space behind the computer station, Dmitry Petrenko saw the project unraveling in triplicate: the flare of frustration in Victor's eyes. The sudden accent of skepticism in Dr. Romfo's voice. Letkov's empty, worn-down expression.

Mr. Zorn was reverting to his own language of obfuscation and justification. Some sort of formula that produced "interim" and "composite" numbers based on statistical computations.

It was Victor's fallback. A way of compensation, for results that were inconclusive or at variance with projections, while furthering the larger objective. Petrenko understood the game. He knew that a person could do virtually anything he wanted with numbers; he could show, on paper, that he was enormously wealthy when in fact he couldn't pay his bills. It had been done often, sometimes very successfully. But it was the sort of deception that Vladimir Volkov abhorred.

Petrenko kept his gaze steady, appearing to be watching one of the small computer screens, as the call was placed, although he was in fact only paying attention to Zorn. Feeling sorry again for the man he had admired all of his life. The man he had grown up with.

"Good morning," Mr. Zorn said. "I am pleased to report that we are seeing the mitigation operations approaching full effect as we speak. The actual numbers are lagging slightly behind the projections, but we are seeing a significant movement in the last thirty to forty-five minutes, which has probably not shown up yet in your tracking data. This indicates that the storm will become in line with projections as the day unfolds, with a possible differential of two to three hours.

"The wind speed has fallen to just over 100 mph, with significant and steady diminishment expected throughout the course of the day. The real effects won't become apparent until after about noon. And so we are going to delay our next report until this afternoon when we have more concrete information."

Minutes later, Petrenko slipped out of the room and into the crisp, wet Virginia air. Facing the valley, he activated his mobile hand-unit and, his eyes misting with emotion, he typed another message to Volkov, who was probably on his plane by now: "Mitigation still under way. Results minimal, at strong variance with projections."

Afterward, he went online to see how the storm was being reported.

Alexander is poised to become a Category 4 hurricane, with wind speeds nearing 130 miles per hour. FEMA Director Shauna Brewster is calling on everyone up and down the East Coast within a hundred miles of the ocean to evacuate their homes.

The National Weather Service warns that Alexander has the potential to grow into a Category 5 hurricane by the time it makes landfall.

Emergency Management Director Carter Wilson said that a Cat 5 storm would have the energy of dozens of atomic bombs.

"For years, we've heard the argument that coastal communities have allowed building too close to the ocean and that one day we will get our payback," he said. "Unfortunately, I fear that we're getting that payback now. I pray we're not, but I urge everyone to prepare for the worst."

FORTY-NINE

DR. JAMES WU SHOOK his head as he looked at the row of monitors displaying radar, satellite, and buoy readings for Hurricane Alexander. Scrolling, changing lines of numbers. Swirling bands of color-enhanced satellite images. The night before, President Hall had instructed his chief science adviser to give the Weathervane Group the benefit of the doubt until eight o'clock in the morning. Now the grace period had passed; Dr. Wu realized that he would have to provide a sobering, real-time assessment. He could see the shift already in the President's eyes, the creeping acceptance of what he was beginning to understand. Minutes earlier, when he was certain that no one was looking, Dr. Wu had turned away and whispered a simple prayer: "Please, God, spare us from this devastation. Thank you, God."

The room in the Eisenhower Executive Office Building seemed to reverberate now with silence as they waited for the President to speak. Outside, the rain had thinned and the sky was a slate gray. But the calm was an illusion. In fact, the storm had been deflected north by an unusual Bermuda high pressure system, making it an even greater danger to the mid-Atlantic coast.

"Okay," the President said, staring at Wu. "I'm looking at the numbers you're giving us and the numbers they're giving us and they're not lining up. They're not even close."

Dr. Wu nodded. "That is correct, sir."

"The numbers they're giving us aren't real. Is that what you're saying?"

Wu waited before answering, as if it were a complicated question.

He summoned his diplomat's persona. "Sir, I've gone through all of the computer models. Two of them do in fact show a turn to the east, of varying degree, by nine A.M.—"

"But that's not what's happening."

"No, not at this point, sir. This high pressure system appears to be pushing the storm north and west."

"And it hasn't lost any strength since their report last night?"

"Minimally, perhaps. Because of an eye wall effect. But not appreciably, no."

"An eye wall effect. Explain."

"Most large storms go through an eye wall replacement cycle. What usually happens is that an outer eye wall will move in and replace the inner eye wall, forming a larger eye. The immediate effect is that the storm will weaken during this cycle and then re-intensify and become even stronger. That's what happened with Katrina in 2005 shortly before it struck land."

He changed the image on the large monitor and pointed to the eastern bands of Alexander, where a counterclockwise system seemed to contain the early stages of another eye wall.

The President turned away. Wu didn't enjoy being the bearer of bad news, and wouldn't have been unless he was absolutely certain. Now, there was no choice.

"What's this about, then?" the President said, at last.

"Maybe they just can't do it, sir."

"They can build it but they can't take it apart?"

"Maybe." Dr. Wu sighed. "As I mentioned earlier, sir, a storm of this size has so many variables. And, in a manner of speaking, its own sense of logic. Or lack of logic. It can behave in ways that may be, frankly, beyond our ability to understand. This storm has something I've never seen before. What almost seems like a survival instinct."

The Vice President snorted, then scooted back in his chair. "Sorry," he said.

"No, that's a perfectly natural reaction," Dr. Wu said, turning to Stanton. "I would never have said anything like that before yesterday. But this storm isn't like any I've ever seen."

"All right," the President said, gesturing impatiently. "What are our options?"

"Options?" Dr. Wu looked at his shoes. "I don't know that that word applies anymore, sir. If this new eye wall continues to organize, I'm afraid that our only real option is to get out of its way."

CHARLES MALLORY LIFTED his head and saw the pizza box and the bottle of merlot on the counter from the night before. He looked over at the other motel bed and saw Blaine. She was sitting up, pillow propped vertically behind her back, gazing at the silent television, wearing nothing but one of his dress shirts, half-buttoned, and her underpants. Except for the bruises on her face, she looked awfully nice.

"What time is it?"

"9:32," she said.

"A long couple of minutes."

"Funny how that happens."

He glanced at the TV screen. A scene of boarded up homes along a stretch of North Carolina coast, then a traffic jam coming off a barrier island. A list of MANDATORY EVACUATIONS scrolled across the bottom of the screen.

"How's the storm?"

"Worse," she said. "I'm really worried. I keep trying to call my son but can't reach him."

She gazed down at the cell phone in her right hand. Mallory climbed out of bed and walked to the window, wearing boxer shorts and a dark polo shirt. He glanced outside, saw the rain dimpling puddles in the parking lot.

"Want to come over and sit with me for a minute?"

He turned. "Sure," he said. "Okay."

Mallory walked to the bed. Her green eyes were keen and damp, watching him.

"I need a hug," she said.

Mallory walked around to her. He met her on the other side.

"Just not too hard. Okay?"

They gave each other a tentative hug, then tried a longer one. It felt good. She pulled her head away to look at him and he kissed her softly and she kissed him back. He breathed the scent of shampoo in her soft hair, and pulled her against him. They folded onto the bed together, touching each other's faces. And then Blaine unbuttoned the shirt and pulled it off and Mallory took off his clothes and they slipped under the covers and held each other. Everything about Blaine excited him. Her skin, her hair, her lips, her courage, the easy way she held him, the way her eyes watched his, the way she pulled him into her. For a few minutes he forgot everything else that was happening in the world.

Afterward, they lay in the covers, holding hands. Then it began to rain harder again. And then harder. And eventually, the outside returned.

"I wish we could just stay here," she said.

"Does it say somewhere that we can't?"

"No." She turned her head to the wall. "Except it's nearing ten thirty."

"And . . . ?"

"I seem to recall you saying something about confronting Easton."

"Well, yeah. Someone has to."

"But the President wants me to come in for an 11:15 meeting about the storm. Dr. Jared Clayton will be there."

"Oh. Really." Mallory propped himself on an elbow and watched her with a new interest. "Where is he?"

"He's at the White House right now. And he's talking. Sending him those memos worked, apparently. He's been talking with the President and Dr. Wu about something. The mitigation hasn't been effective. It's not working."

"Uh oh."

"Yeah. They want to lay the cards out for everyone, apparently."

"You knew all that but didn't tell me?"

"A question of priorities."

"I see."

She smiled, and her eyes brightened with a lovely, warm intensity. "I just needed to stop thinking for a few minutes."

Mallory watched her, frowning now, as she sat up under the covers.

"No," she said, "I don't mean it like that. Really. That was won-derful."

Good, he thought. She reached for him and they held on to each other, and stopped thinking again, for another few minutes.

FIFTY

As Catherine Blaine entered the Data Visualization Center in the Eisenhower Executive Office Building, Dr. Jared Clayton was seated beside Dr. Wu, his elbows spread on the conference table, his eyes intently watching the monitors in front of him; at first glance, Wu appeared to be his young son.

Blaine nodded quickly to the others around the table as she took a seat: Vice President Bill Stanton, Intelligence Director Harold DeVries, Secretary of State Kathryn Milford, Chief of Staff Gabriel Herring, National Security Advisor Nan Sewell, FEMA Director Shauna Brewster, National Weather Service Administrator Kevin Green, and John Hasty, the Director of Emergency Management for the District of Columbia. Conspicuously absent was Clark Easton, the Secretary of Defense.

Normally, an emergency management meeting would involve the heads of FEMA and Homeland Security, not national defense officials or Cabinet members. Blaine wondered if the President was going to bring others into the circle this morning.

She sat between Milford and Herring, and quietly did what the others were doing: she glanced through the update summaries on Hurricane Alexander. The news was not good. Alexander was a still-well-organized Category 3 hurricane, the largest ever in the North Atlantic Ocean.

After several minutes, the door slid open and the President entered, alone, carrying a bottle of Evian in his right hand and a blue briefing folder in his left. Everyone stood until he took his seat at the end of the conference table.

"Good morning," he said. He frowned at Blaine as he sat, and touched a forefinger to his right eye.

Blaine shrugged. "I tripped."

The President's frown deepened. "All right, then," he said. His gaze roamed the faces around the table. "Let's get right to it. I have been to FEMA headquarters and met with Director Brewster, and I think they're doing a great job. I've met with Dr. Wu here and with the folks from the National Weather Service." The President took a drink from his water. "We're going to address several issues this morning, but we'll start with the summary. Jim?"

Dr. Wu, wearing one of his short-sleeved light blue dress shirts and a conservative tie that ended several inches above his belt, stood and clicked the wireless presentation remote in his right hand. Two rows of numbers appeared on the large monitor screen behind him, each showing tracking data recorded over the past twelve hours, relayed from the National Hurricane Center. The smaller row of monitors displayed maps and charts of the system, including one with fifteen computer "spaghetti models" predicting the storm's path; all of them now showed Alexander making landfall in the mid-Atlantic region in approximately thirty-six hours.

"We've seen a shift, a nudge to the left, over the past few hours," he said. "As you can see, most of the projections now have the center of this storm coming into or near the mouth of the Chesapeake Bay. Unfortunately, that would mean that we will probably see a pretty direct hit here in Washington."

"Which would be unprecedented," said Brewster, a sprightly, freckled blond-haired woman in her late fifties.

"Yes." Dr. Wu nodded. As he stood beside Dr. Clayton's chair for a moment, the two men appeared to be the same height, Blaine noticed, even though Clayton was seated. "Quite possibly the worst we've ever had," he said.

"Uh, can you explain that?" said the Vice President, punctuating the question by clearing his throat. "I thought being inland here gives us a buffer that the coast doesn't have."

"No, actually not," said Dr. Wu. "Not if the storm comes up the Chesapeake, and the bay and its tributaries overflow. Much of what is between us and the Bay is sea level or close to it. On this track, we're going to be extremely vulnerable. Much of the eastern shores of Virginia and Maryland are going to be under water. That's maybe less than twenty-four hours away."

"*Under water*," said the Vice President.

"Yes, unfortunately." Dr. Wu took a breath and glanced at the President. "We all heard the criticisms about New Orleans allowing building below sea level. Well, the Eastern Shore isn't much better. With the projected storm surge, much of the land surrounding the Bay is going to be flooded. I don't think there's any other possible scenario at this point."

Blaine saw what had changed: there was no room for caution anymore; Dr. Wu, who had become a likeable resident expert in recent years, was clearly uncomfortable as the bearer of life-altering news. He looked physically ill to Blaine, as if he were about to vomit.

"So what are we looking at?" asked DeVries. "How deep under water?"

"In some areas, a few inches. In others, perhaps ten to twenty feet."

"Jesus H. Christ," said the Vice President.

"And what about Washington?" asked Secretary of State Kathryn Milford.

"Yes, I'm getting to that," Wu said, an unfamiliar edge in his voice. He stepped to one of the workstations and typed a sequence on a keyboard, then stepped back and clicked his wireless remote. "This is the model that we created with the National Weather Service just in the past couple of hours. I'll walk you through it."

Dr. Wu narrated the progression of images that appeared on the large monitor: computer simulated models of the Potomac River flooding its banks, the water then spreading over land, dispersing throughout the city.

"This is the most likely scenario," he began. "Tomorrow afternoon or early evening, the Potomac will begin to flood, first into the streets of Georgetown, Southeast and Alexandria, Virginia."

The simulation focused in on Georgetown for a moment, showing water filling the lower streets and then rising all the way to M Street.

"We've got forty-five miles of riverfront in D.C.," Dr. Wu continued on, "and all along those forty-five miles we're going to see extensive flooding. There's simply nowhere for all that water to go. Hains Point, East Potomac Park, and most of the Mall will be under water by tomorrow evening."

"The *Mall*," said the Vice President.

Blaine looked at the President, who was soberly watching the screen.

"So we'd be particularly vulnerable *here*, presumably," said DeVries.

"Yes. As you can see." Dr. Wu pressed a key to start a new simulation. "This is what we expect overnight tomorrow."

On the screen, a tide of floodwaters rolled steadily east from the Potomac, covering the entire National Mall and the surrounding streets to the Capitol, drowning the South Lawn of the White House, reaching to the top of its first-floor windows.

"There's a basin just south of where we're sitting now," Dr. Wu went on, "which is the lowest point in the city. The flood waters will most likely move north along Seventeenth Street, then down Constitution Avenue and settle into the Federal Triangle area. Everything within the boundaries of Fifteenth Street, Constitution Avenue, and Pennsylvania Avenue will be under water."

"Inches? Feet?" the Vice President asked.

Wu blinked at the President, not looking at Stanton. "Again, that depends," he said. "If you want to stay with worst-case scenario." He paused, glancing at Brewster. "Then we're talking ten feet, minimum."

"Probably a lot more," said the FEMA director.

"This may seem an inappropriate question to ask at this point," said the Secretary of State, "but with this inherent vulnerability, has anyone ever thought of constructing levees to protect the Mall?"

"Actually, we do have levees," Dr. Wu said, in his flat, measured tone. "But they're old and they're not adequate. There's one right behind us, in fact." He pointed out the window toward the Washington Monument. "You may have noticed when you're on the Mall, there's an odd little hill north of the Reflecting Pool, between the World War II Memorial and the Lincoln Memorial."

"Yes?"

"That's part of a levee system the Army Corps built decades ago. Unfortunately, it was never finished. There are two big gaps in it. One is near Constitution Avenue south of Twenty-third Street. The other is at Seventeenth Street. The Park Service is placing sand bags in the gaps right now. But it's only going to be a Band-Aid at best. It's not enough to hold back the water."

"So what does that mean?" the Vice President said.

The FEMA director answered. "What that means," she said, "is that water will surge through those gaps, and downtown will be flooded. There's probably nothing we can do about that."

The National Security Adviser cursed under her breath.

The FEMA director went on: "In fact, much of the National Mall is built on old sea walls that have been crumbling for years. The hit on the Mall is going to be severe, I'm afraid. I don't think there's any way around that."

The President lifted his forefinger. "On a related point: I've been on the phone with the Parks director and the directors of the National Gallery and the Smithsonian, and those buildings are all being secured as we speak."

"So you're saying the Mall is going to be a minimum of ten feet under water and there's nothing we can *do* about it?" the Vice President asked.

When no one answered, Dr. Wu said, "Yes, sir. The real question is going to be how long will the water stay in the city." Everyone watched him, waiting. "The worst case is that, in some places, it stays indefinitely. The boundaries of the city change, in other words. The best case, it recedes, we drain it, and we eventually get back at least a semblance of what we had."

The President nodded at him appreciatively. "Thank you, Jim." He clasped his hands. "So, folks: bottom line, this thing is coming harder and faster than anyone expected. We need to aggressively accelerate our response. We've got mandatory evacuations up and down the coast, as you know. And we're coordinating efforts with all of our coastal states. As Director Brewster tells me, we need to hammer home the message that people within a hundred miles of the coast need to leave immediately. End of story. Staying behind is foolish but it's also illegal. Right now, though, for us, the biggest threat is right here in Washington." The President nodded to the D.C. Emergency Management Director, John Hasty. "John?"

"Thank you, sir." Hasty, a slight, ruddy man with thin, silver hair, clicked on his remote, without standing. "Just to quickly summarize. We have fourteen primary evacuation routes that we will use to direct motorists out of the city beginning at two P.M. this afternoon. Pennsylvania Avenue is the dividing line. Those north of Pennsylvania will be directed to the northeast and west on radial evacuation routes."

He enlarged the map, showing the spokes of the routes out of D.C., none of which crossed.

"To the south of Pennsylvania Avenue, they'll be directed south, east and west."

"Once they leave, no one's coming back in," the President said.

"That's correct. We'll have four inbound routes for emergency vehicles only."

The President's eyes stopped on Blaine's for a moment. He was sizing up her reaction. For a moment, she thought of how this had started: being in West Virginia just last Sunday, seeing the strange message from Kevin on her BlackBerry. *How quickly everything changes. How quickly it's all gone.*

"For the time being, I am going to stay here," the President said. "But we need to begin moving people to other locations. Speaker Davis is on his way to Mount Weather in Virginia as we speak. Bill, I'd like you to move to Bolling Air Force Base overnight."

Silence followed. Blaine understood what he was saying. *Succession.* He was taking precautions, in case the worst happened. The President would go to one facility, the Vice President to another, the Speaker to a third.

"Is this really that bad, sir?" Blaine asked.

"Well. That is what our emergency management officials are telling me we should do. And that is how we're responding. I just met with JOC an hour ago. That's how they've laid it out."

JOC. Joint Operations Center of the Secret Service.

Blaine looked at Dr. Clayton, whose dark eyes were watching attentively.

"This is the hard reality, folks. Okay? On a personal note, get your families and loved ones out of the area as soon as possible, if you haven't already. We're expecting dangerous winds and rains within the next few hours. This is our window to get out. Right now. I am asking everyone who isn't absolutely essential to the emergency response to leave."

He opened the briefing folder he had carried into the room. Let his eyes scan the page.

"Already, we've got, let's see, uh, most of two counties in North Carolina half under water. Ten inches of rain in some parts of Virginia. Trees down, debris blocking roads. And we're seeing some fierce lightning storms, I'm told, that even our top scientists can't quite figure out. And it's all heading this way."

No one spoke. The President's tone left no opening for discussion, although Blaine sensed that his demeanor was not quite in sync with what he was really thinking.

"Okay? That's where we are. Now Director Brewster will convene an additional briefing for you down on C Street at FEMA headquarters. She'll cover the specifics of our evacuation plans, the pre- and post-storm drills, etc. And now, if possible, I'd like Secretary Blaine, Director DeVries, and Vice President Stanton to stay behind for a few minutes. Thank you."

Blaine remained seated, as did DeVries and Stanton.

But she was surprised to see that two of the other people in the room stayed in their seats as well.

FIFTY-ONE

"ALL RIGHT." GRAVELY, THE President folded his hands. "What we just laid out, folks," he said, "was Scenario A. The evacuations, the deployment of FEMA teams and the National Guard. It's the prudent and appropriate response to the information we're receiving on this storm."

Blaine, watching her boss, felt stunned and helpless. She thought of Kevin. *Where was he?*

"Now." He took a deep breath and looked directly at Blaine. "We are also looking at a Scenario B. A different strategy. Different outcome. Which, I'll say right upfront, is probably not as likely as what you have just seen and heard. And which, I might add, is not for public consumption. But I want all of you to be aware of it. First, Dr. Wu, can you tell us where we are with Weathervane?"

Blaine watched the diminutive scientist as he stood again and nodded, his face expressionless. *Did Weathervane even matter any more?* she wondered.

"As you know," Dr. Wu began, "the Weathervane Group yesterday provided us with a series of projections for how their mitigation project would unfold. I've tried to boil this all down into very simple terms." He clicked open a screen full of figures on the large monitor. "The numbers on the top are the projections we were given yesterday by Weathervane." The figures showed barometric pressure in inches, wind speed in miles per hour, wind field size, and thermal wind shear calculations. "The numbers at bottom are the actual real-time numbers. Obviously, there is a consistent discrepancy."

Everyone stared at the numbers, with varying degrees of interest.

"So, it's not working as advertised," said the Vice President.

"No, that's right."

There was a long pause, as he seemed to be waiting for some cue from the President. Blaine studied Dr. Wu's intelligent, unrevealing face, his short, black bangs, and wondered what he really thought. Years earlier, Wu had expressed a stubborn skepticism about hurricane mitigation, once telling a TV interviewer that any money spent studying it "might just as well be dropped from an airplane into the eye of the hurricane."

"Thank you, Jim," the President said. "Now, I'd like to let Jared Clayton explain Scenario B. As you know, Dr. Clayton has been involved in storm mitigation research at the very highest levels for more than a decade. With Lawrence Livermore in California. With U.C. Berkeley. And independently. For the past eighteen months, he was a consultant for the people in this Weathervane Group. That relationship was severed this morning, and I am pleased to say that he is now working with us. He has some thoughts about what we can do—try to do—to mitigate this thing."

"Thank you, sir." Dr. Clayton said. "I want to first just say that I am humbled by what has happened since I last met with you." His expression shifted uncomfortably, as he looked down at his notes. "But let me get right to the subject, as the President requested. At the crux of it is this: there is a chance, still, that we can utilize existing technologies to diminish the impact of this hurricane. And if that possibility exists, the feeling is that we must pursue it."

"But, with all due respect, sir, what about your friends in the Weathervane Group?" asked the Vice President, smiling, a hint of disdain in his voice. "Isn't this what you told us yesterday *they* were going to do?"

"No." Clayton looked down, showing a contrite expression. "Actually, I think they were doing something quite different. Although I did not know that until last night. Which is why we've severed our relationship." He glanced at Blaine. "Scenario B, as the President and I have discussed, is actually a completely different process—and an opportunity that will only exist for a few hours."

"Please, explain," said the Vice President.

"Yes, that's my intention." Dr. Clayton pursed his lips and swallowed. Blaine noticed his unruly gray eyebrows. "Yesterday," he said, "we told you about four mitigation processes. The fourth process involved creating a kind of synthetic, ion-charged bacteria cloud, which could potentially disrupt the storm's inner weather, so to speak, and ultimately cause the eye wall to destabilize. What I'm beginning to understand is that this process, and maybe the others as well, was in fact created in response to an offensive trigger."

"And what does that mean?" asked Vice President Stanton, smiling skeptically.

"Meaning, a self-assembly mechanism was generated first, and, from that, a mechanism to disassemble."

"You're saying this storm was created artificially," said Harold DeVries.

"I think it's possible, yes. Or enhanced and manipulated. And if it was done in the way that I suspect, this storm is, in effect, programmed to be self-sustaining. To have encoded in its structure the ability to continue replicating and growing."

"Don't all storms have that?" asked DeVries.

"To an extent, yes. But not like this. Storms gather strength by absorbing other systems, by feeding off of warm air and warm water. But eventually, they run into something that stops them. Incompatible winds, changes in temperatures or air pressures. That's why we don't get more deadly hurricanes than we do. This system seems somehow immune to the normal obstacle course that degrades a hurricane. It appears driven by something we have not seen before, which almost seems to resemble instinct."

"That's hardly possible, though, is it?" said the Vice President.

Blaine nodded, wanting him to get to the point.

"Well, you tell me what's possible and what's not," Dr. Clayton said, surprising everyone by his shift of tone. "It's being *studied*. Nearly every aspect of the weather is being studied in some form or another. There is a research center in northern California that has been doing independent research of this nature for the past several years."

"Computer simulations, though, not actual weather events," said DeVries.

He nodded.

"But you *did* use mitigation operations on those storms in the Pacific," the President said.

"Yes, that's correct. But with two clear differences. First, the Pacific systems were much smaller than this. And the mitigation began early in the storm cycle. Under normal circumstances, you have the greatest chance of affecting the outcome if you can manipulate the eye early in its evolution."

"Under *normal* circumstances," the President said.

"Right. But in this particular case, there *is* reason to be optimistic." Clayton clicked a new image onto the screen, showing the animated color-enhanced swirl of Alexander. Ragged bands of red, orange, magenta, blue, green.

"What we're seeing here is the potential disintegration of Alexander's inner eye. That's normal, and a rather good sign." He used a red laser pointer to indicate a separate area of organization on the eastern-edge rain-bands. "And what we see *here* is the beginning of an outer eye wall, which will eventually move inside the system, stealing the inner eye wall of its moisture."

"Choking it," the President said.

"Choking it, yes." The corners of Clayton's mouth lifted. "It's what is known as an eye wall replacement cycle. It happens in most major hurricanes when they reach Category Three. What will normally happen," he continued, "is that this outer eye wall replaces the inner eye wall, forming a larger eye, and the hurricane re-intensifies."

"Say that again," said the Vice President.

"Yes." Dr. Clayton nodded. "In large hurricanes, we often see a weakening of the inner eye. The storm, in effect, wants to grow larger, but the eye wall convection is not able to stay organized and the inner eye loses moisture and energy. In other words, one of the ways a major storm system gains strength is by replacing its eye wall. We didn't know that fifty years ago. We do now. It's adjusting, making room to grow bigger."

"And?" asked DeVries, frowning.

"In the models we worked on last year, it was during the storm's formative stages that we were able to bring about small but significant changes. When we were able to alter the structure of the storm as it was forming, and by doing so to alter its outcome."

"But this one's so far along," said the Vice President. "We're not talking about the early stages here."

"No, we're not. But that's what the President means by opportunity.

In effect, we *will be* in the formative stages of this storm as it goes through its eye wall replacement cycle. What it's doing is preparing to start over again. But, you see, until then it's giving us an unusual opportunity."

"Explain," said the Vice President. "An opportunity for what?"

"To do in real time what we've done with computer models," he said. "And what we did in the Pacific last year. We look at the factors that cause the storm to become better organized and we alter those slightly. A small adjustment can sometimes result in a vastly different outcome. We could, for example, steer a potentially deadly storm slightly north, where it would then run into cooler waters or a cold air system and break apart."

There was silence in the room. To Blaine, it felt like skepticism. *How could they be optimistic after what had happened with Weathervane?* Blaine was beginning to wonder if the President might be losing his grip on reality.

"Go ahead, tell them what you were telling me," President Hall said to Clayton.

"Well, what I'm recommending—and what the President and I have been discussing—is utilizing two additional mitigation processes."

Dr. Wu's face was blank, Blaine noticed, his eyelids half-closed. The President nodded for Clayton to go on.

"First, we send a series of solar radar pulses into the existing eye. That's what the President is trying to arrange now. A private satellite company in California has in fact been aggressively developing this technology for about four years. The US military has worked with them on several projects. It's experimental, but it's something I believe could have an impact on the storm."

Blaine saw the Vice President shaking his head. "But if this thing has been programmed to *sustain* itself," he said, "how in God's creation are we going to stop it?"

"You see, that's the point," said Dr. Clayton. "The eye wall replacement *is* part of its sustenance."

"So what would these *pulses* do?" asked DeVries.

"What we hope is that they will alter some of the key defining factors in the storm's eye wall."

"Key defining factors."

"Yes. Storm force, atmospheric pressures, the flow from high pressure to low pressure, wind speed and direction, convection. To slightly alter the equilibrium inside the storm."

"That's the first part," the President said.

Dr. Clayton bit a corner of his lower lip. "Yes. The second process is something we told you about yesterday. Dropping synthetic, ion-charged bacteria clouds into the hurricane, using drone planes. These clouds could in effect feed off of the storm's inner eye wall, disrupting the structure of the storm and ultimately causing it to become unstable. I have close contact with the two labs that are doing this research, and the President is making arrangements for that, as well."

"But isn't this the same thing you just brought us with Weathervane?" asked the Vice President.

"No. The difference," Clayton said, "is the eyewall replacement cycle. That's our window of opportunity."

There was another prolonged silence. DeVries broke it. "What are the odds of any of this actually working?" he asked.

"Well. We don't know," Clayton said, frowning at the intelligence director.

"Just to reiterate," Dr. Wu said, his voice sounding rough and unfamiliar. "This sort of technology has never been tested on a storm of this size. So the chances of it working are not great. It's important that we understand that going in."

"How long would it be before we know something?" asked the Vice President.

"This eye wall replacement cycle is happening very rapidly," Clayton said. "I imagine it will be finished in less than eight hours. The laser process, we are expecting, will begin almost immediately."

The President stood. "In the meantime," he said, "I expect us all to go back to the first scenario. Which, to the outside world, is the *only* scenario. All right? I want you all to make sure that your families are safe and that your homes are secured. And that we're all on the same page in what we say, if anything, to the media." He looked at Dr. Clayton and nodded. "Okay? Let's do it."

Blaine felt anxious again. *Where is my son?*

As the others stood, Clayton make eye contact with Blaine. He moved toward her in an awkward sideways motion around the table and thrust out his hand. "I just wanted to thank you," he said, speaking softly. "For what you did."

"Oh." Blaine shook his hand. His clothes were rumpled, his fingers calloused. She saw that he was about to say more, but the President was gesturing to her.

A Secret Service agent slid a computer card across the magnetic reader and the electronic door opened.

"You know, Cate, I never thought I'd say this," the President told her, as they walked down the marble corridor to the elevator, his hand on her back. "But I'm afraid I don't quite believe you."

"Sir?"

"What you said before we started. I don't believe it."

"Which part, sir?"

"The part about you tripped."

"Oh." Blaine smiled. It made her face hurt.

"Want to tell me what really happened?"

"Sure. Except I need to make a call first."

They walked together through the softly lit tunnel in silence, the President's senatorial features raised by a subtle smile. On the other side, Blaine stepped outside under the awning to the West Wing, breathing the mist of the pouring rain, and she flipped open her phone.

FIFTY-TWO

CHARLES MALLORY DROVE THROUGH the hard gusting rains, along a two-lane rural road that was mostly empty, tree branches and debris scattered across the pavement in places, the traffic signals out, swinging wildly in the wind. Dark clouds had engulfed the suburban sky, making it seem like nighttime when it was still early afternoon. He listened to the static on the AM news stations: Reports of massive flooding in North Carolina, cutting off the Outer Banks; power lost to tens of thousands in Virginia; the damage to marinas, bay-front homes and businesses; tornadoes in Southern Maryland. Winds whipped across the fallow corn and soybean fields, at times pushing his car onto the shoulder, other times causing him to stop and wait it out. The emptiness of this countryside, the encroaching water and storm clouds, made Mallory feel very alone, headed toward something dark and unfamiliar, a feeling he hadn't known in a while. It was as if this violent weather were waking him up, forcing a reassessment. In the past, the storms in this life had made him want to step back and detach, to seek out quieter harbors, and more individual patterns for his life. But in the midst of *this* storm, this very real storm, he felt himself desiring the opposite: to engage. To find something essential and hold on to it. As he sat parked beside the road, waiting out a wild downpour and bursts of lightning, he thought about his brother and how he had gotten here. And then he thought about Blaine again and imagined a life of greater meaning, shared with someone else. With Blaine. Twenty minutes later, he came to an intersection with a gas station and a Home Depot. The gas station was boarded up, but the Home Depot was open. People hurried across the parking lot through the sheets of rain. Mallory sat in the car, formulating a plan. He was about to go in when his phone vibrated.

Blaine.

"Hi," she said. "I'm glad I reached you."

"Me, too."

"I'm about to go into a meeting with the President."

"Okay."

"It's much worse than we thought," she said.

"What's worse?"

"The storm. It's coming right up Chesapeake Bay. It's going to put Washington under ten to twenty feet of water."

"My god. What about the mitigation?"

"Not working," she said. "It's not going to happen. There's going to be a National Weather Service bulletin soon that'll put it all in very stark terms."

Mallory looked out at the rain slanting in gusts across the parking lot lights.

"I need to see you. I need to talk."

"I feel approximately the same," he said.

"Also, I can't find my son."

"What do you mean?"

"I mean, I can't find him. The last I heard from him was yesterday. He texted me last night, saying he might be going to the Shore to 'ride it out.' There's no such thing as riding out this storm, Mallory. But he doesn't know that. I can't reach him. Cell phone service is going out all over the region. Also, I've been having this sort of terrible thought. For the past hour or so." Her voice seemed to crack.

"Tell me."

"That Rorbach did something to Kevin before he got to me."

Mallory took a breath. "Why would you think that?"

"Because the last I heard from him was about an hour and a half before Rorbach attacked me."

"Don't think that."

"Why?"

"Because it isn't true." He listened to the rain, but couldn't think of anything else more reassuring to say. "You're going to meet with the President?"

"Yes. I'm going to ask him about Easton."

"Good."

Blaine was silent. Gusts of wind-driven rain slammed the car.

"Call me when you get finished," he said. "We'll find Kevin."

MALLORY RAN SPLASHING across the parking lot to the Home Depot. Dripping wet, he pushed a shopping cart up and down the aisles. Bought two flashlights, an ice chest and four containers for gas and water. The lines stretched halfway down the aisles. When he finally got out, he drove on through the storm looking for a place to buy gas, water, ice. But the only convenience stores that were open had makeshift signs taped in the windows: NO WATER and NO GAS. Some, NO BEER. He bought what they had left, instead: nuts, chips, sodas, juice.

He kept driving, back toward the Pike Motel, his emergency lights flashing as he tried to follow the lanes of the road, the blinding rain and still-darkening sky reducing visibility to the end of his headlight beams. He listened to news reports of deaths and damages. Thirteen fatalities already attributed to Alexander, even though the storm hadn't actually arrived. He had been through a few deadly storms over the years, several on the East Coast and a couple in the Caribbean, but nothing as large or as potentially devastating as this one.

The rains came in torrents, and the road seemed to disappear in front of him. He parked again and waited it out, turning the radio dial for updates. Mandatory evacuations, he heard, were being ordered throughout the region. "*Everyone within a hundred miles of the coast needs to move. Now,*" the FEMA director said, her sound-bite played repeatedly on every station he turned to.

Several minutes later, his cell phone vibrated again. Chaplin.

"How are you making out?" he said, in his chipper, lilting accent. Mallory heard music in the background. *Madama Butterfly.*

"Not great. Trying to get back to the motel, but the rain won't let me. Surprised you could reach me. Where are you?"

"Me? I'm in Virginia. Two hundred miles from the coast. I'm working on Rorbach's cell phone."

"Oh, okay. What are you finding?"

"A whole series of emails and stored docs. But they're all encrypted. Probably some good material. We're working on it."

"How about my brother?"

"Your brother? How about him?"

"Is he all right?"

"He's fine, yes."

Mallory heard the trees whipping, the hail-like rain thumping harder on the car roof. "Can I talk with him?"

"No. You asked me to protect him, Charlie," he said. "For now, I'm recommending against him talking with you."

Mallory nodded to himself. Chaplin was doing his job. "Okay." He thought about Blaine, going in to tell the President.

"I'll let you know as soon as we break the encryption."

FIFTY-THREE

CATHERINE BLAINE RETURNED TO the Oval Office accompanied by two White House police officers and a Secret Service agent. The President nodded a formal greeting. A new bottle of Evian was on a coaster in front of him.

"I can't find my son," she said, standing in front of the Resolute desk.

The President looked up but didn't seem to see her. "We'll find him, Cate. I'm sure he's fine." He gestured for her to sit. She did. "What else is on your mind? What happened to you, anyway?"

Blaine took a deep breath. "Do you know that Thom Rorbach was killed in Rock Creek Park last night?"

He shrugged, showing nothing.

"Do you know who killed him? Or why?"

The President shook his head. "Don't even know why he was there, Cate. In the middle of this goddamned storm."

"But you have an idea."

"No. No idea. I was told the FBI was out there a few hours ago. Doing clean-up."

"*Clean-up?* What are you talking about?"

The President shrugged again. "Cate, I don't *know*. Okay? I don't know anything about it. Just that none of it's going to make the evening news. For obvious reasons. It's too sensitive. And it's going to take a while to sort through it. And with this storm, who really cares about anything else?"

Priorities. She felt a stab of anger and recalled the foul animal scent of Rorbach as his wet, cold fingers probed her face and her chest and his hard penis jabbed into her face. *All of this will be swept away by the storm*, she thought. *Say what you have to say.*

"Where's Secretary Easton?"

The President raised his eyebrows. Blaine waited. "I don't know," he said. "He hasn't responded to our messages. His wife is at their home in Switzerland. I know that. She left a few days ago."

"Do you know what happened before Rorbach was killed?" Blaine said.

"What do you mean?"

"Do you know what happened before Rorbach was killed?" she said again, her voice rising. "To me?" His face went through a subtle transformation, his brow creasing. "He abducted and sexually assaulted me. He beat me and intended to kill me. The only reason he didn't, I think, is because he wanted to assault me more later."

The President's frown deepened. "Cate, what are you talking about?"

Blaine reached into her purse and took out the list. The seven names. Now nine.

"I just want to show you this. I think this is why he did what he did to me."

She unfolded the sheet of paper and set it in front of the President. The original seven names, followed by Drs. Westlake and Sanchez.

The President seemed to study it carefully. Then he pushed it back toward her. "Is this supposed to mean something to me?"

"Does it?"

"No."

"Do you want me to tell you?"

"All right."

He leaned back in his chair and listened as she told him about Leviathan, and about the nine people who had been killed or disappeared because of what they knew. It was a story that began more than a decade earlier with intelligence reports about storm mitigation research in Russia and China. A story that encompassed the email threats and "natural" disasters. A story which had apparently ended several hours ago in the woods of Rock Creek Park, when Rorbach was killed.

The President watched attentively as she spoke. When she finished, he lifted the sheet of paper again, studied the names and set it down.

"Okay," he said. "That's a dramatic story, Cate."

"It is."

"It's a lot for me to process right now."

"Sir?"

"You're telling me this as we're heading into what my scientists are saying may be the worst natural disaster in our nation's history."

"Yes. I know that, sir."

"At this moment, with all due respect—and I do respect you a great deal, Cate, you know that. But at this moment, why should I care about what sounds to me like a serious police matter?"

"It's not a police matter, sir. And the reason you should care is because there's nothing we can do about the storm anymore except get out of its way. And also because this may be the only time we have to get Easton."

The President's thoughts were elsewhere, with another chess game in his head. "'Get' him?"

"Yes. Easton doesn't know what we know," Blaine said. "He may not even know that I'm still alive. We probably have an advantage right now because of that. Once he knows, he might flee."

"Flee?"

"Flee."

She stared at the President until he was really with her again, angry, disliking him all of a sudden. "He might," he said. "Although, as you know, no planes are flying right now, Cate."

"They're still flying out of Boston. And Chicago. And as soon as this thing passes, God willing, they'll be flying out of Washington again. He may be waiting it out."

"Cate, it's not important," he said, and then seemed to check himself. "I mean, in the context of everything else. Can you let it go until we get past this thing?"

Blaine took a deep breath. "No," she said. She stood and looked outside at the South Lawn.

"I'm sorry, Cate. I don't mean to seem insensitive. I'm very sorry about what happened. Okay?" He waited for her to turn. "So. What are you suggesting?" he said, more softly.

"Send Easton a very specific message. Tell him the mitigation is working. Make it seem like it's a meeting of the inner circle."

"And then?"

"Bring him in."

The President looked past her. "For what?"

"I think you could start with a charge of vandalism," Blaine said. "Deliberately corrupting government-owned SME-PED electronic devices. From there you could go right up to espionage and murder."

"No," he said, barely audible. "No, I have one little problem with that scenario, Cate. And I guess I might as well tell you what it is." The President's eyes narrowed. He regarded Blaine for a long time before he said anything. "We can't do it that way, Cate. I'm sorry. Not at this point."

"Why? Why can't you do it that way?"

He shook his head and averted his eyes. Blaine sat again, flushed with anger. Waiting. *Come on, talk to me. What's really going on here?*

"You told me yourself you were building a case," she said.

"Yes. I did." She watched him as he looked at the backs of his fingers, struggling with what he was going to tell her. "We *have* been building a case, Cate, but I didn't say it was against Easton."

"Against whom?"

"We've been building a case against Rorbach. And Zorn. It seems as if you've accelerated it considerably."

"But Easton was pulling Rorbach's strings. He's the one who brought him in to the Leviathan Project. He's the reason these nine people were killed." She felt her heart racing, felt herself starting to lose control. *What the hell was really going on here?*

"We don't know that, Cate. And it's going to be impossible to prove."

"Yes, we do know it."

"No. We can't do it that way, Cate." A steely look came in his eyes. "Do you know what distinguishes this country from every other country on the planet, Cate? It's our capacity to imagine—and then to use what we imagine to create new technologies. Other countries have occasionally taken what we've created and done it better. But it starts with us. What's going on across the street right now could change the nature of science. And it could change history."

"What does that have to do with anything we're talking about?"

"The case is against Rorbach, Cate. And Zorn."

"No. It's against Easton."

He looked away again, his mouth flattening. Blaine felt her eyes misting with anger. "As I said, I have a problem with that scenario, Cate, and I guess I'm going to have to tell you what it is."

"Yes," she said. "Please."

"I told you that we know about Volkov because we have a source. An informant."

"Yes. You did."

She watched him, leaning forward. Her heart racing again.

"Easton is our source on this."

"*What?*"

"Yes. He's the informant."

1:18 P.M.

Stray bands of Alexander's western edge were already cutting savage dents into the Chesapeake Bay, with wind gusts topping seventy miles an hour, tearing off tree limbs and breaking apart billboards, scattering debris across the Eastern Shore roadways. In dozens of low-lying areas, storm surge had flooded farm fields and rural roads. Three of the five lanes of the two Chesapeake Bay bridge spans were open to westbound traffic only and another, reversible lane, had been reserved for emergency vehicles.

Mallory listened on the radio as he inched through the rolling country back to the Pike Motel. Several miles away, he began to hear a deep rumbling sound, as if the earth were shaking from giant trucks. But there were no other vehicles out in the storm. He turned off the radio and slowed to a stop, thinking it might be his car. He watched the beating rain, thinking. He was startled out of his thoughts by a spectacular display of lightning over the waterlogged farm fields—what seemed like hundreds of tentacles of light shooting down from the clouds.

He drove on and came at last to the motel parking lot. He turned off the engine and waited. Felt the rumbling again as if it were inside the car. A strange, deep, continuous thunder. He looked at the sky above the motel sign, saw the silent lightning flashes jumping from cloud to cloud, dozens of them. Hundreds. He closed his eyes, and the lightning's afterglows seemed to linger, becoming shapes inside his retina. When he looked again, the shapes were still there—giant stick figures walking across the flooded farmland. Mallory gathered his groceries and ran through the rain, up to the motel's third floor, feeling the phone vibrating in his pocket as he went.

THE LAST OF the three thirty-six-foot-long Predator B-003 UAVs, or unmanned aerial vehicles, punctured the western eye wall of Hurricane Alexander at 220 miles per hour shortly after 2 P.M. eastern time. Once it reached the eye, the plane dropped its cargo into the storm, a thousand gallons of synthetic bacteria.

The plane then reversed course, beginning the return flight to its base in central California. But the plane, which was designed to stay aloft for thirty-six hours, did not make it back through the western eye wall. As with the previous two Predator B-003s, each of which carried a $5 million price tag, the third drone became ensnared in a furious net of wind and lightning, which pulled it from its programmed course like a giant, electrified Venus fly trap, and brought it down into a turbulent sea.

FIFTY-FOUR

2:08 P.M.

"FOURTH SERIES OF PULSES has been activated."

Dr. Clayton stood hunched over the row of computer monitors in his rumpled clothes. A headset fed information into his ears, a stream of data from the private satellite operation in California.

His eyes were perpetually intent—although he seemed, to Dr. Wu, disconnected from reality. Unaware of the others in the room or of the carnage that had already been inflicted in the Carolinas. A man who had spent too much time staring into computer models.

Dr. Wu stood behind him, beside Gabriel Herring, the President's chief of staff, trying to fend off feelings of impatience and anger. Both he and Herring, Wu noticed, had their arms crossed in exactly the same manner, right hand cradling left bicep. Dr. Wu self-consciously uncrossed his arms and let them dangle at his sides.

"Some variance now in central pressure," Dr. Clayton announced, moments later, his eyes still on the monitor.

Herring frowned at Dr. Wu, who gave a tiny shake of his head. Wu had not, in fact, detected any changes over the past ninety minutes that were anything but routine. The storm, despite the series of solar laser "pulses" that had been fired into its eye wall, seemed to Dr. Wu nearly unchanged, still churning toward the mid-Atlantic coast on a deadly, uncompromising track.

He felt uneasy and a little dishonest being there, surprised that the President had sanctioned this. Dr. Wu did not share Clayton's optimism. *Couldn't* share it, even though he would have loved to have found a way to prevent what was coming. But the available data simply did not warrant optimism at this point. Dr. Wu believed in science, and he believed in numbers. The science did not in any way validate what Clayton, or the President, thought possible. But Dr. Wu also found himself fighting a darker emotion roiling inside of him. Beyond the issue of realistic outcomes, he resented the steadiness and unwarranted self-assurance of Dr. Clayton. Wu knew that these efforts would almost certainly fail; but another part of him also *wanted* them to fail. Wanted the sort of speculative science that Dr. Clayton had advocated and become known for to be dealt a knockout blow. Dr. Wu harbored a basic difference with Clayton, which reflected nothing so much as a difference in how their minds worked; he carefully and realistically weighed the available data, and did not draw attention to himself by wagering on outcomes that were scientifically unlikely or impossible. It was a fundamental difference.

Dr. Wu turned toward the window, noticing that the drifting clouds had all but turned the sky black.

"Eerie, isn't it?" said Herring. "Looks like it's nine o'clock at night."

"UAV cargo delivered," Clayton announced, typing something on one of the keyboards, his back to them, his legs bent as if he were a runner waiting for the starter pistol to sound. Then he sighed heavily and cussed.

"What is it?" said Herring.

"Contact with third plane lost."

"Lost," said Dr. Wu, snapping back to the present.

"That's three drones lost?" said Gabriel Herring.

"*Contact* lost," said Dr. Clayton. "May just be malfunctioning."

Dr. Wu felt a chill up his back, recalling his friend David Quinn, who had perished with his crew in the belly of Alexander three days ago. Heard his final words again: *Not sure what we're seeing . . . faces . . . figures . . . Not getting out of this.* He thought about his wife Alison and his youngest daughter Melinda, who were driving west through the rain, probably nearing Ohio by now, if they hadn't already arrived. Thought of the possibility that he would be caught here. No, he had to get out. He couldn't let this monster defeat him. Dr. Wu told himself to focus, to study the satellite images as the storm continued to send its sentinels ahead of it, as if to deliver the dire warnings about what was really coming.

"How long now?"

Clayton seem not to have heard.

"How *long?*" Dr. Wu said again.

"The lasers? Close to an hour and a half."

No. Dr. Wu glanced at the clock and saw that it had actually been an hour and forty-three minutes. Funny the way some people fudged the facts unnecessarily when their expectations were raised, as if molding them around what they desired rather than around the truth.

There were several inconsequential changes in the new series of readings from the National Hurricane Center, he noticed. Signifying nothing.

Feeling dizzy, Dr. Wu excused himself and took the marble stairway down to the first floor, his footsteps echoing in the ornate, cavernous stairwell, his breathing accelerated. He stepped outside under an awning, breathing the cold air and gazing toward the National Mall. He listened to the pounding of the rain, the sweep of the wind. The rain-swollen air carried a burning scent now, it seemed, like sulfur or cordite. Suddenly, then, a series of bright lights exploded in the sky to the south, startling him. *Lightning.* Highly charged webs of electricity, shooting haphazardly above the darkness like short circuits. Dr. Wu stared, his eyes transfixed. And then the light began to do funny things—the afterglows forming strange and twisted images inside his eyelids; images that, improbably, grew more defined as he closed his eyes. Giant figures were running mischievously across the lawn. *Insanity.* James Wu wasn't sure, then, if his eyes were even opened or closed, if what he was seeing was in the sky or his imagination. He turned toward the Washington Monument and a spontaneous fountain of light seemed to catch fire in the dark clouds overhead, their undersides burning, the sky becoming a dull orange and then black. This time, in the afterglow, he saw the outlines of a face coalescing in the clouds, its features sharpening for several moments, becoming increasingly lifelike. He closed his eyes, but the face was still there, even clearer. *The face of David Quinn.* Smart, steady. A brilliant man. But his expression wasn't smart right now, it was terrified. Dr. Wu opened his eyes and he became blinded by the show of light igniting the clouds in all directions; he stumbled away, grasping for something to hold onto, realizing that he could no longer see.

2:29 P.M.

Charles Mallory dumped his groceries on the table in Room 321.

There were about a dozen cars in the lot now, more than the day before. The motel Chaplin had found for him was near Parrs Spring, the highest elevation in the county, about eight hundred feet above sea level. Not the safest place on the Eastern Seaboard but far from the worst.

He checked his phone and saw that the last caller had been Blaine. She answered his return call on the second ring.

"Where are you?"

"On my way," she said. "I've got to get some things from my apartment and then I'm leaving."

Good. He listened to the rain for several beats. "Anything more?"

"No." He heard her take a deep breath. "I'm really worried. They're going to send a state trooper out to the place where his girlfriend's family lives. On the Shore."

"We'll find him."

"I'm also just feeling kind of sick. I think it's a delayed reaction."

"What do you mean?"

"To Rorbach. I can't believe he got away with it for so long. Right out in the open."

"Don't think about that."

"I know."

"Be careful," he said. "Everything will be okay."

Blaine sighed. "Thanks."

Mallory opened a quart bottle of Diet Coke and a bag of Cheetos and he turned on the television. The storm was playing on nearly every channel, it seemed, although there was also a John Wayne movie on one and a baseball game on another. At the top of the hour, he clicked on one of the news channels and watched. The NWS alert Blaine had told him was coming had arrived.

A natural disaster of "unprecedented" proportions. That's the word this hour from the National Weather Service, which has just issued an alarming new alert, as Hurricane Alexander continues to bear down on the East Coast.

The news cast cut to FEMA Director Shauna Brewster who was sitting stone-faced in her office as rain cascaded against the windows behind her.

*On a scale of one to ten, this is a fifteen. There is no precedent for
this. The message we want to convey is that if you are within one
hundred miles of the coast, you need to leave. And you need to do
it now. We are estimating that only about half of the homes in coastal
counties have been evacuated, despite mandatory orders issued last night
and this morning."*

    *Earlier in the day, President Hall gave a similar warning, as he left a
meeting at FEMA headquarters in Washington.*

The scene shifted to the President, wearing a dark blue slicker,
standing under an awning against the rain. Just behind him, his eyes
dazed, was the President's chief of staff, Gabriel Herring.

*"The time for deliberation has passed. Everyone needs to get to safety
now."*

    *Already the outer bands of Alexander have caused massive flooding
and substantial damage to homes and businesses up and down the coast.
And there are multiple reports of freak lightning storms throughout the
mid-Atlantic region. Meanwhile, the National Weather Service has just
issued a new alert: A powerful hurricane with unprecedented strength is
roaring toward the Atlantic coast. Most of the coastal region, in at least
six states, is expected to be uninhabitable for weeks or possibly months.*

ON THE STREETS of Frederick, in western Maryland, the rain had
softened to a drizzle, although the sky to the west was dark and lit
with continuous veins of lightning.

    At 3:04, a series of nearly horizontal lightning bolts seemed to
burst out of nowhere, striking trees, parking meters, and several
points along the ground on Court Street, and sending an electric
current down much of a city block, which instantly killed seven
pedestrians and severely burned the legs of four others. An assistant city clerk named Deborah Wattingly, who was standing on
the sidewalk in front of City Hall, captured the moment on her
smart phone.

    Seventy miles away, in downtown Washington, D.C., cell phones
and amateur video cameras recorded the freak, near-continuous
lightning storms that now enveloped the Washington Monument
and the National Cathedral, the two tallest structures in the nation's

capital. The lightning surrounding National Cathedral was flashing more than two hundred and fifty times per hour, according to Washington meteorologist Robin Vance, who was the first to show video of the phenomenon on local Washington television.

By 4 P.M., Vance's broadcast was the most popular YouTube video in the country, followed by Deborah Wattingly's cell phone footage of the deadly strike in Frederick, Maryland.

4:14 P.M.

"Ninth series of pulses has been activated," Dr. Clayton said, his voice resonating with an unwavering energy. He hunched forward over one of the desk monitors, legs bent, and typed in a sequence.

"Nothing substantial yet," said Dr. Wu, blinking numbly at the screens. He still felt disoriented from what had happened outside, his eyes unable to focus properly. The blinding flashes in the sky, the clouds morphing into images, the terrified face of Dr. Quinn looking down at him.

"Well, it's hard to say, actually," Dr. Clayton said, his eyes not quite meeting Dr. Wu's. He began to summarize changes in air pressure, wind speeds and wind field.

None of which is of any significance.

No longer listening, Dr. Wu could hear the blood rushing in his ears. He was relieved when the President finally interrupted, summoning him on his BlackBerry. As he strode into the hallway to the Oval Office, Wu saw Samuel Watson, the director of the Secret Service, and two agents stepping out of the President's office into the narrow hallway. He nodded tersely, but they did not acknowledge him.

Herring was on the other side of the Oval Office, by the windows, standing as erect and still as a statue, facing the South Lawn, talking on his phone.

"Hi, Jim," the President said.

"Mr. President."

"Have a seat. The JOC just told me they want me out of here. How do you like that? They want me to fly to Bolling Air Force Base immediately. I told them to give me until six and they did everything they could not to roll their eyes. Am I being reckless?"

"I can't really answer that, sir."

"No?" The President studied him, his chin lifted, his face drained of emotion. Dr. Wu felt humbled and still shaken by the hallucinations. "But you can give me an update?"

"I can. Yes, sir."

"All right." The President gestured genially.

Herring held up a finger, interrupting. "Sir? The Governor of Virginia?"

"No." The President flapped his hand. "Ten minutes. Go ahead," he said, nodding to Dr. Wu. "What's going on? What are we seeing over there? It's all under way, correct?"

"Yes, sir. It's all active. It's been under way for several hours. As you know. The laser pulses for more than four hours now."

"Please. Have a seat. Can I get you some water? Tea?"

"No, thanks."

Dr. Wu sat on the front edge of the rosewood chair. "Sir, I'm hesitant to tell you this. The latest tracking shows that the storm remains strong and has now taken a slight northwesterly turn."

"Okay." There was a raised, expectant tone in his voice, as if somehow this were good news. "And? So what does that mean?"

"Frankly, sir, not anything good, I'm afraid."

"Okay." The President blinked. "Go ahead."

"The wind field hasn't changed, the wind speed has actually ticked up slightly and the pressure has ticked down. We aren't seeing quite the disorganization of the inner eye that we expected. The latest projections are putting it directly into the mouth of Chesapeake Bay."

The President reflexively glanced away. "Okay. But it's early still, right?"

"Well, yes and no."

"Dammit, I don't want to hear yes and no, Jim." He caught himself. Dr. Wu understood what he was going through. "I want to hear one or the other. What does it mean, what you're telling me? Bottom line."

"Bottom line: no, sir. It *isn't* early. It's late. And the bull's-eye is still on Washington, I'm afraid." Dr. Wu took a deep breath, looking at the presidential seal on the carpet, feeling his heart racing. "And after that, the most likely path has it skirting the coast up to New York City."

"What about this eye wall replacement business?"

Dr. Wu shook his head. He wanted the President to know the truth. That was his job now. Politics was over. "Frankly, sir, Dr. Clayton's efforts have not, so far, proven fruitful. We have not been able to disrupt it. It's an experimental process, as he told you."

"Why? *Why* isn't it working?"

"Well, sir. I don't know. This is such a large system that it's highly unpredictable. And, to be honest, sir, it's highly unlikely at this point that it will take any significant turn." Dr. Wu looked away as he felt his eyes tear up.

"Damnation!" the President muttered. "All right. So what are we looking at?"

"Well, sir, I'm afraid we're still looking at what you told us this morning. Scenario A. Worst case. I just wanted to warn you, sir. I want you to be fully informed."

The President looked as if he had just gotten a whiff of spoiled milk. "I know you do, Jim. So what about this thing Clayton's doing over there? The laser pulses."

"The initial indications are showing no effects, sir. None. I'm sorry."

The two men stared at each other.

"*Shit!*" The President shook his head, looking across the great desk with his dark, tired eyes. This was the first time Dr. Wu had heard the President swear. "So, it's not working."

"I'm afraid not. No, sir." Dr. Wu felt a strange cocktail of emotions again. He watched the President glance at the photos on one side of his desk, knowing what they were: his wife, children, and grandchildren.

"Okay." The President exhaled dramatically, no longer making eye contact. "Okay, I appreciate your candor, Jim. And I want you out of here ASAP. We're going to move downstairs to the Situation Room in a few minutes. I'll be here until six and then I'll be flying out of Washington."

"Sir? With all due respect? I'd like to ask to stay with you until six, also."

The President looked at him quickly, his eyes fluid with emotion, and then, nodding, he turned to the South Lawn, as if dismissing him.

"Thank you, sir. I'm sorry."

Dr. Wu walked outside, and he glanced uneasily toward the Mall. Saw the cocoon of lightning surrounding the Washington Monument. The lightning again beginning to play tricks with his vision, trying to make him look, but this time he turned his eyes to the pavement and rapidly made his way back inside.

VLADIMIR VOLKOV SIPPED a glass of 1945 Mouton Rothschild on the plush divan in the cabin of his private Challenger 604 jet as it quietly carried him away from France, east toward his homeland. On the high-definition video screen, he watched the concert footage of his beloved Anna Netrebko, as Marfa in Rimsky-Korsakov's *The Tsar's Bride* with the Kirov Opera Orchestra.

But Volkov was finding it difficult to concentrate—to feel moved today by his favorite soprano. The update from Petrenko was overdue and the delay could only mean what he had feared: that there was no good news to relay.

He glanced at the clouds for several minutes, then switched to the clips of Anna receiving the State Prize of the Russian Federation from Putin. The anniversary celebration of the Mariinsky Theater in St. Petersburg had been a marvelous event. But it was the same: He couldn't keep his mind on it. He couldn't enjoy her today.

Svetlana, Volkov's mistress, appeared at the front of the cabin and smiled tentatively at him; Vladimir Volkov shook his head. She could see that he was preoccupied by some business trouble and knew not to intrude.

Volkov closed his eyes and waited, thinking, with sadness, about his son Victor. And then, finally, the bad news arrived.

A simple report, conveyed from the United States, confirming that the operation was not succeeding. Would not succeed.

Volkov felt a deep pang of regret over the now certain fate of Victor Zorn.

It was the necessary cost. They had all known it might end this way. They had known that going in.

Volkov then did what he had to do. He typed in the required instruction. One word. Unambiguous, non-negotiable. Pressed SEND.

One word, five letters.

ABORT.

Dmitry Petrenko would know exactly what it meant.

AS CATHERINE BLAINE drove through the rural Maryland countryside in the car Jamie had rented for her, she saw flashes of lightning and bizarre, unnerving images in the distant sky. Tricks of the storm—figures and faces burned into the clouds by sudden backlit bursts of lightning. Like drive-in movie screens in the sky, it seemed. Jagged lines and swirls joined together into sudden clear images, then muting back to darkness. The highway took a sudden turn and she saw a figure seeming to trot through the rain-soaked field toward the road, limping; a man who became Rorbach as he got closer, a larger version of him. Stopping and looking. His eyes dark and center-less, like pieces of coal. Stopping and smiling. *No.* It was her imagination, of course, the fact that she was tired; some trick of the rain. *Stop thinking about it.* But soon she saw another figure, beside the road, hitchhiking. And recognized him. Recognized her son, Kevin. Around another turn she saw him again. Disappearing each time she came close and began to pump her brakes. Another bolt of lightning and she saw him in a front yard, elevated this time, his body swaying in the wind-driven rain from a noose dangling below an oak branch. *No, don't think about it. It's preying on your fears. Don't think about it,* Blaine told herself.

* * *

WE HAVE DRAMATIC *new video. This is from the National Cathedral and the Washington Monument, and what is apparently a continuous lightning storm that has taken root at both locations for more than an hour now. Thousands have gathered in the pouring rain to witness these bizarre freaks of nature.*

Mallory watched in Room 321 as a dowdy-looking, short-sleeved scientist explained the phenomenon using a split screen that showed two live feeds.

In fact, there are many documented atmospheric effects where we see near-continuous lightning. "The Catatumbo lightning in Venezuela is probably the most famous. Where the Catatumbo River meets Lake Maracaibo, there is an atmospheric convergence that creates continuous lightning for 10 hours every day, about 280 times per hour.

Now, what would be causing this particular phenomenon in Washington is another question. Or phenomena, plural. We do think it is

related in some fashion to this monster storm, Hurricane Alexander,
which may well be affecting weather systems throughout the world.
We're getting reports now of similar lightning storms and atmospheric
disturbances throughout Europe this afternoon.

Mallory switched the channel. He watched footage of the storm's
outer bands ripping into the North Carolina and Virginia coasts,
submerging coastal resorts. Power outages, downed trees. More than
half of the traffic signals on the North Carolina coast not working.
Record high tides of seven feet above mean low water reported.

He heard a car door slam and looked out, saw Blaine running
through the rain and felt a surge of adrenaline. He let her in and
helped her out of her windbreaker. They held each other for a long
time, Blaine breathing heavily, her hair wet against the side of his
face. Mallory poured coffee into two motel water glasses. They sat on
the bed and sipped coffee and looked at each other.

"Are you okay?"

"I think so." She shook her head unfamiliarly, staring at the carpet.
"I don't know. It was just . . . It was strange, when I was driving here."
Her voice trailed off. She looked at her coffee.

"What."

"I was thinking about something Dr. Sanchez said to me. He said
natural disasters were all adjustments. That if a severe weather event
happened in one part of the world it would affect weather in other
parts of the world."

"Like the Butterfly Effect."

"Kind of. I don't know. I just feel something really scary is going on."

Mallory nodded. "I know," he said. "Don't think about it."

She turned to him and her eyes searched his.

"Let's go find your son," he said.

FIFTY-FIVE

WHEN IT OPENED IN 1952, the Chesapeake Bay Bridge was the world's largest continuous over-water steel structure. A second, three-lane span was christened in 1973. Nearly thirty million vehicles cross the five lanes of the Chesapeake Bay Bridge every year now. But bridges are vulnerable to high winds and occasionally, during hurricanes, they are closed to traffic. At 1:30 P.M. on Friday, October 7, the State Transportation Administration closed both spans of the bridge indefinitely because of gusts attributed to Alexander—one of which had slammed a small car into a side rail of the bridge, seriously injuring two children.

The White House had given Maryland State Police the location where Blaine's son, Kevin, might be—a beachfront condominium owned by the parents of his girlfriend, Amanda. They were en route to checking it out. If they found him, they'd drive across the bridge and Blaine would meet him at the western terminus. Motion felt better than doing nothing. And Mallory wanted to be with her.

"I know we shouldn't be out in this," she said, as they plowed through an empty, rain-soaked road in Anne Arundel County, toward Highway 50, the east-west route that spanned the Bay Bridge.

"Well, no," Mallory said. "But on the other hand, it'll give us a chance to talk."

Blaine laughed. The wipers beat back and forth. "What do you want to talk about?"

"Everything I forgot to ask you."

"Oh." She looked at him. "You're kidding, right?"

"I'm not."

"All right. Go ahead," she said "Ask."

"Your son's father, for starters."

"Oh. He's living in San Francisco. Remarried. He left me nine years ago. I was too career-oriented. I'm difficult to get along with, he said. I'm not seeing anyone at the moment, if that's what you're asking."

"It is."

"What about you?"

"Ditto."

"Why?"

"Similar reasons, I suppose. I was living with someone. It became complicated."

They listened to the rain. "Although to be honest," she said, "I think I'm becoming a little bit infatuated with you. I'm not sure that's something I should have said."

"No. I'm glad you did." He watched the wipers, beating manically. "How about you?"

"I like career-oriented girls," he said.

Blaine smiled, he could tell. They talked about their pasts for a while, then, answering questions as Mallory plowed on toward the Chesapeake Bay Bridge. Figuring it kept them from thinking about her son or from paying too much attention to the lightning that was illuminating the distant landscape. Nature was acting out, like a child having a temper tantrum, it seemed; or, perhaps, an animal in its final death throes, lashing out at what had killed it, nature's revenge.

A cluster of police cars had set up a roadblock in front of the Bay Bridge toll plaza, blue lights arcing through the rain over wet pavement. Blaine got out and identified herself. Mallory stood beside her. The troopers asked that they wait at a convenience store several miles down the road. They would bring them the news as soon as they had any. Blaine lowered her head and hurried back to the car. She was silent as they drove back against the rain.

The store was the only place open for miles. Its front windows were boarded up. NO WATER and NO BEER signs taped on the front door. Five people sat on lawn chairs inside, wrapped in blankets: two women, three men. Everyone was watching the nineteen-inch television set mounted behind the check-out counter.

"You should see this, son," said the proprietor, a short, square-built man with a ruddy face and close-cropped white hair. "Did you see this? Seven people fried on the street."

The video of the lightning in Frederick.

Mallory turned away. He took a quick inventory of the store. The shelves and coolers were nearly empty. He stood with Blaine by the screen door and held her, looking out toward the bay, rain glittering in the streetlights below the black sky.

"We got beer, son," the man said, a few minutes later. "We're just not advertising that right now. Day like this, I won't even charge you. Go ahead and get a cold one here, if you'd like."

He opened an ice chest behind the counter and showed them. Mallory looked at Blaine. She reached in and pulled out a Bud Light. Thanked him and returned to the front door, breathing the rain.

"Planning to ride it out?" Mallory said to the proprietor.

"Yep."

"Probably shouldn't."

"Been through all kinds of storms, son."

"Not like this one you haven't."

"Well." He made a snorting sound and rubbed his crotch. "What can I tell you?"

"Don't know. Probably not a lot," Mallory said. He stood beside Blaine, who passed him the beer. Waiting. Holding her from behind, watching the rain. Eventually, they saw a set of lights misting through the rain. Growing brighter. A state police trooper, returning with news. Mallory watched the car park, the man emerging, walking toward the store. Taking off his hat. Blaine going outside to meet him.

Mallory stepped into the rain and watched. He could tell from the look on the trooper's face. It wasn't good news.

Blaine turned to Mallory, who was standing ten feet behind her. He saw her face sink.

"THE CONDO WAS empty," he said, driving back on the flooded highway. "Which just means that he's somewhere else. It was one of any number of possible locations."

But Blaine was silent most of the way back, checking her phone frequently, listening to Mallory as he offered up stories about his life. Talking to be talking. At times, the drive was scary, the wind blowing the car off the road or lifting water out of the fields, the rain so heavy he had to pull over and park.

They returned to Room 321, where Blaine took off her clothes and took a long, hot shower. Mallory did, too, then. Afterward, they slipped under the covers in bed and warmed each other. Thunder rumbled as they slowly made love, and occasionally the room lit up with lightning. They were going to devise a plan, they agreed, just not right away.

Then at 5:34, the power went out.

"Just hold me," she said. "There's not much else we can do now, is there?"

"Not much," he said. She seemed to fall asleep as he held her and Mallory lay against her with his eyes open, thinking some of what he'd been thinking earlier. About the family he'd had and the one he didn't have. About the ways he had led his life and the ways he hadn't, the decisions he had made that had somehow steered him to this room, with Catherine Blaine.

"What are you thinking?" she said, turning her head slightly, surprising him.

"Oh, nothing." He lay his head down beside hers and tried to sleep.

Later, Mallory heard something else and opened his eyes. Saw Blaine reaching for her cell phone in the dark. Heard a sharp intake of breath, and in the glow from the phone he saw her face transform.

Dr. James Wu waited until two minutes past six to contact the Oval Office. To his surprise, President Hall took the call directly.

"Sir, I'm getting ready to go."

"All right. Any change?"

"Nothing appreciable. Dr. Clayton will continue monitoring for another couple of hours."

"All right. We'll have a team here overnight, downstairs in the woodshed."

"Sir, can I talk with you before you go?"

"Of course."

"In person, I mean."

"Of course."

"I'll be right over."

FIFTY-SIX

THE FIRST THING CATHERINE Blaine heard was music in the background. A group that she vaguely recognized. The Killers, maybe, or Radiohead. Or Blink 182. One of them.

Then she heard Kevin's voice.

Saying, *"Mom?"*

Blaine listened to him breathe, waiting for him to speak, to explain himself. Anger tempered by joy.

"What's going on?" she said. "Are you all right?"

"Mom?"

"Honey? Can't you hear me?"

"Not well."

"Can you hear me now?" She stood in the open doorway, watching the driving rain.

"Sort of. We have, like, a bad connection?"

"Are you all right?"

"Of course."

"Honey? I've been trying to reach you since yesterday. Why haven't you called?"

"I *tried*," he said, with his customary bristle. "My phone was out. Then the electricity went. Right? I can't believe we just now got reception back."

"Where are you?"

"I'm in—I guess, Delaware? We're in, like, a big house. We're safe, Mom."

"Who's we?"

"A bunch of friends. Amanda's here." After a moment, he said, "Where are *you? I've* been worried, too, you know."

"I know." Blaine looked at Mallory and shook her head. Then she gave him a thumbs up. "Do you realize what's coming, Kev?"

"What?"

"Do you know what's coming?"

"Sort of."

"Sort of what?"

"I mean, our electricity just came back, right? I saw the report from the Weather Service and stuff. Sounds like the usual overreaction."

"No, honey, believe me. It's not overreaction."

She heard someone screaming in the background.

"What's going on there, Kev? Are they all right?"

"Nothing." A woman shouted his name urgently. "It's just a hurricane party, Mom."

"Honey, this is a serious storm. You need to get away from the ocean. Right away."

"What?"

He said something else, but she could only hear a few words. He was breaking up.

"Kev?"

"Bye, Mom. I'll call you in a while."

She pulled the phone away. Her gaze met Mallory's.

"Hurricane party," she said. "Can you believe it?"

Then she looked at her phone and retrieved the message she had just missed. To her surprise, it was from White House Chief of Staff Gabriel Herring.

"What is it?"

"A YARI call. That's odd."

"What's YARI?"

"Your Attendance Required Immediately. I'm being summoned back to the White House." She shared a long look with him. "Want to drive me?"

THEY TOOK INTERSTATE 270, a connector route to the Capital Beltway, back to Washington. The roads were virtually empty now except for police and emergency vehicles. Twice they were stopped at checkpoints and told to turn around. Both times Blaine showed her government identification and they were waved through.

At the White House gate on Fifteenth Street, Blaine was informed that Mallory did not have clearance to enter.

After a confused several minutes, the President's voice came on the gatehouse phone line.

"Cate, what's going on?" he said.

"Charles Mallory's here, sir," she said. "He helped me figure all of this out. I'd like him to come to this meeting."

"Who?" he said. "Hold on."

The President passed the issue on to Gabriel Herring. Another uncertain interval followed, during which Mallory was asked routine background questions, and finally was issued an entry badge.

The others were standing as they entered the Data Visualization Center, hovering around the two scientists. DeVries. Bill Stanton. Herring. The President nodded a greeting, glancing at Mallory.

"I hesitated to convene this meeting, Cate. I don't know if it's worth much, but Jim Wu and Dr. Clayton here are telling me it warrants at least one more briefing before we close down the circus. So here we are."

"All right," Blaine said.

"Basically, we're seeing a small shift in the storm," the President told her, "which may or may not be attributable to our mitigation efforts."

"Okay." Mallory noticed the childlike spark in the President's eyes. He exchanged a look with Blaine, trying to stay out of the way. "Jared?" The President gestured, giving the floor to Dr. Clayton, who stood in the center of everyone like a street performer.

"Thank you," he said, tugging on his sweater sleeves. "I agree with the President that this may or may not ultimately mean much," he said, his eyes moving restlessly, seeming to avoid direct contact with anyone. "But we are, clearly, starting to see some dramatic activity within the eye wall.

"As you know, a series of solar laser pulses was directed to the edges of the new eye wall cycle, beginning at 1:13 this afternoon. One of the intended consequences was to create an elevation in central pressure within the eye wall. The drone planes have also delivered our 37-AQX synthetic bacteria, which appears to be inducing further disruption.

"Now, the most significant change we're seeing right now is this increase in central pressure. And a rather dramatic weakening of the eye wall as well."

"Which was expected," said Blaine.

"Expected, yes. It just took longer than we thought."

The Vice President asked, "What does central pressure mean, exactly?"

The corners of Clayton's mouth turned up wryly. "When air flows into the center of a storm faster than it flows out, the central pressure rises. The effect of these laser pulses appears to have created a pattern of friction within the storm that's causing the winds to 'bend' across the low center, cutting off the storm's source of energy."

"And what in God's name does that mean?" Stanton said. "In English, please."

"Generally, lower pressures correspond to higher winds. By raising the pressure inside this eye wall, we're basically seeing the storm fill up. And slow down."

"Meaning it's working," the President said.

"Well." Clayton pursed his lips. "It would be rather presumptuous to say that at this point. But I think it's valid to say that we're seeing an impact. We get another reading in twenty-seven minutes."

"That's the good news," Dr. Wu said.

"The bad?" Blaine asked.

"At this stage, it may not matter. It may be too late."

MALLORY TURNED AWAY and watched the silent television on a counter across the room while the others waited for the new reports. Storm scenes from everywhere: The cell phone video from Frederick, Maryland. A Virginia farmhouse washed into Chesapeake Bay. The eerie, continuous streams of lightning around the Washington Monument and the National Cathedral.

Several minutes later, Dr. Clayton began to make interested sounds—"mmm" and "uh, okay"—studying one of the GOES thirty-minute satellite readings of the storm's center. Then the animated image from the Space Station. New readings coming in from the National Hurricane Center.

Something is changing. Mallory could tell. He could read it in the separate faces of the two scientists, well before anything was said. And even more clearly when they huddled together and talked in low voices, Clayton crouched down to bring his head level with Wu's.

"What is it?" the President finally asked.

"We're seeing a continuation of the shift inside the eye wall," said Dr. Clayton, nodding toward the large monitor. "As you can see, there's now significant destabilization and also some disintegration evident."

"But we were seeing that five hours ago, weren't we?" Stanton said.

"We were. What's significant now is the activity pursuant to the outer eye wall. Which is also showing signs of disorganization. The question becomes, Will this outer eye wall be able to move in and replace it? My guess at this point would be no."

"Meaning it won't be able to replenish itself," said Blaine.

"That's how it's starting to appear, yes."

"And this is because of these laser pulses?" asked Stanton.

Clayton made a non-committed tilt of his head, glancing quickly at Blaine.

"In a sense, it almost doesn't matter what's causing it, does it?" the President said, trying not to smile. *He's already thinking about how he'll present this to the nation*, Mallory could tell

"Well, let's see what happens in another twenty minutes."

DR. JAMES WU could see that, in fact, the outer eye wall *was* coming apart, a development he hadn't expected and didn't understand. But he knew, now, where this was going, just as Jared Clayton must have known. There wasn't going to be an eye wall replacement cycle. The center of the storm was becoming non-existent and the outer eye wall was tearing apart. The storm no longer had a source of energy, or an organizing force. It had no reason to exist.

TWENTY MINUTES LATER, they saw new activity on the eastern and northern edges of the storm. High levels of wind shear were disrupting the movement of the outer bands and the vertical structure of the eye wall was being smothered, causing a more visible, and obvious, disruption. Without an energy source, Alexander was coming apart.

"It seems like it's getting worse," said Stanton, looking at the President.

"No, the opposite," said Dr. Clayton. "It's a strange storm. But it's clearly losing its structure. Alexander's sin is that he got too big. Too many rain bands competing for the same energy. The wind shear is causing it to lose its rotation and its structure. This is a storm that never should have gotten this big," he said, looking only at the President, who was nodding. "But now that it has, it no longer can sustain itself. I think we may be starting to see the final death throes of this thing."

"But something of this size," said the Vice President. "It isn't going to just break up and disappear, is it? Not at this stage."

"That's precisely what's happening, though, isn't it?" Clayton said. "Look at it. Too many competing winds and rain bands and temperatures." He nodded to the monitors behind him. "Look at the projections now."

Charles Mallory, a silent observer, nearly invisible in the room, felt the shared sense of relief: The new spaghetti models showed a slight shift away from land, with two indicating that the storm was going to take a sharp turn to the east and north, sputtering out at sea.

The President turned to Dr. Wu. "Jim?"

When he responded, it was in a soft but strained voice. "Yes. He's right." His eyes glistened. "I wouldn't have believed this," he said, "but I don't think Alexander has anything to do now but break up and return to sea."

"This storm is unraveling, people," Dr. Clayton said, surprising everyone by vigorously clapping his hands together. "We've stolen its energy. We've outwitted it."

Moments later, the others in the room, including Mallory, began to clap their hands almost simultaneously, breaking out in a spontaneous, energetic applause that didn't want to end.

FIFTY-SEVEN

7:42 P.M.

THE NETWORKS AND NEWS channels all broke in within minutes of one another to announce the news. CNN's Kyra Phillips was the first to come on the air.

> *We have breaking news out of Washington. There are signs that in just the past two hours, Hurricane Alexander has shown a dramatic weakening and we are getting reports that it may in fact take a turn back to sea, according to officials at the White House.*
>
> *Defying all predictions, Alexander has taken a sudden easterly turn and may be downgraded to a tropical storm this evening, according to sources, who spoke to us on condition of anonymity. Officials caution, however, that the storm's path remains unpredictable and that Alexander is still a dangerous hurricane.*

THE TELEPHONE CALL that Dmitry Petrenko expected from the White House finally came at 7:53. The Oval Office summoning Victor Zorn.

Petrenko listened as Zorn took the call in his private room at the Virginia compound. President Hall congratulating him first, Victor responding. The President baiting a trap. Or else, inviting him to come in and join the other side.

Either way, Petrenko would, of necessity, have to provide an alternative.

ABORT.

"Thank you, sir," Zorn said, the persuasive salesman's tone back in his voice. "I am only sorry that the initial projections were not on target."

"Well, the end result is what matters, isn't it?"

"Yes it is, sir. So thank you," Victor said, his eyes lit with naked excitement. "And your part of the bargain, of course, was to make the address to the nation, announcing our partnership. Does that still hold?"

"Of course," the President said. "As we agreed. In fact, I'd love to announce it with you on television at nine thirty this evening. If you can make it here by then."

Mr. Zorn laughed. "No. Thank you, sir, but I am not a television performer."

The President laughed then, too. "Could we invite you to at least be present here with us? I'd love for you to be at the White House when we make the announcement and seal the deal."

"Yes. Thank you, sir. Yes, of course. That would be an honor."

"Very good. Thank you again, Mr. Zorn. And congratulations," the President said. "I believe we are on the cusp of a real breakthrough in science. Of a new era for civilization, really."

"Yes, we are." Zorn was beaming, thinking, as he nearly always did, that he would come out of this on top.

His name, Victor, had been a most perfect choice, Petrenko thought. *Perfect, until now.*

ONE OF PETRENKO'S security officers drove Victor Zorn to Washington through the still-heavy rains in a Mercedes GL450 SUV. Two D.C. police cars accompanied the vehicle the last twelve blocks and in through the White House gates near Fifteenth Street. The car arrived on the White House grounds shortly after 9:15 P.M.

Mr. Zorn and his driver were detained by White House police immediately as they stepped out into the rain, and transported to the military prison at Marine Corps Base Quantico in Virginia.

From Zorn's house in the Virginia foothills, Petrenko activated a remote electronic prompt just minutes before President Hall began his talk to the nation. It released a synthetic endotoxin from the implant in Mr. Zorn's left arm, which quickly seeped into his bloodstream, shedding bubbles containing concentrated toxin. Within seconds, the poison had given him an irregular heartbeat and was causing blood vessels to leak throughout his body. As the blood vessels hemorrhaged, Mr. Zorn's lungs and kidneys were destroyed.

Six minutes after the activation, Victor Zorn was dead.

FIFTY-EIGHT

"GOOD EVENING," PRESIDENT HALL began, seated behind his desk in the Oval Office, gazing at the teleprompter that scrolled through the speech he had finished writing that evening with Dr. Wu. "I would like to update the American people tonight on the fate of Hurricane Alexander.

"Just twelve hours ago, many of the world's leading climate scientists and weather forecasters were predicting that Alexander had the potential to become the worst natural disaster in this nation's history. Its unprecedented power, we were warned, was capable of destroying dozens of cities along the East Coast of the United States, resulting in tens of thousands of lives lost.

"This evening, I am able to report to you that this tragic scenario has been averted. While the remains of Alexander still pose a serious threat to some mid-Atlantic and New England regions, the unprecedented disaster that many had feared was inevitable has been avoided.

"I've just met with a team of the country's leading weather scientists from FEMA, the National Weather Service, and the National Hurricane Center, and I am pleased to announce that as of twenty minutes ago, Alexander has been downgraded from a hurricane to a tropical storm, with all projections showing continued weakening through the overnight hours.

"Threats such as Alexander remind us of our nation's vulnerabilities—and of our own vulnerabilities as human beings. They are a clear testament to the power of nature to disrupt our lives and our livelihoods. Today, however, I am able to announce that some important and exciting new strides have been taken that may eventually render disasters such as Alexander obsolete."

The camera came in for a closeup.

"In fact, I am both pleased and humbled to tell you this evening that some of the credit for averting Alexander may in fact belong to American science, rather than nature.

"For the first time, the federal government of the United States, working in tandem with a consortium of research centers, was able to implement a program of comprehensive storm mitigation. Specifically, we engaged cutting-edge solar laser technologies that were designed to alter the structure of hurricanes, cutting off Alexander's energy source, increasing central pressure and, as a result, degrading the hurricane's eye and diminishing its overall strength. Although I am not able to offer definitive proof to you tonight that these efforts were the sole reason that Alexander is no longer a hurricane, I *am* able to announce that this is a viable new science and that the United States will pledge all of its resources, ingenuity, and imagination to becoming the world leader in this field. Eventually, this new science will enable us to eliminate drought and heat waves, providing significant assistance in crop production and mitigating various other natural disasters.

"The destructive force of storms such as Alexander makes it imperative that we take the lead in exploring and developing this new realm of science and technology, so that in the future we may harness the power of nature for good rather than be at its mercy. It is our American responsibility—to ourselves, to our nation and to our future.

"It is in this spirit, therefore, that I am today announcing a new international organization that will pool resources and research to fully explore the dynamics of climate and weather science. It is our goal that within a generation, massive hurricanes such as Alexander will no longer pose a danger to these shores, to our lives, or to our livelihoods.

"However, I want to close by saying that Tropical Storm Alexander remains a potent threat to the United States. I would urge residents in the mid-Atlantic and lower New England coastal areas to take all necessary precautions. And I assure you that the United States of America will pledge all of its available resources toward assisting any and all regions affected by this storm. Thank you for your time. And God bless America."

TROPICAL STORM ALEXANDER took a northeastern jag overnight, missing the Chesapeake and turning back into the Atlantic Ocean, although its western bands slammed the coasts of Maryland, Delaware, and New Jersey on Saturday, with fifty-mile-an-hour winds and gusts topping eighty. In those three states, the storm destroyed dozens of beachfront homes, knocked out power, and flooded streets.

Blaine and Mallory watched from the Pike Motel, where they had decided to "ride it out."

"Feels kind of funny being in a motel room like this," she said, after they woke in the still of mid-morning.

"Yes. You said that before."

"Think any restaurants are open? Stores?"

"Sure."

He gave her a sideways look. The sun was high again through the blinds, accenting the planes of her face.

"There are still a few things we haven't talked about, you know," she said.

"Like?"

"Like what you're going to do with yourself."

"Suggestions?"

"Some."

"Do they all involve me staying in Washington?"

"I think so. Is that a possibility?"

"It could be." He listened to the whisk of cars moving past the motel on the wet street. "Yes," he said. "I definitely think it could be."

FIFTY-NINE

THE SATURDAY AFTERNOON BREEZE was balmy and laced with a fine mist as Catherine Blaine drove them through the narrow streets back to Washington. Traffic was heavy, and there was a palpable human energy in the D.C. suburbs. Families sat on front lawns and raised their fists, gave thumbs-up signs to passing travelers, who responded with celebratory whoops and honking horns as if everyone were sharing in the giddy aftermath of some sports victory. What people were sharing was of a higher order, though, than the outcome of a ball game. It was as if they were celebrating getting their lives back; having another chance that they hadn't expected. As Mallory and Blaine came through Bethesda back into the District, Joseph Chaplin reached Mallory with the news about Thomas Rorbach. He'd deciphered thirteen documents and emails on Rorbach's cell phone, he said. The most significant had been written three days earlier: a two-page memo succinctly explaining the project and his, and Secretary Easton's, roles in it. Leviathan, the murders, Zorn and Volkov. He had realized that he was in trouble, evidently, and chose to leave a record. It was tantamount to a confession, Chaplin said.

"What about Easton? Do we have any idea where he is?"

"Yes, actually." What he said next was drowned out by a burst of revelry from the sidewalks. Mallory raised the windows. "This might all work out naturally, Charles. On its own."

"How do you mean?"

"Planes are flying again."

"Okay."

"His Continental flight to Geneva left eleven minutes ago."

"So he gets away?"

"No. He doesn't get away."

"What do you mean?"

"I've obtained the passenger list," Chaplin said. Mallory heard the Toreador song from *Carmen* playing in the background. "Dmitry Petrenko is on the same flight. I don't think that is a coincidence."

Petrenko. A name he recognized. He was trying to remember how. Then it came to him. "Volkov's man."

"Yes. He's in charge of security and clean-up. Volkov's right-hand man, actually. Mr. Zorn died yesterday evening. If Petrenko's on that plane, I'm fairly certain Easton will be dead within twenty-four hours."

Monday, October 10, 3:27 P.M.

"That's a remarkable story," said Roger Church, looking up from the printout of Jon Mallory's draft, his face creasing into a network of wrinkles. "I don't know how you managed to pull it together."

"Sources." Jon Mallory shrugged. "That's all."

Two of the sources were in Church's spacious corner office at the *Weekly American* in Foggy Bottom—Catherine Blaine and Charles Mallory. Another was Steven Loomis, the first name on the list and the "S.L." in documents Dr. Keri Westlake had sent to Jon Mallory.

Loomis had started the chain, sharing his concerns about Leviathan with the project's assistant administrator, Frank Johnson, in 2004 and later with a journalist named Michael Dunlopen—two of the names on the list. Loomis and Johnson had both worked for Thomas Rorbach and Environmental Atmospheric Research Systems, observing firsthand the evolution of the Leviathan Project.

Jon Mallory was titling his piece "Story of an Unnatural Disaster—the Leviathan Memos." He would describe it with a series of documents passed down through the years, beginning with Loomis's.

Among the earliest of these documents was an email linking Thomas Rorbach and Clark Easton to experimental radio tomography research in Alaska that may have inadvertently triggered a devastating earthquake and tsunami in the Indian Ocean. Shortly before his disappearance, Loomis forwarded this email to a scientist named Deborah Piper, who then shared its contents with a colleague, Susan Beaumont. Their concerns received a little play on the Internet at the time but were never taken seriously. Email exchanges between lobbyist David Worth, who had also worked with EARS, and Dunlopen, however, indicated that the journalist was at work on an in-depth investigative story about the Leviathan Project at the time of his death in 2007. Several of those emails were obtained by Atul Pradhan, a scientist Dunlopen apparently knew in passing.

The earliest memo, titled "The Leviathan Effect," had been written by Loomis in August 2004. In it, he expressed concerns about the lack of international oversight for climate and weather modification research and warned that efforts to manipulate geo-physical phenomena might produce unwanted and unpredictable results.

I am troubled that the technological advancements inherent in the Leviathan Project, which have the ultimate potential of mitigating natural disasters that every year exact a toll of millions of lives and tens of billions of dollars, may instead be used irresponsibly for political gain.

A pre-requisite to the use of this technology must be a comprehensive understanding of how atmospheric systems work, and how they may be affected by these sorts of adjustments. Unfortunately, as you know, there is much about these processes that is still not understood.

When weather is altered to benefit one group or region, adverse effects may result in other regions. This is what I refer to here as the Leviathan Effect. I am afraid that as we continue to explore the complex science of climate and weather, we will increasingly make ourselves susceptible to this effect if we do not first raise global awareness and implement global safeguards.

Even research supposedly conducted in our own backyard may have chaotic and potentially disastrous effects elsewhere in the world, in ways we might not be able to anticipate. That is my primary reservation about the Leviathan Project as it stands today.

I do believe that climate and weather research is essential to our future and should go forward at an accelerated pace. This is a science that could be used for great gain or for great ill; it may even one day hold the keys to the survival of our planet. But this is why I believe it is essential that it be explored transparently, and with international oversight.

Stephen Loomis's warnings about the Leviathan Effect may have been borne out by the spate of severe events that accompanied

Hurricane Alexander. These included torrential rains in China that caused the evacuations of two million people; deadly earthquakes in Pakistan and Iran, which killed thousands; record downpours in Mexico, Argentina, and the Midwestern United States; and unprecedented lightning storms in Tanzania, Sumatra, Bolivia, and elsewhere, responsible for several hundred deaths.

The most recent memo, found on Thomas Rorbach's smart phone, succinctly explained the roles of Rorbach, Zorn, and Easton in the Leviathan and Weathervane projects. "This is our mission," it concluded. He signed it, "A soldier."

CHARLES MALLORY AND Catherine Blaine walked into the blue shaded autumn evening. As they came to Constitution Avenue, she reached for his hand. Mallory felt lifted by the warm-cool currents of the air, and by just being with her. Everything had changed, and he had no particular interest in leaving again.

They walked through the soggy parkland and across the National Mall, stopping to look east, toward the World War II memorial, the Washington Monument, and the Capitol. The Mall was a giant rectangle of land that told the American story better than any other. A piece of property that was projected to have been twenty feet under water right now.

They strolled past the monuments and the cherry trees into West Potomac Park, stopping finally at the Tidal Basin, where they sat on a bench and gazed out across the choppy reservoir waters, lit with the orange-gold glows of the fading sun. Mallory was surprised to see the vague outlines of a new life; things he'd never done, places he'd never been; adventures he would share with Blaine.

When she spoke, her voice was soft, surprising.

"It's not really over, is it?" she said.

"I don't know. Probably not."

"It's nice to stop thinking about it for a while, though, isn't it?"

"It is."

They sat there for a long time, marveling at the sky's shades of blue and gold glimmering in the water, hearing the cars passing over the wet streets and the waves splashing on stone, the breeze coming in currents. He thought of saying more, but decided not to.

The birds were high in the air again, Mallory noticed.

EPILOGUE

Beijing, China

PARAMILITARY GUARDS STOOD OUTSIDE the imposing southern gates of Zhongnanhai as a shiny black Hong Qi limousine pulled onto the park-like grounds of the Chinese leadership compound. Inaccessible to the general public and media, much as the Forbidden City had been during the Imperial era, Zhongnanhai was the seat of the Chinese Communist Party and the residence of the President. The sprawling, rectangular complex, set behind vermilion-colored walls, was a strange blend of blocky gray office buildings and ornate Qing dynasty palaces set on the shores of two giant artificial lakes.

Just inside the Xinhuamen Gate, the limousine passed a concrete wall with the famous slogan SERVE THE PEOPLE, in a giant facsimile of Chairman Mao's calligraphy. The car sped past the South Lake, where stone bridges led to an ornamental island, and a series of whimsical pavilions with names such as Zhanxulou, the Pavilion of Placid Pleasure, and Penglaige, the Fairy Isles Pavilion, before stopping at the massive Western-style building known as Qunzhengdian, or the Hall of Diligent Government.

The man in the back seat of the limousine was the country's Vice President, one of the nine old men known as the Politburo Standing Committee who determined much of China's national policy.

In his briefcase he carried a message for the President, his friend and former rival. It was a message that he had received approximately thirty minutes earlier on his mobile phone, which he knew the President would want to see immediately. A message signed Janus.

The Vice President held various titles in the Chinese government, including propaganda minister and Vice President of military affairs.

He had also served for years as a top-rank intelligence official and knew as well as anyone that Janus did not, in fact, actually exist. He knew this because he had been one of the six men who had invented Janus, a fictitious super-hacker who could infiltrate Internet networks of other nations and corporate entities, including the Dalai Lama's organization and the White House in Washington, without seeming to have any connection with the Chinese government.

But he was naturally concerned that someone—probably an American, or "the Americans"—was now appropriating Janus's identity and using it to threaten his country.

He was ushered in to the President's large but austere office, with its recessed lighting and leather chairs, where he remained standing as the country's ruler read and re-read the email message.

Mr. Vice President: Three days ago, a deadly hurricane struck the East Coast of the United States of America. This was the sixth in a series of so-called natural disasters.

Within the next week, another major disaster will devastate a portion of North America. You have the power to stop this trend. It is up to you. If not, the next disaster will be on Chinese soil—an earthquake worse than any you have ever experienced. We will be in contact soon with further instructions.

—Janus

Sochi, Russia

In a hillside villa above the Black Sea, Vladimir Volkov listened to Prokofiev's "Dance of the Knights" on his iPod while enjoying the warm-cool currents of air from over the open sea. Two of his mistresses had fixed the house for him and he expected to stay here for the next three nights.

Volkov was waiting now for the arrival of his only surviving son, Dmitry Petrenko, to discuss their plans for the next phase. Dmitry was coming from the cold of America to meet him here, where the weather was still pleasant and would be for the duration of his stay.

Volkov had given his other son the opportunity that he had requested. But Victor, it turned out, could not produce the prize. He had the desire to do big things, but he lacked the ability. He was like most people, who strove stupidly after what they could not achieve;

who became regressives. Mankind was still a regressive creature, Volkov believed. For all of man's ingenuity and accomplishments, nature was still capable of reducing him to a veritable caveman.

That was something that could change. That *would* change. Volkov knew exactly how to do it. How the world could become more civilized. He just needed the right general to carry out his mission. *The Project.*

Once again, the Americans had not been paying attention, he reflected, looking up at the cumulous clouds, as he walked along a ridge beside the sea. It was almost amusing to him: for all of their wealth, their knowhow, their arrogance, aggression, and resourcefulness, the Americans had not even read the last warning properly. They had become so consumed with their notions of success and winning that they hadn't even processed the last note carefully. It had been stated very clearly: *The next two events will be on American soil.*

Vladimir Volkov turned from the water and gazed up the lawn. That's when he saw his son, the good son, Dmitry Petrenko, walking toward him. What he really saw was the future.

ACKNOWLEDGMENTS

I am grateful to Laura Gross for her support of this series and of my writing.

Thank you to Bronwen Hruska and the staff at Soho Press for their creative work on the book.

Special thanks to my editor, Juliet Grames, for her incisive editorial suggestions, which made this a better book.

And thank you to Janet, China and Tibbie for their continuing friendship, encouragement and humor.